THE FERNDALE SECTOR

LAWRENCE KADOW

Also by Lawrence Kadow

The Button Boy

ISBN: 1468123009
ISBN-13: 9781468123005
Library of Congress Control Number: 2011963365
CreateSpace, North Charleston, SC

With heartfelt appreciation,
I must thank those who made my job much easier

Cathy Holmes
Jasvin Singh
Skyler
Petar
Dag
Bree
Cindy
Mohammed

PROLOGUE

James levered the crowbar under the nail's head, pulled firmly, and felt the stepladder shift slightly. Common sense told him not to take unnecessary risks; not this day or ever. Feeling with his toe, he found a lower rung. Four nails out, two to go. Dropping the first one in his coat pocket, he turned to reach for another nail when he detected a tiny flicker in his peripheral vision. So small and quick, that had he winked, he would have missed it. Gently laying his crowbar on the top step, he concentrated on a road far to the south, nearly three miles away. Nervous anticipation pushed out all other thoughts and actions.

This hillside home was chosen for its 280° view. The original owners must have paid dearly for the luxury. A cloudless day was not typical, at least not this early in the spring. Luckily for James it was not a typical day. At first, there was nothing he could find with the naked eye; no spark of light. But experience warned him not to ignore this apparition. They had enjoyed almost six months of peace, he'd always known it couldn't last, not in these times. Briefly glancing skyward, he estimated it was well before noon, mid-morning perhaps. Without a working watch, James could only guess. Staying on the ladder, he stared to the south, waiting, ever vigilant when instinct told him a threat might be near.

It was the final week of March in 2031, and although the winter was officially behind them, the temperature remained cooler than it had before the Change. Yet it was safe enough to expose a couple of windows, maybe two for now, but not all. The rest would wait; hidden behind their plywood shutters, protected from the cold winds should they return. The other windows, the ones on the north side, would probably forever stay shuttered. He and Lara had spent the winter in the dark, waiting for spring, waiting for the storms to abate. Now they could finally allow some light in.

During this second winter, James felt the need to make his own calendar; the dates copied from a store-bought relic. He'd written a large 'AC' to the right of the year; it reflected 'After the Change'. In the last two years, everything changed. There was no longer any form of government. All public utilities had faded away with the economic collapse. The seasons, mostly because of the winters, had also been altered. The winter of 2029-2030 could have been summed up in one word: polar. This last winter had not been quite as unkind—high winds and sub-zero temps came in spurts with periods of stillness separating the storms. Had the oceans cooled just a little because of the previous winter? James had long ago concluded that the ocean's warmer temperature had brought about the nuclear winters. Mankind had been warned, decade after decade, year after year, that an epic change was coming. The colder air was pulled in by the rising heat, producing the hurricane strength winds. However, this year's snow melted away almost twenty days earlier than last year. Could this be another sign that Mother Nature wasn't as angry as she had been? More than recording these changes, the calendar gave him hope.

James, still alert to the flash of light he had seen, kept his attention directed toward Slater Road. It took maybe five minutes, but as he suspected, he finally detected the movement again. "There's something there," he thought to himself. In most any other circumstances it would have been a congratulatory discovery. At this distance, it appeared no more distinct than a shadow on an overcast day. A chill ran down his spine. What frightened him most was that if it were just a single person, he'd never have noticed anything at this range. The fluidity of its movement and its size meant more than likely that he was looking at a group.

James wasted no time running inside. He grabbed the binoculars from the countertop, ignoring Lara's concerned expression. Once back on the deck, he rested his elbows on the rails to steady his hands. Using his fore-finger on the focusing wheel, he eventually found what had caught his attention; the mass was moving fast, traveling from east to west. Since cars no longer roamed the roads, its speed could only be compared to someone running; it was moving much faster than that. Sunlight glinted off metallic components defining the width of the group. Still, at this distance, he could only assume that their number exceeded ten; too many for him if they were looking for trouble.

Lara appeared alongside him, "What do you see?" A slight breeze lifted wisps of her short blonde hair from her face. A few years older than him, her femininity was difficult to disguise even without make-up and women's clothing. Dressed so thinly, James knew she wouldn't be outside for long.

He paused as he tried desperately to count the riders as they changed positions every couple of seconds. "A bunch of people on bicycles headed west on Slater."

"Good or bad?"

He looked up from his glasses knowing that if he said the wrong thing, it would cause her to worry unnecessarily. "They're too far away to know. I guess it's good because they aren't traveling in our direction."

Satisfied with his answer, she turned and went inside. A moment later, she stuck her head back out and asked, "Have you ever thought about trying to find a bicycle?"

James pondered the question. "Not really. I guess I hadn't really considered it."

Lifting the binoculars to his eyes again, he watched as the mass moved behind a rise in the terrain and vanished. The speed in which they were traveling made him more than a bit nervous. For their survival, he had to assume that they were up to no good. Why else would they be on the move? Grabbing the crowbar, James returned to the task of removing the plywood from their bedroom window. This one window would do. His attention never quite left the valley, checking every few seconds for any signs of more Wanderers. That's what they called them, those who didn't produce their own food, instead, preying on those who did. James had not had to spend a night outside since last October. Knowing that Wanderers were nearby once again, he had no other choice than to pass the night hours sitting on the deck, keeping a watchful eye for those who had only one purpose.

James, now aware that danger lurked in their area, wished that they weren't alone. Normally, Skyler would be here. Their young friend, orphaned at the age of thirteen, had been with them since the terminus of that first catastrophic winter. His skill with both the bow and rifle, along with his unsettling lack of fear, had made him an integral part of their survival through that first year. Skyler, taking advantage of the break in the weather, was away for a few days, probably fishing or hunting. He was their sole source of fish and meat prior to their isolation through the winter. James, grateful for the game Skyler brought to their table, now wished more than ever that the boy were here.

As he pulled the last nail out, he deftly lowered the plywood to the deck, being careful not to drop it on its edge. He looked around once more. This time, instead of scanning the valley for the riders, he inspected the terrain around him. Their house was well situated on a hill; surrounded by fields on three sides—open spaces that could only hide someone at night. It would be difficult to attack this place without warning. That is, it used to be that way. The neighboring house, burned down during an attack just a few months ago, left no one to guard his blind spot. He felt another chill and wondered if he would ever feel warm again.

CHAPTER 1

March 25th, 2031
10:45 am

James stayed on the deck for no reason other than to observe. And not just the valley below. He observed the yard with the gardens waiting to be tilled again, but it was Lara who occupied his thoughts. They'd worked and fought hard to make this place their home. If this sighting proved to be what he feared, hadn't she suffered enough? If they were attacked, could she keep it together? She appeared to be as tough as any woman he'd ever met, carving a life from the debris left by the storms and the Change. But James knew differently. Lara wasn't as fragile as a snowflake, but she didn't handle adversity well. He intentionally kept his fears from her just to avoid any unnecessary stress on her part. She had survived unmeasureable terrors over the last two years; James wasn't sure how much more she could take. He stood there scanning their layout, occasionally looking back at Lara. To his relief, she appeared unconcerned.

She would expect him to open up more windows. He'd have to find some excuse for stopping after the first one. Lifting the one large piece of plywood, he maneuvered it down the stairs to store in the garage. Leaning it against the wall, James could now continue with what he started up on the deck; taking inventory of his defenses. He walked around the house, checking on the few windows and doors that were boarded shut. They were already sealed when they'd acquired this place the previous spring. Once the property of some bank before the Change, it was one of the few houses that had survived the riots and then that first winter. As long as he left the bottom of the house boarded, the only way in would be up the single flight of stairs to the upper deck. That was one of the reasons he liked this place; it made him feel safe.

Satisfied with the security of the lower floor, he glanced over the back yard. Once a green lawn used for family gatherings, it was now completely turned into garden space. The winter had packed the earth, leaving it as hard and brown as a coffee bean. It had proved to be sufficient size for the three of them. Keeping a count of their food stores, and monitoring their consumption, told him they had slightly more than enough to get them through the summer. Still, he felt the need to expand on what they tilled. He wanted a bank of food, enough to get them through hard times should their growing season be cut short.

He rounded the last corner; before him stood the trunks of twenty-five dead cedars. How he missed the scent of evergreens. Would he ever get the chance to smell one again? Like all the trees, these had probably died during that first bad winter; their tentacle-like roots frozen by the constant sub-zero temperatures. The two houses that harbored them from the high winds was the only reason they were still upright; the other trees had been snapped off like twigs. Their boughs were already turning from green to brown in the short time that James had lived here. His only reason for not cutting them down sooner was the barrier they created between his house and Mike's. They'd given him and Lara some privacy. Now with Mike and his house gone, burned during an attack last fall, these trees—or rather their charred skeletons—were only a false curtain to the west. They needed to go. To expand his garden and improve his security, he'd want to open up Mike's yard to claim it for his own. His only hesitation was the blackened foundation of what remained of Mike's house. Each time he looked upon it, he'd pause and take a deep breath, pushing back the rush of memories from that one horrible night.

Finding his ax in the corner of the garage, James began chopping away at the first tree in the row. He liked the mindless work. The aerobic exercise made him feel younger and gave him time to think. His thoughts went back to their security and how he would tell Lara his fears. His train of concentration was constantly interrupted by his need to look out over the valley below. Had the riders found what they were looking for or would they come here? Each time he'd glance up from his work, the blackened foundation would also enter his field of view.

By mid-afternoon, two-thirds of the trees lay pointing west away from his place. Between the hard work and the afternoon sun, James had shed his coat, yet still wore two layers to shield him against the biting cold. Lara had come down only once to ask him why he was removing the cedars. This time she wore her coat; her head covered by a wool ski cap.

"We could use them for firewood," was his only answer, not yet willing to alarm her about his fears with their apparent lack of security.

"Well, I'll be up on the deck planting seeds in paper cups. If we can start the tomatoes early enough, they might turn red by harvest time."

"Aren't you worried about them freezing at night? It's still pretty cold after dark."

"I'll bring them inside until it's safe to start the garden. I'm hoping this year we can have them in the ground as early as late April."

As James watched her walk away, he felt a familiar tug on his heart. They were as close as two people could be without being lovers. Yet he realized how much he'd cared for her when she had been abducted and taken from him last fall. As much as he disliked violence, he'd killed one of the men, holding no regrets about his actions. Their second winter together was uneventful, without attacks, except from the intermittent storms. Their platonic relationship remained stagnant because of the tenuous life they led. These were new times, different times, and surviving had become their predominant drive. However, in his own way, he adored her. It wasn't her beauty, but her balance that he yearned. She filled voids that he didn't know existed until he'd met her.

Picking up his axe, he glanced to the south once more—still, no sign of the riders, the ones that now plagued his subconscious. As he worked, he thought about the weaknesses in his defenses, seeking answers to this predicament. Because his mind was so busy contemplating his options, he failed to notice when he dropped the final cedar. Arms and shoulders sore, sweaty from the hard work despite the chill, he returned the ax to the garage. That was enough for one day. If he was to spend the night on the deck, he'd need a few hours of sleep first.

An hour before sunset, James dressed in his heavy coat, grabbed his hat, and went out on the deck with his blanket. The wool blanket, thick and coarse, was for his legs. He sniffed the air once, testing it for an odor that would soon arrive; the smell of thawing decay. Something he'd grown to appreciate last spring; a sign that the cold nights would soon be retreating. He repositioned his chair, an old, unpainted Adirondack found in the garage. Lara, bundled in her winter coat, came outside carrying a dining room chair, positioning it so their knees faced each other. James shared the blanket with her, thankful for her company. After fifteen months of living in close quarters, they never tired of each other's companionship. He read to her, a habit acquired when they first met. Something small that he could do for her after all she had done for him. Books weren't in abundance, but James had collected what wasn't destroyed by water or fire. To him, books were the only record of their history. He considered the knowledge they held as invaluable. The reading would last until the sun finally set, when he would be forced to put the book down. They talked for a few minutes longer, reflecting on what they had accomplished, books they liked, and their upcoming birthdays. He would turn forty-one in the summer. Her birthday—a few weeks to come—would be her forty-fourth. Finished with their time together, she finally stood, touched him on the shoulder and retreated back inside. She would sleep while he guarded their house.

With his compound bow and rifle at his side, he scrutinized the fields with both his eyes and ears. They'd moved here just over ten months earlier after an unexpected middle-of-the night attack at their former residence. That was when James realized how vulnerable they were by living on a dead-end street surrounded by wind-damaged houses. This new location, this formidable house, had been built on the west side of Ferndale. It sat alone over a hundred yards from the nearest structure. They were two miles from the Interstate, and less than a mile from the downtown, which was located just down the hill. From any given point on the deck, James could observe most, but not all of the openness of the terrain around him. He passed some of the time moving his chair about the L-shaped deck trying to find the best location to watch the front, back and sides all at once. No matter where he sat, there was always a blind spot. Having to contend with this handicap made it difficult for him to relax. When Mike lived next door, there was an unspoken sense of security that kept this fear at bay.

Compared to what he'd found elsewhere in the area, living here made surviving viable. The town of Ferndale was built in the 1800s in the northwest corner of Washington State along the Interstate—a ribbon of highway that ran north-south on the west side of the Cascade mountain range. Although they were only fifteen miles from the Canadian border, there was no longer any real boundary. Canada's fate had followed the United States and possibly the rest of the world when the Change took place. Many of Canada's surviving residents followed the Interstate south in search of warmer climates, as did most of the surviving locals from this corner of the state. James had presumed that the overabundance of immigrants to the southern West Coast would overwhelm the infrastructure there. Unless proven otherwise, staying in Ferndale was still his safest option.

This night, uneventful as it was, gave him time to think. James spent much of the night contemplating their security. Each issue became a hurdle that he mentally had to leap over before moving on to the next. Like a detective collecting clues, he had to anticipate every possible scenario. By the first hint of dawn, he'd formulated a plan—one that should allow him to sleep a bit easier. He'd still have to spend nights guarding the house, but at least they'd have a fighting chance if there came under attack.

Shortly after the sun peeked over the horizon, he quietly stood, stretching as he took one last look around. Only after he was sure it was safe, did he descend the stairs, careful not to disturb Lara. He walked over to the neighboring foundation. He'd avoided it before, as if it were a coffin, a vessel that carried nothing he wanted. That was true until now. He inspected its concrete walls and pushed some of the rubble around with his boot. Satisfied, he returned to the deck to wait for Lara to wake. When she was up, he finally allowed himself to sleep, knowing she would keep watch and alert him if necessary. A rainless day. Lara would be busy outside, possibly turning over soil in preparation for planting. Days like this were rare in the spring. She would want to take advantage.

James needed to make a trip up onto the hill above them. His plan required the cooperation of those that lived there. At the top of Church Road was a family of eleven that he'd bonded with last fall. They included four men, three of which were war veterans. Back during that awful time when Lara had been abducted and James had been left for dead, the men had risked their lives to help him, asking for nothing in return. During this last harsh winter, James had gone to visit them on two occasions when the winds had paused long enough to allow the short trip up the hill. They had welcomed him as a friend, willing to share their food, offering space in their already overcrowded house, an act of kindness that came unexpectedly. James always declined, knowing that though their generosity was unlimited, their resources were not. James, Lara, and their house mate Skyler, had canned enough vegetables to get them through the winter, spring and most of the upcoming summer. They didn't feel right about accepting such an offer from a larger family that probably had fewer provisions than they had. The connection they'd made with the people on the hill, one of the few things that kindled hope for the future, seemed to become stronger each time he visited them.

In addition to this family, there was only a smattering of survivors just outside of town. Through Skyler's hunting trips, James had learned of other families lucky enough to have survived the winter of 2029 and the summer that followed it; the summer when the soldiers came, taking what they wanted without self-reproach. James didn't know the numbers, but they had killed entire families who hadn't cooperated. What the winter storms hadn't destroyed, they had. Now, a new possible threat crossed the valley. Once again, James needed help protecting what he'd acquired.

Smoke escaping from the chimney indicated that Lara was awake. She would soon be preparing their breakfast, a bit earlier than usual. James had been anxious for the night to end, eager to move forward with his plan. Climbing back up the stairs, he looked around again, and felt some hope that his plan could succeed. Picking up his blanket, bow, and rifle, he headed to the front door.

"How was it?" Lara asked. She stood in the kitchen, bundled from head to foot, stoking the fire in their wood stove.

"Boring as hell. Just the way I like it." He leaned the rifle and bow inside the door, folded the blanket, placing it on a table. "As soon as I eat something, I'm going to hit the sack right away. Can you wake me before midday?"

"Yeah, sure. Why?"

She always asked why. For this reason, he thought of his replies in advance. The answer had to be neutral in nature to keep her from kindling a spark of worry. "Today would be a good day to walk up the hill to visit Petar and his family. I haven't seen them in almost two months. Want to go with me?"

"I'd like that. I hope Skyler stayed up there last night. I expected him back yesterday. Besides, I'd like to see Brandy again."

Two weeks earlier, Skyler hiked out to some ponds in search of migrating waterfowl. The ponds, located four miles to the west between two abandoned refineries, were still iced over with patches melting near the centers. The boy's desire to hunt and fish seemed to override any respect of the cold. He hadn't reported that any ducks were seen, probably because it was too early for a northern migration. Skyler had returned with his fishing pole. After breaking a hole through the ice near shore, he had caught a handful of small crappies. Each trip out had been a one-day excursion, with Skyler always returning with a string of fish. The protein it provided had been a welcome change in their diet. A week ago, with his small tent and sleeping bag stowed in his backpack, he set out to catch a quantity of the fish. Taking them back alive, he intended to transplant them to the pond that sat in the field near their house. As he'd said he would, Skyler returned the next afternoon with two five-gallon buckets half-filled with fish and water. Because of multiple rest stops, it had taken him over four hours to complete the return trip. It occurred to James that they were now officially fish farmers.

Three days ago, Skyler left for the ponds again, buckets in hands, camping gear on his back. His goal was to deliver live fish to the people on the hill. When he didn't return home by the second night, James and Lara could only assume that he'd spent his last night up on the hill, as he often did. Skyler and Brandy had grown closer through the winter. Like Skyler, she too was an unfortunate orphan as a result of the first catastrophic winter. Through the winter, he stayed with her family for up to a week at a time; their pairing viewed as a bright spot amid a sea of turmoil.

As promised, Lara woke James from his well-earned sleep. She took the initiative, preparing him a lunch of spiced carrots and beets. Wasting no time, James wolfed down the food before putting on his boots. Since the attack last fall, he'd almost always slept fully dressed. Once out the door, he noticed that the day was warmer than expected; no wind to carry the chill down from the mountains. Lara, as usual, was dressed to disguise herself as a man, a ruse she developed last spring to prevent herself from becoming a target. After they left the house, his pace quickened with determination, and Lara matched him step for step. Finally, in what she would have called a personal record, they arrived at the log barricade. Built from large power poles atop Church Road, this structure formed a barrier that spanned the road. It was constructed at a time when these people wanted no visitors.

After taking the path around the wooden structure, it was another five minutes before they reached the entrance into the development. As they walked down the street lined with the vacant, wind-battered houses, they spotted Skyler with Brandy and two young children. He was teaching them how to shoot bows. James could see that the bows were not anything like the compounds that he and Skyler carried, but were handmade from some kind of hardwood. They sported long cylindrical shafts with no recurve, carved from a single tree limb or small trunk. They had enough power to pierce a plastic jug with only blunt tips on their arrows.

"Skyler, where did you get the bows?" James asked.

Skyler smiled at the sight of his friends. "Brent and I made them. He had a book with pictures and a description. I found the dried limbs out near the ponds." His boyish face, darkened by spending most of his time outdoors, was framed by light brown hair that had gone uncut through the winter. His lean body was topped by muscular arms cultivated by the countless hours of shooting his bow and carrying buckets of fish over long distances.

Brandy had lowered her bow as did the two younger archers. Brandy handed hers to James for him to inspect, allowing her to exchange hugs with Lara. James hefted the weight of the bow before pulling back on the string to test its strength—it was surprisingly taut. The string itself looked to be of some type of parachute cord. The whole thing was nearly four feet in height. A grip was made using the same parachute cord by winding it around the shaft multiple times. James noted that every arrow was homemade, probably carved from split cedar. Crude as they were, they flew straight. Unless James could find a supply of the aluminum shafts, he would soon be using hand-carved arrows also.

"These are nice, but you realize how difficult it will be to sneak up on a bird with something as long as this." James handed the bow back to Brandy.

"They're not just for hunting," said Brandy. "Our supply of bullets won't last forever. Brent wants us to see if these can be an alternative."

James nodded in approval. He'd once taught Skyler that bows were man's first weapons and would probably be the last. So far, he was right. And now, Skyler was sharing the knowledge with the family that they had grown to trust.

James hadn't seen Brandy in two months. He was surprised at how tall she'd grown; her height almost matched Skyler's. He also noticed that her forearms were no longer soft looking like a young girl's. With her hair cropped like Lara's, the only hints that she wasn't a young man came from her softened facial features and voice. Both she and Skyler would be turning fifteen within the next couple of months, yet they didn't look like children to him.

"Where's the rest of the crew?" James asked. "I need to talk with them as well as the two of you."

"They're in the house with Scott. I don't know if you knew this, but he's not doing so well."

This caught Lara's attention. She moved a step closer to the younger woman, motherly in her action. "What's wrong with him?"

"He's lost a lot of weight and he complains about stomach pains. The pain is so bad that he can't sleep. We're all really worried about him."

James' face took on a look of concern. Lara, formerly a nurse, also appeared alarmed and said without hesitation, "I'd be glad to look at him, but we didn't bring any medical supplies."

Skyler and Brandy led the way as the four headed down the street leaving the two younger children behind to hone their skill. The development was composed of over seventy homes before the first storm hit in December of 2029. Now, only one structure was inhabitable. As they rounded the corner, James could see that one of the collapsed houses had been partially dismantled; the lumber stacked in piles on the street. 'They must finally be getting around to repairing a second house for their family,' he thought. All eleven of them had been living together in that one house. The cramped quarters had not appealed to Lara on the few occasions they were invited to stay on the hill.

The house that Brandy's family lived in had not changed since the first time James had seen it last fall. Except for an intact roof and shuttered windows, it appeared no different than the surrounding homes, debris scattered everywhere around it. They wound their way toward the front porch through the maze of garbage intended as a subterfuge to camouflage their abode. Skyler swung back the large sheet of plywood that hid the front door. James held the door open long enough so the other three could see their way through the dark living room crowded with beds and couches. Leftover from an extended winter of wood burning, a smoky odor, mixed with the smells of human habitation, enveloped the room. They walked through toward a lighted doorway, into the sunlit kitchen, finding the six adults at the large dining room table. Scott sat at the head of the table with his head in his hands. James could see the despair on the other five faces as they looked up in recognition.

"James! Lara! Welcome back!" Petar exclaimed. He stood, reaching out to shake hands with James. He was the unspoken patriarch of this family. His body was lean and his height was taller than average. A not too handsome face was adorned by dark foreboding eyes that didn't match his outgoing friendly personality. Gray hairs flanked his temples. Besides Scott, there was Petar, his wife Ella, Brent, Lydia, and John McBride.

Lara moved around the table, touching each person she passed with a gentle hand to acknowledge them. When she reached Scott, she placed her hand on his back, which caused him to look up at his visitors. James' heart sank when he saw the toll the illness had taken on Skyler's former teacher and oldest member of this family; he was the only male member of the family who wasn't a war veteran. All of them were thin from their meager diet, but Scott looked like a skeleton with pale white skin stretched over the bones, making him appear older, more frail than his actual age of forty-eight. Scott feigned a slight smile at the sight of Skyler's family members.

Addressing Scott, Lara asked, "What were the first symptoms when you started feeling ill?"

Scott paused a few seconds while he collected his thoughts. "I had a tender area down in my lower abdomen that hurt when I tightened my belt. Then it got worse. Sometimes, I would get quite nauseous and couldn't hold down any food or water."

Brent's wife, Lydia, spoke up. "He also seems to be running a fever most of the time." She was at least a dozen years younger than Lara; yet, raising two small children during the Change had stolen her youthful attractiveness. Her hair was also cut like a man's and she wore a pair of denim bib overalls over an old wool sweater.

"Well, in a way, that may actually be good. A constant fever means that it's probably not cancer. Maybe it's something that's curable," Lara said to the group. "My first guess is that he might have an infection in the colon. It can happen when food gets trapped in small pockets in the colon wall. Has he been eating any seeds or nuts?"

This time Brent answered for the group. "We don't have either of those items in our food supply. Since Scott became ill, his diet has been entirely composed of cooked vegetables." Brent was the youngest adult male seated at the table. Like Petar, he was also a veteran. His short military career had ended ten years earlier, placing him back in Ferndale without a job in a dying economy. A resourceful man, Brent had found work in construction and stayed employed until that final year when the degradation became exponential.

"What can we do for him?" Lydia pleaded.

"Antibiotics might help, but he needs to get some relief from the pain so he can sleep and eat again. Ibuprofen would dull the pain, reduce some of the tissue swelling, maybe even allow some food to pass through. We need to search the other homes around here for these medications," Lara said as she looked at everyone, including James.

Ella, Petar's wife, had remained quiet throughout the discussion. A petite woman, maybe five feet tall at tops, spoke only when she had something important to pass on. She gently raised her hand and said, "Little Brent and Bekka have crawled through every structure surrounding us. They know more about these houses than we do."

John McBride stood to get everyone's attention, his demeanor less broken than the others. In his mid-thirties, he was tall with the chiseled features of a soldier; a look that he made no effort to change. He kept his hair cut, not allowing it to grow more than an inch in length. Clearing his throat, he said, "Let's start looking right away. We can split up and cover more houses that way. We can even enlist some of the younger children to help by making it a game to find pills."

James held up his hand as if to stop everyone from rising and said, "Wait, before we rush out of here, I need to discuss something with all of you. I'm worried about something I saw yesterday."

At the mention of the word 'worried', McBride sat back down, waiting for James to continue. Everyone else also gave James their full attention. Lara pulled up an empty chair next to Scott, eager to hear what had been on James' mind since yesterday morning.

12

James began by saying, "Yesterday, I watched a group move along Slater Road at a fast pace. They appeared to be riding bicycles and heading west. I tried to count the riders, but could only guess that there were maybe up to a dozen or more." He paused after seeing that he'd truly caught everyone's attention. "I realized that if this group is hostile, they could ride right down to my house and attack us without warning. I no longer feel that Lara and I are safe."

Petar spoke up first. "You know that you've always been welcome to move up here with us."

"I know that and I'm grateful for that option. However, Lara and I like where we live. We had some security when Mike was alive and living next door. It's now obvious that without their house on our blind side, I can't fully protect our house. What I'd like to do is rebuild their house. The foundation is a daylight basement and appears to be in good shape. If one or two of you could help me, we can construct a house on the existing foundation before summer is out. I can't do it by myself as long as I'm awake all night ensuring our safety."

The group before him remained quiet. Brent and Lydia looked at each other, as if they were having a silent conversation. Finally, Brent asked, "Who would live in this house once it's built?"

"Whoever helps me the most can have first rights to living there," James replied. He knew that Lydia and Brent had not liked living in such a crowded home, now glad that Brent was curious about the offer. "I also have one other favor to ask," James added. "While we are out looking for antibiotics and pain relievers, can you gather any old bicycles, bicycle parts, and tire pumps that you find?"

"What for?" asked Petar.

"If we're attacked, it would take you ten or fifteen minutes to run to our rescue. If you had bicycles, you could arrive within three minutes."

Once again, the group sat speechless as they digested what James had just asked of them. Brent, Petar and McBride had joined up with James and Skyler when Lara had been abducted last fall. They had fought alongside him and Skyler, defeating the soldiers who once terrorized the area.

There was no question as to whether or not they'd do it again. What few families remained had to look out for each other. There were still roving bands of survivors, Wanderers, who chose hunting over harvesting, and they hunted for those that had food.

James looked at the group, adding seriously, "We also need to talk about starting over. We've survived two winters since the Collapse. What do we want our future to hold? The way I see it, we need to organize ourselves and form some kind of pseudo-government that can make decisions. Skyler has connected with other families not far from here. We should get their input and support."

Petar's family nodded in agreement. James could see the hint of a smile form on Lara's face. She approved with what he was asking.

Brent stood, directing his question at James. "If one of us agrees to help you build the house, where would we stay during those months?"

Lara spoke before James even had a chance to open his mouth, "With us! We have a large master bedroom in the lower half of our house. We would love to share that space."

James was surprised at her offer. He hadn't really thought that far ahead. His main concern had only been enlisting someone to help. But relocating someone to his house would mean he'd have help with the chores and overnight guard duties. He worried that these people might reject his appeal, but now, it looked like a possibility. Finally, he said to the group, "Let's go do some scavenging for medicine and bicycles. We can talk more after we get Scott comfortable again."

CHAPTER 2

March 28th, 2031
9:15 am

Over the next couple of days, James spent a few hours each morning cleaning out the foundation of Mike's house. He had stayed away from the detritus of his neighbor's home since the fire last October, fearful that he'd find the charred remains of the couple that once lived there. He'd tried to warn them, warn them of the soldiers' intent, but Mike wouldn't listen. As he shoveled the wet ash intermixed with melted bits of metal and glass, he was relieved to find that everything had burned completely.

Skyler, as expected, did not return with Lara and him. He'd stayed on the hill for numerous reasons, most of which were centered on Brandy. The bows that he was making were evolving, the children were being trained. He was also helping them with the rebuilding of a second house. James could have used his help, who was still spending his nights on the deck, leaving him with only a few hours each day to work on the project. They had the gardens to dig, firewood to collect, leaving little time for him and Lara to enjoy their friendship. However, James harbored no ill feelings about Skyler's absence knowing that he, too, was staying productive.

James, busy with end-of-winter tasks, never stopped thinking about building the new house. The lumber, insulation, and hardware, would come from abandoned houses that were beyond repair. He already knew that to find windows that were fully intact, he'd have to do some serious searching. Only after accumulating a collection of doors and windows, recording their sizes, could he consider its design, and create a makeshift blueprint. The roof, the most difficult problem, could not exceed a size greater than the amount of attainable roofing material. What excited him about this project, more so than the safety of having neighbors once again, was that they could build something made for the new environment; a house that wasn't threatened by high winds and extreme cold. The roof could collect water from rain and warmth from the sun. The hillside it was being built on was perfect; dirt surrounded the eight-foot concrete walls on three of its four sides. It would be much easier to keep warm than a conventional house.

James strained as he lifted a full bucket of wet ash in each hand. Setting them in place, he noticed Lara, using her weight to drive the spade, turning the soil in her garden. Before he'd cut down the row of trees, they had formed a barrier separating the yards; now their yard was larger, the visibility much better. Watching Lara turning over the sod, he thought about the fact that it wasn't 'their' garden. Other than hauling buckets of water up from the pond, he neither planted seeds nor pulled weeds. It was all hers. She worked the soil, planted the seeds, and canned at harvest time. Last fall, they stored almost three hundred quart jars of beets, carrots, corn, tomatoes, and cucumbers. She also managed, with a small spud supplied by Brandy, to grow one potato plant. She wouldn't allow anyone to eat any of the potatoes when it was harvested: the eight spuds it produced were saved for seeds for this upcoming garden. As hard as she worked, she never once complained. The garden gave her purpose.

James was about to quit for the morning when he noticed Lara looking up in terror, dropping her shovel.

"James!" she screamed.

James dropped the buckets, hopped over the foundation's wall, fumbling for the pistol in his coat pocket, his heart racing as fast as his feet. Lara stood frozen with fear, unable to move. Within seconds, he positioned himself in front of her, raising his pistol in the direction that she was staring. Two bicycles were coming at high speed down the short street directly toward them. James aimed at the first rider, following him with the sights. Only then did he recognize him; it was Skyler. He quickly lowered the barrel and turned to Lara with a grin. She must have recognized him at the same time, exclaiming, "It's just Skyler!"

Brent was on the second bicycle. Both pulled up to the edge of the concrete just thirty feet from where Lara had been digging. Skyler had his bow over his back while Brent wore a rifle with a sling. Skyler shouted to them, "One hundred and thirty five."

"What do you mean?" asked James.

Brent answered for him. "It took us one hundred and thirty-five seconds to get here from the barricade. You were right; we can arrive in less than three minutes once we know you're in danger."

James and Lara walked over to where Skyler and Brent were straddling their bikes. Brent was on a mountain bike with fat knobby tires, while Skyler had a multi-speed road bike. Both bikes had been painted a matte black finish that covered everything, including the reflectors and spokes. James noticed there were no shiny parts visible.

Skyler, breathless and obviously pleased, added, "We managed to assemble six like these. We've found enough tires to last us for years."

"Nice work!" Lara said, but her tone became serious when she asked, "How's Scott doing?"

"Somewhat better," said Brent. "The ibuprofen we found kicked in later the other night after you left. He was able to eat a full meal before finally getting a night's sleep. Lydia woke him every four hours and forced him to take more pills. He still has some cramping, but he's out walking around and says he's feeling better. He wanted me to express his thanks for what you did for him."

James had been hoping that the medications still had some potency. Before he and Lara had left the hill, they had found about a dozen bicycles in various sizes, and only a handful of outdated jars of aspirin, ibuprofen, antibiotics, and other medications. There was maybe enough ibuprofen to last Scott three or four weeks.

"He's not out of danger yet," Lara said. "The anti-inflammatory won't cure the infection; it can only give him some relief. We'll need to have him relax for a while and drink lots of water every day. I appreciate that you came all the way down here to update us."

"That wasn't the only reason we came," said Brent as he dismounted. "I want to see this house that you plan to build. Lydia and I are considering taking you up on your offer. That is, if you think you can handle my two kids living with you."

Lara smiled at this. "Your son and daughter are so well behaved that I don't even have to think twice about it. Of course, you are all welcome to live with us. This house is surprisingly spacious, and we can fix up the garage as a playroom for the children."

Brent looked toward James. "Well, are you going to show me around?"

"Sure. Follow me." They walked the fifty feet over to the blackened concrete walls. "I'm almost finished with cleaning out the foundation. The concrete appears to be stable, but there are some cracks from the high heat." James pointed at the tall back wall where the dark lines resembling varicose veins ran from top to bottom. "I think we can seal those with some kind of filler so that water won't leak in."

Brent scrutinized the back wall as he contemplated what James was showing him. "I did concrete work for a year after I got out of the Marines. I think a better way to stop those cracks from becoming a problem is to dig out behind those walls and slide some kind of water-proof barrier over the outside of each wall. It should only take us a couple of days to do it."

James appreciated that Brent seemed very interested. He continued with the plan he was working on. "The first thing we'll need to do is round up doors and windows. Once we have them, I can draw up blueprints. The next step is to compose a list of the different sizes of boards we'll need. There are three damaged houses nearby that we can dismantle for the building supplies."

"What about a roof?"

"I'm still deliberating about that. Whatever we do, it has to be just about bombproof and will need to funnel rain to one side. The only shingles available are old and damaged."

Brent seemed satisfied with James' plans. "Can you show me the living quarters where Lydia and I will be staying until it's finished?"

The two men walked back over to the house and climbed the stairs. Once on the deck, Brent stopped and took in the view, "My God, I can see forever from up here. No wonder you like this place so much."

"It makes it easier to defend, but in the winter we have no shelter from the wind."

James led the way through the house, grabbing a candle on his way down to the lower level. "We'll need a light, since I've kept the ground floor boarded up for security reasons." Once down the stairs, James took him to the doorway between the large bedroom and family room.

"Holy cow, this is as large as our house up on the hill!" exclaimed Brent.

"You can see why we didn't have any qualms about you moving in. With your family living here, we can remove some of the boards from the top of the windows. That way, you'll have a natural source of light. If we can find a toilet that isn't cracked, we might be able to make the bathroom work for you as well."

"I know where there are two. I came across them when we were rounding up medicine."

"Good, we can save the second one for the new house—that is, if the heat from the fire didn't damage the sewer pipe. I'm getting the sense that you and your family are going to make the move down here. Would that be a correct assumption?"

"Without a doubt! Lydia and I are anxious to have our own space. We'll come down tomorrow afternoon and get settled in."

"That's great. Let's go tell Lara."

When the two men stepped out onto the deck, they could see Skyler and Lara in the yard below, pointing at something south of their house.

"What are you guys looking at?" shouted James.

The sudden loud question startled Lara, but for only an instant. Still pointing in the direction of Slater Road, she said, "I thought I saw something down there off in the distance. Now I can't find it again."

James and Brent scanned the expansive fields below for any movement. Suddenly, Brent pointed to a moving shadow near the intersection of Slater and Imhoff. "There it is."

James ran back inside, returning with the binoculars. Handing them to Brent, he said, "Take a look. That's the same group I saw down there a few days ago."

Brent described what he could see to the rest. "They're definitely on bikes. There must be at least ten or more riders." He continued to watch even as he handed the binoculars back to James. "You'd better look again; they just turned up Imhoff and are headed this way."

James grabbed the glasses. They were slightly less than three miles away, but at that speed, they could be in Ferndale in fifteen minutes. "What do you think we should do?" he asked Brent.

"Let's take some of those logs lying on the side of the house and spread them across the entrance. It might be enough of a deterrent to keep them from turning in here."

Lara and Skyler had just made it up on the deck. James handed Lara the binoculars. "Keep us posted as to their location. We're going to try to block the road into here." Both men ran down the stairs and disappeared around the corner.

The cedar logs were all about fifteen to twenty feet in length; the width varied from eight to ten inches in diameter. Each of them grabbed the ends of one of the logs, jogging it out toward the intersection at Main Street. Laying it across the entrance, its length was maybe half the width of the street. James estimated they used up five minutes on that single log. "That took too long," he panted. "We need to work faster."

"Then let's each drag a log out there," said Brent.

Each man hefted a log by the heavy end and started dragging it toward the street. Once they were on asphalt, the resistance diminished and the work became easier. Still, that much exertion all at once made them break out in a sweat.

No sooner had they positioned the two logs to fill in the gaps, when Lara shouted at them. "They just disappeared behind the hill! They're only about a quarter-mile from Main Street!"

Brent pulled his rifle from his back. "I'll hide behind that house there and keep an eye out for them. You go back and set up your defenses. We won't know what we're up against until they get closer. Be sure to arm both Lara and Skyler."

James was happy to take orders from Brent. His military background and years spent fighting in the Middle East had made him an invaluable asset. When James was younger, he'd avoided joining any of the armed forces. He had almost no knowledge of the best way to defend against an attack from multiple persons. As he reached the house, he took the stairs three at a time. Lara held the .22 caliber pistol that she carried when James slept during the day. "Put that in your pocket for now," he told her, "I'd rather have you use a rifle. That pistol is only accurate up close." He didn't need to say a word to Skyler, who was already armed with his bow and arrows.

Moments later, the three of them were crouched down below the rail of the deck as they watched Main Street. From their vantage point, they could see Brent as he stood peeking out from the corner of a house that sat only a few yards off the road. Part of the roof of the house leaned against the same side of the house that Brent was watching from, affording him a place to take cover if they did come this way. They watched Brent closely for several minutes until he turned and signaled that the bicyclists were coming up the hill.

The logs they'd laid on the road were not the deterrent they had hoped for, but they would require the bikers to dismount if they were to cross them. James hoped that they would continue up Main Street, bypassing the entrance to their home, but knew that might be unlikely. They were hunters of a sort. Survivors with homes grew vegetables with little reason to venture out through the surrounding area. These hunters were the opposite; they had every reason to roam since they didn't take the time to grow and harvest crops. To those that did grow food, storing it away in preparation for winter, these marauders were their greatest threat.

Within a few minutes, Brent backed away from the western side of the house, repositioning himself behind the next house. Whoever was coming up the hill had to be drawing near. James could see a gap between the corner where Brent hid himself and the next damaged structure. As he watched, through the thin gap, he could see several cyclists laboring up the hill at a slow pace. Every two or three had a rifle slung over his back. James looked at his companions and could tell that they had also seen what was coming. No sooner had the last ones crossed the narrow field of view, when the front riders came into the open just before the intersection. James raised his binoculars, inspecting the intruders closely. When the entire group reached the road that led in toward them, they all came to a stop. James could see a couple of them pointing toward their house, talking among themselves. James counted twelve of them. What surprised him was their age—the youngest was maybe ten years old, while the oldest could not have been more than eighteen. Of the twelve, three, possibly four, could be girls.

The riders stood their ground for only a couple of minutes before continuing up Main Street. When they disappeared from sight, James told Lara and Skyler to stay up on the deck. James wanted to see if they were going to stay on Main Street or turn up Church Road. Both were long hills, but Church Road had a steeper grade and would require them to dismount. James ran down the stairs, sprinted past the garage and over to the foundation of the new house where he could see the intersection and the rest of Main Street before it disappeared over the hill. He saw the riders stop once again near the opening of Church Road, but eventually kept going on Main until they disappeared from view. By the time James made it back over to their house, Brent had arrived with his rifle in hand.

"What do think they're looking for?"

"Food. What else? They looked awfully skinny. Only one had a real rifle. Three others had pellet guns," answered Brent.

"Any idea why they didn't turn in here?"

"Yeah, I heard them talking. They didn't like the looks of the situation. Maybe the logs in the road made them think twice. Regardless, if it came down to a fight, we had them out gunned."

James thought about that last statement. As long as Brent and Skyler were here, they did have them out gunned. However, what if they came back tonight before Brent and Lydia moved in? Something else was nagging him; where had they come from and where were they going? They were just kids, no different than Skyler when he'd met him. James once again felt the melancholy of a world turned upside down, where hungry, orphaned children resorted to any means for survival, even if it involved violence.

"Did you get a sense of where they came from?" he asked.

"Judging by the fact that three were wearing hockey jerseys, and one had a maple leaf on his backpack, I'd guess that they came out of Canada."

James looked at Brent. "Do you still want to move in?"

"Hell, yes. They didn't concern me that much. If they get their hands on more weapons, then we could have a problem. I'm thinking that they'll move on when they see that there's no food being handed out around here."

Skyler and Lara grew tired of waiting on the deck, so they came down to listen in. As they approached, James said, "I need to get some sleep before tonight. Skyler, will you hang out here this afternoon until I'm up for the night?"

Lara, concerned, asked, "What about those riders?"

James was quick to answer. "They really weren't very well-armed, and I doubt that they'll attack us, but we still need to stay alert. They're just a bunch of hungry kids scrounging for food."

The answer seemed to assuage Lara's fears. Finally, Brent slung his rifle back over his shoulder and said, "I need to start walking up the hill so Lydia and I can begin packing. I'll see you two sometime tomorrow."

"What about your bikes?" asked James.

"Those can stay here. We have four more up at our place. Maybe tomorrow, we should move a few more logs out near the intersection, just in case they do get desperate."

Lara returned to the garden to finish turning the soil. Without the wind, this was their warmest day so far this spring. Before James made it to the bedroom, Skyler stopped him. "I'm a little worried about some of the families west of here. There are two in that general direction where those riders were headed. Would you mind if I made a quick trip out there this evening to warn them about what we saw?"

"As long as you wait until I'm up, and you promise to return tonight. I'm a little nervous about being the only sentry here."

"I'll make it a quick trip. Try to get some sleep."

James' fatigue had been replaced by a rush of adrenaline when the riders had passed near their house. Now he found it difficult to relax and fall asleep. Something was bothering him, and he couldn't quite put a finger on it. Each time he thought about those kids, their ages, their disheveled appearance, a sense of foreboding swept over him. What wasn't he seeing? Were they really a threat or could they become an asset? He tried to take his thoughts elsewhere, but the image of Skyler the day he'd arrived at their house kept reappearing. The boy had been just as emaciated as them, if not more so. James would have liked to bring them in, feed them, but that was out of the question. What food he, Lara and Skyler stored, needed to last them until the next harvest, six months away. Besides, in this new era, you trusted no one. Finally, the adrenaline rush was replaced by exhaustion. James drifted off into a deep sleep.

CHAPTER 3

March 28th, 2031
4:00 pm

No sooner had James come out of the bedroom when Skyler updated him on the current status. His report was simple; the riders had not passed by again. This meant little except that they didn't know their whereabouts. They could be west of here, the direction in which they were headed, or they could have gone off in any direction once they'd crossed over the hill. Lara appeared in the doorway; hands dirty from working the garden, she headed for the wash bucket.

"There's still about three hours of daylight left. Are you rested enough for me to go check on those other families now?" Skyler asked James, once again acknowledging James as a surrogate father.

"Yeah, do that. Just make it quick and be careful. One more thing, can you ask one or two members of each family to come here for a meeting tomorrow afternoon? We need to discuss our future, our security, and the possibility of organizing ourselves."

Skyler nodded, wasting no time in picking up his bow, hooking his quiver on his belt, and running down the stairs. He was about to jog up the street when he remembered the bicycles. Slipping the compound bow over his back, he grabbed the bike he'd ridden down on and took off. Once he was on Main Street, his plan was to walk the bike up Church Road because there would be less chance of running into that group of riders. By crossing over Church hill, he could take the Thornton Road west. Both families, the Lopatnikovs and the Jensens, lived off there. Thornton had never been cleared of debris. It would slow him down to lift the bike over the power poles and other obstacles. It was logical that the riders would more than likely travel only on roads that they could easily maneuver.

Pushing his bike up the long hill, he thought back to that time last summer when he'd met both of those families. He'd been returning from the ponds one afternoon when he saw a thin wisp of smoke a couple of miles to the north, far from his route between the house and the ponds. It sparked his curiosity, his natural inclination to connect with other survivors. A week later, after shooting two ducks in one day, he'd gone out there searching for the source of the smoke. Skyler was familiar with the terrain, once having had a friend who lived in the area, but could not remember the names of all the roads; the signs long ago snapped off by the high winds. This friend's house, visible from the road he followed, like the trees, no longer stood erect. It still amazed him to see the damage that the winds were capable of doing, much like the tornados of the Midwest. The only difference was that here, there was no end to the devastation. Vast areas of wooded acreage, once providing shelter to so many wild and domestic animals now lay flattened as far as the eye could see.

On that day, he had continued north until he came across a graveled driveway. A driveway jutting from the road caught his attention. Dead trees were piled high on both sides of the curved driveway, limiting his view. Someone had cleared this path and was keeping it clear. Skyler cautiously walked down the driveway, a gauntlet of sorts. He soon broke out into an open area. From there, he had seen a tall house that looked intact surrounded by acres of garden. The house stood two-stories high, painted mostly white, its windows bordered with thick wooden-hinged shudders. Mismatched boards lacking paint hinted that it had only recently been repaired. A large barn behind the house looked as if it had been partially collapsed, but it was clear that it was being rebuilt. There had even been a coop with chickens. The people who lived there must have been well pre-pared for the Change, because this had been the most prosperous habitat he had come across. Skyler, his bow still slung over his back, untied a duck from his waist. He walked toward the house, holding the duck out in front of him, displaying his gift, when he heard the sound of a pump shotgun being readied behind him. Skyler stopped immediately, holding his breath and waiting.

"What you want?" asked a man with a thick foreign accent.

Skyler, having gone to school with several Russian children, thought he recognized the accent. He held up the waterfowl without turning around. There was an uncomfortable silence, the man obviously waiting for a verbal answer. Skyler cleared his throat. "I want to give you this duck."

"Why?"

Skyler had to think about his answer. Why had he come here? Curios-ity? The need to connect with other humans? "We may need each other someday."

The man shouted, "Dimitrey!"

A few seconds later, a boy of about ten ran out of the house. He didn't seemed surprised about finding a stranger standing in his yard, but had focused on arriving at the man's side as quickly as possible. Skyler still had his back towards the man and heard him speak to the boy in Russian. The boy stepped out in front of Skyler and asked, "What do you want?"

"I want to be friends. I don't want your food, and I don't want to hurt anybody."

The boy translated in rapid Russian to the man; it seemed to take twice as long to translate. The man said something much shorter in return to the boy. Skyler feared that it would translate into 'get out.'

"My father says, 'Welcome!'"

Dimitrey's family, large in size and numbers, had stepped away from their chores to meet this stranger. Skyler had counted eighteen in all, most of them knowing little or no English. Through Dimitrey, Skyler learned of another family just a mile further down Thornton; a friendly family that he was told he need not fear. Short on time, Skyler had bid good-bye before heading down the road to meet the family they called the Jensens. As expected, the second family was just as receptive as the Lopatnikovs. This had been the only time since the Change that Skyler had met friendly people outside of those who lived on the hill.

Now, Skyler reached the top of Church, remounted his bike, and peddled across the crest of the hill. He realized he had not visited either the Lopatnikovs or the Jensens since early October, and looked forward to seeing how they had fared through the winter. He'd felt an urge to stop in to say hi to Brandy, but reminded himself of his promise to James to return before dark and hurried on.

It was almost a half-hour before he reached Thornton. Skyler found that this last winter's force had deposited more debris on this road. Lifting the bike over every pole crossing his path soon became a nuisance. However, knowing there was a route he could ride home on, and that it would be downhill most of the way, he continued on. He never quit looking ahead or behind for strangers; he often felt wary when traveling alone, but the sightings earlier that day had heightened his awareness. Almost an hour after he'd left the house, the smell of wood smoke drifted his way. He was soon looking up the Lopatnikov's driveway. As Skyler walked the narrow road, he heard footsteps come from behind. Cautiously turning, he saw a man loosely cradling a shotgun. Skyler recognized him from last summer as Dimitrey's uncle. Together they walked up to the house. Soon, a dozen members of the Lopatnikov family appeared from various places.

Spotting Dimitrey and his father at the forefront of the crowd, Skyler asked the young boy to ask his father if they'd seen a group of teenagers on bicycles. Dimitrey translated for Skyler. The older man shook his head.

"Tell your father to be aware that there are twelve of them that they are probably looking for food. Can you also ask him if he will come to a meeting at our house tomorrow afternoon? My friend James feels that it is important for everyone to meet and discuss our future."

Skyler watched as a long conversation went back and forth between Dimitrey and his father. Finally, the boy turned to Skyler. "My father needs a map to your house. We will come for tomorrow's meeting."

"Good. I can't stay as I need to speak with the Jensens as soon as possible." Skyler drew them a crude map on a sheet of paper provided by one of Dimitrey's aunts. He noticed that the boy's father seemed to be the decision maker for this large family. Skyler handed him the map, the older man nodded, signifying that he knew where to go. His map would lead them down Thornton, where they would then turn right onto Church. Skyler made a mental note that he would need to alert Petar that there would be friendly strangers passing through the barricade.

Leaving the Lopatnikovs, Skyler continued west on Thornton, dismounting and remounting every one hundred feet or so. When he came to a crossroad only a quarter mile from the Jensens, the road ahead suddenly became clear of any debris. Obviously, they had been busy since Skyler's visit last October.

The Jensens were a non-related family in that no member had any blood lines connected with any other members; their only reason for living together was the need for food and protection. The old man who owned the place, Dag Jensen, had come to the United States from Norway when he was just a child. Skyler had befriended him shortly after meeting the Lopatnikovs the previous year. Dag, who mistrusted no one, had immediately taken a shine to the young boy. Skyler had guessed his age at seventy-five, but he could be older. After Dag's wife had passed away three years earlier, the old man had taken in stragglers, people to help out with the chores, creating gardens as food became scarce and expensive. Dag Jensen was considered 'too kind' since he feared no one and welcomed everyone without caution.

A thick stand of large conifers on three sides of their house had protected it during the first harsh winter over a year earlier. The trees did not withstand the winds, but the graveyard of thick timbers formed a protective bay much like a boat harbor. The Jensens, as Skyler called them, learned to cohabitate, depending on each other, falling into familial roles with Dag as the patriarch. Eventually, their number grew to eight. There were four men and an equal number of women. Only by chance were there no children to be found on this farm. Dag would have welcomed them too.

Skyler entered the yard and sensed something was wrong. The late afternoon, sunny and warm compared to most days, should have given them reason to be outside. All the windows were still shuttered, which also seemed odd. He became tentative about knocking on the front door. It had been six months since his last visit, yet nothing outside the house revealed what could have happened during that time.

Finally, Skyler shouted a loud "Hello," toward the house and waited. The door opened a crack and a rifle barrel appeared.

"What do you want?" a man's voice barked.

Skyler didn't readily recognize the voice and knew that it didn't belong to the older Norwegian.

"It's me, Skyler. I came to see if everyone is alright."

The barrel retreated back through the crack, the door slowly opening. A man with a woman hiding behind him appeared. He recognized the man's face as one of the family members. "Where's Mr. Jensen?" asked Skyler.

"He's sick in bed. Dag has not been feeling well for the last month."

"Where are the others?"

"They've been missing for the last two weeks. We sent them off to Bellingham to see if they could find some help for Dag. They never returned. Now there are only the five of us left."

By now, the woman hiding behind him had stepped in the open. Two other faces peeked out occasionally. "I came to warn you about a band of bicycle riders that might come out this way. They appear to be scavengers passing through, more than likely looking for food."

The man forced a sarcastic chuckle. "You are a little late with your warning. Twelve kids on bikes came through here an hour ago. They caught us working in our garden. The oldest one held the four of us at gunpoint while the others ransacked our house. It scared the hell out of us and the old man."

"What did they take?"

"All the food they could fit in their backpacks. It was all in Mason jars, so they didn't take much. To us, losing the Mason jars was more important than the food in them."

30

"Anything else?"

"They wanted to take my rifle, but the older boy wouldn't allow it. He was pretty adamant that none of the others were to touch any of the guns."

"Did you see which way they went after they left here?"

"West. They headed west. We only cleared the road down to the next intersection, so I suppose they'd have to turn south or north once they got there."

"I'm sorry that I wasn't able to warn you sooner. My friend James wanted me to invite a couple of you to a meeting at our house. The meeting is tomorrow in the afternoon. The Lopatnikovs will be coming as well as a few other people. James wants to discuss organizing ourselves."

"Sorry, but we can't afford to leave this place unguarded. Nor can a couple of us go while leaving only two behind."

"I think that James wants to figure out ways that we can all protect ourselves and each other. If you can't make it, then maybe we can get word to you about what was said."

Skyler had the attention of all four people, yet not one of them strayed beyond the doorway. Whatever had happened here an hour earlier had really shaken them. He realized that if these four were easily surrounded and robbed, Lara and James could also be in similar danger. Skyler now understood why James had been on high alert over the last few days. Pulling a piece of paper from his pocket, he drew a map of the route to their house. Once again, it directed them through the barricades on Church Road.

"Hang onto this; it's the safest route to our house. You'll pass through another friendly community like yourselves. If you can make it, I'm sure James won't waste your time. If not, you can find us here if you need our help." Skyler had to reach in through the doorway to get them to take the map. Just then the old man appeared. Other than looking tired, he didn't seem much different than last fall.

"Skyler, I thought I heard your voice. How are you?" asked Dag.

"I'm good, Mr. Jensen, but I hear that you've been sick."

The old man managed to grin at the comment. "I was, but I'm getting better. What do you know about these kids that came through here?"

"Sorry, but not much. James spotted them for the first time a few days ago. We only saw them up close this morning."

The old man shuffled closer to the door. "Just be careful when you leave here. We don't know which way they went. I heard what you said about a meeting. We'll do our best to make it there."

Skyler thanked him and turned to leave. It was getting late; James was expecting him back before dark. He mounted his bike and retraced his route, being careful to check the road before entering it. He wondered what could have happened to the three who hadn't returned after leaving for Bellingham.

Not knowing the whereabouts of the bicycle gang, Skyler's nervousness stepped up a level on his return trip. When he reached the intersection where he could turn left to reach the Lopatnikov farm, he had intended on going straight toward Church Road to update Petar and his family about the meeting. The road ahead was strewn with obstacles, while the road to his right was clear all the way to Mountain View and on into Ferndale. If he went right, he'd be home in much less time. He was now close to being overdue. James would worry. Turning right, Skyler decided he could visit his friends on the hill in the morning.

The first quarter mile was pedaling up and down small hills. The terrain, not the best for fast travel, limited his view. If he came upon someone, he would get little or no warning. The downed trees alongside the road increased his anxiety as he could become boxed in if surrounded. Once he made it past the series of dips and hills, feeling relieved that they were behind him, he started down a long hill that would lead him to Mountain View. His speed increased with the gentle grade until his cap threatened to fly from his head At the rate he was going, he estimated he'd be home in less than ten minutes.

Skyler was within two hundred feet of the intersection at Mountain View when he caught movement in his peripheral vision. Suddenly, he locked up the brakes. Off to his right, less than a quarter-mile to the west, on the same road he needed to get home, was the bicycle gang. When he'd turned to look, they were jumping on their bikes, pointing in his direction, the taller boys urging the slower ones to move faster. Skyler, taking only a second to weigh his options, continued ahead toward the intersection instead of retreating. He'd have almost a quarter-mile lead, and he was maybe a mile and a half from home.

Choosing not to slow when he made the turn, Skyler still caught a quick glimpse of his pursuers; the pack was already stretched out. At least three or four were pedaling hard to close the gap between themselves and him. The road, level for almost a mile, would eventually descend into town. He pedaled hard, breaking into a sweat, aiming for that point on the horizon where the road disappeared. Fear of the unknown, fear of what they wanted of him, drove him to push past his point of exhaustion. Like an athlete, he drove his body beyond its limitations. Each time he turned to look back, a couple of them appeared closer. Their intentions, whatever they might be, could not be good. Knowing that they had at least one rifle, and that they severely outnumbered him, kept him from dismounting and taking a stand.

Sweat rolled down his temples, salt stinging his eyes, as he saw the last small rise a few hundred yards before him. He stole a glance behind him; only one rider remained ahead of the rest. All he could tell was that this rider, taller than his companions, was much closer than when he last looked back. A rifle was slung over his back. Every instinct told Skyler that the guy was menacing.

The crest of the hill seemed to take forever to reach. Skyler finally reached the last sixty yards as the pavement rose at a steady incline to meet the crest. His speed diminished rapidly as he'd spent most of his reserves just trying to stay out of the grasp of the lone pursuer. Could that rider be close enough to stop his chase and use his rifle instead? The crest was now only thirty yards away, the grade having increased significantly. Skyler could hear someone behind him closing the gap. His lungs screamed, fighting for every oxygen molecule they could find. With only yards to go, within seconds of reaching the downgrade, he heard the rider breathing heavily behind him. Finally, he reached the crest, and despite his exhaustion, his speed increased as the road leveled out. Just as Skyler reached the far slope, he took one look back and saw the tall boy with broad shoulders, his face full of rage. Whoever he was, he was not much older than himself. With his heart wanting to explode, Skyler stood on his pedals, gave three strong power pushes, nearly doubling his speed as the road dropped away from the hill; the sounds of his pursuer fading behind him. In less than a quarter-mile, he'd make the turn into the street that led to their house. James would be there, undoubtedly armed. He realized that the noises following him had disappeared.

It wasn't until Skyler had to slow for that final turn that he looked back up the hill. The lone rider had not continued the chase after cresting the hill. Instead, he just stood there watching Skyler from the high point. Skyler, finally catching his breath, had to wonder why his pursuer had stopped, especially when he was so close. Stopping his bike at the intersection, knowing that safe harbor was nearby, he glanced back up the hill in time to see other riders joining the lone pursuer. Skyler's heart still raced, but the fear that had overwhelmed him only seconds before decreased rapidly. Then he realized why the chase had ended. The entire group of twelve was now coming down the hill, picking up speed by the second. Their leader, if that's who he was, had waited for the rest of the pack. Skyler lifted his bike over the logs and sprinted the last short distance. By the time he stood in front of the garage, he watched as the pack passed by on Main Street, slowing only enough to glance in toward him. Their direction continued on down the hill as they disappeared from sight.

Skyler dropped the bike and was about to rush up the stairs when James came flying down four steps at a time.

"I was watching the top of the hill with binoculars when you came over the crest. Are you okay?" James asked him.

"Yeah, fine." He was still breathing hard; it would take a little time before he could articulate a longer sentence. Then he blurted, "They robbed the Jensens."

James saved his other questions until they were back upstairs. Only after a tall glass of water did Skyler resume telling him about the evening's events.

"I went to the Lopatnikovs first, and they said that they hadn't seen any groups on bicycles. Mr. Lopatnikov said he'll be here for the meeting tomorrow. Then when I went to the Jensen's, I found only five of them left. Dag's been sick in bed for the last month. Three of them made a trip to Bellingham two weeks ago to get help for him. They haven't returned. Four of them were working in the garden when those kids caught them by surprise. The leader held them at gunpoint while the others took what food they could carry."

"Did anybody get hurt?" asked James.

"No, but they were pretty scared when I got there. They said that the amount of food taken was small. They said they wouldn't starve."

"Will they be here tomorrow?"

"I think so. They said that they couldn't afford to leave their place unguarded, but Mr. Jensen came out and said he'd try to send someone."

"Anything else happen?" asked James.

"Yeah, something strange; the man at the Jensens said some of the riders wanted to take their guns, but the oldest one forbade them to touch them." He paused for a few seconds, "I'd think that they'd want to disarm them considering they are thieves, and guns have some value. The leader of the riders almost caught me at the top of the hill, but when I descended, he quit chasing me. If he had gotten that close, why not finish the job."

"Any idea why he gave up?"

"Yeah, I don't think he wanted to be separated from the others. I think there's a connection with him not wanting them to carry real guns and not wanting to risk being separated from them."

Just then, Lara came in the door holding the binoculars. "I can see them going down Imhoff. They're headed back the way they came."

James stood and walked out on the deck. Even without the binoculars in the fading light, he could see the mass as it moved south. He finally took the glasses from Lara, scrutinizing the group more closely. He turned to his housemates and said, "The tallest one is riding behind the others."

The trio stood out on the deck, watching as the group of riders continued south. Skyler tried to envision where they might be headed now.

Since they'd been in that area for at least a couple of days, they must have found a place to stay. He had not ventured anywhere east of Imhoff, so he had only a little knowledge about where their hideout might be.

Skyler split the night watch with James, allowing James to get some sleep before the upcoming arrival of Brent's family, and the expected meeting with the others. At dawn, Skyler made a quick trip up the hill, pushing the bicycle up the steep grade. He needed to extend James' invitation to the upcoming gathering. He also wanted to warn Petar to expect the Lopatnikovs and possibly the Jensens to cross over on Church Road. He'd intentionally wanted the visitors to pass through the barricaded community, hoping that they would meet and make a connection. If it didn't happen up there, then it would surely take place when the different parties arrived for that afternoon meeting.

CHAPTER 4

March 29th, 2031
1:20 pm

The first arrivals, burdened with bags of clothes and toys, made their appearance shortly after mid-day. The group was included Brent and Lydia, their two children, Little Brent and Bekka, and finally, Brandy and Petar. The latter two had carried some of Brent's meager belongings, eliminating the need for a second trip. Lara met them at the bottom of the stairs, warmly embracing each and everyone, including the children. As she followed them up the stairs, she looked back to see if anyone else was coming.

Lydia, following Brent, was wide-eyed and speechless at the house her family was going to move into. Lara, trailing the couple, felt Lydia's excitement as she silently admired her surroundings. Brent, anxious to show her the bedroom, led his wife downstairs. James enlisted Petar's help pulling the plywood from the downstairs sliding glass door and repositioning it so that light would enter the large bedroom from the top twelve inches of the door. For their security, neither James nor Brent wanted any doors or windows on the lower level fully exposed.

Perhaps the new surroundings stimulated Lydia's memory when she saw the bedroom her family would occupy. Turning to Lara, she said tearfully, "This place is far nicer than I could've imagined."

Lydia soon found that there was enough room in the dressers and closet for all of their belongings. Lara pulled open a closet to reveal some clothes left by the former inhabitants. While the men adjusted the outside windows and doors, Lydia helped Lara clean up the dusty surfaces, shake out blankets and give the room a thorough cleaning.

Lying down on the bed, feeling how comfortable it was, Lydia remarked to Lara, "I just realized that this will be the first time in a year that Brent and I will be able to sleep in the same bed together. Now I know why you and James hate to give this place up."

Lara was unsure how to respond, if at all. She wondered if Lydia assumed that she and James were lovers. They did share the same bed together, but their relationship was purely platonic. Neither one of them had asked for anything more than that from each other. Maybe it was the new times, or the uncertainty of the future that kept their relationship static. Lara found herself wondering if their relationship would ever evolve into something beyond what they were experiencing now. Had it been a different time, maybe it could have been something beautiful. Her train of thought was quickly interrupted when Skyler shouted down the stairs.

"Someone's coming!" His voice was excited and not fearful.

Both Lara and Lydia ran up the stairs, followed by Lydia's children, and gathered with the three men on the upper deck. A man, woman, and boy were walking toward them from Main Street. The woman wore an ankle-length dress with a heavy overcoat, while the man—tall, bearded, formidable— wore insulated coveralls and carried a double-barrel shotgun.

"It's the Lopatnikovs. They've brought Dimitrey," said Skyler.

Everyone but the children descended the stairs to meet the trio. Skyler made the introductions as Dimitrey translated what each person said. After the introductions, Mr. Lopatnikov cleared his throat before saying in carefully practiced English, "It is good to meet you."

Lara was about to usher everyone upstairs and into the house when Lydia spotted others walking their way. Two men carrying rifles, barrels pointed downward, coming from Main Street were headed in their direction. Both wore heavy clothing and cowboy hats. As they drew close, Lara saw that they weren't men after all, but women, wore their hair tucked up inside their hats. She stepped forward, hand outstretched. "Welcome to our home."

The introductions began once again with Dimitrey translating for his parents. The two women, Beth and Lindsey, explained that after much deliberation, Mr. Jensen, understanding how important it was to band the families, had decided that two of them should attend the meeting, especially after yesterday's events. Lara was surprised mainly because the two women were young, maybe in their mid twenties. They went on to say that Mr. Jensen, wanting to take part, was still recovering and too weak for the round trip. The two other men of their family, Carl and Robert, felt the need to stay behind to guard the house should the bicycle gang return.

When Lara finally got all thirteen people into their large living room, she was surprised at the conversations that started; everyone seemed to relish escaping their isolation, if only for this one afternoon. All the adults, including Dimitrey's family, wanted to tell the others what they'd been through during the last two years. Petar was engulfed in the stories that Beth and Lindsey wanted to share, while Lydia spoke to Mrs. Lopatnikov through Dimitrey. There were at least four or five speaking at the same time; even Lara let her guard down and joined in, clearly enjoying herself.

Twenty minutes passed before James realized the need to get the meeting underway. "Can I have your attention, please?"

The small crowd fell silent as they waited for him to continue. He smiled at the people before him. "I want to thank you all for coming here today. It's good to see you warming up to each other rather quickly. We have a lot to discuss. First on the agenda is providing support for one another. Beth and Lindsey, along with the three others living with them, were robbed yesterday. As we all know, there isn't anyone who is going to look out for us other than ourselves. I need to know that if we are up against a sizeable force, how many people at your site could be used to help defend another family."

Petar spoke first. "With Brent moving down here and Scott ill, sending only one or two people is the best we could do."

Dimitrey's father had his son tell the crowd that he had eight men and five women capable of 'inflicting severe damage if necessary."

Beth and Lindsey offered that if their assistance was requested, they needed to keep at least two persons behind to guard their remote home, leaving only two to help any of the others.

James looked around and said, "As it stands for now, there are three men and two women living here. I would be available as well as Brent and Skyler. This would leave Lara and Lydia behind to guard the house."

At once, they all seemed to have a lot to say. James raised his hand to get their attention. "Since we don't have any way for a family to communicate with another family, we need a system that we can use to alert one another in case of an attack. From here, Petar's family on the hill can hear if we've fired shots. Judging by where the Lopatnikovs live, I can only assume that shots from their farm could be heard by Petar's group. Beth and Lindsey's farm is a bit remote, but the sound of gunfire should reach the Lopatnikovs. I think that if any of us are attacked, we should fire three rounds spaced two seconds apart to alert anyone within earshot."

Again, their voices erupted until Petar stood and posed a counter-point to the crowd. "If one of the smaller families is attacked, they may not be able to get off a three-shot warning. I suggest that any firing of weapons should be investigated and that we use the three-shot system to let others know that everything is all right."

This turned into a discussion until Skyler pointed out the fact that not everyone was at the meeting. "If we are being rescued by Dimitrey's uncles, how will we know that it's them and not more attackers?"

The crowd resumed their deliberation until it was finally agreed that any family member stepping outside of their own area would wear a red armband. That way, regardless of where you were, any member could be identified as friendly if encountered by any other member from the four families represented at the meeting.

That will have to do for now, James thought, as he prepared to speak once again. "Our safety is not the only thing we need to discuss. Another item I feel is important is our future. As you've noticed, we no longer have any form of municipality or infrastructure for the town of Ferndale. Like it or not, we are the government. Any decisions about how we handle things are up to us. I'm not suggesting that we need to rebuild at this time, but there are things we need to discuss here and now."

At this point, everyone grew quiet except for Brent's children who had discovered an old jigsaw puzzle. James continued, "For those items that we need to vote on, I think we should decide how many votes come from each family."

Mr. Lopatnikov whispered in his son's ear. The small boy stepped forward. "My father would like to see that each family gets one vote for every member."

Almost everyone tried speaking at once until Brent raised both hands to get everyone's attention and then asked Dimitrey, "How many people live on your farm?"

The boy looked to his father for approval to speak before answering, "Twenty."

"In that case, whatever the Lopatnikovs voted for would win. They outnumber the rest of us combined." Brent pointed out.

Beth stood and asked, "What if we limit the voting to legal age adults?"

James responded, "I have two issues with that. Brandy and Skyler act and work as adults, but they won't be eighteen for more than three years. I think that their vote is necessary and valid. Second, if only adults could vote, that still gives the Lopatnikovs the majority."

Petar stood and said, "To make this fair to everyone and to keep the process democratic, I suggest that there be one vote per family, but that one vote is decided upon by the members of that family and not just one person. In both the families and this newly-formed council, the majority vote wins."

The discussion opened up once again, and only after Dimitrey finished translating what was said into Russian, did Mr. Lopatnikov agree to Petar's terms. Everyone was now in agreement with the one vote per family rule.

"Good", James said. "Now that we have that settled, I have one more thing to bring up. What are we going to do about these damn kids on bicycles? They've only been around a couple of days. They've already robbed the Jensens, and they tried to run down Skyler, both events occurring just yesterday. We can't allow them to stay in this area. Does anyone have any ideas on how we should handle this situation?"

Beth stood up. She was visibly angry. "I say we shoot them. The next time we see any of those thieves, we are going to open up on them until the last one is dead!"

James was stunned by her deadly solution. Yet, he could see that some of the group were in agreement with Beth. Mr. Lopatnikov was nodding in approval after his son translated Beth's rigid statement. Brent also appeared to be in favor, as did Lindsey.

Skyler stood, asking for everyone to be quiet for a moment. He looked around at the faces and asked, "What if I was one of them, would you still feel the same?"

No one attempted to answer his question, so he continued. "When I met James and Lara, I was no different than those riders. I did what I could to survive. Lara and James could have shot me and continued on with their lives. The fact that they didn't is why I am standing before you today. I'm the one that visited your families and brought you here. These riders are thieves because they have no other choice."

The mood suddenly went somber, until Beth said, "You're right. They didn't hurt anyone and all they took was food. I'm ashamed that I suggested what I did."

"Then what do we do?" asked James.

Mr. Lopatnikov stood, looking over the crowd; he said several sentences to his son before sitting back down. Dimitrey stood and said, "We give them a choice. They become farmers or they leave."

Everyone seemed to be in approval of this new option. Once again, multiple conversations erupted at once until Brent stood and asked loudly, "How do we go about doing that?"

Skyler, like a young diplomat, said, "I think I know where they are living, at least a general idea. I can scout out that area, and when I find their hideout, we can surround them early one morning. We would then need to separate them from their leader because I think he holds some kind of control over them."

James could barely wait for him to finish, asking, "Why go looking for them? Why not wait for them to appear? Most of the roads around here are visible with no trees to block our view. The next time I see them coming up Imhoff, we send someone up to alert Petar and McBride. By the time they reach Main Street, we can have an ambush set up and trap them."

Lindsey noted, "That will only work if they use Imhoff, and in the meantime, we're still vulnerable."

"I don't like the idea of having Skyler sneaking around in a strange area, and I don't think we should just sit and wait either. Let's have Skyler find out what he can, then, if they show up, we can still pull off some kind of ambush. If they don't, we can go after them." Petar's solution was simplistic, yet well thought out and articulated, as usual.

James looked about. Everyone seemed to be in agreement except Lara and Brandy. Neither one of them wanted to see Skyler risk his life. James, seeing the dissatisfaction on their faces, asked, "Is there anyone here more qualified than Skyler to go looking for their lair?"

The crowd went quiet once again. Finally, Skyler stood and added, "I'll keep my distance and I'll only look at night. I should be able to find them by locating the smoke from their fire. I think I can do this without them knowing that I'm looking for them."

"Should we vote on this issue?" James asked. Only after Dimitrey translated for his father and gave the group Mr. Lopatnikov's approval, did he continue. "The motion before us is to set up an ambush and take the cyclists by surprise. Once we have separated them from their leader, we give them a choice of farming for their food or leaving."

All four families voted in favor of the motion.

James proposed the second item. "Do we allow Skyler to scout out their whereabouts?"

Once more, the members of the different families discussed the proposition among themselves. Again, James asked for their vote. He looked to Brent, Lydia and Lara for their opinions. Lara had been the only one from their household who didn't like the idea of Skyler being used as a scout, but she agreed, given his past, that he was the most qualified. As before, everyone present voted unanimously in favor of Skyler being the one to find the Wanderers' place of hiding.

James was about to adjourn the meeting when he decided to update the other families on what was happening at Lara's and his place. "The reason I called this meeting is because for the last few days, I have felt pretty vulnerable living here with only Lara and, sometimes, Skyler. To remedy this, Brent and Lydia have agreed to move in with us while Brent helps me build a house next door. I now feel much safer knowing that we have twice as many people living here." He then looked at both Beth and Lindsey. "If any of your households feel that you are living in an unsafe place, let us know. We may be able to provide you with housing until we can get you relocated closer to the other families."

Lindsey stood and looked down at Beth before fixing her eyes on James. "Thank you. That was what we were hoping to hear when we made the decision to come down here today."

"Good. Then unless any of you have anything else to say, our meeting is officially adjourned."

The ten adults and Dimitrey milled about, while reliving their stories of the last two years. It was another half-hour before they finally worked their way to the front door. James and Lara watched from the deck as the Lopatnikovs, Brandy, Petar, Beth and Lindsey walked each other back toward Main Street and eventually up Church Road. Brent and Lydia returned to the basement to finish unpacking as their two children played on the deck kicking a ball, with Skyler as goalie.

That evening, Skyler stayed on the deck watching for intruders while the others shared their evening meal together. He'd volunteered for the first of three shifts—no one bothering to question why. Sometime around midnight, Brent came up to relieve him. They talked briefly in hushed tones before Skyler returned to his room and closed his door. Moments later, he emerged wearing dark clothing, bow strung over his back. He stopped out on the deck to let Brent know what his plans were and asked him to tell James that he should be back before first light. Brent started to protest, but Skyler told him that he chose this night because no one would lose sleep over him being gone. A moment later, he disappeared into the darkness.

CHAPTER 5

March 30th, 2031
1:00 am

Skyler, in a race against the dawn, mounted his bike and headed out of the driveway. His breath formed mists of vapor in the cool night air warning that the puddles would ice over before he returned. The sky, clear enough to reveal a bright half moon, gave him plenty of light to see where he was going, but not enough to see more than thirty yards ahead. Still, he rode at full speed down the hill. If anyone was walking the roads at this time of the night, he would scare them as much as they would scare him. He was pushing himself harder than he had planned, working up a sweat, while his mind was elsewhere.

He wanted to find this group of kids who, having lost their families and loved ones were veering down a path toward an even more dangerous existence, if any. Skyler wasn't looking for a confrontation with their apparent leader, who was more than likely self-appointed, either by his size and age or experience or perhaps all; instead, he wanted to help them. Knowing that they too had past lives, probably not much different than his own —homes with mothers and/or fathers, siblings, grandparents, people who loved them—some barely out of grade school to roam aimlessly, sufferers of an event of such epic proportion as to leave them with depersonalized labels such as "Wanderers," their given names swept away on an arctic wind and, with them, their search for stability leading them to a life not much different than primitive man. He'd felt an emotional tie, a kinship, to the ones that followed the leader. He knew that it would only be a matter of time before someone acting in self-defense would not care that they were simply children trying to survive.

Just before reaching downtown Ferndale, he turned off onto Douglas Road where it melded with Main Street, the same route the riders had taken only two days earlier. The first 150 yards of the road were criss-crossed with power poles and debris, forcing him to dismount until he reached Imhoff. During the ten minutes he lifted his bike over each obstacle, Skyler felt exposed and vulnerable. A row of apartment buildings on his right, all but leveled by the winds, created a dark threatening shadow. With both hands needed to lift the bike, he would not be able reach his bow quickly or silently. He was aware of every small sound he made. As far as he knew, no one lived down the hill from their house. What he feared were those who traveled in the dark trying to elude detection by others. Anybody out at this time of the night would surely be armed and nervous.

The entrance to Imhoff could not have come soon enough. Skyler remounted and coasted down the small slope that eventually turned into a flat, uneventful three-mile ride. The tops of some power poles lay in such a fashion that they jutted out into the road, but there was still plenty of room for his bike. Skyler counted off the seconds so he'd know just how long it would take on the return trip. When he reached Slater, he'd counted to eight-hundred and sixty—slightly less than fifteen minutes.

Each time the riders had passed by here, they had come from the east, and when they returned, it had also been in that direction. When he'd hunted waterfowl, Skyler had been down to Slater on several occasions, but he'd never ventured east of Imhoff. Between here and the freeway, there were only a scattering of houses, each of them out in the open, exposed to the winds. Between the winds and the flooding, it had become a "no man's land"; there was little chance that they stayed on this side of the river. Brent had mentioned that he thought the riders came out of Canada so it made sense that they'd traveled this far along the Interstate. Perhaps they'd found some place near there. He traveled east, across the flat plain, like they had, to search the area between the river and the freeway.

Along the way, Skyler passed the remnants of the cigarette store owned by a family belonging to the Lummi Indian Tribe. Nothing remained in the parking lot except some cinder blocks the trailer once sat upon. There had been a real building on the site, but severe flooding over the last ten years had forced the family into a mobile store. The location, within three-quarters of a mile of the river, and at nearly the same elevation, was vulnerable whenever the river spilled over its banks. Towing the store to higher ground and returning it when the waters subsided had become too frequent of an event. Skyler's mother had explained to him how, in years past, the river only flooded once every two or three years and even then it was minor. As the climate changed, the flooding occurred more frequently, often no less than twice a year, covering a vast area of farmland when it did so. The land, perfect farmland for crops like carrots, potatoes, corn and peas, was now useless; the mobile cigarette shop became the family's only remaining source of revenue. Skyler remembered before the Change seeing a picture on the Internet news of a truck towing the trailer through eighteen-inch deep water while the owners struggled to save their business.

Before long, Skyler was within sight of the bridge. The moon-lit, snow-covered hills, miles beyond the bridge, helped to outline it. As Skyler drew closer, the flat road began a gradual incline, and his speed naturally slowed. The road within the bridge was a tangle of fence posts, trees, and barbed wire, forming an impassable obstacle. The river had obviously flooded recently, leaving a smooth thin layer of wet silt covering the road. Even in the moonlight, he was able to see the trails left by multiple bike tires. Skyler came to a halt. He stood there staring at the darkened interior of the bridge, looking for an open path through. The riders had to have come through here because there were no other spans crossing the river for several miles in both directions. He followed the trail in the mud and spotted a metal rail that had once protected pedestrians from traffic. The metal rail was the terminus for most of the debris; the sidewalk it protected was clear enough to walk a bike through.

Skyler was halfway across the bridge when he heard a noise downstream. He stopped. Listening, he could hear the swirling waters create a babble that was like background music. Then a new sound that could only be described as a 'kerplunk' came from his right. The moon, reflecting off the midline of the river, blocked his ability to see either bank. With the dimmed light, Skyler could not pick out the source of the noise. It occurred every ten or fifteen seconds. Faint as it was, it portended something ominous. He finished crossing the bridge, silently laying his bike on its side; he was determined to investigate further.

There had been a dike along both sides of the river. The dike on the eastern bank had a trail running its length. A short service road led from the edge of the bridge down to the dike. There was just enough moonlight for him to find his way down to the trail. Once he was on the dike, he stepped cautiously, willing his body to make every move in total silence, synchronizing the bend of a knee with the inhalation of a breath.

The last time Skyler had seen the dike was before the first bad storm. It was summer, the one before the Change, and two summers before that first horrific winter. Back then, except for the narrow trail, the dike was overgrown with brush. His cross-country team had come down here to run, not knowing that a homeless camp had blocked the trail further down the river. They had been running in a tight pack most of the way until they came to the thick brush, forcing them into a serpentine string of runners. Skyler, the youngest on the team, was the last runner in the line. He remembered focusing on the trail just in front of each foot when he suddenly bumped into the runner in front of him. That runner had also come to an abrupt halt because the entire team ahead of them was at a standstill. Whispers and low voices were heard as each runner turned to go back upriver. Skyler was able to steal a glance at what had stopped them. The trail had abruptly ended onto a sea of tents, dirty children, and dirty adults. There must have been over a hundred tents pitched on or

50

alongside the trail. Weary faces, hungry and sad, followed them as they turned and headed back to town.

Skyler worked his way through the darkness, noticing that all the brush was gone. Not just some of it; all of it. The dike was a clean mound of hard-packed dirt that dropped off both sides like a hog's back. After a short distance, he realized that his silhouette could be seen above the dike, so he dropped down on all fours before continuing further. The distinctive noise that had originally caught his attention could still be heard and it was getting closer as he crawled south. Skyler estimated that it was around one in the morning; he had about four or five hours of darkness to shroud him. Now that he'd been off of his bike for several minutes, his sweat turned to chills, and he could feel the cold night's air through his clothing. He came to a point where the sound was just below him, on the river side of the dike. Looking down, he could see a small beach reaching into the river from the bank. It was dark where the bottom of the dike met the beach. He listened, watched, and waited for the next 'kerplunk'.

Before he heard the noise of a stone hitting water, he saw a small hand arc through the moonlight from the shadows, releasing the stone. Whoever was throwing the stones was only twenty feet directly below him. Skyler listened for several minutes trying to detect the presence of more than one person. The stones had been tossed at regular intervals since he'd left the bridge, but now they'd suddenly stopped. Still too dark to see, Skyler couldn't tell if there was a tent or any camping gear for that matter. Then he heard an involuntary rapid inhalation followed by a sob. Whoever was below him had stopped throwing stones and started crying.

Skyler lifted his bow from his back and fitted an arrow onto its string. He wasn't sure what he was up against; he wasn't going to be caught unarmed. He listened for a few more minutes before he finally walked down the bank. The sounds of the river hid his steps in the silt covered sand. When he was within ten feet of where the person lay hidden, Skyler's boot snapped a twig; he froze. He heard a clambering in the dirt just ahead of him, then a small boy stepped out into the moonlight.

"Who's there?" The voice was small—a child's. It shook with fear.

Realizing that he was still by the shadow of the dike, Skyler stepped out into the moonlight and said, "Don't worry. I'm not here to hurt you. I heard you throwing rocks into the river. Why are you here?"

Skyler guessed the boy to be about ten years-old. He shivered from the cold. He was very thin, pale, obviously scared. His hair was long and unkempt. Coatless, Skyler could see in the moonlight his clothes were thread-bare. The two stood silently looking at each other until Skyler placed his arrow back into the quiver.

"I thought you came here to shoot me," said the boy.

"No, I just wasn't sure who was down here. Why are you here?"

"He kicked me out of the survival club. He said that I was too slow, and that they always had to wait for me."

"Who is 'he'?" asked Skyler.

"Brandon."

"What is this survival club?"

"Brandon says that if I tell anyone, he'll kill me."

"Don't you think he's already done that by banishing you without a coat? Let's start over. My name is Skyler. What's yours?"

The boy paused, swallowed hard, obviously contemplating his situation. Finally, seeing that the boy's teeth were shattering, Skyler removed his coat, handing it to him. He waited patiently for the boy to continue.

"My name is Devon. Our survival club is going to California. We heard there's lots of food there. We stopped here because we ran out of food."

"Where did your club come from?"

"Vancouver."

Realizing that this boy was probably one of those who had chased him yesterday, Skyler asked, "Does your club ride bicycles?"

"Yeah, we did. Brandon took my bike away when he said I had to leave."

"Well, I'm getting cold without my coat. Let's walk up to the road while we talk."

"I can't go with you," said Devon.

"Why not?"

"I told my sister that I'd wait here. She's in the club too. Brandon wouldn't let her leave with me. He told her that if she left, he would shoot me."

"Then show me where they're staying. I have friends who can help us get her away from Brandon."

When the boy heard this, he seemed eager to follow Skyler up to the road. Skyler questioned Devon about the club and his sister as they tread quietly in the darkness.

"She's two years older than me. We've been in the club since last spring. We'd been living in a church run by a priest who cared for us during the first winter. Everyone in the club had been living there." Devon, his grief palpable, admitted that he didn't know what had happened to his parents—they didn't come home the night that the storm arrived. The church was just down the street, and it was the only building that remained erect after that first week. Devon and his sister had to run for the church after their own roof dissipated in the wind. The priest, Father Michael, had taken in several other children. Brandon was already living there when Devon and his sister had arrived.

Devon went on to say, "Father Michael had stored away enough food to get us through the first winter. He was always kind to everyone. When spring arrived, our food was running out. Father Michael and Brandon got into an argument. Brandon wanted to leave for California and take all of us with him. Father Michael told him it was foolish. They started yelling and got into a fist fight. Father Michael made Brandon leave the church. A week later, Brandon came back with a gun and told Father Michael that he was taking us with him."

"What happened then?" asked Skyler. The taller boy who almost caught him yesterday must be Brandon. Now he was beginning to understand why he hadn't continued the chase.

"None of us wanted Brandon to kill Father Michael, so we left the church and stayed in a house with Brandon. He got us to steal food and to beg from people we saw that weren't starving. The bicycles came later when Brandon said it was time to leave."

Skyler stopped briefly and asked, "Have there always been twelve in your club?"

Devon's face looked pained as he struggled to answer, "No, there were more of us when we lived in the church. Brandon wouldn't take everyone. We also lost some on the trip here. Twice, we were attacked on the highway. We had to ride as fast as we could. I think we lost four or five before we made it to here." Skyler could only imagine the evil Devon had already witnessed since the Change.

By now, the two had reached Slater Road. Skyler stopped the boy. "Where are they staying now? Can you show me?"

"It's not far but I don't want to go back there. Brandon said that if he saw me again, he'd shoot me."

"Just show me from a distance. I'll need to see this place if we are going to try to get your sister out of there."

They left the bicycle at the bridge, walking in silence, because they had little to say, both fearing what could be laying for them in the dark. Skyler could not be sure that there wasn't anyone else out on this cold night. When they crossed the railroad tracks, Skyler recognized the area: they were nearing the old refuse station. It too had quit operating almost two years earlier, another outcome of the economic situation just before the Change. No one could afford to pay someone to burn their waste. They turned up the road that led past its entrance, a road that snaked its way back to downtown.

Finally, Devon came to a stop. "This is as far as I'll go."

"Where's the house?"

"Over there." Devon pointed down the road to a squat one-story building alongside a collapsed barn.

"Does Brandon ever post guards?"

"No, everyone has to stay inside with him."

It was too dark to make out any details except that the building did have a roof. Skyler motioned Devon to stop. "Wait here. I want to take a closer look."

Skyler walked silently along the road until he drew near the house. He eyed the surrounding area. The house, a single story, appeared to be made of cinder blocks that were painted with shiny green enamel. Moonlight reflected off its glossy surface. It had only one door that he could see. The windows, recessed into the concrete blocks, had been blown out and shuttered from within. Skyler found this odd until he realized that putting plywood on the outside of the windows would have been difficult since the structure was made of concrete. When he was forty feet away, he saw what he needed to know; there was only one door in and out, and it wasn't actually a house, but rather some type of maintenance building. He'd stopped when he felt he'd seen enough and turned back. Skyler found Devon waiting exactly where he'd left him. Together, they silently began the walk back toward the bridge.

"Do you know how long they will be staying here?"

Devon stopped and looked up at Skyler. "Brandon said that they were leaving soon, probably today. They have enough food to last two days."

They continued on in silence as Skyler thought about the situation. If the bike riders moved on, it would solve their problem. They wouldn't have to worry about them attacking any of the locals. What bothered him was Devon's sister: he would probably never see her again. Skyler was an only child, not knowing what it was like to have a sibling, but he'd always wished that he had. It sounded to him like she was being kept against her will, that she would have chosen to be banished with her brother. And what about the other kids? How many of them had any choice about staying with Brandon? When he banished Devon, he didn't allow him to take his bike or even a coat. The kid could have frozen to death by morning. An uneasiness needled Skyler about whether Brandon's thirst for power was greater than the need for a more stable supply of food. If so, then more children could follow Devon's path.

By the time they reached the bridge, Skyler was cold. He needed to start riding again. They walked across the bridge, then he had Devon ride on the handlebars of the bike as they retraced his route down Slater and back up Imhoff in the dark.

Devon was quiet most of the way, except for one brief question. "Where are we going?"

"To my house. You'll be safe there. You won't have to steal anymore." Before Devon could ask his next question, Skyler added, "I have friends who will help us get your sister away from the club."

They arrived at the house just as the dawn silhouetted the mountains to the east. Skyler climbed the stairs, followed by Devon. They startled James enough that he pulled his pistol out and had it pointed at them.

"Easy James, it's just me."

"Who's with you?" he asked as he lowered the pistol. Brent, too, had been alerted, his rifle leveled at the boys.

"This is Devon. He was with the bicycle gang." Skyler had to turn almost completely around to find Devon huddled behind his back.

James looked at the boys before turning to Brent. "Did you know that Skyler wasn't in bed?"

"He told me that he wanted to find where the bicycle gang lived tonight and didn't want to wait."

"I found Devon along the way. He'd been banished from the group and left without a coat or food. His sister is still with the group. The oldest boy with the gun makes them steal food for him. Devon says that they'll probably leave today."

"Good, our problem is solved," said James.

"No, it's not," replied Skyler. "Devon's sister is being forced to leave with them against her wishes. We need to help him get her away from the group before it's too late." His desperate voice, so unlike the Skyler they knew, surprised both James and Brent.

The golden glow of a new day was just beginning to lighten the eastern sky. James had slept almost eight full hours, but Brent needed more sleep. The plan had been that today they would start dismantling the local houses, collecting the materials needed for the new house. James stood silently as he deliberated the situation in his mind.

He turned to Brent. "Do you have enough energy to pull off a rescue mission before we start working on your house?"

"Yeah. I doubt that I could sleep knowing what I do."

James added, "We'll need to wake Lara and Lydia. Take Devon inside and stoke up the fire. Maybe they can feed him while we're gone."

James and Brent both went inside. Skyler went in behind them, but saw that Devon wasn't following. He stopped and asked, "What's the matter?"

"I don't know. If you get my sister back, where will we stay?"

"Probably here with us. We'll decide that later. James and Lara won't banish you like Brandon did. They took me in over a year ago. They're good people."

Devon, no longer tentative, entered the dark warm house behind his new-found friend. Two candles provided just enough light to outline the furniture. James emerged from a bedroom the same time Brent came back up the stairs. Both men were carrying rifles and had donned lighter clothing. Lara soon stepped from the bedroom fully dressed, her hair still tossed. She walked over to Devon and introduced herself. She was very warm to the young boy and asked him to sit near the wood stove while she made him some tea.

"Where's this house that we're going to raid?" asked Brent.

Skyler found a piece of paper with enough space to draw a map. When he completed it, he showed it to James and Brent under candlelight.

"I know where this is," said James. "We can get there faster if we cut through downtown and take Labounty Road."

"But we wouldn't be able to ride the bikes that way!" added Skyler.

"Doesn't matter, we only have two bikes and three of us are going. There will probably be four of us returning."

"Then go without me. I would rather have you get there before they're awake, than later when they might already be gone."

James looked to Brent for some guidance. Finally, Brent asked Devon, "How many real guns are in that house?"

"Just Brandon's rifle and he only has a few bullets left."

"Alright, Skyler stays here and we'll take the bikes. It looks like we can get there in just under one hour if we stick to Imhoff and Slater. If we rush the door, we can surprise them and be out of there rather quickly. How will we know which girl is your sister?" asked James.

"Her name is Virginia. If you call her 'Gia', she'll know that you spoke with me."

Skyler was anxious for James and Brent to depart. He'd wanted to go but could see that it was more important that they get there faster by using the bikes. He figured that on the return trip, Gia could ride on the handlebars like her brother had, or maybe she could ride her own bike. Skyler watched as the two men rode off with rifles slung over their backs, estimating that if it went well, they should be returning in about two hours. Lara, wanting to monitor the time, produced a wind-up egg timer, setting it for one hour. Neither boy could sit still while they waited. Skyler got his tent out and assembled it on the deck. By the time he finished erecting it, both of Brent's children were awake, wanting to play in it.

Two hours came and went. Skyler, scanning the valley below, could see no sign of his friends in the distance. Maybe they chose to return by a different route? By now, it was fully light out with the sun peeking over the top of the Cascades. Skyler noticed that both Lara and Lydia were whispering to one another and a bit edgy. Still, there had not been any sounds of distant shooting. Devon, having been awake so long, fell asleep on Skyler's bed while Brent's kids played outside in the tent. The egg timer dinged for the third time signifying that three hours had passed. Finally, Lara was the first to spot a mass coming up Imhoff. She scanned the road for several seconds before handing the binoculars to Skyler. From this distance, they couldn't identify if James or Brent were in the group coming their way, but the entire mass was on bikes and moving fast. The group was much larger than just three riders. This didn't make sense. Skyler worried that something had gone terribly wrong. He went back inside to wake Devon. The boy, startled by the intrusion, jumped right out of bed. Lydia brought the children inside while Skyler and Lara rounded up what weapons they could.

As the group of riders came to the closest visible point before disappearing behind the hill, the only thing Skyler knew for sure was that there were about a dozen of them. The low sun made silhouettes of the riders. As they neared the end of Imhoff, they rode out of his field of view. Skyler estimated that they had about fifteen minutes if the riders were coming this way. Surely, they must be. Both Lydia and Lara were holding rifles now, only after assigning Devon to keeping the children occupied. Skyler collected five more arrows from James' quiver, giving him a total of ten, then positioned himself on the deck while both Lydia and Lara chose to stand at ground level, each using a corner of the house to hide themselves.

Just when they were expecting the group to appear on Main Street, Lara stepped out on the parking pad and announced, "As soon as they turn in here, I'm firing a shot to alert Petar!"

Both Skyler and Lydia agreed with her before she returned to her position. Another minute passed, and they still couldn't see any sign that the riders had decided to come this way. Then Skyler detected movement on the street through a gap in the houses along the road. Voices could be heard coming from that direction.

"Get ready! Here they come!" he shouted to the others.

When the first four bikes appeared, Skyler didn't recognize any of them. As more bikes appeared behind them, the front bikes turning in toward the house headed straight for the logs. These first riders had rifles slung over their backs. Lara, assuming the worst, fired a warning shot over their heads.

Skyler, hoping that someone from Petar's family would hear the shot, wondered if this would be enough to bring reinforcements. As soon as the shot was fired, all the riders came to an abrupt halt. Then Skyler saw the last two appear from behind the house and move to the front. It was James and Brent.

Both men dismounted at the logs and lifted their bikes over. Skyler could see that the rest of the riders were tentative to move forward after hearing Lara's shot. James continued toward the house while Brent attempted to herd the other ten riders into the cul-de-sac. No sooner had the last of the bikers crossed over the logs, when Petar and McBride appeared on bikes moving at a high speed. By now, both Lara and Lydia had figured out that the men had not just rescued one child, but all of them. They stepped out from behind their hiding places, rifles lowered to show they meant no harm. As James rode up to them, Petar and Brent dismounted at the intersection, their rifles poised for action. Skyler saw Brent turn and wave them in. Both men stood their ground looking confused.

"Did you just shoot at us?" James asked Lara, the hint of a smile spreading across his face.

"No, I fired once to alert Petar that we were in trouble," she said matter-of-factly, a rebellious tinge to her tone.

James smiled at her and Lydia. "I would have called, but you know, the phones haven't worked in two years. So I guess that this is a good time to break the news to you. We've just adopted eleven kids."

By then, the crowd in front of the garage grew to six adults and ten children varying from twelve to seventeen years in age. Skyler briefly stuck his head inside the house, calling for Devon to come out. When Devon saw his sister, he flew past Skyler and ran down the stairs. Everyone had dismounted, bikes strewn everywhere. McBride and Petar had already shouldered their rifles, joining the group. As these two separate tribes of survivors met one another for the first time, James attempted to remember everyone's names, introducing them as he went along. All the children wore backpacks. Some were quick to lower them to the ground.

Skyler finally saw who Gia was when Devon embraced her. Listening through the excited voices, he heard James as he fought to remember the names. Besides Gia, there were also two other girls named Bree and Marly. Every child seemed excited to see Devon again. The constant chatter became a dull roar.

Skyler watched as James pointed to each boy and pronounced their names. "There's Kai and Sebastian, and this here is David and Thomas, whom I can't seem to get straight. Then there's Petey, Joe, and Joel, my new carpenters. Petey's the oldest at seventeen." James was pointing to three boys who were taller than Skyler, yet gaunt looking. Their eyes showing the strain of the lives they'd been leading.

Skyler looked toward Lara and Lydia. He half expected a look of dismay on their faces. After all, they now had eleven more mouths to feed, more clothes to wash, and eleven more kids to put to bed at night. He saw only smiles as both women reached out, touching each child on the head or shoulder as they tried to make them feel welcome.

Petar and McBride stayed only long enough to hear the story of the rescue. They wanted to return to the hill so that the remainder of their family wouldn't worry. Brent filled them in on what happened that morning. When he and James had arrived at the house, it appeared that no one was awake yet. They had walked right in, lifting the rifle away from a sleeping figure that was soon identified as Brandon. After waking all the children, they told them how Devon had been found. He was now staying at their house, and that they were there to get his sister Gia to return with them. What they didn't expect was that every child wanted to go with them. Brandon was the only one who objected to the intrusion, attempting to remind the others that they were in his club that they couldn't leave. James placed himself between Brandon and the children, telling them that they had a choice, but if they chose to leave the club, they would have to quit stealing and start learning how to grow and harvest their own food. Not one child stayed behind with Brandon. The timing of the encounter, following Devon's cruel expulsion, was the deciding factor in their decision to return with James and Brent.

The rest of the day was filled with trying to create makeshift beds, collecting more water, and helping the children settle in. Skyler gave up his room for the three girls. He and Devon would sleep on the couches. Two of the oldest boys, excited by the change, eager to contribute, wanted to stay in the tent, offering to help out with the nightly watches. The remaining five boys would need to sleep in the garage until different arrangements could be made. Before Petar had left, he'd offered to accommodate a few children, but needed to consult with the other members of his household. Their family had dropped from eleven to seven when Brent and Lydia moved out. He didn't think that they would have a problem; the extra hands would help with their rebuilding project up on the hill.

Skyler took the first watch that evening, and was relieved by James a few hours later. Both the boys in the tent had fallen fast asleep before it was completely dark. James took a chair next to Skyler. Resting a hand on the teenager's shoulder, said, "You did a good thing last night by going out there when you did."

"Why do you say that?" Skyler asked in a quiet tone, trying not to awaken the boys in the tent.

"Had you not snuck out when you did, they would all have moved on and probably never been seen again."

"Are you angry because I didn't ask?"

"No, not really."

"You seemed reluctant when I first asked you to rescue them."

"When you first asked, I did question it. Now I'm glad that you did."

"Aren't you worried that we won't be able to feed all these mouths?"

"No. When I took you and Lara in, I thought that my food supply would quickly dwindle away. However, both of you have contributed so much that you proved me wrong. These kids will do the same. We just have to get through the summer until the next harvest. We'll need more gardens, and we'll probably have to ask for help from the Lopatnikovs and the Jensens, but we'll make it. We do have a lot of work ahead of us. Besides, do you honestly believe that I could have said no to them?"

Skyler felt a great weight come off his shoulders. He went inside, being careful not to wake Devon. Since he no longer had a blanket, he left his shoes and coat on to help stay warm. He lay on the couch for a few minutes allowing the excitement of the day to escape, waiting for sleep to take over. His last thought was something his mother had once told him. He couldn't remember it exactly, but the last line went 'teach a man to fish and you feed him for the rest of his life'. That was what Skyler needed to do, he would teach them to fish.

CHAPTER 6

April 1st, 2031
7:40 am

The first night in the overcrowded house went relatively well. Occasionally a child would get up needing to relieve themselves. Their inclination was to find a door leading outside. James had the watch from midnight to first light. Much of his time was spent redirecting the new guests back inside to the working toilet. By the time James had been relieved by Brent in the early hours of the morning, he had found Gia sleeping on his side of the bed snuggled up to Lara's back. He managed to get two hours on the third couch between Devon and Skyler before the house came alive once again.

Lara awoke that morning, a bit surprised that James had been replaced by Gia. Without waking the young girl, she slid out of bed, headed for the kitchen. She started the day by making a large pot of oatmeal with beets and carrots mixed in. There was a small amount of sugar left in the pantry. Lara felt tempted to add it to the pot. These were children and she feared that her bland porridge would be rejected. There weren't enough dishes, so the children ate in shifts with the younger ones going first. No one complained about the meal. Gia and Devon, two of the first to finish their meal, pitched in, helping Lara with whatever task she passed on to them.

It made her think. She wondered if they had adopted her as their surrogate mother. Once they'd all eaten, Lara started addressing their hygiene. She soon found that only two of the children had tooth brushes, and that they'd rarely used them. She had seen several toothbrushes when they were scrounging for medicine. She would need to contact Petar to see if they could collect some from the houses in their neighborhood.

Throughout the rest of the morning, Gia searched for ways to help Lara out. She was constantly at Lara's side, never venturing more than a few feet away. Finally, Lara squatted down to her eye level. "Why are you following me around?"

"I don't want to leave here," replied the girl. Tears began welling up in her large eyes.

"Trust me, you and your brother are not leaving. I appreciate your offer to help, and you will be asked to do a lot of work at times, but for now, please wait until I ask you. I need to get used to the fact that I have a lot of children to look after."

Brent, feeling the pressure from Lydia to find a toilet, announced that he would soon be leaving for the hill. Lara, seizing the opportunity, asked Brent to search for toothbrushes while he was up there. To facilitate this, she sent Kai and Bree with him. Before they departed, Lara coached them on where to look for toothbrushes. She was emphatic that they do it safely, staying near Brent or another adult during their search. Lara was determined that, by the end of this day, all of the children will have brushed their teeth. And this was only the beginning.

James, feeling the need to mend bridges, led Skyler and two of the older boys, Joe and Joel, down to the garage. All the kids had left their packs in the garage the day before. Opening each pack, Skyler found several empty Mason jars complete with lids.

"While we were liberating this bunch, I had them pack up every useable jar and lid before we left that house. There are actually more jars here than what was taken from the Jensens. I'd like it if the three of you hiked back up to the Jensens and returned them," said James.

Joel's face look mortified. Skyler noticed and asked, "What's wrong?"

64

"What if they're still mad?" he asked. "We had Brandon to protect us before."

"Nobody's gonna hurt you," said Skyler. "I'll go up to them first and make sure it's okay."

James added, "I also want you to tell them of our situation. We're going to need food donations to get through the summer. Offer to help them out for the food you stole and please offer them an apology."

"Would you mind if we took the fishing poles with us? After we finish up there, I think we'll have time for a trip to the ponds. We might be able to catch enough fish for dinner tonight."

"Do that. Any food you bring back will be helpful."

When the packs were emptied, they repacked the three largest with the jars. The canning jars, now more valuable than gasoline, were necessary for preserving meats, pickles, carrots, and whatever else they could hunt or grow during the warmer months. The three boys, two sporting fishing poles, took their bikes, heading west up Main Street with Skyler leading the way.

Petey stood by watching silently as the boys rode away. He'd been quiet since James and Brent overpowered Brandon. Petey lacked the confidence that Skyler exhibited. James' first thought was that, besides being unsure of his surroundings, the kid was a little introverted. Since Petey wasn't doing anything, James decided to take him along as he searched the row of wind-damaged homes along Main. James carried a crowbar and hammer, just in case they had the opportunity to remove a window. They were also good weapons if needed.

They approached the first damaged house. They stood before it, looking at how the house had been twisted by the winds, destroying all of its doors and windows. Petey remained as silent as a shadow. James eyed the boy for a few seconds and asked, "Something on your mind?"

At first, Petey didn't answer, just staring off into the distance.

"Petey? What's bothering you?"

The abruptness of the question caught the boy's attention. He turned to face James and blurted, "Why are you being nice to us?"

"Well, you and I are both survivors of two harsh winters, not to mention the collapse of our society, if not the entire world."

"No, I mean, why?"

"Petey, I don't need to tell you that there's not many of us left, at least not in this part of the country. You can either be my friend or my enemy. It's your choice. Before yesterday, you were my enemy. That didn't work well for me. So I want to take a stab at being friends."

Petey stared into James' eyes as he contemplated his words. The boy remained quiet as they circled each structure searching for windows that still had unbroken panes within their frames. James noticed that the Petey was actively looking over each structure. "Why don't you go to the next house? If you find any intact windows, come back and tell me," James instructed.

Petey, maintaining his quiet demeanor, disappeared around the corner. James finished circling his house, an older home; a two-story craftsman built in the 1980's. Finding no windows intact, he moved to the next one. James expected to find Petey there, but was startled to find he was nowhere in sight. He looked out over the fields behind the houses. Not knowing Petey, uneasiness fell over James as he wondered if Petey had taken off, if he was trying to make his way back to Brandon. Petey's shout from three houses away assured him that he was wrong.

"Found two on this house!"

James ran toward Petey's voice, excited over the possible find, but slightly miffed that Petey had worried him. Petey stood there with his arm raised, finger pointed to two windows, smiling at his accomplishment. They were small, measuring two feet by three feet each, but the glass was indeed intact; perfect for the new house. James considered scolding the boy for leaving the house he had been assigned to, but realized that the kid had taken the initiative to move on when he saw there were not good windows to be found there.

"Those are perfect! Now let's see if we can get them out without breaking them."

For the rest of the morning, James sensed that his earlier conversation with Petey had made an impression on the boy. They worked together, bound by their desire to find and reclaim whatever James felt they could use for the new project. Still quiet, yet now tenacious, Petey seemed to be grateful for the opportunity to work by James' side.

Brent returned pushing a wheelbarrow, borrowed from Petar, loaded with a fully operational toilet. Kai and Bree marched behind Brent, proud of their work, carrying their find like they were trophies. They had collected almost twenty toothbrushes with varying degrees of wear. Since most were frayed from overuse, Brent wanted Lara and Lydia to decide which ones to keep. Both Bree and Kai, with their energetic personalities, were a big hit with the smaller family on the hill. When Brent and Lydia had moved down to James' place, they hadn't brought any of the food supplies at the insistence of James. Brent spoke briefly with Petar about 'loaning' out some of the children to help with the gardening. This would free up Petar and McBride to work on their second house, Also, their current supply of food was still large enough to handle the extra mouths to feed. Petar said that he would come down to their house by the next day to discuss the matter.

Skyler's trip out to the Jensens took a detour when they reached Thornton Road. Since they were so close to Lopatnikov's farm, Skyler thought this might be a good time to let them know that the problem with the thieves on bikes had been resolved. It would also be a good opportunity to make Mr. Lopatnikov aware that they might need some food subsidy over the summer. The three boys left their bikes at the end of the driveway and walked in. Once again, a man emerged from the bushes behind them, following them from a short distance. Both Joe and Joel appeared nervous at first, but Skyler told them to "get used to it." Almost the entire family dropped what they were doing to hear the story as Dimitrey translated Skyler's version of the rescue. When one of the uncles noticed the fishing poles, he had Dimitrey ask them where they were going.

"Out to the ponds between the refineries, there're still some fish in them."

Dimitrey translated this to his father and uncles. There was much discussion between the adults. Finally, Dimitrey asked Skyler, "May I go with you? My father would like it very much if you taught me to fish."

Skyler responded, "Sure," but he was uneasy as he was the only one of the three carrying a weapon. He hadn't seen Dimitrey carry any type of weapon ever, while most of the Lopatnikov men were either armed or standing near a rifle or shotgun. An odd feeling crept over Skyler. He didn't know of any threats in the area, but while going from the Jensens to the ponds, they would be traversing a road he'd not traveled on before. If they found themselves in a dangerous situation, he would have to protect all three of them.

Dimitrey ran into the house. He came out, his face flushed, brandishing a bamboo pole with a ten-foot length of monofilament tied to the small end. Skyler looked it over and gave the boy a thumb up. At Skyler's request, Dimitrey retrieved a bicycle from their garage. Seconds later, all four boys were riding down Thornton toward the Jensen farm.

They soon came within sight of the small farm. The two older boys, nervous about the upcoming meeting, started to lag behind Skyler and Dimitrey. Skyler halted the group. He had promised the two boys that he'd approach the Jensens first. It was still early enough to be considered late morning, so the Jensen family should be outside doing chores. Skyler, walking his bicycle, entered the driveway alone. Two men, shirts soaked with sweat, were to the side of the house turning the soil over with shovels. The crunching of gravel caused one of them to look up and see Skyler. He instinctively gave a curt warning to the other who pulled a pistol from his coat.

Skyler threw up both hands and shouted, "It's just me, Skyler."

Both men relaxed, and dropping their shovels, walked over to meet him half way. They shook hands, glad to see him for the second time that week. "What brings you out this far?" asked the taller man.

"We caught up with those boys who robbed you. They had been forced to do it by that older boy with the gun. I have two of the boys with me.

They'd like to apologize, if that's okay with you. I'm sorry, but I've forgotten your names."

"I'm Carl and this is Robert," said the taller of the two men.

"Can I invite them in?" asked Skyler.

Robert looked to the other man as if it was his decision. Carl didn't seem overly thrilled before saying, "Tell them to come on in. We'll be civil."

Beth and Lindsey stepped out of the house in time to wave to Skyler as he walked back out to the road. A moment later, the three boys apprehensively followed Skyler into the yard. Neither Carl nor Robert smiled or showed any friendly gestures as the boys approached. With Dimitrey standing behind them, watching, the older boys stepped forward, removing their backpacks.

Joe spoke first, "We're sorry that we took your food. We've brought your jars back."

Joel stood there, too scared to move or say anything. Carl looked over at his other three housemates before replying, "We'll accept your apology on one condition, you two owe us for the food you took. Since I'm sure that you have nothing to pay us with, I expect you to help us dig up our garden."

"Today?" asked Joe.

"Yes, right now. Do you think I'm being unfair?"

"Uh, no, we can help," replied Joel.

Robert walked over to the tool shed attached to the side of the house, pulling out two more shovels. Beth and Lindsey collected the jars from the packs and carried them inside. As the four boys stood there, Dimitrey asked Skyler, "Aren't we going fishing?"

"Not yet. Since we have to wait on them, let's help them with the digging."

Soon, all four boys were turning over the soil from last year's garden. The winter storms had repacked the dirt, making it difficult work. Carl and Robert followed behind them with hoes, further busting up the larger chunks, leveling the ground. An hour later, dripping with sweat despite the chilly day, they'd reached the far end of the garden.

The upturned soil created a rich dark patch amid the tan and green field. Carl, leaning on his hoe, looking back at the accomplishment, turned to the boys. "You're good workers. I'm thankful. I think you did more than your fair share."

Lindsey came out of the house carrying two bowls of soup, handing one each to Dimitrey and Joel. She went back inside and came out with two more bowls. The first one she handed to Joe, then she held Skyler's bowl with both hands for him to take.

Skyler took the opportunity to ask Lindsey, "How is Dag doing?"

"He appears to be a little stronger. At the moment, he's sleeping, but earlier, he was up. He even went outside for a spell. I need to go back inside and see if he's ready to try to eat something."

Joe and Joel had relaxed, downing the soup in record time. Dimitrey, anxious to fish, drank his like water. Skyler told Robert and Carl the story of how James and Brent had brought eleven Canadian children, all separated from their parents, into their home. As promised, he also relayed to them that they needed help feeding them. Finished with the soup, and in a hurry to go fishing, the three boys picked up their empty packs. They were about to mount their bikes when Skyler asked Carl, "Do you have any idea where in Bellingham your other three family members went?"

Carl's expression visibly changed. His lower lip quivered a bit when he spoke. "We don't know exactly where they went. When they left that morning, their plan was to venture into the medical district to see if they could find a doctor or some medicine. It's been seventeen days now."

Skyler realized that he'd touched a nerve. "I'm sorry for bringing it up. If we hear anything, I'll make a trip up here and let you know."

They said their good-byes, the boys thanking the men for their understanding and hospitality.

The trip out to the ponds was uneventful—to Skyler's relief. He supposed that the Lopatnikovs had not seen the many dangers that the other survivors had witnessed. After all, the Lopatnikov farm was a bit more remote and their numbers outweighed any of the other surviving families.

He wondered if Dimitrey's father sent his son off not fully aware of what unknown dangers existed.

This acreage between the two refineries contained a total of five ponds large enough to support fish, with a handful of smaller ponds that could dry up over the summer. Since there were four of them and only three fishing poles, Skyler would act as the teacher. Once they were catching fish, he'd visit the other ponds in search of crows or waterfowl. Leaving the bikes at the entrance, they bypassed a pond that Skyler had fished previously, knowing that the number of fish in it would be small.

The next pond up the trail, having only a small patch of ice on the end shadowed by a tall bank, proved to be fruitful on the first few casts. Skyler spread the boys along the bank, coaching them for the first half-hour. The crappies, small from a lack of insects to feed upon, made up for their size with quantity. Skyler wondered if insects would return soon, if ever. The Alder and Maple trees surrounding these ponds had died two winters ago, leaving a tangle of dead wood. The winds had all but flattened the once green forest that shielded the ponds from the sun. It was last fall that a fire had come within a few hundred yards of the ponds, swallowing up any dry wood in its path. All that saved the ponds from being engulfed in that inferno was a patch of barren field just to the south. Skyler was sure that had the fire reached the ponds, there wouldn't be any fish here now.

The three boys were as focused on the sport of fishing as if they were playing their favorite video game. Skyler, convinced that the boys had figured how to catch and string the fish on a stick, pulled his bow from his back. He set out through the maze of trails between the ponds. His route, often blocked by fallen trees, sometimes stopping him completely, led him up to a clearing by the next pond. To his delight, he spotted fresh new trees sprouting from the soil. The most common was alder—a tree that grew easily from seed and made good firewood. There was also the occasional conifer that Skyler couldn't identify because they all looked the same to him. The new growth was a good sign. He'd be sure to tell James when they returned home.

Skyler came to an abrupt stop. He'd reached another pond, larger than the previous along the trail. On the far side of the pond, oblivious to his presence, were two white swans. These were the largest birds that Skyler had ever seen up close. James had taught him that there were two types of swans that migrated through this area; the Tundras and the Trumpeters. The latter of the two species were the largest, known only to travel in pairs or trios. The two birds, all white except for dark beaks, had to be Trumpeters. At the water's edge, between him and the swans, stood a large root ball from a downed tree. Skyler crept up to the tree to get a closer look.

He was torn about what to do. The meat from one of these birds would be enough to feed their current household population for a day or more, while on the other hand, this was a mated pair, and he knew that their species must have become endangered over the last two winters. He had seen a few pairs of swans fly overhead the previous summer, but he had never seen one on the ground. The other dilemma was his supply of arrows. The jumbled mass of downed trees surrounding the ponds would surely hide whatever he shot. He had too few remaining arrows to lose knowingly.

Through the winter months, their intake of protein had been minimal. The winter storms were severe enough to freeze the ponds and inhibit the migration of birds. Only recently had Skyler been able to fish and hunt, even then his bounty was meager. Taking the risk that it might upset James; Skyler decided he'd shoot one of the swans. The other, he would allow to escape with the hope that it would find another mate. With his first issue resolved, he contemplated how he could take down the bird without losing an arrow in the process. Skyler retreated back to the other pond to get a fishing pole.

In the short time that he'd left the other three boys alone, each sported a heavy string of fish. The boys were so excited that they all tried to speak at once. Skyler put a finger to his lips asking for silence, then said, "Joe, I need you to follow me to the next pond. I'll need your fishing pole to help me shoot a swan."

All three boys wanted to follow, but Skyler told them that it was imperative that they stay where they were and keep their voices down. Joe followed him through the maze of limbs and dead trees to a spot near the edge of another much larger pond. Skyler didn't need to point out the large birds; they were as obvious as two cars on a barren street. He had Joe release the drag on the reel so that the thin monofilament flowed freely from the tip of the pole. Joe watched silently as Skyler unscrewed a broad head from an arrow shaft, tied the end of the fishing line to the base of the arrow head, and screwed it back on. Since the string was attached to the front of the arrow, the slight drag could alter the arrow's path, causing him to miss. Skyler peeled a piece of tape from the riser of his compound bow, using this to secure the line to the tail end of the arrow. It was a flimsy alternative, but he hoped that the arrow would now travel straight enough to reach the large bird. The distance to the birds was just about a hundred feet, an easy shot in any other situation.

Skyler motioned for Joe to stand behind him and aim the tip of the pole toward the nearest swan. Drawing back on the bowstring, he sighted in on the bird. Skyler hesitated only long enough to estimate how much to aim above the birds broad back, allowing for the drop during the flight. The twang of the string seemed loud against the surrounding silence. Both boys witnessed a slight jerk to the bird, followed by a small splash as the arrow pierced the water on the far side. Instantly, both birds, sensing danger, opened their enormous wings and pushed themselves up off the water. The fishing line clearly led to the body of one bird. As the swan reached a height of twenty-five feet, its wings seem to fold, and it dropped violently back on to the water's surface. It lay there unmoving.

Joe locked down the reel and gently turned the handle forward. At first, the bird stayed stationary as Joe reeled the excess line through the bird. As the arrow reached the mortal wound, the bird began to move towards them. Joe began pulling the bird in by swinging the pole back and then forward again as he wound up the slack.

"Don't get in a hurry," Skyler cautioned him, "We don't want to lose the bird and my arrow."

A few moments later, Skyler and Joe were walking back down the trail with the large bird tied to the outside of Skyler's pack. After sharing the story with the two other boys, Skyler had them pack up their catches—they were finished here.

The boys, chatting constantly, reliving the fishing trip, rode down Mountain View like they would have any other day before the Change. The three talked about how much they liked fishing, wanting to know when they could return. Skyler realized that he needed to teach these boys how to shoot. He couldn't send them out here alone and unarmed; running into someone hostile would happen sooner or later. Skyler was also quick to caution Dimitrey about returning without an armed escort. He told the younger boy, "Take one of your uncles with you if you go."

After parting with Dimitrey and his fish at the end of the Lopatnikov's driveway, Skyler led Joel and Joe back down the Thornton Road toward Church Road. All three were forced to stay off their bikes, lifting them over the evenly spaced power poles. Eventually they reached the barricade of stacked power poles. Joe and Joel became apprehensive about walking past the ominous barrier.

"Don't worry, these are good people. You two might be spending a lot of time up here helping them this summer."

Entering the street that led into the development, Brandy, Petar, and McBride came out to greet them. Skyler introduced the boys to Brandy as his 'girlfriend', so that there wouldn't be any confusion. When he reached into Joe's pack to pull out a string of fish to hand over, the trio got a full view of the bird tied to his pack.

"Jesus, that swan you shot is huge," said Petar.

"That's why I can spare giving up some of the fish. I hope that James doesn't get angry because I shot it," he replied. "You're welcome to join us for dinner. I'm sure that there's going to be enough for everyone."

"Some of us might be able to come down, but Scott isn't having a good day," said Brandy. "The ibuprofen seems to have stopped working. The cramping has returned."

"Brent and two of the kids just left here an hour ago with a toilet. We requested that he ask Lara come back up in the next day or so to check on his condition," said McBride.

Both men looked worried suggesting that they weren't telling the whole story. Skyler knew that Scott was feeling a little better after taking the anti-inflammatory drugs, but then, Lara had warned them that it might be temporary.

When they left the hill, Brandy rode down with them. Unlike Skyler's first trip on the bike, he was not out to break any speed records. With the weight of the bird on his back and Brandy riding alongside, he was not in a hurry.

Lara was the first to greet them as they entered the upstairs. Upon seeing Brandy, she gave the young girl a brief hug. The swan and the string of fish impressed her but she carried no excitement in her voice. James, along with the rest of the children, was nowhere to be seen. It was his way of helping. "James spent most of his day with Petey collecting windows, doors and anything else that could be used in the new house," she exclaimed. "I had been keeping the six youngest children occupied through most of the day and I am exhausted."

She was smiling, so Skyler knew this to be a good sign.

"I also taught the stronger children how to fetch water from the pond for the garden. Since Brent is in the basement attempting to get the toilet functioning, some of that water will be needed to flush the toilet."

Brandy shed her coat and set to work helping Lara prepare dinner for the large clan. The swan, large as it was, took a couple of hours to cook, making for a late meal. By the time they sat down to eat, the once musty odor of the house had been replaced by gamey smell of the swan.

Skyler, feeling a bit guilty about shooting the bird, relived the events of the hunt to James.

"I doubt that I would have thought of using a fishing pole. Don't get me wrong. When I first saw what you carried on your back, I was a bit disappointed. I am grateful for the amount of meat you brought home. I just hope that we didn't further endanger a species on the brink. However, I am proud and pleased that you allowed the other swan to escape."

After dinner was finished, Brandy stayed long enough to help was the last round of dishes. Without any places left for guests to sleep, Skyler apologized for not inviting her to stay for the night. After saying her good-byes, Brandy headed for the door with Skyler close behind. They both had looked forward to this time. Having him walk her home would be the one time that they would be alone without the others surrounding them. As they walked their bikes up the hill, they took their time, often so close together that their shoulders were touching.

"I was surprised to learn that they aren't all a bunch of delinquents," Brandy commented. "Most of them seem eager to help, and there weren't any fights. Will they be staying with you all the time?"

"I doubt it. James wants to teach them survival skill like hunting, fish-ing, and farming. Eventually, some of them might move up to your place to help."

Dusk was settling as they reached the barricade. Instead of following her in, he gave her a kiss and said that he'd see her the next day. This wasn't the first time that he'd kissed her, but those moments were rare because they were almost never alone. Now, with eleven more added to their fami-lies, they would need to consciously seek solitude once in a while. Glanc-ing at the first star to appear, Skyler hopped on the bike, allowing gravity to carry him down the steep hill. Pulling up to the house, he bounded up the stairs. James was leaning against one wall, two candles burning on the mantle next to him, providing enough light while he read aloud from a book. Before him, listening intently, sat all eleven children, Lara, Brent, Lydia, and their two children. Skyler noticed that this was not the same book that he'd read from two nights earlier; more likely something left here by the previous owner. Skyler quietly crept back to his bedroom to change his clothes; he had the first shift of watch for the night. Instead of immedi-ately heading out onto the deck, Skyler slipped into the living room floor, taking a spot next to Devon. He listened as James read them a story about a man named Tarzan, who was the king of all the apes.

CHAPTER 7

April 2nd, 2031
7:25 am

The morning after the feast, almost everyone was awake at first light. Lara spent her first hour feeding their large clan, then trying to get everyone into the habit of brushing their teeth. By mid-morning, James, who had slept through the earlier noise, was awakened from the nap that followed his turn at the watch. Both he and Brent were anxious to sit down and draw out the plans for the new house.

Despite the constant interruptions from the children, Lara was intent on hiking up the hill to see how Scott was faring. She wanted all the children, including little Brent and Bekka, to accompany her. Most of the children were still wearing the same clothes that they had arrived in. Feeling it was up to her alone to monitor their hygiene, she wanted them to pick through the houses for a second and cleaner set of clothing. She also knew the house up on the hill still had a functioning shower. Cold as it was, the shower was a slight improvement over washing up in the pond. She asked Skyler to go with her. Lydia would stay behind, taking a break from all the children, including her own.

Eleven curious children followed Lara and Skyler, along with Little Brent and Bekka, up the long grade without issue. Upon reaching the upper house, Skyler asked Brandy to bring out all the long bows and as many target arrows as she could find. Lara took the younger half of the group with her while Skyler and Brandy, assuming the role as instructors, focused on teaching the older boys how to shoot a bow. With only five long bows, the six boys took turns aiming their arrows at the empty plastic milk jugs used as targets. Being the eldest of the new arrivals, and possessing the hubris of young men, they took to archery like a fish takes to swimming. Skyler was impressed at how well each of his students improved in an hour and a half. Still, they were no match for Brandy when she turned their lesson into a contest. Lara returned with the seven younger children, now with clean clothes, faces, and hair, looking so much different than when they had arrived.

The older boys did not want to lay down the bows to go "shopping." Lara put both hands on her hips and, like she'd been barking orders to children most of her life, snapped, "I am not going to have a bunch of smelly kids running around my house. Get yourselves cleaned up and maybe I'll see if Petar and John can spare a bow for us to take back down to the house."

Before she could return to her task, Skyler stopped her. "How's Scott?"

"Not well right now. He has only a slight fever, but his pain seems to have returned with a vengeance. At this point, I don't know what more we can do for him."

Skyler was torn. He wanted to visit his former teacher, but he didn't relish the thought of seeing him ill and frail. He remembered what he looked like only a week earlier, and it scared him; he'd lost so much weight that his skin stretched over his bones like a tent. Scott had known Skyler's mother before the Change. He had liked her. Skyler could not bear the thought of losing Scott, his last tie to a past that he wasn't ready to part with. Scott was responsible for making Skyler as much a part of this family as any of them. Scott was also the brains behind much of the improvements that were adopted here. Their water system was his idea, which enabled them to have running water through half of the year.

Skyler and Brandy didn't have as much luck training the youngest children because not all of them were interested in shooting the large cumbersome weapons. The three girls, enamored by their new clothes, wanted nothing more than to continue scrounging for clothes. The boys simply lost interest. Devon and Kai weren't as tall as the bows, making it difficult for them to aim. Little Brent and Bekka, content to be in the company of other children, became a distraction. Skyler didn't get the satisfaction for his efforts as he had with the older boys. Lara finally returned with the older boys, some of them were carrying plastic bags containing everyone's old clothes. Skyler took this as a sign that they would soon be returning home. It was just past midday. There was still time to break ground for more gardens. Skyler wanted Brandy to return with them, but she declined, saying that she needed to get their own gardens tilled.

"Besides," she added, "Petar says that we'll be going down to your place this evening. He wants to discuss moving some of the kids up here to help us."

Back at home, Lara broke out three jars of pickles, beets, and carrots, chopping them together in a bowl. She hadn't mixed these vegetables in this fashion before, and the combination of sweet and salty mixed with vinegar tasted delicious. The quantity of the lunch, small when divided into eighteen servings, only needed to hold them over until dinner. There was still some of the swan meat remaining, and she was saving it for their evening meal. Without refrigeration, she would need to re-cook the meat before serving it a second time. Lara and James had decided that any meat should always be eaten within twenty-four hours. If it sat at room temperature more than eight hours, it had to be re-cooked. So far, nobody in their house had gotten sick following a meal.

Joe, Joel, and Petey were assigned to help Brent and James collect lumber for the new house. Both Joe and Joel balked at first, knowing that Skyler was intending to return to the ponds. Petey seemed to relish working with James once again, his eagerness so infectious, he soon convinced the other two into accepting the task of joining him in the hunt for acceptable boards. Equipped with hammers and crowbars, the three boys set out for a row of collapsed houses off Main Street with a list of dimensions necessary for the initial frame. Both Brent and James followed along, measuring tapes in hand, acting as security.

Lara was set on enlarging their garden. Left with the three girls, Bree, Gia, and Marley, and two of the younger boys, David and Thomas, she assigned them to ground work. She laid out a big area of the yard, one that had not yet been tilled, dividing it up into six smaller sections. Each child was assigned a section, and given a shovel. The ground was covered with a brown carpet of dead grass. She showed them how to cut the sod into strips, and then roll it up as it peeled away from the earth. Lara pointed out that if their strips were too narrow, they'd have to make more cuts in their sections, and if their strips were excessively wide, they might not have the strength to finish rolling up the strip.

To make it more fun and, more importantly, to keep them focused, Lara turned the job into a race. Whoever could clear their section of sod first would be declared the winner. The rules were simple: they could team up and work together, or even recruit little Brent and Bekka. The winner would be exempt from any more chores that day. They had to be careful because the last two to finish clearing their sections would have to wash the dinner plates that evening.

Lara finally said, "Go!" and the race was on.

Lara used a spade to make her cuts, noticing that each child was glancing over, copying her technique. Marley was the first to lay down her shovel and strike a deal with Thomas, promising to do his share of the dishes if he took the time to help her finish ahead of the others. Soon after, Gia recruited David, leaving Bree to work on her own. Bree continued to make her cuts, but didn't stop and roll up each strip like Lara was doing. Instead, she made all of her cuts at once and soon disappeared around the side of the house. She returned a few minutes later with Bekka and little Brent in tow. As she used her shovel to pry up the edge of each strip, the two younger children worked together to roll the sod. Within twenty minutes, Bree had caught up to Lara and was gaining on Gia and Marley.

Lydia came out into the yard to watch and soon was soon solicited by each girl and Lara. Lydia finally joined up with Lara, helping her just enough to finish in a tie with Bree. Now that the race had two winners, the two boys abandoned their female partners to focus on their own plots. The piles of sod grew quickly, and the two boys finished their sections only seconds behind the girls. Lara looked at their accomplishment, congratulating them on clearing a twenty-foot by forty-foot section of the yard in less than two hours. The only downside was that these once clean kids were now covered in dirt again.

While the others worked around the house, Skyler, Sebastian and Devon rode out to the ponds. Knowing that they were too young to hunt for lumber, Skyler could find no reason that they couldn't fish, as long as someone went along for protection. Arming the boys, something that still plagued the back of his mind, needed to be addressed. He couldn't be expected to be everyone's personal guard. Devon and Sebastian were too young to train for any sort of defense, but Joel, Joe and Petey were as capable as he was. Even David and Thomas were about the same size as Skyler when he first met James and Lara. He didn't learn to shoot his bow overnight, but his strength and skill grew with practice. He silently wished that there were smaller compound bows available. Skyler knew that finding another would be a fluke, and even if they did, the elements would have damaged it by now.

Inside his backpack, Skyler carried the small crossbow used for hunting ducks and crows. James had made a special bolt with a frog gig tip that attached to a reel located under its stock. The small crossbow was meant to be held with one hand by a pistol grip. Skyler brought it along because he didn't want to risk losing one of his own arrows. The crossbows arrow could be reeled back in if it didn't find its target.

Skyler took the boys to the same pond where he'd taught Joe and Joel to fish. Within minutes, both boys were reeling in fish. For only the second time since he'd found Devon, he saw the boy smile. Even Sebastian was grinning as he showed his fifth fish to Skyler. He left them on the bank and walked up to the pond where he'd shot the swan. Upon nearing the pond, Skyler took off his pack and withdrew the small compound bow. Before he stepped any closer to the water's edge, he quietly pulled the lever back that cocked and locked the string. Hiding behind the same root ball as he had the day before, Skyler peered out and could see five small ducks clustered at the far end of the pond.

At this distance, the small crossbow was highly inaccurate. Skyler wasn't even sure if there was enough line within the reel to reach that far. Besides, this was a 'one of a kind' bolt. James wouldn't appreciate it if it was lost over a small duck. If he could get closer, he knew that the risk of losing the bolt would be minimized.

He backed away from the water's edge and retraced his steps to the main trail. Walking parallel to the ponds edge, he sought out the far side. Trees and limbs, strewn everywhere, made it difficult to move quickly or quietly. Eventually, Skyler worked his way around just as the ducks sensed his presence and made a dash for the opposite corner. Frustrated, Skyler turned to make his way back to the younger boys when he noticed a large berm overshadowing this side of the pond. Could there be one more pond above this one? He climbed the steep bank expecting to see more dead trees and water, but was surprised to step from the darkness of the tangled trees to find a chain-link fence.

Stepping up to the fence, he looked down into a large hallowed out basin with a dilapidated warehouse sitting below the level where he stood. This was the remains of the old aluminum smelter. The strong winter winds, the same ones that had decimated so many houses, had removed most of the thin sheet metal skin, leaving a network of steel beams. Some of the beams had been twisted by the winds, but the framework was still intact. Beyond the warehouse, crumpled like pop cans, were the enormous buildings that housed the smelting pots.

Curious about what could be found in this place, Skyler scouted the surrounding area for any sign that he might not be alone. The yard before him, once a tiny part of the smelter, now appeared as he imagined a ghost town would look like. He was about to try to climb the fence when he remembered the boys he'd left at the pond.

He raced back to get Sebastian and Devon. Both boys, in the same place where he'd left them, were still pulling in the crappies as soon as their hooks hit the water. Skyler eyed their string of fish. "We're done here. Leave the poles and fish, and follow me."

"Where are we going now?" asked Devon.

"We're going exploring. There's an old factory on the other side of this hill. I want to see if we can find anything useful there."

The thought of scrounging through an old building excited both boys. They readily left their gear along the bank and followed him. Skyler made them bring their packs, in case they found something worth hauling home. Before long, all three were at the fence, fingers poking through the wire mesh, looking down on the warehouse and the storage yard that surrounded it. The fence, a full seven feet in height, topped with another foot of barbed wire, would be impossible to climb over. Devon spotted a gap in the fence on the far side of the basin where a large maple tree had fallen. Skyler led the way, following the fence and entered the old smelter by climbing onto the tree. Exploring this place generated as much excitement as the fishing had. This was a new territory for all three of them; each of them moved forward with a little fear.

To reach the warehouse, they walked through rows of aluminum ingots, stacked in bundles, awaiting a sale that would never happen. Each bundle was made of small ingots that were maybe three feet long and stacked about three feet tall. The bundles were stacked three high making a nine-foot wall wherever the wind had not knocked off the top stack. A four-digit number, faded by the weather, was spray painted onto each bundle: Skyler guessed that since all the numbers were in proximity to one another, they must reflect the weight of each bundle. Several times the boys had to retrace their steps; their route blocked by bundles that had fallen between the rows. But what piqued the three boy's interest was the building frame and what it contained within.

Nearing the frame, Skyler could see where the large sliding doors had once covered the entrance. The enormous doors, having been ripped away by high winds, lay twisted in the corner of the basin.

Devon looked around, asking in a hushed voice, "What is this place?"

"Yeah, where are we?" asked Sebastian.

"I guess they used to make aluminum here. That's what's in those stacks we just walked through. I think this building stored the stuff they used. Let's look around for tools or anything else that we might be able to use."

Upon entering the open doorway, the three spread out. The interior was strewn with pieces of crumpled metal sheeting peeled from the walls and roof. The material was light enough to push out of the way or lift. Skyler made the first discovery; a pallet of shrink-wrapped boxes. Using his pocket knife, he cut the plastic and opened one of the upper boxes. Inside were six cans of spray paint, the color matching the numbers on the bundles outside. When he removed a cap and pressed the nozzle, nothing came out. After testing several other cans that failed to function, he gave up.

"Skyler, come look at this," shouted Sebastian. He was holding up a large long armed tool that resembled a bolt cutter.

Skyler and Devon worked their way over to him, discovering that he was using the tool to cut pieces of steel banding. It was the same material used to encase the bundles of ingots. Sebastian was standing on one of the handles as he used both arms to press down on the other handle to make each cut. He was a cutting a long piece of the steel banding into smaller pieces.

"Too bad we don't have a use for this," said Devon as he fingered one of the small pieces of banding. The metal band was over an inch wide and extremely stiff.

Skyler ignored his statement as he lifted a sheet of aluminum to discover another shrink-wrapped pallet. This was different from the first one. It was smaller, and whatever was under the plastic was as round as a tire. Using his knife, he slit the side to expose a stack of several spools of the steel banding. He counted twenty four spools stacked evenly, one atop the other. "Hey, can you guys look around to see if there are other tools for working with this stuff?"

"What for? There's nothing you can use this for."

"Maybe it can be used to hold two boards together so the wind can't rip them apart. James might be able to use it for the new house."

A minute later, Devon opened a small chest revealing a variety of other tools. He held two of them up in the air. Skyler climbed over to his location. The first tool was some kind of crimping device. In the chest were several green colored metal sleeves, just large enough to fit over the ends of the bands. Skyler took two pieces of banding, slipped a steel band over those and used the tool to crimp the sleeve. It made the two bands impossible to separate. The second tool was a bit more difficult to figure out until Devon showed him that the flat side was meant to sit on the ground while the arm moved. Skyler set the tool on the only clear spot on the floor and started working it up and down. It didn't take long before he realized that it was used to manually tighten two bands together before crimping them.

"Sebastian. Could you hand that to me?" Skyler asked as he reached his hand out for the cutting tool. As the smaller boys watched, Skyler snipped off the two small bands holding the roll together. The large spool expanded from the spring action of the steel being released. Locating the end, he cut a four-foot strip of the banding, bending it to make a loop. At the place where the two ends overlapped to form the loop, Skyler set down the tightening tool and began working the lever. The tool made a ratcheting sound as it made the loop smaller. Devon found a block of wood and set it inside the loop as Skyler tightened the band around it. When the band was so tight that it cut into the wood, Skyler quit pumping and picked up one of the metal sleeves. He realized that if he wanted to crimp the sleeve around the band, he needed to have the sleeve over the band before he started tightening it.

Skyler reversed the ratchet, and after loosening the band, pulled everything apart and started over. With Devon and Sebastian watching, he slid a sleeve over both ends and tightened the band once more. When he was finished, he held up a block of wood with a metal band squeezing its center so tight that the banding was embedded into the corners up to a half inch deep. Skyler knew this was something James could use.

Using his boot to measure, Skyler cut several four-foot strips of banding, stuffing them in his own pack. The cutter, the crimper, the tightener, and a quantity of sleeves went in the boy's packs. He wanted to show James what this set up was capable of doing. He envisioned being able to use the banding to lash a roof to a frame or for joining walls together. The steel bands would bind the house frame much stronger than nails would.

Retrieving their poles and fish, they were soon back on their bikes and headed home. The two younger boys had a string of crappies inside their packs along with the banding tools that Skyler gave them to transport. Devon and Sebastian talked constantly about how much they liked fishing while Skyler rode along in silence. His mind was elsewhere that afternoon. Something about the metal bands in his pack was pressing on his thoughts.

Arriving back at the house, Skyler was able to impress both James and Brent with the metal bands and how well they could bind the roof and walls together. He also told them about the endless amounts of sheet metal that once sheltered the warehouse and other buildings. Both men were interested with this discovery. They had already laid-out boards to form the framework for the walls, but were still perplexed by what to use for the roof. Sheet metal had not been a viable option, until now. The boys may have provided a solution for that final dilemma.

The stack of recovered lumber and the expanded garden amazed Skyler. So much had been accomplished in the few hours he'd been away. Having the bikes made the trip out to the ponds a half-day affair instead of a full day. Still, the work completed by the others was phenomenal.

Exhausted and sated after a dinner of swan meat, pickles, carrots, and fish, everyone lay about on the living room couches and floor. A knock on the front door startled James causing him to jump to his feet and reach for his pistol. Lara, seeing a face through the small glass portal, motioned him back down as she stepped over the smaller children on her way to the door.

"It's Petar and Brandy," she said as she reached for the deadbolt.

The door opened. Brandy entered first, her eyes, red and swollen, obvious signs that she'd been crying. Petar followed behind with a pained look on his face. They stood there quietly as if they were searching for the correct words. The looks on their faces halted the usual barrage of hellos.

Finally, Petar cleared his throat once and uttered, "Scott isn't doing so well. His fever was one-hundred and four when we left."

CHAPTER 8

March 30th, 2031
6:55 am

Brandon opened his eyes to find a strange man pointing a rifle at his chest. His first thought was that he was about to die; his second, betrayal. He had trained these kids how to beg and steal, and now they had allowed these two men to walk right in and take his rifle. To add to the treachery, when the men said they wanted to reunite Gia with her brother, all of them wanted to go with them. He protested, but the man called Brent kept him pinned to the floor while the other one called James helped the others load their packs with empty jars. He couldn't believe what he was seeing. He'd kept these kids fed and clothed for the last year, and yet, they were willing to walk away with two strange men.

The children filed out leaving Brandon alone with the two men. James handed Brandon a full jar of cut carrots. He still harbored a pent-up look of anger on his face. "This will keep you from starving right away."

The other man, the one called Brent, unloaded the rifle and pocketed the cartridges before leaning the gun against the wall. He'd already searched through Brandon's pack and coat pockets, finding nothing. "You can keep your rifle and your bike, but I'm taking your bullets. If you're smart, you'll continue traveling south. If I ever see you again, I won't hesitate to shoot you."

With that, both men exited the small house. Brandon watched from the open door as the two men rode away with his ten former companions. He was now on his own and his existence was more precarious. Brandon stayed long enough to contemplate on what to do next. He fought the urge to follow them, thinking that maybe he could talk them into coming back. Did they really believe that these two men would feed them? Others had tried the same thing before they left Vancouver, only they were more upfront and said their need for a child was for other purposes. Brandon could have sold any of the children, but hadn't. They were more valuable as a means of keeping him fed indefinitely. That was, until now. He gathered what little was left and placed it in his pack with the jar of carrots. Bellingham was only a few miles away, and they had been planning on going there today anyway. This was all Devon's fault. He knew he should have sold that boy when he had the chance.

Tall for young man, Brandon relied on his height to intimidate others. His dark-brown hair, once curly, lay matted to his head. Short dark whiskers covered his face making him look older than his eighteen years. His temper, hardened by years of abuse, had kept the children in check. When angered, his assertiveness towards them, or anyone else that crossed his path was not to be taken lightly. His earlier years were pock-marked with arrests for petty crimes, most of which involved assaults, and all of which involved younger and smaller victims. By definition, he was a bully.

The day was still early enough that he could bypass Bellingham altogether and possibly make it to Burlington, the next town on the I-5 corridor. Brandon didn't know what to expect, but without any bullets, he was defenseless. The cities to the north, Blaine, Whiterock, and Surrey, each had their own unique predators, and the thought of what lay before him made him fearful. Could he possibly find more children? He'd have to start by exploring each city that he passed through. As long as he acted like his rifle was loaded, most would believe that it was. Locating bullets would be difficult but it was something that needed to be done. It was by pure luck that they had ended up near Ferndale. What survivors they found were isolated and easy to steal from. There was that boy they'd chased into town and that house off Main Street. He bet that was where James and Brent were taking the children. He'd remember that place. Maybe when the kids discovered what those men really wanted, they'd be willing to come back to him.

With his rifle attached to his pack, it made him top heavy with that one jar of carrots, his sleeping bag and a his extra clothes. The children had packed the water jars with them; he would need to find a clean source before the day was out. Abandoned cars adorned the sides of the freeway. The fences and guardrails, embedded with wind-blown debris, created a channel much like a dry canal. He felt relief not seeing anyone since leaving Ferndale, yet, the day was still young. As he neared the Bellingham city limits, he recognized the area that he was passing through.

He'd been here once before the Change. Five years earlier, his mother brought him down across the border to the city's mall to make purchases for the upcoming school year. He protested about making the trip; he wanted to hang out with his friends. His mother became angry and insisted that he go. She wasn't about to pay the higher prices in Canada. It was always about her and her needs; even now the thought of her made him angry. That trip had almost been canceled at the border. The border guard, an armed man with a crisp uniform, motioned them to park off to the side. Another guard led them into the customs building for questioning. It turned out to be a routine check. Brandon was sure that they'd have known about his previous arrests, but they only questioned his mother, asking how long she was planning on staying in Bellingham as they studied her I.D. They were soon released to continue their shopping trip.

That same mall was now off to his left. The main structure, the only part he could see from the road, had been completely caved in. The parking lot, uninviting, was still filled with abandoned cars used by people that had lost their homes. Brandon remembered arriving at the mall and how disgusted his mother had been with the quantities of displaced people. Now it was a ghost parking lot, full of broken cars, perhaps more than a few with frozen occupants, victims of the Change that may be exhumed decades later, if ever. Except for the lack of people, and the collapsed structure in the background, the parking lot didn't look different today. Brandon focused on the road ahead, avoiding the memory of his mother. She was dead to him long before she was killed by the storm.

Two kilometers later, Brandon saw that the highway ahead was blocked; the overpass spanning it had collapsed. Brandon turned and peddled up the off ramp. All the traffic signs, long ago blown away, left him guessing at his exact location. At the top, he found himself at a four-way intersection. He looked around; remnants of homes, many burned to the foundation, lined the streets to his right and straight ahead. To his left was the abyss left by the fallen overpass. This was as good of a time as any to look for water, shelter, and maybe some food. He turned to the right, watching for signs of danger as he weaved his bike around a myriad of obstacles. All the houses and trees along the road were damaged; what hadn't burned, the high winds had broken up and swept away. Nothing habitable appeared to have survived.

The street curved gently to the left as the grade allowed him to stop peddling and coast. Another intersection loomed ahead, the road beyond it blocked by cars that had been torched. Whatever had happened here looked more like a war than a storm. Approaching closer, the road to his left was also blocked. Brandon hesitated; he felt like his direction was being controlled for a reason. Wary, he turned to the right and rode a little further. Two blocks up ahead, a large building made of steel and concrete, stood up above the many single-story structures that once were homes.

Two men with rifles stepped out into the street, barrels pointed at him. Brandon stopped the bike and spun it around, intending to escape the same way he'd come in. To his surprise, four more men with rifles blocked his only exit. Glancing about, he looked for an open alley; they had chosen this place for a reason. There was no way out. Brandon's rifle rode high on his pack. He let it fall from one shoulder when a shot was fired. The bullet tore through his backpack. He froze. Six dirty and malnourished men surrounded him.

"Step off the bike and take off your pack," barked the man who was man who clearly their leader. The man's eyes were wide like a drug-crazed maniac. His skin, so dark and dirty, left Brandon guessing at his race.

Brandon said nothing as he did exactly what he was ordered to do. A second man tore into his pack, while a third pulled the rifle from its ties and opened the chamber.

"Who were you planning on shooting with this? This stupid kid is packing an empty gun!" The rest of the men laughed, lowering their barrels.

The jar of carrots was held it in the air for all to see. The appearance of food brought on a frenzied search of the inside of the pack. Two men groped the pockets of Brandon's coat and pants. These men were clearly starving.

"You can have the carrots. Just let me go, please?" Brandon asked no one in particular.

Mo, their leader, held the jar out and asked Brandon, "Where did you find these?"

"There's a little farm outside of Ferndale. They had plenty more. Let me go and I'll draw you a map on how to get there."

Mo grinned, exposing a full set of yellowed teeth highlighted by his dark skin. His unshaven face populated with patches of long black hairs growing from pocked, dirty pores. "No, I'm not stupid enough to fall for that. I think that maybe you should take us there!"

Brandon remembered the warning that he'd just received earlier that morning. The words, "If I ever see you again, I will shoot you," still echoed in his head. Going there with six armed men might give him the opportunity to get those wretched kids back under his command. And he wouldn't mind settling up with Devon for bringing all of this trouble onto him. Then, there was that boy on the bike that he'd almost caught. He obviously wasn't starving like these guys were.

"I can take you, but you'll need bicycles. It's at least twenty kilometers from here."

"Are you Canadian?" Mo asked.

Brandon gulped. "Yes."

"Stupid fucker!"

One of the men picked up the bike and started walking toward the big building at the end of the street. Mo poked Brandon in the back with a rifle barrel and commanded, "Follow him."

"Where are you taking me?"

"To the hospital, we're gonna get you checked out!" he said with a chuckle.

As they moved closer to the building, looking up at its glassless windows, Brandon now feared for his life. Except for the man pushing the bike, everyone else stayed close to Brandon as they wearily eyed the surrounding area for any new dangers. They followed the signs that once directed the public to the Emergency Room, and walked through a large door frame, passing through a foyer. Brandon entered a gigantic room that must have been a waiting room. An entire wall that had once been all glass had become a cavernous opening. Broken glass and garbage covered the floor. Two men seated in wheelchairs, rifles positioned on their laps, were watching the entrance and parking lots. They nodded to Mo as he passed, showing no interest in his prisoner. Brandon made a mental note that there were now eight bandits. Water dripped from the floor above.

They led him to an interior staircase entirely lined with concrete walls. Two candles were lit before they climbed the stairs to the next floor. Water trickled down the stairs, probably from the roof. Except for a single path up the middle, garbage all but hid the steps. A rusty green metal door adorned the landing. Mo opened it and Brandon was thrust through it. Someone pushed him down a carpeted hall past a series of doors that looked like patient's rooms. They reached a door that Mo used a key to unlock. Once open, they pushed Brandon into the dark abyss causing him to stumble to the floor.

Mo's silhouette, ominous even in shadow, blocked the open door. "This is where you'll be staying while we round up the bicycles. For now, you are a 'prospect'. You'll be allowed to join us if you can lead us to food. If you're successful, we might let you live." His voice trailed off as the door was slammed shut and locked.

The room was completely devoid of light. Feeling his way around, Brandon determined that this had to be some kind of janitorial closet. He counted out the feet between each wall and guessed the room to be two meters by three meters. The floor was almost entirely covered with paper wrappers and discarded bottles. There were empty shelves along one wall, and a deep sink jutted out across from them. He turned the taps on the faucets and found them already open; a drop of water dripped out every five seconds. Finding a plastic bottle, and not caring if it was clean, Brandon positioned it under the tap until he heard the drop land inside. After a long period of time, each drop now made a splash as it landed. Waiting for either the bottle to get full or for someone to open the door, he laid on the floor. Eventually, he fell asleep atop the garbage. A not too distant noise, possibly a gunshot, pried him from his sleep. He lay there listening for more shots, but heard nothing but the methodical drip from the faucet, an aquatic metronome to mark off the time. He stood and stretched not knowing even what time of day it was. Feeling around for the sink, he found the bottle. The liter size bottle was about a quarter full. The contents had a putrid and bitter taste, but he didn't care. This was the first water he'd had since the night before he'd left Ferndale. It must have taken over half a day to collect this much water.

Hours later, he felt the need to defecate so badly that he was certain that the water had been tainted. Banging on the door, he pleaded for someone to let him out, but no one came. He finally defecated in the far corner away from the door. His stool was almost as watery as the fluid he'd drunk from the bottle. The room smelled rancid when he was first thrown in, but now it was intolerable. Brandon felt weaker and more ill as each moment passed. His stomach tensed, plagued by dry heaves. He was sure that he had a fever as he shivered in a corner near the door. Brandon fell onto the garbage that covered the floor, curled up in the fetal position, and fought the continuous waves of nausea that rocked his body. He went through episodes of sleep only to be woken by chills that caused him to shake violently. He was awakened by a foot pushing on his shoulder.

"Did you shit yourself? Gawd, it stinks in here!"

Two men picked him up by the shoulders, drug him out into the light and dropped him into a wheelchair. He was driven down a hall, barely conscious of where he was or what was happening.

"What's the matter with him?" asked Mo. He was seated in a chair, rifle laid over his lap, watching the parking lot and entrance below.

"I don't know, but it smells really bad in that closet. Maybe he ate something he shouldn't have. You know, it ain't no good to starve someone if you want to use them later."

"Shut the fuck up!" screamed Mo. "He was fine when we parked him in there."

"So what do we do with him now? Dump him with the rest of the bodies?"

"The kid says he knows where we can find food. Put him in one of the rooms with a bed. Give him nothing but clean water and keep the door locked, if he lives, he'll owe us for saving his ass."

CHAPTER 9

April 3rd, 2031
11:15 am

Lara, anxious to check on Scott, took the three girls and the two youngest boys, David and Thomas, with her. James ignored a tug at his heart he could not entirely explain. He was noticing that between the night watches, being constantly surrounded by children, and Scott's illness, they were not spending time alone together. Since Lara could be gone for several hours, he enlisted the five oldest boys to help him and Brent with the new house, work they would have been too young to do before the Change. Skyler, for safety reasons, walked Lara and her group up the hill. Seeing both Brandy and Scott had been his goal. But knowing the inevitability of situation, he turned and walked back down alone; not willing to see Scott in his current state. Brandy had spent a few moments with Skyler before taking the children to free up Lara. As she put the kids to work cultivating their gardens, Lara went in to see Scott.

The former teacher lay on his bed, pallid, clammy, unconsciously laboring for each breath. Both Petar and Ella sat near him. Seeing Lara, Petar excused himself, claiming he needed to relieve McBride from sentry duty, convincing neither woman of his true reason for leaving. Ella, like a young nurse yearning to learn more, stayed with Lara.

Lara checked Scott's temperature and pulse, cursing the lack of a blood pressure cuff. The daily reminders of all that had been lost during the Change plagued her. She recalled something about estimating the blood pressure by finding a pulse at certain points. Knowing it was not an exact science, she couldn't be sure with her findings. Even if she did know his pressure, what could she do with this information? If his pressure fell to low, his body wouldn't perfuse blood to his vital organs, and he would slowly die. This could be happening now with his level of consciousness being so low. Frustrated with not knowing, she shook him and shouted, "Scott!"

He opened his eyes, staring at the ceiling as if searching for what had disturbed his sleep. He turned his head toward her. He met her gaze, made a slight smile at the sight of her, and uttered a near silent, "Hello."

"Scott, can you show me where it hurts the most?"

Obvious that he was using all his strength, he lifted his right hand, placing a shaky forefinger on a spot at the lower left side of his abdomen, just inside the wing of his pelvis. Using only two fingers, Lara pressed gently around there until he grimaced. "If it is an abscess, this is where it's located." She thought to herself, being reminded of how cruel their existence had become.

Lara, having worked in a nursing home, had seen this same condition appear in some of her patients. Each time, the patient would be transferred to the hospital where they'd undergo a series of tests and treatments. The patient would usually be placed on antibiotic therapy right away. Almost always, once the abscess was located, a physician would either 'tap' the abscess with a needle or drain the pus using an actual drain tube. Lara knew about the procedures from the reports that were added to the patient's files, but had never witnessed the procedure. Without any antibiotics available, Scott's chances were dim. His only hope was for her to perform some sort of intervention to drain off the pus.

Lara checked the drawer next to his bed to see what kinds of medications were available. There was still a small quantity of ibuprofen. Giving him anymore wouldn't improve his condition. She found a bottle of amoxicillin prescribed for someone's dog by a veterinary clinic. The dark-brown glass bottle had been opened previously, yet appeared to be full. Lara knew enough about pharmaceuticals that the only real difference between veterinary and human antibiotics was the strength. She also knew that if amoxicillin wasn't stored properly, it would be useless. The bottle came with an eye dropper for dispensing. Aware that it had been contaminated when it had been opened, she unscrewed the lid, pouring half of the bottle's contents into a glass provided by Ella. She helped Scott move it to his lips. In four hours, they would have him drink the other half. This might reduce his fever temporarily, but she knew it would not be enough. Lara weighed her options as she watched Scott fall back into a deep sleep. Scott was dying, that she had no doubt. She pressed on his abdomen again. He winced even in his sleep. Yes, Lara thought. Something extreme would have to be done to save him.

Skyler was back at the new house by midmorning. With the help of Joe, Joel and Petey they busied themselves collecting the lumber that would soon become the walls. Devon and Sebastian, crowbars in hand, were sent back to the damaged homes to look for fiberglass insulation. They were instructed to drag anything they found outside to lay in the sun to dry. James, still uneasy, warned them to stick together. If they saw anyone, they were to run back right away.

Brent came up with an idea on how to make the structure stronger and better insulated. The original foundation, a daylight basement, had been constructed with a solid concrete floor with concrete walls of varying heights on all sides. Originally, the walls they would build would sit on top of the concrete walls. Brent pointed out that this created a weak spot in the structure and that the floor, being concrete, would always be very cold in the winter. Instead, he suggested they construct a sub-floor that would sit directly on top of the concrete. Next, they would build the walls within the foundation's walls, securing these walls to both the new floor and the outer concrete walls. It didn't take much to convince James that this approach would be more beneficial. While the boys collected more boards, James altered the blueprints so they could get started.

The sub-floor went in first and soon after, the walls were being raised and secured. The steel banding Skyler had found worked perfectly for multiplying the strength of the walls. They quickly used up the small supply of bands that he'd brought back. By late afternoon, all the outside walls had been erected, but only half were secured with the banding.

"Skyler, how do you feel about riding out and collecting more of that banding?" asked Brent.

"No problem, I can probably be back in a little over an hour," he replied. "Can I take Joe with me?"

"Yes, take him. It would be nice if we could start on the roof by tomorrow. I've marked a band at the perfect length. When you cut the bands, don't make them so long. We wasted about a foot off each piece."

Skyler had previously cut four-foot pieces; not knowing just how much was needed. If he cut only thirty-inch pieces, he could fit more into his pack. Looking through the tools, he found one of the tape measurers, slipped it into his pack along with the cutters, grabbed his bow and quiver, and headed toward the bikes, calling for Joe to join him.

Skyler and Joe were soon riding side by side headed west up the hill that separated them from the refinery. The last time he'd gone into the old aluminum smelter, he'd entered through the ponds behind the plant. This time, rather than taking the long route, he planned on short-cutting the route by riding straight in through the main entrance. The yard where they found the warehouse was just off the left side of the road leading in, which would enable them to get in and out much faster. Skyler brought Joe along as an extra set of eyes. He feared getting too caught up in cutting the bands, making himself vulnerable. For all he knew, people could be living in the plant. The area it covered was vast and there were many other buildings situated throughout the pot lines.

Entering the refineries' compound, they rode up a small hill, stopping near the large Maple tree that had fallen across the fence. Skyler, leaning his bike against the tree, pulled his bow from his back before climbing up on its once majestic trunk. Joe knowingly stayed silent, following Skyler's actions as they walked into yard.

Skyler located the roll of banding and pulled the cutter from his pack. He'd already laid down his bow and quiver within reach. He measured the first thirty inches on the roll and made a cut. This piece was to act as a template. After Skyler cut twenty of the shorter bands, he had Joe take a turn while he collected his and placed them in his pack. Lifting a handful of the bands, he set the end on the ground to see how accurate he was at cutting the lengths. All five bands measured within a quarter of an inch of each other. Attempting to fold the stack to fit inside the pack, he found it quite difficult. The combined strength of the banding was much like the older car springs. He realized what had plagued him the day before. A single piece of banding was like a weak spring, if not bent too far, it would spring back to its shape. However, when he layered several pieces together, holding them as one, it became a much stronger spring; strong enough to launch an arrow.

Skyler took over the cutting once again, instructing Joe to place all his cut pieces into the packs. He then measured and cut three pieces measuring twenty-four, twenty, and sixteen inches. Using these as templates, he cut ten pieces of each length. Joe placed these in his pack along with several of the crimping sleeves. The boys donned the heavy packs and headed for their bikes.

Skyler and Joe rode up to the construction site, dropping their packs in front of the crew. Skyler emptied the contents, separating the shorter pieces from the ones cut for the framing.

"Why'd you make all those pieces so short? I doubt we can use them," James asked.

'These are for me. I think I've figured out a way to make crossbows." He picked up a stack of five bands, demonstrating to James how difficult it was to bend them.

"I guess I can live without your help until we start on the roof. Go ahead and see what you can come up with."

Skyler lined up five of the sixteen-inch lengths. He then slid a crimping sleeve over each end, crimping the ends together. Locked together, the strength was more than adequate. The next problem was mounting the spring to some kind of stock. He needed to be able to attach this to the end of a board. In his haste, he overlooked the need to install a hole for this. Since this set had already been crimped together, he would have to start over with another set. He moved his operation into the garage where most of the other tools were kept, knowing that he needed to leave the crimper with James for now.

Using the twenty-inch pieces, he measured to the exact center of each band, punching holes through the center that were large enough to drive a screw through. Skyler spent the rest of the afternoon in and out of the garage. At times, he went over to the new house in search of short boards or to borrow the hand saw. He also sent Devon and Sebastian into the houses where they'd found insulation, to search for old paintings that used braided wire for hanging pictures.

That evening, Lydia served vegetables and rice to the hard-working crew. Skyler was absent from the table as was Lara. Dusk approached. James, concerned, walked downstairs and entered the garage looking for the boy. The garage, normally kept tidy, was now strewn with pieces of banding, wood chips, and sawdust. There was no sign of Skyler. James stepped out onto the pad in front of the house. He finally spotted Skyler fidgeting with a large wooden cross. It was Skyler's turn for the early watch.

"How's it coming?" he asked as he walked over to him.

Skyler nearly dropped the crossbow he was working on. "You startled me. I think I'm finished. I was just about to test fire it for the first time."

James looked over the contraption. It wasn't as lightweight looking as the small crossbow they used for duck hunting, and the stock was rather crude. The spring or bow was made of several lengths of banding crimped together. The lengths started out long, progressively became shorter like the old-style car springs. The bow string was braided steel cable with a leather patch fastened in the center. "I notice that you don't have any arrows to test it with."

"Don't need them. I made it so you'll be able to shoot anything you can fit in this groove in the stock. Nuts, bolts, and rocks included."

James watched as Skyler pulled back on a lever attached to the top of the stock. As he pulled, the lever caught the stainless steel cable, stretching it as the bands bent from the pull, and the cable fell behind the two prongs at the back of the stock. James noted that Skyler had to strain to cock it, yet the crimped banding moved only inches. Once the cable was safely held by the prongs, Skyler pushed the lever down and out of the path of the cable. He then fished two large steel nuts from his pocket. He set one in front of the leather patch, lifted the stock to his shoulder, taking aim at a nearby house. When he pulled the trigger, they both felt the crossbow release its energy. James instinctively flinched to protect his eyes from a ricochet. The nut, flying so fast that they lost sight of it, punched through the siding and outer wall completely. They both heard the thud as it impacted against a wall within the structure.

"Jesus, that thing is powerful!" exclaimed James.

"Watch this." Skyler's grin was as wide as a Cheshire's cat. He quickly pulled the lever back, locked the string, moved the lever forward and dropped the second nut into the slot. No sooner had it landed on the wood, he pulled the trigger again. The second nut flew toward the house, punching an identical hole through the wall only inches from the first. "I can shoot this thing almost as fast as I can shoot my bow. If I can add a spring to pull the lever back after cocking, I think I can get off a shot in less than two seconds."

James looked on in astonishment. He reached out his hands. Skyler handed the crossbow to him. It felt heavy compared to their own bows, but not too heavy. He pulled back on the lever to cock the string, discovering that it took some effort. "What do you plan on using this for?"

"I want to make three smaller ones for now. I can't ride shotgun every time someone wants to go somewhere. If Joe, Petey, and Joel each has their own, and practice, they'll be armed enough to go out to the ponds without me."

James reached down, picking up a rock slightly smaller than a golf ball. He set it in front of the leather patch and aimed it at a section of the roof that hung off the side of the structure. He pulled the trigger. The jolt as the crossbow released the cable was startling. The rock hit one of the two by sixes, shattering it.

"That would have killed someone!" said James.

"That's the idea. Those long bows we made would probably only wound an attacker. A crossbow like this could be deadly, and it can use anything small and heavy for ammunition. I need to make another trip out to the refinery tomorrow. I've got an idea for making arrows for this thing, ones that we won't have to worry about losing."

Petar rode up to them on a bicycle, his expression grave. James was surprised to see him this late in the day; it would be dark in a matter of minutes.

"Lara sent me," Petar said panting. "She's going to stay with us tonight and keep an eye on Scott. She wants you to find something for her."

"Sure, what is it?"

"She wants you to go and search any of the doctor's offices in the downtown. She needs a hollow needle at least three inches long along with a syringe. She wants it as soon as possible."

When James looked back at him quizzically, Petar said, "I think she's going to make an attempt to drain some of the pus out of Scott's belly."

"Is he that bad?"

"Yeah, he's that bad. I have to get back right away. I left my post to come down here."

"Before you leave, Skyler has something to show you." Looking at the boy he asked, "Do you have another one of those nuts in your pocket?"

Skyler had already fished one out. James cocked, loaded and fired the crossbow. Like the others, the nut went through the wall without slowing.

"Jesus!" said Petar.

CHAPTER 10

April 4th, 2031
5:45 am

Brent gently shook James. As tired as he was, James jumped to his feet instantly. The room was still dark except for the candle that Brent was holding.

"Are you sure you want to go this early?" Brent asked. He had relieved James just four hours earlier from his turn at watch.

"Yeah, I feel safer at this time of day. I want to get back here so we can start work on the house." James found Skyler in the living room and gave him a shake, "Time to get up."

Each ate a hardtack biscuit, washing it down with cold tea. Before Skyler could finish eating, they were out the door. Brent would stay and catch some sleep while Lydia watched for any intruders, allowing James and Skyler to look for the supplies requested by Lara. The morning sky cast just enough light for them to ride fast.

This was James first trip to downtown Ferndale since the previous year. The weight of the hallowed out buildings, signs that other survivors had stopped there searching for food, leaving hungry and lifeless like specters of a forgotten civilization, was more than he could bear. He grew to fear this area.

When they reached Third Street, they came to a power pole that stretched across the road. If they were at all tired when they started out, their senses were fully alert now. They laid their bikes alongside the large pole, carefully glancing around as they did so. From this point, they would have to walk. James didn't know of any clinics on their side of the river. They would need to pass through the downtown to cross the river. On the other side, were the remains of two veterinary hospitals and a large family clinic. James knew that all three places had been looted long ago, but there might be something useful in the debris of unwanted items. Former businesses, now the skeletons of civilization, were littered with the things that carried little or no value. James walked holding his rifle in hand; Skyler, an arrow resting on the string of his bow.

They reached the bridge unheeded, crossing it with a sense of urgency. Adjacent to the bridge was a railroad trestle that once offered an alternate way across. Recent flooding entangled the large steel beams with multiple trees, limbs, and fence debris. One or two more floods would create a log jam, causing a disastrous effect upon the path of the river. The bridges could become useless if the river changed its course. But, there a positive side to this: any Wanderers would be prevented from crossing from the other side. On the other hand, any Wanderers from the north would be stopped from continuing south. James feared this new dilemma more than losing the bridge.

The first animal hospital they reached was a brick building, its flat roof collapsed within. Looking through a large broken window in the front, they could see no way to get past the waiting room. The ceiling hung from timbers, blocking the doors leading to the interior examination rooms. They walked around to the back, checking for any means of entry. They found a steel security door, still locked. They had no tools and neither wanted to attempt to kick it in.

"There's that other clinic just a couple of blocks from here. Let's keep moving," James whispered to Skyler.

Skyler reached out and touched James' arm. He pointed to the back of the parking lot where a dumpster sat in a brick alcove. It had to belong to the animal hospital. Lifting the lid, they found the remnants of garbage bags already torn apart by someone looking for food. They found empty pill bottles, used bandages, sodden papers, but no syringes or needles.

Their next hope was the family clinic. They needed to cross the road and travel east for only a couple of blocks to reach it. It sat near the highway, increasing the possibility of running into someone, especially in full daylight.

They stayed in the shadows until they were reasonably sure that no one was watching them. The clinic was a newer brick building with a pitched roof, half of which was collapsed into the interior. All of the windows had been blown out or shattered in some other fashion. They circled the building looking for the best way in. Again in the back, they found a door that was still intact. James turned the handle. The door opened to reveal a long narrow hall. This portion of the building sat beneath the intact half of the roof. The hall was surprisingly clean except for a small amount of water on the floor. The interior did not have that wet musty odor James had smelled in other buildings. Then James froze. Skyler followed suit. An unlocked door leading into a clean building was not expected.

Just ahead were two doors directly across from each other. Both were closed with no light escaping from beneath them. James reached inside a pocket and pulled out a candle. He hated to waste a match, but neither was he about to search these rooms without any type of light. Nothing was said as James struck the match and the hall lit up before them. Grasping the knob of the door leading to the right, James slowly turned it. It swung open easily.

A loud scream came from within the room. James clambered backwards nearly knocking Skyler over. In his rush to get his rifle raised, he'd dropped the candle. The hall became dark once again. Skyler stood to James' side, legs firmly planted apart, bow drawn, aiming directly at the voice.

"What do you want?" A gruff shout from a voice distinctly that of an older man.

"We're armed, but we're not here to hurt you. We just need to find a needle and a syringe," James said, keeping his rifle leveled at the doorway. He fought the urge to flee, avoiding any kind of an altercation. The man's voice indicated surprise but not aggression, mitigating James' own fear.

"Are you a junkie? If so, you're in the wrong place."

"No," James replied, "A friend of ours is sick."

Skyler lowered his bow, waiting on guard. They heard some shuffling from within the room. The light appeared from beneath the doorway. Soon a haggard face materialized. "Are you a doctor?"

"No, we have a friend who's a nurse. She asked for the supplies."

The man stepped out into the hall. He held the stub of a candle. He was very thin, his clothes dirty and threadbare, yet his hands and face were clean. James guessed his age near sixty-five, but the Change, along with trauma and a lack of food, could make someone look older than their years. He assumed that he was a Wanderer who had sought shelter for the night.

"I have a needle and a syringe, but I won't let you take them with you. You'll need to bring the patient here."

James picked up on the man's use of the word 'patient'. "Are you a doctor?"

"I am."

"We can't bring him here. He's too sick to move."

"Then he'll die. If he's too sick to move, there's nothing I can do for him."

James was suddenly taken aback by the man's callous remark. Lara was no surgeon; anything she did for Scott would be a last-ditch effort. This man claimed to be a doctor, gave off the impression that he was a loner with no ties, but indicated he was unwilling to let his tools or himself to leave the premises. Suddenly angered, James raised the rifle's barrel to the man's chest and said, "I need you to come with us."

"You won't shoot me; you have nothing to gain by killing the only surviving doctor for who knows what distance."

"No, but I can drag your ass up there. Either way, I'm not going to let our friend die just because you aren't willing to leave here."

Skyler stood in wonder at the situation unfolding before him. James had rarely shown his aggressive side. Now he was making threats to someone, who until moments ago had been minding his own business.

"Relax; you can put the gun down. I'll go with you. I won't work for free. I'd like to be paid with some food."

"We can do that," replied James. "I'm sorry about pointing the rifle at you. I don't think I've ever threatened to shoot anyone before. Please gather what you need and let's leave as soon as possible. It will take us an hour to walk up there."

Without hesitation, the old man grabbed his backpack, and they headed out the door. "Don't you want to lock this place up?" James asked.

"No, it wasn't my office. I came out of Canada only a week ago. Each time I pass through a town, I find clinics and look for supplies. You happened to catch me about an hour before I was to leave here."

"Where are you headed?"

"Don't really know, maybe a warmer climate. From the people I've met, it sounds like the entire continent is in chaos."

Outside, James noticed that the man appeared older than when he first saw him in the building. His eyebrows were long, unkempt, while his ears were nearly covered with a gray mat of fine hairs. "My name is James and this is Skyler. There are only a handful of families scattered to the west of this town. You'll probably get to meet most of us today."

"Despite our initial encounter, I'm glad to meet both of you." He paused briefly and then added, "I used to be called Dr. McKenzie, but that now seems all too formal. Call me Ian."

Walking back toward the bridge, James and Skyler kept a vigilante watch as if their new companion was a valuable dignitary. A layer of clouds enveloped the sun while the temperature dropped slightly. Skyler, glimpsing over to Ian, finally asked him, "Don't you carry a weapon?"

"No son, I don't think it's necessary. When people find out that I'm a doctor, they usually treat me squarely. I've survived by offering my services in trade for food."

James asked, "What was your specialty before the collapse?"

"Pediatrics, most of my patients were under the age of eighteen. Before you go making up your mind, thinking that I can't help an adult, I was a surgeon for the first twenty years of my career. I gave up surgery because I found that most of my patients didn't respect the body they were born with. It frustrated me to no end. I figured that maybe if I influenced children to take better care of themselves, surgeons wouldn't have so much work to do."

Reaching the bridge, James removed his rifle from his shoulder. He held it in front of him with both hands. The trio fell silent as they passed through the gauntlet of empty buildings. James noticed that Ian didn't tire like he expected—his pace as steady as his two escorts despite his large backpack. When they reached the place where they'd left the bikes, they picked them up and continued walking west.

"So James, how have you and young Skyler managed to survive?"

James had to ponder this question, wondering when he crossed the line between existing and surviving. "Before the Change, I saw a dark future. I knew that our entire food supply depended on oil. When the price reached a certain point, we'd no longer be able to sustain our current population. I cashed in all of my assets and bought staples, seeds, guns, and outdoor clothing. I didn't expect that first winter storm to be so harsh, but I made it through it."

"What about you, Skyler? What's your story?"

Skyler looked up at the old man not really knowing where to begin. Finally, he said, "I guess that I was just lucky. I had gone to search for my mother when the storm hit. I stayed in a house near where James lived. If he hadn't taken me in, I wouldn't be standing here now."

The old man glanced from Skyler to James with a look of satisfaction upon his face. Then he turned his attention back to Skyler. "Are you good with that bow?"

Before Skyler could utter a word, James said, "Better than you can imagine."

"Well good. The problem is that everything we have now is no longer being produced. Someday, you'll need to replace that bow. Those bikes are also going to be dinosaurs when there aren't any parts left to keep them working. If our race can last another fifty years, we'll be back to living the way early man did during the Bronze Age. Your bows and arrows will all be carved from a knife that you made by melting iron. Our clothes will be leather if there are any animals left to hunt. Cherish what you have because it won't last forever."

"Sounds like you don't believe that we will ever recover from this," said James.

"I don't and it's not because I'm pessimistic. Our world needed a certain number of people to maintain our infrastructure. I suspect that we've lost over ninety percent of the world's population in just the last five years. We no longer have the resources or the energy needed to build factories, produce products, and ship them to other parts throughout the country or overseas, for that matter. For now, we are merely survivors. As communities rebuild, they will become silos; they'll grow and manufacture what is needed only for themselves. Someday, these silos might trade with neighboring silos, but only if they are within walking distance. The internal combustion engine was the tool that propelled us from being hunter-gatherers into the space age. We are now hunter-gatherers once again."

The three walked in silence as James and Skyler digested Ian's words. This was the first time that they'd met someone from outside their area who had professed what they already suspected. They were walking up the long grade toward Church Road when they came to the street that led to James' house. James waved an arm knowing that someone would be watching the road. Seconds later, Brent came running down the stairs, then jogged up the street to greet them.

"Brent, this is Ian. He's a doctor, and has agreed to take a look at Scott."

Brent stopped to catch his breath before reaching out with his right hand. "Glad to meet you, Ian. I hope that you can help him."

"I don't want to get your hopes up. From what I've seen since the collapse, it's difficult to save the really ill. Without technology, medicine is now the same as it was in the 1800s."

Understanding that James was in a hurry to ascend the hill, Brent said, not unkindly, "I sense that you'll still do whatever you can. I don't expect a miracle, but I can still wish for one."

The trio continued on, making the turn up the much steeper Church Road. Thick clouds were coming in from the south. The gentle breeze had changed to a gusty wind. When they arrived at the top of the hill, Petar stepped out from behind a pile of dead brush. Introductions were brief. Anxiously, he led them down to the house, not looking back at his followers, as if their presence caused some discomfort. As they entered, Ian admired how they disguised the house to look abandoned. The old man seemed to be taking in everything as they passed through the living room and kitchen. When they reached the bedroom, Lara asleep in a chair, jumped to her feet. Scott lay there unmoving on the bed next to her chair. His breathing was labored.

"Lara, this is Ian. He's a doctor," said James.

"You must be the nurse who requested the needle and syringe?" Ian asked.

She nodded.

"Can I see your patient up close?"

Lara stepped aside as Ian lowered his pack to the floor. He pulled back the blankets. Ian squeezed Scott's hand before moving to his wrist, searching for his pulse. As he did so, he watched Scott's chest rise and fall. He moved up to Scott's face, feeling his forehead, and looking under both eyelids before peering into his mouth. Scott still wasn't responding. He finally turned to Lara and asked, "How long has he been like this?"

"Since I arrived here yesterday morning, he's become less cognitive. I think he's been going downhill for a couple of days before that. I gave him some oral amoxicillin yesterday, but his condition hasn't improved."

Ian looked at Scott's lower abdomen and started pressing until he found a spot that made Scott wince. He pressed around that area watching Scott's face for a reaction.

James, Skyler and Petar slowly backed out of the room and regrouped in the dark living room.

James looked around and asked Petar, "Where is everyone else?"

"They're planting seeds. The kids finished tilling the gardens late yesterday. When we saw the clouds move in, we decided to get everything planted before the rain fell."

They heard muffled voices come from the bedroom. Lara appeared in the kitchen doorway, her face carried a look of worry. "Ian wants us to open Scott's abdomen. He says that it's our only choice besides waiting. Can you guys stay outside and make sure no one comes in the house until we come out?"

"Sure, do you need anything?"

"No, Ian has a small surgical kit in his pack. I'll sterilize everything in boiling water. If we need anything, I'll let you know. Just stay close."

"Are you okay with this?" James asked her, uncharacteristically reaching for her hand in a quiet gesture of tenderness.

"Yeah, I don't see what else we can do at this point."

James and Petar followed Skyler out the door. Petar needed to return to his post, so James sat upon the steps of the porch while Skyler went in search of Brandy and the others. A half-hour passed, Lydia arrived with little Brent and Bekka, along with the five boys who were going to help Brent with the house. She approached James with a look of worry on her face, "Brent says it looks like rain, so he won't be working on the house. I think it's just an excuse. He's too worried about Scott to get anything done. He said that we could come up here while he stayed and guarded the house."

"Good, maybe Brandy could use some help in the gardens. They decided to plant seeds before the rains come. Take the boys and go see if you can find her."

Another half-hour passed before Lara came out the front door in tears. She nodded to James that they were finished. James put two fingers up to his mouth and gave a loud shrill whistle. Moments later, a crowd of fifteen adolescents and five adults stood in front of the porch. Ian stepped through the door while drying his hands with a towel. He stared at the crowd below him. The expression on his face told James that he wasn't prepared to say what he needed to such a large group, especially one so young. He leaned over toward James and whispered something to him.

James stood and addressed everyone first. "As most of you have known, our friend Scott has been very ill. Many of you have not met Scott since you just arrived here recently. The man standing next to me is Ian McKenzie, and he's a doctor. He needs to speak with Scott's immediate family. Can I ask the rest of you to return to the gardens for now?"

The crowd shrank to a small cluster in a matter of seconds. Those who remained moved up closer to the porch so that they could hear what the doctor had to say.

"First of all, I want to commend Lara and the rest of you for doing the best that you could under the circumstances. Scott's condition had deteriorated so much that my only option upon arrival was to open his abdomen and see if there was anything we could do. I regret to say that nothing more can be done to save your friend. His colon has become so infected that much of the tissue is necrotic, and his blood is now septic."

The crowd stared at the man waiting to hear more, but he said nothing. Brandy took a step forward and asked, "Is he still alive?"

Lara put a hand on Ian's shoulder to let him know that she preferred to answer that question. "He's alive, but he's not expected to last until tomorrow. Ian was able to spare a small amount of morphine so that Scott will rest easier during his final hours."

"Can we see him?" asked Petar. His eyes began to moisten.

"Yes, you are free to go see him. I've done all I can do here. I think that maybe it's probably time for me to return to the other side of the river."

"James," said Lara, "When you take Ian back, will you drop everyone off at the house with Brent and tell him what's happened? He'll probably want to come up here before the day is finished. I think Petar and his family need to be alone this afternoon. I would like it if Skyler stayed with us this evening. He can walk me down later."

Brandy, fighting back tears, rounded up all eleven of the children and told them to follow James and Ian down the hill. Joe and Joel rode the two bikes as the other nine kids entertained Ian with questions. James noticed that the old man was taking pleasure with the attention he was receiving from them. It appeared that he genuinely liked their questions. Halfway back to the house, rain began to fall slowly and unevenly at first. With each step, the drops seemed to increase in size and frequency. By the time they reached the bottom of the hill, all eleven of them, including Ian with his large backpack, were in a full run for the house. They ran up the stairs, surprising Brent when they threw open the door. Ian told Brent about Scott's prognosis, suggesting that he try to make it up there to say his good-byes.

"What do we do about your payment?" James asked Ian.

"I'll take any canned food that you can spare. I don't have much room in my pack for more than a few days' worth."

The rain came down heavily. The sky darkened further, reflecting conditions would not improve before nightfall. James glanced out the one open window and asked, "Are you in a hurry to get back?"

"No, I didn't have anything left back at that clinic. I was just going to continue my trip south from here."

"Will you stay here with us until the weather improves?"

Ian glanced around at all the eager faces of the eleven kids who had returned with him. He looked at James and asked, "Are all these children yours?"

"No, we took them in about five days ago. We are quickly turning them into farmers, fishermen, and carpenters."

"That is truly commendable. I think I will stay till the weather improves, if it's not too much trouble. And while I'm here, why don't I take inventory of everyone's health."

James smiled and thought about the moment only a few hours earlier when he pointed his rifle at Ian's chest.

CHAPTER 11

April 4th, 2031
3:15 pm

Brandon estimated that it had been at least five days since his capture, if not more. His fever was gone, but he felt weak; too weak to attempt an escape. For three days, he had been kept in a dark filthy room with an actual hospital bed crammed into its small quarters. Someone had pulled the sleeping bag from his pack, leaving it in the room for him to keep warm. There was just enough daylight coming in under the door for him to see his surroundings. The only other piece of furniture was a bedside table. On top of it sat an old two liter pop bottle half-filled with water. At first, he'd been tentative about drinking from it, but thirst and dehydration slowly whittled away at the apprehension. A bucket he'd been using as a toilet sat in a corner of the room. It hadn't been emptied yet, the stench repugnant enough to make him nauseous. From the light under the door he knew that his room had to be situated across from a window—a possible avenue of escape once he felt stronger. He wondered just what they had in store for him. He was still alive, but for how long?

He heard footsteps coming down the hall; footsteps foreboding with each touch of the floor. Someone fumbled with a key in the doorknob.

Brandon was nearly blinded when the door was opened. When his eyes adjusted, he recognized the silhouette before him. It was Mo.

"So my little friend, how are you feeling today?"

Brandon sat up in the bed, twisting his back in both directions as he stretched. Brandon's voice was hoarse, unused and dry; it felt rusty. "I'm better than a few days ago, but I haven't had anything to eat in at least five days. I feel really weak."

"I'm not about to waste any food on you, unless I think that I could get something in return. We have five bicycles ready to roll when you are willing to show us those places in Ferndale."

"I can't be expected to ride twelve or more miles out there and back again like this," Brandon said, holding his arms up as if displaying his body. "Besides, what will keep you from killing me once you have the food?"

"My word. I'll stick to my deal if you help us score more food. Otherwise, you can die right now for all I care," sneered Mo. "The reason I came up here was to offer you an opportunity to earn some food before we ride. Interested?"

"Sure, go on."

"One of my men just reported three people coming this way. They're moving slow, so we still have some time. Two men with rifles on foot, one is towing a woman in a wagon. The other man is pushing a wheelbarrow with a tarp over it. My guess is that they're coming here to barter for medicine."

"What do you want from me?"

"When they arrive, you do whatever you need to do to get their food. You can eat whatever you take as long as my men and I get the rest."

"What if I refuse?"

"Then I drag you through this door and toss you out that third-story window behind me."

Brandon didn't have to ponder the offer. He swung his legs over the side of the mattress and gingerly stood. He kept a hand resting on the mattress until he was sure that his legs would remain upright. He looked for his shoes, but they were nowhere to be found. "Where are my shoes?"

"I'm keeping them until I'm sure that you aren't going to try to run away."

"Can I use one of your guns? You can't expect me to do this unarmed."

"No, you can't use one of our guns." Mo said sarcastically. He reached into a pocket and pulled out a plastic bag filled with different colored capsules and tablets. "I suggest that you play doctor and sell them these pills for whatever they have in that wheelbarrow." He tossed the bag to Brandon.

Five minutes later, Brandon was walking through the main entrance of the hospital, trying not to step on any of the broken glass. Mo had said that this was where they would probably tow the woman since all the other entrances to the hospital were at a higher elevation. He thought about running, but knew that someone in the waiting room had a full view of this area. Besides, he had no shoes or coat. Plus, he was hungrier than he'd ever been since the Change. It was several minutes before he saw the two men appear. Their heads emerged first as they pushed and pulled their cargo up a small rise. Both men, armed with rifles, walked doggedly in Brandon's direction. Brandon noticed that the wagon was one of those carts from a home-improvement store. Since each man had his hands full pushing or pulling, their rifles were slung across their backs. The woman was sitting upright, looking particularly uncomfortable.

The small group stopped once about fifty yards from the entrance as the men caught their breath. Before they started up again, Brandon had come up with a plan. Brandon could see that the woman was probably in her late fifties, as was the man towing her. She coughed uncontrollably from time to time. The other man pushing the wheelbarrow was several years younger than his companions, perhaps their son. As did most survivors of the Change, they had that hollowed out look, wearing filthy clothes that hung loosely from their frames. Seeing no other avenue, the trio came right up to Brandon.

"She looks sick. What can I do to help you?" Brandon asked them.

"Are you a doctor?" asked the older man, eyeing Brandon with a hopeful but wary look.

Brandon had already known that his age wouldn't allow him to claim he was a doctor. Weak as he was, he needed to focus on standing straight, not allowing them to see that he might be ailing more than the woman."No, I'm a paramedic. There are no doctors left. I can treat some things, but not everything. What's wrong with her?"

The younger man lowered the wheelbarrow to the ground, but left his rifle on his back. The older man looked down at the woman briefly before returning his gaze to Brandon. "This is my wife, Sarah. She's had a high fever and a cough for two weeks. This morning, she was too weak to walk. Can you do anything for her?"

Brandon knew little to nothing about medicine or treating illnesses. His plan was based solely on the fact that these men knew less than he did. "I have some pills that will make her fever go away. She should start getting stronger in a day or two. If you can wait here, I can collect enough to last her until she's better."

The older man glanced at the younger one before he turned back to Brandon; his face reflecting that he was pleased with Brandon's offer. "We'll try whatever you suggest. We've brought food to pay you with."

With a tone of quiet desperation, Brandon replied, "I don't need your food, but I'll trade those pills for one of your rifles. I need protection more than I need food."

The older man looked to his younger companion for guidance. The younger man leaned over and spoke softly, not making any pretense that he approved of such a trade. They bantered quietly not wanting to disturb the woman that appeared to have fallen asleep. Finally, having said their arguments, the two stared at each other for a few seconds before the old man pulled the rifle from his shoulder. He held it out for Brandon to examine. It was a small .22 caliber semi-automatic carbine. "Would you accept this in trade?"

"Yes, let me get the pills."

Brandon disappeared back inside the large open entrance. Hidden from their view, he pulled the bag from his pocket, scanning the contents. Most of the medications were green and yellow capsules. He picked eighteen of these from the bag before returning to the hospital's entrance. As he stepped back outside, he noticed that the sky was darkening, the wind had picked up.

"Here, I'm sorry, but I don't have a container," he said as he held out his open hand.

The older man looked at the pills like they weren't quite what he'd expected. Finally, he reached out his open palm to accept them.

"Give her two right now, two more tonight, then two each day until she's better." Brandon added, trying to sound convincing.

The man pocketed the pills before reluctantly handing the rifle over to Brandon.

"Is it loaded?" he asked.

"Yes, it holds ten rounds, and it's full."

Brandon looked over the rifle, found the safety and switched it off. Raising the barrel, he fired four quick rounds into the younger man's chest, sending him toppling backwards. Instantly, he swung the barrel towards the older man, firing four more times in rapid succession. With both men on the ground, he fired the last two shots into the woman's head. Brandon, feeling urgency, stepped over the older man, pulling the younger man's rifle from his back. He clicked off the safety, praying it was loaded, and leaned it against the handles of the wheelbarrow. Pulling back the tarp to conceal the second rifle, he exposed about fifteen jars of canned foods. Most were filled with what appeared to be meats. As he looked at the treasure in front of him, raindrops splattered on the lids of the jars.

Mo came walking through the entrance. His rifle held low but pointed at Brandon. He stopped about twelve feet from Brandon, parked the rifle under his arm, and clapped his hands in a slow applause. "Nice job, boy. What did these nice people bring us?"

Brandon had already laid the .22 across the top of the wheelbarrow. He picked up a jar and after looking through at its contents, he said, "We have some canned salmon." With that, he tossed the jar to Mo.

Mo had to take his right hand from his gun to catch the flying Mason jar. As he did, Brandon reached for the other rifle, quickly raised it up and fired into Mo's chest, knocking him back several feet. The jar shattered as it hit the floor. He rapidly worked the bolt action, feeding a second round into the chamber. Mo fell onto his back, not moving. His rifle lay a respectful distance from his body.

Brandon cautiously walked over to pick up Mo's rifle. He glanced out the opening of the foyer at the dark rainy world outside. He wondered if he should take Mo's shoes and make a run for it. How long would it take before these other men would catch up to him? Using his foot, he pushed at Mo's lifeless body. Confirming that the former leader was dead, he looked up at the open windows and shouted, "Who wants to join me for some salmon? And who wants to quit going hungry?"

Eventually, all seven of the remaining bandits appeared with their gun barrels pointed to the ground. Brandon had already pulled the wheelbarrow inside and opened a jar. As he ate smoked fish, he passed a jar to each grateful man. Brandon, enjoying his first meal for several days, stopped briefly to say, "Permit me to introduce myself properly. My name is Brandon, and I'm going to teach you how find food and quit going hungry." He looked about for any signs of disagreement, then added, "Tomorrow we'll ride out to Ferndale and get enough food to last us a month."

CHAPTER 12

April 5th, 2031
9:10 am

Lara returned from the hill the following morning. She'd stayed long enough to administer the morphine until Scott's breathing finally ceased late the night before. John McBride escorted both her and Skyler down, but hurried back up the hill. Lara did not need to announce Scott's passing, her return to the house said enough. She was a bit surprised to discover that Ian had stayed through the night. He was surrounded by all the younger children as they tried to coax another story from him. Kai came up to her an announced that Ian had read to them the night before, and that he read better than James did. James let her know that Ian's stay had stemmed from an invitation since it was raining rather hard. Now that the sky was mostly clear once again, the old man didn't seem to be in a hurry to move on. Perhaps more importantly, during his exams of one of the children, he had discovered that one of the girls, Bree, was near-sided enough to prevent her from reading. This explained her curiosity of everything in the house, holding the smaller items close, and never flipping through any of the books. Ian had carried a few pairs of reading glasses he had found during his travels. One of them was close enough to the strength she needed. These glasses, a token of what Ian was capable of providing, seemed to forge a link between him and the children.

Lara looked at James, "Petar and John wanted me to speak to you about moving some of the children to join their family."

"With only six people left up there, I'm sure that they could use the help. How many can they handle?"

"At least four; two or three of the older boys and maybe one or two girls. I already told them that Gia and Devon were staying here."

"I think we could do that." James hated giving up any of the older boys. They were proving their value and would soon be able to help with defense. He was looking forward to the day that he'd not have to stand watch out in the cold night air. However, he also knew that Petar and John needed help with the construction of a second house. But nothing was carved in stone; the children could be moved back and forth depending upon their needs. "Let's take Joe, Joel, Marley, Bree and Thomas up there later this evening."

Lara smiled. She didn't like to part with any of the children. She didn't want them to feel that they were being warehoused, their only worth that of child laborers. The needs of building a strong community and increasing their production of food required everyone's cooperation and commitment. The time she had spent with the other family had allowed her to see their needs. She liked them and looked forward to a long relationship between their two families. She could allow some of the children to move away because she knew that she would be seeing them regularly.

Ian appeared with Gia on his back, Devon racing behind as he tried to pull her off. Ian looked into Lara's eyes, as if he was trying to read her thoughts. She extended her hand and took hold of his. "You seem to like it here. Please tell me that you don't have to leave right away."

Ian smiled at her indirect invitation. "I've seen families of survivors all along my way south. They live in dismal conditions. They're malnourished, and they carry a look like they are waiting to die. They don't smile, and they don't have fun." He paused before continuing. "After meeting the survivors here in Ferndale, it has given me the hope that someday all people can live in harmony once again. I don't have to leave now, but after seeing what you have accomplished, I will want to continue my sojourn someday to tell other families of how you live."

"It's agreed then. You can stay as long as you like."

James and Brent, taking advantage of the nice day, and having the three older boys to help out, returned to work on the house. They made it a goal to build the frame for the roof before Joe and Joel were to be transplanted to the hill. Both boys had learned a lesson from Petey, that the work they did was something to be proud of. All three boys were waiting on the work site for the two men.

James and Brent arrived carrying a large beam extracted from another house. James looked around and asked, "Where's Skyler this morning?"

Joe, being the least shy, was quick to answer, "He's in the garage making something."

James remembered the large heavy crossbow and how Skyler was determined to make smaller models for the boys. He decided to leave Skyler alone unless they needed him—the five of them should be enough to get the roof up.

Lydia had dispersed the remainder of the children among the gardens. She was to monitor their progress as they planted seeds. It was still a bit early in the season, but it would take a week or two before sprouts would appear. The children, having been trained the day before by Brandy, seemed to have forgotten what their goal was. Lydia found that she ran from one plot to another, shouting instructions and corrections, as the children seemed to do as they pleased. The last thing she wanted was to see any of the seeds go to waste. She put a halt to all planting, and returned to the house to enlist the help of Ian and Lara.

"I have to confess, I've never planted anything in my life," Ian said in reply to her request.

"Doesn't matter," said Lydia. "Just make sure that they plant them four inches apart, two inches deep, and it's done in straight lines, so we know where we can expect them to sprout up from the soil."

"Ian, I'm surprised," Lara remarked. "This is the one skill that can keep you alive if you ever decide to settle down. I can see that we need to teach you some things before we can allow you to leave here."

Both groups worked into the afternoon with their designated projects. Brent and James, reluctant to take a break, worked harder than the previous days, especially when they saw that the clouds had thickened once again. Skyler came out to help, following behind the carpenters, banding the trusses to the structure. Petey stayed one step ahead of him, wrapping the banding around the joists and installing a crimping sleeve. Skyler then would only have to attach the tightener, lever the handle, and crimp the sleeve when the banding was tight. When they finished, there were still a few hours of daylight.

Skyler asked James, "Can I borrow some of the boys for the rest of the afternoon?"

"Sure. Did you finish making the crossbows?"

"I've made two. A third is almost finished. I want to take David and Thomas out to fish while Joe and Joel help me make arrows. The smaller crossbows aren't as powerful as the first one I made. They'll only be worthy if they shoot arrows."

Petey, listening in on the conversation, wasn't disappointed that Skyler had not chosen him for their afternoon excursion. He liked helping James and Brent, looking forward to getting the roof finished. He'd never been involved in any kind of construction before. Working on the project made him feel his life was worth something, that he wasn't just part of a ruck. While the other boys were anxious to learn how to hunt and fish, Petey looked forward to finishing this house. As soon as the others were headed out to Main Street, Petey grabbed his tools, following James and Brent into the rows of damaged houses in search of good plywood. Considering that these structures had used conventional building methods, the only plywood would be found under the siding, in the sub-floor, or beneath the roofing material. Either place, it would mean a lot of nail pulling to get one good sheet.

The hours slipped past quickly. Before long, Skyler and the others returned with their packs full. Both David and Thomas had caught enough fish to feed everyone that night. Skyler dropped his pack in front of James, pulling out a ten-inch aluminum shaft. It was solid, not hollow like their aluminum arrows; its diameter was noticeably larger. The only thing that kept them from outweighing their conventional arrows was the short length. Skyler disappeared into the garage, returning a few seconds later carrying a small crossbow in each hand. Like the prototype, they were crude looking compared to the factory-made weapons.

"So where did you find these arrows?" asked James.

"There were these large rolls of this aluminum wire out there. All I had to do was cut it to length, and then we hammered on the pieces to get the curve taken out. If this works, I found enough there to last us for years."

Skyler handed Joe and Joel each one of the crossbows and instructed them on how to pull back the string by cocking them. Once they had their crossbows ready to shoot, Skyler had them lay an aluminum shaft in the groove at the top of the stock. Like their prototype, there was a leather patch to serve as the launching pad for the wire cable, much like that on a slingshot. He told them to aim at the damaged structures by the road, but James stopped them.

"Skyler, could you redirect their targets? Those nuts you shot through the houses a few days ago destroyed the plywood beneath the siding. Try to use a different target for any future practice shots."

Skyler ducked into a broken-out sliding glass door. He dragged an old wet mattress through the wide frame, leaning it up against a row of mailboxes. Joe fired first, and except for a shudder from the target, the arrow appeared to have disappeared when it reached the mattress. Joel was next with the same result. Skyler ran over to the mattresses and inspected the backside where the arrows would have exited. He found both shafts protruding from the backside. He easily extracted them. To his relief, the impact did not damage the arrows. The boys made a few more practice shots, discovering that they could reasonably aim the arrows as long as their distance to the target was less than thirty yards.

Skyler disappeared, only this time he returned with the larger original crossbow. He cocked it, set an arrow in front of the string before shooting it into the mattress. Like the others, the arrow disappeared when it contacted with the target, but this time, they heard it ricochet off the corner of a house about forty yards behind it; everyone witnessed it arc through the air and disappear. Both Joe and Joel were in awe of the larger weapon, both begging for a chance to shoot it.

Petey had been standing back watching the routine unfold, seemingly uninterested in the new devices. Skyler, seeing him standing there and not taking part, called him over for a turn to shoot. By now, others from the house came out to watch. Ian and Lydia were there, as were most of the kids except Gia, Marley, and Bree, who had stayed behind to help Lara.

Petey picked up one of the smaller crossbows first, successfully firing the silver-colored shaft into the mattress. He seemed unimpressed. Then Skyler handed him the larger crossbow. Instead of using an arrow, he had him load it with a rusty colored three-quarter inch nut. When the nut impacted against the mattress, the implosion violently shook the mattress. The entire target collapsed onto the ground. For the first time in the week since Petey had arrived, Skyler saw the taller boy smile.

Petey turned to Skyler and asked, "Do you think it would be possible to make an even larger crossbow?"

Skyler deliberated the question only briefly. "We could make a larger one, as long as we're strong enough to cock it."

Soon enough, the mattress was re-erected. All the boys, including Kai and Devon, were taking turns at shooting the crossbows. Skyler noticed that even the youngest boys could successfully cock and aim the smaller crossbows. His original plan was to make only three, but now he could see that each boy could use one.

Too soon for the boys, Lara yelled out to the group that the fish was ready and to come inside to eat. Skyler collected the bows, returning them to the garage before heading up the stairs. The plan was that once dinner was finished, James would escort almost half of the children up the hill. Feeding the entire group meant spreading them out through the dining room and living room. They still didn't have enough plates for everyone so Lara had enacted a rule that the youngest ate first, the oldest last. This meant Ian had to wait. While he sat there watching the children, he said to the adults, "You know I worry about our diets now that we don't import or fortify foods anymore."

"What do you mean?" asked James.

Well, for instance, the milk we bought in stores. It was enriched with vitamin D only because it was added during processing. Now with the lack of sunshine, we need vitamin D more than we ever did before. Yet, store-bought milk is extinct. The same goes for vitamin C. Most of our sources came from fresh imported fruits."

Lara was quick to interrupt him. "We grow enough tomatoes to help with the vitamin C. If I can get my hands on some pepper seeds, we can plant them and grow peppers. They would be another good source. The carrots have a lot of Vitamin A. However, I don't know what will substitute for the vitamin D besides exposure to sunshine."

James had been listening thoughtfully. "The new house could use more windows!" he exclaimed. "I could put some additional windows on the south side of the house. Since we can't synthetically make Vitamin D, then maybe we need to focus on getting more exposure from the sun. Most of the year, it's too cold to sit outside without being totally bundled up."

"Well so far, no one here appears to have any of the maladies associated with vitamin deficiencies, but I do agree that it would benefit this group to be proactive," said Ian.

Lara stood from her chair and walked to the kitchen. She pulled open one of the cupboards, searching through the collection of spices left by the previous owners. Finally, she found what she was looking for, pulled the small jar out, holding it up for everyone to see.

"Pepper seeds! I knew I had seen these somewhere. The former occupants must have used them to spice up their food. If I can get just one seed to germinate, I can harvest a whole bunch of seeds from a single pepper."

After the last of the dinner plates were washed and put away, James had Joe, Joel, Marley, Bree and Thomas round up their packs and extra clothing. The kids grabbed their bikes, but since it was an uphill trip, they would need to walk most of the way. While he and Lara followed the five up the hill, the others stayed behind. Skyler and Petey, taking advantage of the remaining daylight, snuck away to work in the garage. Soon, all that was left in the upstairs were Brent, Lydia, Ian, and seven children. Brent moved a chair out onto the deck since the first watch was his. Bekka and Gia took over Skyler's tent, allowing Ian the opportunity to sleep in Skyler's bed. Ian remarked that he was looking forward to this night. He hadn't slept in a real bed for almost eighteen months.

The chaos of the last few days seemed to suit James and Lara. They were both experiencing a sort of contentment for the first time since the Change. As James walked up the steep road, with Lara close by his side, the children often running ahead in anticipation, he realized that, for the first time in months if not years, he was at peace with himself. Not a feeling that he'd been familiar with since years before the Change. The sun peeked through the clouds on its way toward the horizon, calling for the end of another day. He looked over at Lara, somehow knowing that she too was experiencing the same euphoria. Her mood, since the arrival of the children, did not reflect someone running from the darkness; the darkness that neither of them could get accustomed to. As they passed the barricade, James' mood turned to melancholy, a melancholy he could not explain. Like a feather catching flight on the wind, the feeling passed as quickly as it appeared. Was it because some of the children were leaving them or was it something less tangible? He felt his guard go up again, unable to hold onto the belief that days like this could be their future, in which the constant battle against the elements, and desperate survivors, would never cease.

They were greeted warmly by the entire remaining six members of Petar's family. Joe and Joel were quick to show off their new weapons. Skyler had given each of them a crossbow, along with ten arrows apiece. John McBride looked over their newly acquired weapons. "Petar told me about the first crossbow that Skyler made. If these are half as powerful, they'll make a fine weapon. When can I see you shoot these?" Joe and Joel wasted no time dragging John outside for a demonstration.

With twilight looming shortly, Lara prodded James away from the other men. Her excuse was that she didn't want to miss out on another reading performed by Ian. They stood outside saying their good-byes when a single gunshot interrupted the evening's tranquility. It came from the area below the hill.

"Lara, you stay here. I want one other man to ride down to the house with me," James knew instinctively that someone needed stay behind to guard their own house.

John McBride was the first to leave; a rifle slung over his shoulder. James borrowed Petar's bike, riding hard to catch up. Both were around the barricade in record time. They listened intently for more shots as they rode, but heard nothing. Coasting down the steep grade, both men were at the bottom of the hill turning onto Main Street in what seemed like only seconds. With nerves on edge, they slowed for the sharp turn, allowing them to consider what might be waiting for them. They had to be careful about riding into an ambush.

Seeing that everything was clear, both men pedaled their bikes forward, finally reaching the house. Brent stood on the deck holding the binoculars in one hand, waving them up the stairs. On the deck, Brent led them to the rear of the house, handing the glasses to James. Before raising the binoculars to his eyes, he instinctively followed the Imhoff Road down Slater. Detecting movement, he raised the binoculars. What he saw in the gloaming light frightened him. Just as it had happened the previous week, a group of bicycles was coming up Imhoff; only these riders were larger, adults instead of children. He kept focusing on the group as they continued north. It became clear that each rider had a rifle slung over his back. The exact count of the group was hard to determine because of the dim light, and their shifting movement like a school of fish. Still, James was able to narrow it down to seven or eight riders. A few minutes later, just as dusk settled in, they disappeared behind the shoulder of the hill as they entered Ferndale.

CHAPTER 13

April 4th, 2031
5:30 pm

Brandon could not have asked for a better situation. Not only were these seven men capable of murder, they *needed* a leader to guide them in their pursuit of food. Brandon was younger than most of them, but he'd earned their respect by killing Mo. Not one of them challenged his newly acquired authority. It was fortunate that he procured the canned meats to share; feed the starving and they'll do anything for you.

Feeling it necessary to establish his leadership, Brandon took over Mo's room. The room, cluttered with litter, was still the nicest available. Located centrally, it was dry and quiet. Two candles shed enough light for him to view his surroundings. Weathered magazine foldouts, pinned against the walls with chipped pea-green paint, depicted naked women in various illicit poses. The remainder of the magazines, the ones the pictures were apparently torn from, lay neatly stacked on a nightstand next to the bed. Brandon pulled the pictures from the walls, gathered the magazines, as well as Mo's other possessions and tossed them out a nearby window. He had no use for them and wanted no reminder of Mo. Having retrieved his own back pack and sleeping bag, he'd brought them up to the room. A collection of guns leaned against one corner, guns most likely taken from unexpected victims seeking help at the hospital. Upon his inspection, Brandon found mostly odd calibers, little use for what he needed.

Brandon had not wanted to kill those three people. He saw no way of getting out alive if he'd let them walk away leaving him holding a rifle and no food. What he'd done had gnawed at him, but he hid his feelings from the other men, not wanting to show any sign of weakness. The woman probably would have died soon anyway; her two male companions would not have lasted long in this city. From what the others had told him, most of Bellingham had burned during the riots. The only survivors left in this once beautiful city surrounded by mountains, lakes, islands, prayed on others. Brandon and the children had not been violent murderers like these men. Killing Mo was different; he almost found pleasure in taking his life. Mo had brought him to the brink of starvation while deriving pleasure from control over his captive.

Lying atop the bed, Brandon wasn't ready to fully relax. His first order of business would be to send the men out for two more bikes and some packs. The cloudburst had passed, leaving them with a clear day to travel. Brandon had no desire to stay at the hospital or ever return, for that matter. He could still smell his own vomit and feces from his incarceration, and the metallic taste of blood from the two men and woman whom he'd shot lingered in his mouth. His intent was to lead the men to the outlying rural areas where survivors grew their food. The ones with food lived in well-fortified seclusion and were always armed. As he learned when the children were following his bidding, it was easier to get around barriers or sneak past guards by sending a child scout or two ahead, then using whatever information they brought back to plan what to do next. Now that he had seven men backing him, he no longer had to place himself in such a dangerous position. Once he finally blew the candles out and laid in total darkness, he found it difficult to shut his mind off, ruminating on the following day and thereafter. Several hours after nightfall, with only a few hours before daylight, he gave up trying to plan what his next step should be and succumbed to sleep.

In the morning, Brandon rationed out the last of the food from the wheelbarrow. He was surprised to find four jars instead of five. Someone had snuck out during the night and stolen one. Brandon was mad as hell about the theft but there was nothing he could do. He would get nowhere with this group. These men were thieves, and lying came natural to them, as natural as if they had never known what living a life of truth was. His best plan was to observe them eating and see if one of them appeared sated. Only then would he know who the thief might be. He made a mental note to keep an accounting of whatever food they acquired, and to sleep in the same room with it. What was left in the wheelbarrow was all the food they had. These men lived day to day, relying on the occasional survivor to wander into their area. Brandon thought about what they might do once they suffered real starvation. He shook the vision from his mind.

Two more bikes had been found. Brandon decided it was time to move. It was almost midday before they left the hospital, heading to Interstate Five. Some of the men balked about traveling north instead of south. Brandon noticed that as soon as they voiced a complaint, their voices started dying, seemingly expecting a reprimand. He assumed it had stemmed from how Mo had treated them. He noticed that they were quick to challenge every decision he made, so he changed his tactic and shouted at no one in particular, "We'll go south when I say we will. For now, let's collect from the farms that we know exist."

Traveling the highway in the middle of the day with unarmed children had always made Brandon nervous. He had become accustomed to moving his group early in the morning to avoid thugs and highwaymen who lay in wait. Now, the thugs and highway men were with him, and as long as he kept them fed, they would stay with him. Brandon would have to lead then to a source of food or these men would turn on him like vultures. When they arrived in Ferndale, they would need to find a place to stay; a location that could be defended if needed, but not too far from the outlying farms. He thought about the cinder block house where he'd last stayed and quickly nixed the idea. These were men. They wouldn't take to everyone huddled in one small room.

For no uncertain reason, Brandon exited the Interstate just a few miles north of Bellingham. He was back on Slater Road, not far from that cinder block house. The territory was familiar to him and it would lead them into the town. They continued west past the road, the one the house was on, and walked their bikes over the bridge. A few miles further sat the old casino; one of the largest buildings in the area, every bit as large as the hospital. He'd ridden past it before with the children, but they hadn't stopped there because they were looking for farms. Considering this new situation and traveling with men, the casino's location could be advantageous as a place to stay.

It was late afternoon before they pulled the bicycles into the parking lot of the casino. They all looked up in awe at the massive building. One-half of the building was a vaulted, three-story high structure that housed the restaurants and gaming rooms, while the other half had been a seven-story hotel. The parking lot, as large as any, was a sea of abandoned cars, tattered motor homes, and debris from the winter wind storms. The local native tribe had built this once profitable and grand gaming palace just as their income from fishing was noticeably declining. Shortly after it was built, frequent flooding from the unsettled climate decimated the salmon run, the tribe's mainstay for the last several centuries. The casino was more profitable than fishing, which is until the local economy followed the same terminus as the salmon. Following Brandon's queue, they dismounted and walked their bikes through a maze of vehicles to get to the entrance. The hotel half was a cavernous shell with every window blown out. Torn draperies, still anchored inside some of the windows, blew outward like ghosts. They had no desire to go inside. It would provide no more shelter than camping outside.

They dropped their bikes at the bottom of the long rows of steps below the casino's entrance. One of the men tentatively asked Brandon "Is this where we'll be staying?"

Brandon, annoyed by the question, held back so as not to antagonize the men. "We'll see."

Tall, double-doors once marked the entrance, had long since been sucked out by winds or riots with no telltale sign of one or the other. Through the darkness, all they could see was one cavernous room.

The gaming area had no windows to remind patrons of the time of day; it remained opaque without its artificial lighting. Brandon pulled a candle from his pack, lighting it with his only source of flame, a Zippo lighter. As they moved into the room, an all too recognizable smell assaulted them. Not the death pall of the recently deceased, but the musty decaying stench that grew stronger with each step inward. They picked their way through corpse after corpse like a parquet floor of skeletons and dried rotted flesh. Most of the bodies had weapons, hunting rifles and shotguns rusted with time, lying near them. Many were shot through the head. This was the site of a last stand in a fight for food and shelter. Brandon turned to leave, and the men followed without dissent or comment.

"Let's head north to Ferndale," Brandon ordered, yet shaken by what he had just seen.

"Brandon?" One of the men stepped forward wanting a word with him.

Brandon recalled he was the one called DJ. He didn't know what the initials stood for and didn't care. He also noticed that whenever he turned to look in DJ's direction, he was watching him. The other men looked up to DJ. Brandon felt unsettled by this. DJ, slightly shorter than Brandon, made up for it in musculature. He now gave DJ his full attention. "What do you want?"

"I used to work security at hotels. Each floor should have one or two supply rooms. They kept linen, soap, and toilet paper in these rooms. These rooms often had secure lockers for the food that went into the mini-bars. Can we check them out?"

Brandon looked up at the tall hollow building. As uninviting as it appeared, it wouldn't hurt to look. However, he didn't want to spread everyone apart. If one of these men were lucky enough to discover something, he'd quickly fill his belly before alerting the others. "Let's split up into two groups. DJ, you take those three with you, and I'll take these three. Let's also go room to room and see if any of the mini-bars are still locked."

"Then maybe you'll need one of these keys," said DJ. He had reached into his pack and pulled out two small pry bars, about a foot long each.

Brandon, taking the tool, entered through the hotel's side entrance. DJ and his group had already agreed to check the lower four floors, while Bandon's men would cover the top three. Locating the stairs was easier than climbing up through the debris that filled them. The supply rooms were found at each end of the long buildings; it was obvious that they'd already been ransacked. The hall leading through the extended corridor of rooms was lit only by the light from open doors that had been blown from their hinges. The carpets were soggy with water, and splattered with white chunks of gypsum from the wall board that drooped from the ceiling and walls. Brandon ducked into the first room on the fifth floor, finding a small refrigerator in a cabinet under the television. It was still locked.

About one-third of the rooms they checked had mini-bars that had lain there for over two years undiscovered. Almost all had a brown liquid leaking from the door. The pry bar easily jammed under the plastic gasket and broke the cheap locks. The bottles and cans of soda pop and beer had long ago frozen, rupturing their containers. However, in most units, they found one-ounce bottles of whiskey, vodka or gin—a token gift for the guests in exchange for gambling away their money. Packages of potato and corn chips, still vacuum sealed, were found in literally every locked refrigerator. Cigars and cigarettes were also collected if the quagmire of liquids hadn't penetrated their folded cellophane wrappers. Some of the mini-bars reeked of rotting food. Still, they were soon filling their packs with packaged nuts, chips, chocolate bars, tobacco products, and several small bottles of liquor.

When they met up in the stairwell, DJ and his group had fared almost as well. The first floor had no guest rooms, but as they moved up from one floor to another, their bounty increased. They returned together out to the front steps, emptying their findings into a pile. Moods changed as they viewed the food and drink before them; a feast for kings. Some of the men already opened up the small bottles, swallowing their contents in a single gulp.

Seeing this, Brandon stood and pointed his rifle at the pile. "Don't open another bottle until we find a place to stay tonight. Eat some of the chips and let's re-pack." He paused, waiting to see if someone objected.

"We'll ride up to Ferndale and find a building to take shelter in, and then you can finish off the liquor for all I care."

This seemed to be agreeable to all of them. As they picked through the sealed bags, eating stale snacks, Brandon picked up their names as they spoke to one another. What he didn't already know, he worked at memorizing. They all went by nicknames for reasons unknown to him. Besides DJ, there was also Okie, who had a southern accent. Another named Postal left Brandon guessing at the source of his name. Two brothers, Ink and No Ink, named accordingly for first one's fondness for tattoos, while his older sibling thought they were a waste of time. Another they called Weasel because of his aptness to pilfer through the other's belongings. The smallest one of the group was called Mouse, and except for his size, Brandon could see no other resemblance. And then there was Einstein; a cruel title labeling the group's simpleton.

DJ tore open a pack of cigarettes and passed them out. Brandon was the only one not interested in the white sticks. He had smoked once out behind the gym when he was in junior high school, but had not found anything desirable about it. The odor they emitted wasn't the slightest bit aromatic. As cigarettes were passed, each man was asking another for a light. It soon became obvious to Brandon that not one of them had any way to start a fire. He pulled the Zippo from his pocket, handing it to DJ with the instructions, "Light yours and then have them light theirs off yours. I don't want to waste the fuel on cigarettes."

Most of them hadn't smoked in almost two years if not longer. Some coughed each time they inhaled, but they continued as if this were a just-deserved treat. Brandon let them finish before he began stuffing his pack with the remaining food and drink. It wasn't long before each man leaped in, fearful of not getting his share.

They remounted their bikes and Brandon led the way back along Slater. The sun was low on the horizon; it would be dark within the hour. A bank of clouds was moving in from the south, signifying that it might rain within the next day. From where they re-entered the Slater Road, Brandon estimated that they were still four miles from the downtown area. If they could get there, it would suffice for the first night. A short time later, they turned north on Imhoff. Brandon, familiar with this road, kept the group moving forward, the small town just ahead.

It was close to dark before they passed a sign, its metal pole bent by past winds, welcoming them to the city limits. They came to an inter-section, turning right on Main Street, coasting their bikes down into the town until the road became blocked by a large power pole intersecting the street. Three blocks of buildings, deserted, dark and foreboding like a modern-day ghost town, lay before them. Leaving their bikes there, they split up and began checking the darkened structures for habitable shelter. They went door to door, quickly checking each building, keeping in verbal contact with the group that checked the other side of the street.

DJ shouted to Brandon from a corner across the street, motioning to what he'd found. He stood just outside a tavern that had closed long before the Change. The front door had been forcefully removed and the inside was light enough to see all the way into the back. Debris, covering most of the floor, made it appear that others camped in here previously. Brandon understood its desirability immediately; it had a fireplace, a real fireplace.

They gathered up wood from nearby buildings and sat around the open flames eating, drinking, and smoking. Brandon knew he was fortunate they had found food and shelter. The fireplace was an extra bonus he hadn't counted on. Had it gone differently, his term as the favorable leader might have ended abruptly. His mind drifted away from the party-like chatter as he thought about what tomorrow might yield. He remembered that large house that was occupied just outside of town; it sat nearby, just up the street from where they camped tonight. The place where he'd almost caught that kid before he escaped his grasp. Once they rested for the night, they would investigate what kind of defenses those people had. The last time he was there, small logs had been placed across the road going in. Taking that house would be easy with these men behind him. From there, they could go after the others.

CHAPTER 14

April 5th, 2031
6:55 pm

"Where do you suppose they went?" James asked Brent.

"Don't know, but there were only two ways they could have gone, and they didn't come this way, not yet anyway."

The three men, watched and waited, rifles ready, expecting the riders to come into view. It had been twenty minutes since the party had disappeared behind the hill; the tension was so high that the children fled to the downstairs. James knew that if there were at least seven men with rifles, quite possibly eight. They were clearly outnumbered. The bulk of their defense consisted of McBride, Brent and himself. Skyler was good with his bow, but was no match for someone with a rifle unless it was at close range. Lydia could and would shoot, but she lacked both confidence and experience with guns. James, glad that he'd left Lara up on the hill, had enough to worry about with the children. Then he remembered Ian. Like so many others who had led non-aggressive lives before the Change, James wondered if he would he hold that course if the worst happened? Would he pick up a rifle to protect the children?

James turned to the two other men. "Since both of you are ex-military, what should we be doing?"

Both Brent and McBride looked at one another before McBride finally spoke. "There's too much that we don't know. We don't know who they are, how well they are armed, or how much training they've had." He paused and looked to Brent to see if his former family member agreed or not. Brent nodded his head so McBride continued, "All we *should* do for now is to prepare our defensive position. They could be a hundred yards down the road waiting for dawn or scouting an alternate path to here. I doubt that we'll see them tonight."

"Why so?" asked James.

"Would you go out after dark and creep up on a group of armed men when you didn't know their numbers or their exact location?"

"Yeah, I see your point. Should one of us go out and see if we can locate where they're staying tonight?"

"What if they have a sentry? Our scout would most likely be seen before he sees them."

"Then our only course of action is to wait?"

Brent took over at this point in the conversation. "I don't see any other option. We need to prepare for an early-morning attack. They are eight children staying here, and bullets will cut through this house like it's made of paper. We need to get them out at first light and up the hill before anything happens. We also need to alert Petar, the Lopatnikovs and the Jensens."

Skyler had joined the group moments before and was taking in everything that was being said. When James saw him, he asked him, "Would you be willing to make a trip up the hill and spread the word tonight?"

"I don't think I should. Most of Dimitrey's family doesn't understand English. They could shoot at me if I enter their driveway late at night. The same with the Jensens; they were already nervous after last week. I don't feel good about visiting them until daylight."

"My worry is that Petar will come down here if he hears any gunshots. Should we at least warn him?"

"He won't come down," McBride jumped in. "It's a clear rule in our group that one defender is to stay behind regardless of what happens. He's the only protection they have, so he'll stay and guard the road."

"May I suggest a plan for the night?" asked Brent. "The women and children sleep downstairs tonight. They should stay dressed and ready to run. One of us could stay in the grass half-way between here and the road, acting as a forward sentry or listening post. The moon is behind the clouds, we won't know if someone is attacking us until they're up close. As soon as it begins to lighten up a bit, we wake everyone who can't or won't fight, and move them up on the hill. They can warn the others for us."

"I agree," said McBride.

James knew that Brent's last remark about those that won't fight was referring solely to Ian and no one else. "That works for me but I still want one sentry on the deck. Just because we know that there is a potential attacker who could come in from the east does not mean someone else couldn't try it from the south."

"I suggest we split up the night so we can all try to get at least a little sleep," said McBride.

As McBride had predicted, there was no sign of the attackers through the night. He and James had taken the second shifts earlier than necessary only because neither man could fall asleep. Anticipating the scenarios they could face was on both of their minds. Sometime during the night, a light rain fell as the clouds continued to thicken. Likewise, Lydia and Ian were laying awake downstairs with the children, ready to rouse them if necessary.

The first light of dawn crept in. They waited until they could see the road from the house. McBride sat up from the grass, stealing a glance down Main Street before returning to the house. James lit a candle and walked down the inner stairway to find that Lydia and Ian had already started the process of helping the children pack their belongings.

"No breakfast this morning," James ordered, not unkindly to no one in particular. "As soon as everyone is packed, we'll head out through the garage." He obvious reasons, he didn't want a fire in the stove. His plan was for them to cross the yard to the construction site, utilizing the old driveway for the escape. At the very least, it would afford them some cover until they reached Main Street. From there, they would cross Main to reach Church Road. He had thought about who should shepherd them up the hill since Lydia and Ian were not armed. Skyler would be his first choice, but he changed his mind. They needed someone that could hold an attacker at bay from a distance; someone with a rifle and scope. Brent and McBride, with their combat experience, were the obvious choices to stay behind. James didn't have time to ponder options; he would chaperone them just to the top of the hill, returning immediately. Someone from up there would need to alert the other families.

It took only minutes before everyone was ready to move out. James raced upstairs only long enough to let the others know they were leaving. He grabbed his hunting rifle, his only weapon equipped with a scope. Ian had already opened the large garage door nearest to the west side of the house. Lydia ushered the children into the neighboring yard. Each child carried three or four Mason jars inside their packs making them appear top heavy. James mandated that they remove as much food from the house as possible. Walking past the newly constructed frame, James could only wonder if they'd ever be able to finish the house. This latest exposure to impending danger was another reminder of the heightened need for families to live clustered together if they were to have any quality of life.

Lydia led the way while James took up the rear. Twice, Ian had to remind the younger ones to stay quiet. James noticed that Petey carrying the large homemade crossbow. He wondered if he'd asked Skyler for it or just took it. This wasn't the time to question him about this action. Minutes later they emerged out of the long gravel driveway, standing on the edge of Main Street looking directly up Church Road. James scouted the road leading towards town. Assured that there was no danger, he motioned for Lydia to start crossing with the children. Just as the last child scurried across the road, James detected movement. The combination of early dawn light and clouds afforded him little visibility. While the others waited safely across the intersection for him to cross, he stayed back. Holding up his hand in a halting gesture, he stared unblinking down Main Street. He saw nothing at first. Lifting the rifle to his shoulder, he used the scope to scan the sides of the road below their location. Then he saw it. A rifle barrel was sticking up out of the ditch, moving purposefully back and forth like an upside-down pendulum: at least one person was crawling up the ditch less than a hundred yards from the entrance to their cul-de-sac.

James held up a single finger signifying the number one and pointed down the hill. Lydia's eyes widened, understanding the message instantly. He pointed up Church and motioned for them to leave without him. James was sure that, whoever it was, had seen the children cross the road and took cover. Apparently, they hadn't seen James with the rifle because they were still moving forward.

After watching Lydia and Ian lead the children to safety, James ran back down to the house to alert Skyler, Brent and McBride. At a full run, he reached the house in less than a minute, entering through the garage instead of the front stairs.

"Something's up if you're back already," McBride, alarmed at the unexpected sight of James. He had been in Special Ops before the Change; a soldier's soldier. Little frightened him. He never felt fear for his own safety. He knew before probing that James had run into the enemy.

"I saw someone inching their way up Main Street in the ditch on the other side of the road. I think there's just the one, probably to scout us out."

"Do you think that he might be aware that he was seen?"

"Probably not, he kept coming this way. Shall we try to capture him?" asked James.

"No, if he doesn't return, they'll have to assume that we've got him. We need to know where they are staying. Our chances improve with the more information we have. One of us should try to shadow him back and see where he goes."

Brent, the only one left out on the deck, well hidden by the rail, crawled back in through the front door. Skyler, watching the road from a crack in the shutters, turned to join the others. Together, the four formulated a plan with McBride taking the lead. Skyler would follow the old driveway back to Main Street. From there, he would have a clear view of the ditch along that road He was instructed to stay there until the interloper returned the way he had come. Skyler would then follow him as far as he safely could, hopefully, near where the bandits were holed up. The other three men would be poised covertly with rifles, awaiting his return.

"Leave your bow here," said James. "I don't want you carrying more than you have to." He pulled the pistol from his coat pocket and handed it to the youth, a man, nonetheless, in this new world. He was secure in knowing that Skyler knew how to use it, and any shot fired by Skyler would be heard by the rest of them.

Skyler left through the garage door, ducking into the depression in the neighboring yard. Once he was sure he couldn't be seen by anyone on the road, he sprinted up the old driveway. Reaching the point where the gravel met the asphalt, he dropped, scouring the entire length of the road below him. At first blush, there was nothing amiss. Just as Skyler began to feel he'd missed the opportunity, he saw someone standing behind the corner of one of the damaged homes along on their side of Main. Whoever was there, they were clearly watching James' house. The dim light hampered his acuity; Skyler could only tell that it was a tall male. Whoever he was must have seen what he was looking for, because seconds later, he turned and ran down the hill, making no attempt to stay hidden. Skyler got up, sprinting after him, staying as close to the edge of the road as possible, ready to make a dive for cover. The runner never once turned; he just kept heading for the downtown.

The distance from the house to the downtown was roughly one mile. In the ten minutes that it took that person to run there, he'd gained another hundred yards on Skyler. The closer they came to the downtown, the more nervous Skyler felt. This was not a place for someone to wander into alone. His biggest fear was that his quarry would cross the bridge. If he did, Skyler would have to decide on following him further or turning back. Up ahead, Skyler spotted about half a dozen bicycles scattered around the same place where he and James had left theirs only two days earlier. He relaxed a bit knowing their lair had to be close.

Skyler halted his pursuit before the runner slowed; he knew instantly where they'd stayed the night before. He could smell it as well as see it. Smoke was rising from a brick chimney above the old tavern on the corner of Second and Main. Skyler remembered seeing it just two days prior. The tavern had only one entrance. They had peered into it as they walked past. It was located on the building's corner where the side street met Main. These guys chose the worst possible place to defend. It spoke to Skyler about their lack of leadership.

Without hesitation, he turned, retracing his trail back up the street. The information he gleaned had just given them the upper hand. He already knew what their next step would be—they would need to make a pre-emptive strike as soon as possible. Whoever they were, they were planning on raiding the locals starting with James' house. Sending a spy was all the proof any of them needed.

As he ran in the entrance of the cul de sac, he made out James and Brent as they stood from their prone positions on the deck. Skyler trotted up the stairs to address them. "I know where they're at!"

CHAPTER 15

April 5th, 2031
9:30 pm

It had been a festive atmosphere that Brandon had wanted no part of. These men were not at all like him. Thugs that lived day to day without thinking about tomorrow, and most had spent part of their lives incarcerated. After settling into the tavern, the men had built a large fire in the old stone fireplace, immediately passing around the small bottles of liquor. Their gluttony disgusted Brandon as he watched them openly waste food. Tearing open bags of chips and nuts, dropping them on the floor like they didn't have a worry in the world. It appeared to him they were driven to finish off all the food they'd recovered from the casino before morning. A few asked him for a light for their cigarettes, but Brandon refused, merely pointing to the large fireplace without a word. Their behavior exhausted him, and they would soon suck up his remaining energy if he did not get away from them.

Looking around the tavern, Brandon found a small room insulated from the noise. Lacking of furniture, its only contents was debris that wouldn't burn. There were no windows; Brandon would not know when dawn arrived if he slept here. Pushing aside empty cans and bottles, he unrolled his sleeping bag. Shutting and latching the only door muffled the constant chatter; enough to convince him to stay in here for the night. He'd wanted to make the first raid early the next morning, but now he didn't favor trying to wake the other seven men. He hoped that they would finish off the liquor and cigarettes so that they could get on with what they'd come for. At first, the thought of having these men doing the stealing was more attractive than getting those kids back. Now, he was having second thoughts. At least with the kids he had some control.

Brandon awoke in total darkness, his bladder screaming to be emptied. He groped around the dark room for his rifle, finding his shoes and coat in the process. Silently cracking the door, he discovered what he had expected. The others, amid a sea of cellophane wrappers, snored and farted in their sleep. Even as they slept, they disgusted him. Rifle in hand, Brandon made his way to the only door that led outside.

Out on the street, all was still. A cloud cover had stalled the dawn. The remnants of a light rain left a sheen on the sidewalk. Brandon could only guess at what time it was. "Early, too early for those bastards," he thought out loud as he looked back through the doorway. What would they do now that they'd wasted the opportunity for an early-morning strike? Rushing the house that sat just up the road, the one the boy sought cover at, would have been so much easier if they had done it early. Soon, it would be full daylight. To try and take it in broad daylight would be nothing more than an act of suicide. Brandon looked at the bridge and then back up the road they'd come in on. Maybe this would be a good time to scope things out. A little walk up the hill might reveal something useful. Looking back at the tavern, he realized he had no reason to hang around, waiting for the men to wake up.

They'd left the bicycles a block further up the street, and as Brandon passed them, he felt a little relief that no one had disturbed them through the night. Tempting as it was, he decided not to ride up the hill. It was only about a mile at the most, and having the bike under him meant he'd need to stay on the road. It was impossible to be stealthy on a bike and Brandon needed stealthy. He strained his memory for what the place had looked like when he'd passed by there over a week earlier. He remembered that it was a large house with three garage doors on the north side, but not much more than that. Whoever lived there had dragged small logs out into the opening of the street. Did they really believe that some twigs would thwart an attack? He was pretty sure that this was where James and Brent lived. What right did they have to take the kids from him? A surly look appeared on Brandon's face. They were more likely using them for much worse purposes than stealing. He bet they were a couple of perverts.

Fifteen minutes later, Brandon was getting close. He'd been walking on the north side of Main Street staying close to the ditch. The trek was proving to be uneventful, yet Brandon kept his rifle ready. He had stopped to survey the scene when he saw someone run across the road about two hundred yards up ahead. Brandon dove for the ditch. Lifting his head, he caught a glimpse of several children crossing at the same place. He lay with his face pressed against the damp ground. He stood briefly to get a better view, but a shoulder of the hill blocked him from seeing where they'd crossed to. He waited, but nothing more crossed the road.

Could they be on their way up to raid someone else? Could James and Brent be using them to steal for them? He'd seen at least one or two adults, maybe three. Brandon could think of no other reason why they would be out so early on this cloudy morning. He needed to move up a little further and get a good look at their house. With that many leaving the house, it might be easy for his men to take it, even with their hangovers. Brandon stayed low in the ditch, crawling, holding his rifle off the ground. When the house was in full view, he looked for a sentry on the deck but there appeared to be none. He was still several hundred feet away. A pair of binoculars would have been useful to confirm this. Looking around and seeing no one, Brandon leapt to his feet and ran across to a damaged house on the other side of the road. He looked up and down Main before peering out around the corner. The big house stood alone at the end of the cul-de-sac. There wasn't any smoke coming from its chimney. There was no movement of any type. It was as if the place had been deserted by those he'd seen crossing the road.

Maybe this was the opportune time to attack. If he went back for the men, they could be waiting for James and Brent to return with the children. He would love to be sitting inside their house when they came back. To see the look on their faces when they encountered eight rifles pointed at their faces. That would teach those fuckers. Maybe this would be a good day after all. Brandon stayed only a few more minutes as he worked out how they would attack the house. The main problem was getting from the street to the house; they would be in the open for a quite a distance. If someone saw them, there was nowhere to hide should they be fired upon. He'd have two of the men make the initial assault, and if they made it to the house, he'd have the rest run in.

Brandon felt his heart racing. He needed to get back into town and wake those filthy bastards up. Without hesitating further, Brandon looked both up and down the road before taking off in a sprint. He ran down the hill allowing gravity to increase his speed. The sooner he got back, the better. He liked running again and realized that it had been quite a while since he'd done this much. As weak as he'd been two days earlier, his recovery came quickly. He kept his eyes open for any dangers, but really expected to see nothing. A light rain began to fall, too weak to change the color of the dry pavement.

Brandon jumped over the first power pole, passed the parked bikes, and continued running. He didn't slow until his feet touched the sidewalk in front of the tavern. His pace was still fast as he entered through the door, nearly colliding with one of the men. It was Okie. His eyes needed to adjust to the dimly lit room. Two of the men were already up. One had stoked the fire.

"Everyone get up now! We have an unguarded house just a mile from here. We need to get up there as soon as possible." Brandon watched as the three still on the floor slowly raised their heads and looked about. Mouse sat up, the only one that looked alert enough to be ready to leave. Then he noticed that DJ was missing.

"Where's DJ?" he asked Mouse.

"He went out to take a dump. He'll be back in a minute."

The men on the floor were now awake, but no one made an attempt to stand. Furious, Brandon shouted one more time, enunciating each word as if speaking to a deaf person, "Get up now! We need to get moving if we're going to take that house!"

"Did you know that you were followed back here?"

Brandon spun around to confront the voice behind him. Standing in the well-lit doorway was DJ's distinct silhouette. The words he'd just said were not making sense. "What do you mean by that?"

"Just as I said, you were followed here. I saw you running back down the road. There was a kid running a couple hundred yards behind you. As soon as you passed the bicycles, he turned and split."

The excitement that had carried Brandon back to the tavern quickly drained from his body. All the men were now standing and staring at him. How could he have been so stupid as to not look back? Who could that kid have been? Was it Joe or Joel? Or was it that kid they'd chased down that afternoon before Brent and James abducted the kids? Either way, this changed everything.

DJ interrupted his thoughts with a question. "Where'd you go this morning?"

Brandon paused as he thought about what he could say without looking even more stupid. "I went to check on a house. I saw several people leave that area and assumed that the house might be vacant for the next couple of hours. If we took it, we'd be in a great position to raid the other houses."

"Well, whoever followed you ran back the way he'd come from. I suspect that everyone and their brother knows that you were up early and spying on them." He paused before adding, "I, for one, do not look forward to going up there just yet."

Brandon suddenly realized that whoever had followed him probably knew where they were staying. Even if he hadn't seen Brandon walk into the tavern, he surely saw the smoke coming from the chimney. Maybe that explained why the kids were on the move. Maybe they knew that Brandon had brought men into the town. They were preparing for an attack. If they went back up there now, it would be anyone's guess what or who would be waiting for them.

"May I make a suggestion?" asked DJ. He waited for a response from Brandon, but got nothing. "We need to get our asses out of here really fast. That kid knows where we are staying, and this place has only one door. If even one man comes after us with a rifle, we're trapped." He turned, speaking directly at Brandon. "When I was watching you, I came across a building two blocks up from here that's hollowed out. It has about four doors leading in and out, and it's made of bricks. We can sit there for the day and decide what to do next."

"That would put us even closer to them. I'm thinking we should head the other way and cross the bridge." Brandon responded.

DJ looked around the room. He was about to take control of the group, and Brandon was too naïve to notice. He took his time because he now held all the trump cards. "If we are sitting in that brick building, anyone who wanders down this way will walk right past us. We'll know where they are, and they won't know where we are. We can eliminate them without going up to meet them. I'll bet my left nut that kid has already reported back that we're staying here, and they won't be able to resist the urge to stomp on us today."

Everyone in the room except Brandon seemed to be nodding in agreement. Without waiting for Brandon to say anything more, DJ announced, "Pack up your shit and let's move! Someone throw more wood on the fire. I want it to look like we're here waiting for them!"

CHAPTER 16

April 6th, 2031
7:15 am

"I agree with Brent. We move while we know where they're at," said McBride.

Of the three men, James was the only one uncommitted to pulling off a raid right away. He also lacked the experience of the two seasoned veterans. It had already been determined that Skyler would stay behind to watch the house—someone had to.

"I just think it's a good idea to enlist a little more help. Three of us against seven or eight of them is not what I call favorable odds," said James.

Brent felt strongly about their plan now that there was a steady rain coming down. He was sure that the bandits would stay in the dry tavern at least until the weather broke. "Our odds are best if we pick the place of battle, especially if we catch them all in one building. If we can trap them in there, they'll either have to come out fighting or surrender. Either way, they can't win."

Skyler sat there and listened to their arguments. As much as he would have liked to be a part of the assault team, he also could see the importance of staying behind. As soon as any shots were fired, the other survivors up on the hill would be compelled to come and aid those down here. Skyler's job would be to make sure no one went into the downtown area, and no strangers came out. The food they'd stored last fall was their gold; his job was to guard it.

"James, if we are to do this, we need to move now. We can't sit here and deliberate or wait until help arrives. As soon as this rain quits, they'll come out of the building, and most likely, they'll come this way. We can either fight them down there or up here. It's your choice." McBride crossed his arms signifying that this was his final plea.

James glanced out the window. Copious amounts of water ran from one of the downspouts, into their rain barrel. He didn't like going into battle and probably would never get used to it. The previous fall, he had fought alongside both men against much greater odds and won. However, at that time, he had a reason to attack; the soldiers they fought had taken Lara from him. This was different. They were to be the aggressors; these bandits having done nothing more than send up a spy. He felt like a wishbone being pulled in two directions, but he knew his friends were making their decisions based upon their desires to protect the sector. It would be selfish for him to hinder their stronghold.

"All right," James replied. "Let's get this over with."

Neither Brent nor McBride smiled at their victory. Both men had seen combat in the Middle East. They knew that there were risks. It was Brent that had come up with the plan; catch them in the building, shoot anyone who comes out holding a weapon, and if they refused, they would throw in a flaming can of kerosene. The objective was to get their weapons and allow them to walk away alive. However, if this wasn't acceptable to the bandits, they were prepared to terminate them.

Within minutes, James dumped a collection of dark clothing on the floor. Some of it was waterproof, but not enough for all three of them. The heavy rain meant that they were going to be wet until this ended.

James found his supply of kerosene. He poured his last two liters into an old plastic milk jug. If they needed to use the kerosene, they would stuff a rag down into the opening and use it like a Molotov cocktail. The difference being that the kerosene would not explode, but would burn at a

154

slower rate. The building the bandits had secluded themselves in was brick on the outside, while the interior was lined with wood from floor to ceiling. Without a water supply, the men inside would not be able to stop the spreading flames.

To Skyler, it seemed like only minutes had passed before all three men stood inside the kitchen ready to carry on the offensive attack. Each was armed with a rifle slung over their back and a pistol in their coats. Dressed in dark clothing, including their stocking caps, faces painted with grease, they stood in a semi-circle. Brent held out the crudely drawn map in front of him.

"Let's go over this to make sure we're all on the same page," said Brent. "We ride down the hill and turn when we reach city hall. From there, we go on foot one street below Main until just before Second Avenue. I'll cut up the alley behind the bank building and aim for the entrance to the tavern. Once I'm in place, you two are to go up Second Avenue and position yourselves precisely outside the entrance. Then it's up to you to inform them that they are surrounded."

Both James and McBride nodded their understanding. As much as James hated to be one of the two that approached the building, he didn't relish Brent's job: shooting anyone who came out holding a weapon. It was time to go.

With their rifles slung over their backs, each picked up a bike and started peddling toward Main Street. From there, the grade allowed them to coast at a fast pace. The rain stung their eyes, impeding their vision as they rolled silently; each man alone with his thoughts, yet constantly on the lookout for the unexpected. Reaching the first stretch of flat terrain, they peddled just enough to keep their momentum going. When they could see the slight downward curve of the road with the city hall before them, they were in enemy territory.

Brent was the first to bring his bike to a stop and dismount. They hid their three bikes behind a sign that had been blown from the roof of the large building that once housed the office of the mayor. Rain continued to pound them, making enough noise to muffle their actions. There was no need for stealth, not yet anyway; the place they stood was still two blocks from the tavern and sheltered from view. If the bandits did have a sentry, which they must assume, most likely he'd be posted up closer to where they were hiding. By staying off of Main and coming in from the parallel street below, they had a greater chance of evading detection.

Using only hand signals, Brent had the other two follow him behind the large building and over onto Fourth Avenue. The sky was a dull, dark gray, shadowless and foreboding. The lack of contrast and the dim light worked to their benefit. Each man carried their rifle with both hands except McBride. His right hand held the rifle at its mid-point while his other hand held the jug of kerosene. The destructive winds from two prior winters dropped an incredible amount of debris on the street between the city hall and the old gas station. The three men had to find their way around the entanglement until they were on the street that ran one block down from Main.

The destruction caught James off guard. In the year that he'd been living just less than a mile away, he had never bothered to venture down here below Main Street. This area sat lower than the downtown and had been flooded by the river so many times that the grade school and most of the homes had been abandoned long before the Change. There was nothing of value that the river had not washed away. Everything up to a height of eight feet had a layer of silt covering it. Piles of dead trees mixed with other items that floated were washed up against the sides of the few buildings that hadn't been pushed off their foundations. Mud covered every visible piece of ground.

They reached Third Avenue without incident. All was quiet except for the rain. The smell of wood smoke could now be detected. The tavern sat diagonally from them just one street above. There were several cars off the side of the street, carried by the flood waters to where they now rested. All were coated with mud, including any windows that remained intact. It reminded James of the floods that followed volcanic eruptions. As if a wall of mud had had passed through here painting everything it touched. They were getting close to where Brent would part from them. The funeral home sat just off to their left, and the next building would be the bank. If it was passable, Brent would make his way up the alley between these two buildings.

At first glance, the alley appeared to be filled with detritus from the roof of the bank. Brent approached the obstruction, finding that he could walk in and around the large obstacles. He disappeared from view for almost two minutes before reappearing and giving the thumbs up signal. McBride held up three fingers signaling to James that they would allow Brent three minutes to get into position before moving forward and crossing Second Avenue. They picked their way in front of an old squat cinder-block building. Once a dentist's office, the concrete blocks proved their worth in this catastrophic environment. Off to his right, James could see the shell of the grade school. Its roof must have caved in completely because daylight could be seen through each blown-out window. Large chunks of wooden structures and trees were piled over twenty-five feet high on the side that faced the river. The brick structure had withstood the strong forces of the flood waters, but everything else around it had been washed away long ago.

McBride held up one finger. James checked the safety of his rifle. He already clicked it off when they'd dismounted, but found that he kept checking it. He was nervous and scared, yet he overrode his fears to keep pace with McBride. From where they stood, they could peer around the dentist office and see all the way to the entrance of the tavern. There were no signs of movement anywhere on the street above them. The rain continued to fall at a steady pace. Smoke from the chimney was now visible as it wafted down to the street in front of them. Second Avenue was littered with enough cars and pickup trucks to afford them some protection. Until now, James had been distracted by the damage of the storms. Now, they were to move on an enemy that they knew little about.

McBride went first running from one car to another. James followed suit, staying one car behind him. Both men kept their heads as low as possible, just in case there was a sentry on the street above. So far, they had not heard anything come from the area where Brent was positioned. They took this as a good sign. The distance between the dentist office and the tavern was only a half of a block. They were close to being within fifty feet of the tavern's door. McBride motioned for James to move up to his position. The sound of the rain hitting the cars made it impossible to hear any noises coming from within the building. They both ducked down behind the same car.

McBride leaned closer to whisper to him. "You cover me. I'll position myself outside the door. I expect that they'll shoot out through the open door. Stay out of their way and don't shoot unless you have a target." He then handed James the plastic jug of kerosene.

Before James could respond, McBride left the safety of the vehicle's cover and ran to their side of the entrance into the building. As soon as he reached it, he threw his back up against the brick wall and leaned in toward the open doorway. As James watched, McBride turned back to face James with a worried look on his face. It was clear to him that McBride sensed that something was wrong.

As James moved to the spot that McBride had just vacated, a bullet shattered the car window right where his head had been only a half second earlier. James instinctively ducked down as a hail of bullets forced him and McBride to the ground. From James' position, he could see under the car and that his friend had probably escaped getting hit. Whoever was shooting at them had followed them in from the street below. McBride stood and returned fire down Second Avenue. He had taken shelter by using the corner of the building, firing at the cars just a few yards away from where James lay hidden.

"James, get over here! NOW!" He shouted.

James grabbed the kerosene and waited until he heard two successive shots from McBride's weapon before running out from the cover of the car. With bullets impacting against the bricks just above his head, James dove past the tavern's entrance, landing behind the same wall where McBride had taken cover. No sooner had he arrived when more shots came from Main Street near where Brent was stationed.

"What the hell? We walked right into a trap!" said McBride.

The shooters in the cars below must also have heard the other shots. They halted firing their weapons as soon as the other shooting started. McBride kept peeking around the corner but could not find a target worth aiming at. Another volley of shots was fired further up Main, and both men could clearly hear Brent's return fire. Then a bullet hit the bricks just between them sending chards of red brick into their unprotected faces. McBride grabbed James' arm, jerking him to his feet as he took two large steps into the tavern's open doorway. Bullets splintered the door frame as they passed through.

After coarsely depositing James on the floor, McBride turned and raised his rifle out the open door. He fired once at a target across Main and then waved his arm at something in his line of sight. A barrage of rifle fire opened up and McBride stood back as Brent came diving through the door almost knocking into James as he attempted to stand.

"What happened out there?" asked Brent. He clearly looked shaken by the sudden turn of events.

"We must have been followed in. They came up from behind us and started firing. I knew something was wrong as soon as I stood outside this door. There wasn't anyone in here when we arrived."

Two more bullets came through the doorway at no particular target. The three men, finding themselves victims of their own trap, moved toward the back of the tavern, looking for something to take cover behind. The room, still warm with the fire burning, offered them no protection. Its only advantageous trait was that it was as dark as a cave.

They could hear voices coming from outside the tavern. Men were gathering outside their line of sight. The only windows, small and positioned up high on the walls, couldn't be used to view their surroundings. They kept their rifles leveled at the one open doorway that was their only way out. They finally heard someone shout just outside the door.

"Hey, if you guys would like a chance to live, we'll make you an offer."

CHAPTER 17

April 6th, 2031
7:15 am

It was Mouse who had first spotted the three bikes coming down the hill. At first, his stammer annoyed the others as he tried to get their attention. He finally got their attention. They were on the second floor of the brick building with open windows and a leaky ceiling; a torrent of rain soaking them as they sat and waited. DJ had rigged a couple of boards in a glassless window allowing them to see up the street without being seen. As DJ had predicted, armed men were coming down the hill and headed into the downtown section of Ferndale.

DJ expected more than three. Then he smiled; three could easily be handled. However, instead of riding past and getting closer to the tavern, they pulled up short, stashing their bicycles near the old City Hall. He wondered if they might do a door-to-door search as they made their way up the street. This brick box, across from the trio and the town's hall, gave no hint to what it possessed within. Entering their stronghold would not present a problem for DJ; it would just spoil his initial plan.

DJ watched closely as the three disappeared behind the former City Hall. "Nice tactic," he thought to himself, "Sneaking in from the lower part of town for a surprise attack."

All the men, including Brandon, took a turn at the window to view their would-be attackers. Each one showed no fear, and a few even smiled at the prospect of ending this wait. When Brandon finished looking, he turned to DJ and said, "I recognize two of them. They're the ones that took the children away and left me without bullets."

DJ looked around the room to make sure everyone was listening. He directed his comment to Brandon to reinforce to the men that he was now in control. "Had I not witnessed that kid follow you back here, we'd be sitting in that tavern waiting to die." He paused to see if Brandon's face showed any sign of anger. "From now on, you do not leave my sight unless I say so!" It was not necessary to raise his voice; the punctuation was enough. Even though he hadn't used the words, the message was clear; disobey or die.

Brandon stood speechless neither accepting nor denying this new decree. DJ stared at him for several seconds before turning back to the window. The other men in the room didn't utter a word. Brandon had relinquished his control of them just as quickly as he had taken it from Mo. DJ, the new Alpha male in charge, was calling the shots, and it was clear what his expectations were.

"We'll leave the packs here. Take your rifles and plenty of ammo. Mouse and Postal, you'll steal up Main Street, preventing those men from escaping back this way. Find a dry spot on the other side of the next street and wait. The rest of us will follow those three."

The eight men exited the building, staying close to the wall until they saw the trio reappear crossing Fourth Avenue. It was as DJ had surmised; they were taking the side street into the downtown. He waited until he witnessed their disappearance behind a row of buildings before sending Mouse and Postal up Main. The heavy rain would help conceal any noise they made. He turned to the five men with him and said, "We'll run until we get to the end of that street. Once we're there, I'll move forward. If the coast is clear, I'll wave to you to move up. No one is to say anything. One slip-up can alarm them. If this happens, it's every man for his self. Is this clear?"

As if to show they agreed, no one said a sound. DJ, nervous with antici-pation, started out jogging across the street. Five men followed as they struggled to keep pace. The heavy rain helped to drown out the noise of their boots as they rumbled across Main and onto Fourth. They stayed close together not realizing that it made them an easier target. Their route was tortuous through the street filled with debris. Quite often someone would bump into a large piece of plastic or sheet metal, giving DJ cause to turn and throw a look of disapproval. Finally, DJ slowed and put up a hand to halt the other five as he moved forward a few steps. He peered up the street. Turning back to the men, he used his forefinger to signal them to move up.

Staying low, using cars as shields, they congregated behind the funeral home. DJ pointed his finger up the street, and in a hoarse breathless voice, he whispered, "Looks like they are about to get the drop on us."

They could see the three men a block up ahead, moving from car to car, slowly working their way along the mud covered street. Even if they couldn't see the men, their footprints in the muddy silt gave their route away. DJ allowed them to get a little further ahead before moving forward. He held up a hand as a silent message to the others not to follow yet. Then, he watched as one of the men split away and entered the alley. The other two stood in the rain for a few minutes before moving on to Second Avenue. Once they were around the corner, DJ waved his men to move up to his position.

"Okie," he whispered, "Follow the guy that went up this alley. Make sure he doesn't return."

When Okie was out of sight, DJ crept over to the corner of the cinder-block building and slowly peered around its corner. Cars pushed about by floodwaters were haphazardly scattered about Second Avenue. At first, he thought that he'd lost sight of the two remaining men—he couldn't see any sign except their footprints disappearing between some cars. As of now, the rain was as heavy as he had seen in a long time, remembrance of the monsoon like storms that preceded the Change. He motioned for Brandon and the other three to move up to the corner.

"I'm going up ahead alone," his voice virtually drowned out by the rain, hung in the air for minutes. "Stay two cars behind me until I stop. Then spread out so we have the street covered."

DJ squatted to keep his head low, crab-walking from car to car as he followed the disappearing muddy prints up the incline. Every few feet, the silt became visibly thinner until he could see wet asphalt beneath his feet. He caught a glimpse of a head briefly popping up just thirty feet ahead of him. DJ dropped onto his knees, peering beneath the car. Between the rows of flattened tires, he could see two pairs of boots moving out of his line of sight. They were very near the entrance to the tavern. He looked back and saw Brandon's head visible over the hood of the car behind him. It angered him that Brandon made no effort to stay hidden. Suddenly, Brandon raised his rifle and fired over DJ's head. The other two men, following Brandon's lead, opened fire as both the cars and the brick building were assaulted with a barrage of bullets.

DJ, trying to get a shot at his prey, found himself in the undesirable position between the shooters and the target. A bullet forced him back down when it ricocheted off a fender near his head. Whoever Brandon had been shooting at was now returning fire, and DJ was caught between the two sets of combatants. He cursed under his breath, swearing that Brandon would pay for this second mistake. Just then, shots from another location on Main Street could be heard. Was it Okie, or Mouse and Postal? The new battle was taking place maybe a hundred feet up to the left. DJ was thankful for the distraction because Brandon and the two others had stopped shooting for the moment. He got on all fours and began crawling down the hill to re-group with the others when the shooting started up one more time. Almost all the shots came from Brandon's side of the car, and DJ could see the barrels of their rifles following a fast-moving target up the street.

As soon as the firing stopped a second time, DJ ran around to their side of the car, grabbed Brandon by the coat, and shouted, "Who in the fuck told you to start shooting?"

164

Brandon had been standing in a row with the two other men. Their forearms resting on the bed of a pick-up, rifles pointed at the tavern. All three went wide-eyed when DJ suddenly appeared with rage upon his face and in his voice. Brandon was slammed against the side of the truck, making no attempt to defend himself.

DJ repeated his question, "Who told you to start shooting?"

Brandon ignored his question, simply replying, "They're in the tavern, and we have them boxed in."

DJ turned and looked up the street in time to see Okie crossing the intersection. His rifle pointed at the tavern's door. He was visibly limping; blood soaked the lower half of his right pant leg. Before DJ could get his attention, Okie fired two rounds into the open door before taking cover behind a downed power pole. Seeing that the three men they hunted were now hidden inside the brick building, DJ started barking orders at the three men with him. "One of you better get your ass up there and tie something around Okie's leg before he bleeds to death. Keep a rifle aimed at that open door and absolutely no shooting unless someone comes running out."

Brandon started to walk away when DJ grabbed his arm, jerked him back, furious with Brandon's refusal to respect his authority. "You are staying with me. That's twice now that you've almost gotten me killed. You and I are going to see if there are any droplets of blood outside that door. You better pray to God that you hit at least one of them."

Brandon followed DJ until they neared the dark doorway. Mouse and Postal were now walking toward them with their rifles ready. DJ flagged them to get out of the sight of the open door. Both men veered over to his side of the building.

"What the fuck happened?" asked Postal.

DJ tipped his head toward Brandon and said, "This dipshit opened fire before we were in position. All three made it inside here. The only way out is through this door and it doesn't appear we wounded any of them."

Brandon quickly retorted, "I had to shoot. I saw one of them aim their rifle at us."

DJ snapped back with the same anger he'd carried since the shooting started, "They didn't have a fucking clue that we were here. If they did, they wouldn't have begun an all-out assault on the tavern!"

Brandon held his tongue and lowered his eyes. He reached into his pocket, pulled out four bullets and began feeding them into the magazine.

"How many bullets do you have left?" asked DJ.

As nonchalantly as he could, Brandon answered without looking up. "Huh? Four, I think."

DJ shook his head in disgust. He didn't dare to ask the others how many bullets they'd fired. He didn't want to know. The rain was finally letting up. With two rifles aimed at the entrance, DJ had the remaining five men gather around him.

Okie asked, "Should we go ahead and burn them out?" His question intended as a suggestion.

There was silence for several seconds as DJ accessed this idea. Then Mouse spoke up, "Why don't we offer to let one of them leave. Whoever goes has to bring back a wagon loaded with food before we let the others go."

"That's stupid. What if they go get help and surround us?" stated Brandon.

DJ smiled. Brandon obviously wasn't using his head again. "It's not stupid. We won't really let one leave. As soon as he comes out, we hold a gun to his head and threaten to shoot him unless his friends drop their weapons and come out."

"What if they refuse?"

"We shoot him anyway. Then we'll only have two left to kill."

There were no looks of disapproval. DJ stepped closer to the door while keeping his back up against the bricks. He looked to see that two men were still lying behind the power pole with rifles aimed at the door. The rain had now quit completely. DJ knew it would be difficult for these men to stand around in wet clothes all day. He needed to end the stand-off as soon as possible. If they could get these men out of the tavern, there was a warm fire within waiting for them. Then, without these three to stop them, they'd have a much easier time raiding what houses were left up the road.

166

DJ leaned his head closer to the doorway and shouted, "Hey, if you guys would like a chance to live, we'll make you an offer."

Almost a full minute of silence passed before a voice from within the dark room asked, "What's your offer?"

"We'll let one of you leave unarmed. Whoever goes has to bring back thirty jars of food. If you do, we'll let all three of you go."

Another silence followed this last statement, only this time it took longer for a response. The same voice as before shouted from the back of the tavern. "Go fuck yourself! We'll stay here and wait for our friends to arrive."

As chilled as he was beginning to feel, DJ was still able to muster up a wry smile. As long as these three couldn't leave the confines of the tavern, there wasn't anything to stop DJ's men from taking what they wanted from their houses. Finding something dry enough to burn them out would be near impossible at the moment. He walked back over to Brandon and said, "Time for you to make yourself useful again. How far is the first house from here?"

"Maybe fifteen minutes."

"Listen up!" He looked until all seven had their eyes pointed in his direction. "I want Okie and Mouse to change into some dry clothes and return back here. Your job will be to keep these three busy while the rest of us pays a visit to their house."

It was a half-hour later before Mouse and Okie arrived back and resumed their position behind the power pole. Okie's wound was only to the flesh of his right calf, needing nothing more than a dressing. The sun finally cut through the clouds. Its warmth was welcomed by those still covered in sodden clothes. The three hidden in the confines of the tavern had not been heard from since the offer had been rejected. While DJ waited for Mouse and Okie to return, he fired a bullet into the dark open doorway once every ten minutes. A reminder of what waited outside should they decide to come rushing out.

He looked at the motley two that were staying behind. "Don't take your eyes off the open door. Fire a shot into the tavern once every ten or fifteen minutes. That way, I'll know that things haven't changed. If I hear more than that, we can be back down here in a matter of minutes."

DJ led the other five men back up the street to where they'd left the bicycles. He intentionally kept Brandon close at hand, not only because of his knowledge of the area, but also because of his lack of trust. He would have just as soon killed him on the spot for that last error if it wasn't for the fact that he was the only one that knew where two of the houses were. He cursed himself for not having him make some kind of a map. DJ had already decided that as soon as Brandon was no longer useful, he would be terminated.

CHAPTER 18

April 6th, 2031
7:55 am

Skyler estimated that it had been at least a half hour since James, McBride and Brent had left before he heard the first sounds of gunfire. From his distance, the reports were barely audible in the heavy rain. He was nervous, uncertain of what scenarios could play, what could go wrong. He'd given up waiting inside. Instead, he stood under the outside stairs, out of the rain, and listened. His hope was that they would return without conflict, having found that the bandits had moved on. Hearing the explosive, even though muffled, gunfire disintegrated what little hope he had for an uncomplicated mission.

He estimated that following the first shot, there had been up to twenty-five rounds of gunfire exchanged in the first minute of the firefight. After that, another small hail of five or six shots was followed by silence. At first, he wondered if it was over. Then several minutes later, another single round was fired, followed by several more minutes of silence. Skyler was torn as to what he should do. The not knowing was gnawing at him; what seemed like seconds, turned into minutes, and then into what felt like hours. Waiting became a hidden terror that ate at him from the inside. Should he venture down the hill for a glimpse of what might be happening or run to the top of Church, collect whoever was willing to join him in an unplanned rescue attempt? He wasn't even sure if his friends needed to be rescued. However, the amount of shots, and the subsequent single rounds told him that the raid had not gone as planned.

As he stood with rain water dripping off his parka, a lone bicycle appeared entering the cul-de-sac at a fast speed. Instinctively, Skyler had an arrow nocked and drawn in a second. At the speed it was moving, the cyclist could only have come from the hill above. It stopped briefly at the logs before clearing the obstacle and continuing on. Skyler relaxed the string and pointed the arrow downward. The rider was dressed in heavy rain gear, making it impossible to recognize who it was until he dismounted before him. It was Ian.

"Petar sent me. He thought he heard shots coming from the town."

"Ian, you don't know how glad I am to see you. I don't know what is happening. James, Brent, and McBride went down into town after you and Lydia took the kids up the hill."

"Why would they do that?" His tone insinuated his disapproval.

"After you crossed the road this morning, James spotted someone spying on us. I went out and found the man just before he returned to town. I followed him and was able to locate the building where the rest of this bicycle gang was hidden." He took a deep breath before giving a full report of the events as he knew them. "Brent and McBride wanted to attack right away, saying that if they didn't, the bandits would eventually come up here and come after us. They convinced James to go with them saying that there wasn't time to get more help. Judging by the amount of shots fired, I don't think it went as planned."

Ian assumed a protective, almost fatherly stance. "I need to run back up the hill and alert the others. I want you to come with me."

"I can't and I don't want to leave here without knowing what is happening down in the town."

"How are you going to find out? Are you planning on going down there?"

"No, that would be stupid. I just want to wait a little longer. I'll walk with you out to the road and if James doesn't return within the hour, I'll come up the hill."

Ian reluctantly agreed, picked up his bike, and the two of them walked briskly out to Main Street. At the intersection, he was about to throw his leg over the bike's frame when he saw Skyler staring down the street. "What is it?"

"Quick, get off the road! There's a group of bikes coming this way!"

Ian did what he was told and backed the bike up. "Could it be James and the others?"

Skyler was leaning his head out using the row of houses to shield him from being seen. "No, there's too many of them. This isn't good."

They watched the small cluster until they were sure that they were headed in their direction. When they were just over a half-mile down the slope, Skyler said, "You better not go back up the hill. They'll see you and might follow you. Let's go back to the house. If they come in here, we can escape out the back."

Both took off at a fast pace for the house. Skyler took the stairs two at a time with Ian surprisingly close behind. Both immediately rounded up what weapons were left behind. Skyler had Ian carry James' bow and the small .22 pistol, while he grabbed the .22 rifle and the rest of the arrows.

"Follow me downstairs," said Skyler. "We'll need to open up the back door."

The downstairs shutters had been recently modified to allow some light in. Skyler could see his way around without the aid of candle light. They entered the bedroom where Brent and Lydia had been staying. Skyler unlocked and slid the large glass door open. It was covered with two sheets of plywood positioned to allow light to enter through the top six inches.

"You push on that side while I push on this," Skyler directed him.

They almost pitched forward through the opening as the plywood fell away.

"Where to now?" asked Ian.

Skyler handed him his bow and quiver. "Hold this; I'm going to buy us some time. When I run back here, we'll drop down the hill and cut over behind the new place. From there, we should be able to work our way up to Church Road without being seen."

"Wait a minute. What are you going to do?"

"Just fire a few rounds at them. That should keep them back long enough to allow us to escape."

Ian had a look on his face like he was about to protest, but Skyler turned and darted back up the stairs before he could utter a word. At the top of the stairs, he ducked into the kitchen and quickly glanced in the pantry. There were only four full jars of carrots and beets remaining—just enough to make these bandits think they'd found their stash. He ran to the front door in time to see six men on bikes turn off Main Street. Skyler waited until they stopped at the logs. Stepping partially out the front door, he raised the .22 to his shoulder, and opened fire. At this distance, it would be pure luck to hit someone and even greater odds at making a fatal wound. What it did was to force the six men to dive for the scarce cover provided by the logs. Skyler immediately bolted down the stairs, taking three at a time, landing in the basement, just as the bandits returned fire. Bullets ripped through the walls of the upper floor. Skyler and Ian wasted no time as they stole out the back door.

Running through the tall grass, Skyler said to Ian, "I'll bet it will be twenty minutes or more before they make it close to the house."

The older man remained quiet as they made their way along the trail, cutting below the frame of the new house. When they reached the bottom where a large stand of trees had once stood, they stopped long enough for Skyler to re-load the .22. From here, they would need to climb a small, yet steep hill. A rising path before them was the one critical place where they could be seen if the bandits had moved closer to the house. Skyler wanted a full magazine before making the twenty-yard dash. Yet, he felt sure that the bandits would still be hugging the ground behind the logs. Other than the initial barrage of gunfire, the bandits had not fired any more shots. As they reached the apex of the trail, neither Ian nor Skyler could see any sign of anyone approaching the house just yet. Their gambit was working.

Ian clapped him on the shoulder and said, "Nice job of making them nervous."

Upon reaching Main Street, both had to be careful before they could consider crossing the road. The bandits' position, only a hundred yards down the hill, was hidden by a rise in the terrain. Skyler couldn't be sure that they wouldn't back out of their current location and try coming in from another direction. When they were sure it was clear, he and Ian ran across together, dropping into the ditch along Church. Another shot rang out from the area of the downtown. "So someone is still alive down there," Skyler thought to himself.

With their heads down, they made haste climbing up the steep hill. Skyler was truly impressed with Ian's ability to keep up with him. He realized that the older man must have stayed athletic all of his life because he wasn't slow by any means. When they neared the barricade, Petar stepped out and directed them behind the logs.

"What's happening?" he asked Skyler.

Petey was with Petar, carrying the large crossbow that he was so fond of. Skyler quickly caught his breath and recounted the turn of events since early that morning.

At the beginning of the story, Petar looked shaken. He listened patiently before asking him, "Do you have any idea if Brent, McBride or James are still alive?"

The reality of the question made Skyler swallow hard. He hadn't taken the time to ponder this most painful scenario. "I think that at least one of them has to be. I hear a single gunshot once about every ten to fifteen minutes. It makes me think that they have someone pinned down and their able to prevent them from escaping. The way those bandits came riding in, it looked like they assumed no one was home. My guess is that James and the others are pinned down, so these six others thought they had a free run of the place."

"Let's hope you're right. We've got to think of some way to get down into town and help them before it's too late. Without Brent and McBride, we don't have a chance of going up against that many armed men."

"We still have the Lopatnikovs and the Jensens. I can make it over to their farms and be back within the hour. If I can get them to help, we will have enough."

"Do you think that they'll help us? It's not even their fight."

"Eventually, it will be. That's how I'm going to pitch it."

CHAPTER 19

April 6ᵗʰ, 2031
11:45 am

It took a half-hour for DJ and his men to get within a stone's throw of the house. Not knowing what lay before them made them apprehensive about moving in closer. They hadn't expected a teenage boy to come out shooting—another error that DJ blamed Brandon for. As quickly as he appeared, the boy disappeared, a reminder that if they were to take this house, they would have to be willing to risk getting shot at again. DJ had to wonder if the boy had been shot during the return fire, or if he somehow escaped. His greatest fear was that he lay in wait at the top of the stairs, or worse yet, there was more than one shooter waiting for them to move closer.

"Brandon, since you were the one that said that we could walk right in, how 'bout you being the first one up those stairs?" DJ's statement was more of a demand than a question.

"I'll go first, but I want a rifle with more than four bullets in it," he answered. Brandon had felt nothing but anger and disgust come from DJ since early that morning. Accepting the challenge might just buy him a little respect, a first step in regaining control over this group.

The six men were scattered within sixty yards of the northern side of the house. Since there was no cover to use, they stayed apart, keeping their rifles aimed at the house at all times. DJ instructed Postal to swap rifles with Brandon. If someone armed was lying in wait and popped Brandon, it would serve two purposes for DJ—getting rid of Brandon, a burr in his side, and establishing a better idea of what they were facing. He suspected that Brandon secretly wanted them killed. Why else would he have led them to Ferndale? There were too many close calls in the past several hours. The only reason Brandon had been accepted into the group was because he'd killed Mo. Could this trip here have been a ruse to lead them into a trap?

In full daylight, Brandon stood, and sprinted for the north side of the house. He took refuge at a three-foot section of wall between two of the three garage doors. He was no longer visible to anyone watching from a window. With the others watching, Brandon reached for the handle of the door farthest from the stairway. Giving it a tug, but as he suspected, it was locked from within. Brandon was careful about not standing directly in front of a door, having figured out that anyone within would see his shadow crossing the bottom crack between the door and the concrete. The thin aluminum door would not offer him any protection. Brandon ran for the next pillar of wall and tried the middle door before moving on to the last. Finding all three doors locked meant that he would now be forced to use the stairs.

As the others watched, rifles trained at the deck, Brandon crawled up the stairs. He would have to pass under a large boarded window before he could reach the top. Brandon hugged the shadows, attempting to conceal his location. Upon reaching the deck, he leaned over and placed his ear against the wall. He held it there for over a minute before reaching into a pocket and throwing a rock down the length of the deck. Seconds later, he stood and ran into the partially open door. As they looked on, no sounds came from within the house.

Brandon finally reappeared, fully standing outside the door; his rifle relaxed. He scanned the area until he spotted DJ. "Come on up," he yelled, not a little boastful. He wanted to send a message that he was the reason this stand-off had ended. "Whoever was here has escaped out the back door."

DJ had two of the men stay outside to watch for any sign of trouble. A scattering of clouds was still apparent, but it hadn't rained for over an hour. DJ led the way up the stairs. He entered the house, letting out a low whistle as he looked over the leather couches and the large open window facing south. "Whoever *lived* here has it made," he said to no one in particular. "Look around guys. This is our new house, so don't ruin anything."

Brandon led DJ down the inside flight of stairs to show him the back door. The plywood cover was ripped from its nails; the large glass door still open. They both stepped out onto the patio with rifle barrels leading the way. The possibility of a trap still existed, which was foremost in their minds. From here, DJ could see most of the gardens and wondered, ignorantly, if he should take over the task of cultivating what they had planted. Then he thought about the harvesting and canning, realizing he didn't know enough about it. It would be much easier just to take someone else's food.

Brandon wandered to the back of the yard before the hill fell away to the flat valley below. Off to their right was a framed structure, something that had to be fairly new since it couldn't have survived through the winter winds. As he glanced around, DJ asked him, "What are you looking for?"

"I was wondering if I could see a trail, but there are too many ways that he could have gone."

"Which way do you think he ran?" asked DJ.

"Up that steep road," Brandon pointed in the opposite direction at Church, the top half of it just visible past a tangle of dead trees and debris. "Somebody must be living up there. That's where that group went early this morning."

DJ glanced up at the road but said nothing. The steepness would dictate a slow ascent; not something you wanted when you were the attacker. It also meant that whoever lived up there could come down quickly—too quickly.

Brandon glanced up at the rear of the large house and added, "We'll need to place a guard on the deck. Whoever was here could be planning on coming back after dark."

DJ jerked his head toward Brandon, "Please don't think that we'll be taking orders from you, especially after what's happened today."

The tension in the air suddenly became noticeable. Brandon didn't reply to DJ's statement simply because there was no reason to escalate this into a confrontation. He had hoped that being the first one to enter the house had repaired the bridge between the two, but it obviously hadn't. The sound of another round being fired off from the town below was enough to cause DJ to change the subject.

"We need to find some kind of combustible material so we can burn those guys out. The sooner we get rid of them, the faster we can get on with collecting food from that farm. You start by looking in the garage. Let me know if you find something we can use. Meanwhile, I'm going to see what kind of food these people left us."

Upon entering the house, Brandon stepped into the garage. DJ turned and went back up the stairs. One of the men already laid out the contents of the pantry on the kitchen counter. There was only a handful of Mason jars containing carrots. Also found were a few containers of tea, coffee, spices, and some flour. Upon seeing this DJ ordered the other two in the room, "We need to search every nook and cranny in this house. There is no way they could exist until the fall harvest on just this. They must have more food stashed somewhere. There could be a hollowed out box spring mattress or a hidden space in a floor or wall. Just find it."

Both men turned and went into separate rooms. Brandon came running up the stairs carrying a one-gallon metal can with the words 'Paint Thinner' on the label. He shook it in front of DJ showing him that it was almost half full.

"That'll work if we use it correctly. We'll need to find a large bottle and turn it into Molotov cocktail. Once it starts burning inside that old tavern, they'll either have to come running out or burn to death." He took the can from Brandon without saying thanks or acknowledging that he had come through again.

It wasn't until the search for food had moved downstairs, that one of the men had removed the filter on the furnace. He got the credit for discovering over a hundred jars filled with various vegetables. DJ lifted a few out to see what they held within and smiled when he saw that carrots weren't going to be the only course for dinner that night. He collected four jars and carried them upstairs to be placed with the others.

Brandon returned to the garage to search for a bottle. He returned carrying an old one liter champagne bottle. DJ took it from him without expressing any gratitude.

Taking a strip of cloth from a curtain, DJ stuffed the end into the bottle to test the fit. Satisfied, he turned to Brandon and said, "Give me your lighter."

With only a little hesitation, Brandon reached into his pocket and fished it out. He handed it to DJ without looking directly into his eyes.

"I want everyone upstairs in here for a minute," DJ announced loudly.

The two men standing guard outside were summoned to listen in as well. Soon, all six men were standing in the living room.

"I want four of you to go back down into town to help Okie and Mouse finish those fuckers off. Fill this bottle to the top with this paint thinner," he held the can up for everyone to see, "and stuff this rag into the top. Once the rag is damp, light the rag and toss it inside the tavern. Be sure to throw it hard so the glass breaks and the liquid spreads out. Once the fire's going, they'll either have to run out or burn to death"

He looked about at the five men before asking, "Any questions?"

Not one of them responded, so DJ continued, "Nobody is to leave there until those three men are out of the way. Brandon and I will stay here and make sure no one returns for the food. Once your job is finished, grab your gear and haul your asses back up to this place. We'll have plenty to eat here. This is where we will be staying for now."

DJ handed the champagne bottle, the paint thinner, rag, and lighter over to Postal and asked, "You know what to do with this?"

"Yeah, nobody is getting away."

As the others moved out onto the deck, DJ grabbed Postal by the arm and kept him inside until they were out of earshot from the others. "If you hear a single gunshot come from here, don't come running. I have a little business to take care of once you leave. Tell the others for me."

Postal nodded before following the others out the door and down the stairs. DJ joined Brandon on the deck, watching as the four men mounted their bicycles and peddled out to Main. Once they made the turn, the bikes quickly picked up speed on the downgrade and disappeared.

"Go find a chair and make yourself comfortable. I want you to keep an eye out for anyone coming down that hill," DJ said. "I'm going to watch the back in case someone tries to sneak up on us from that way. As soon as those guys finish and get back up here, I'll feel much safer."

DJ watched as Brandon went inside and grabbed one of the dining room chairs, carrying it out onto the deck. The sun had just peeked through the clouds again, finally adding some warmth to the afternoon. Brandon took his damp coat off and laid it over the rail to dry. He sat with his back toward the area where DJ had placed his chair.

DJ didn't really expect that anyone would ride down the hill with the intent of reclaiming ownership of this house. He wanted Brandon to be occupied. As soon as he was sure that the three in the tavern had been silenced, he was going to place a bullet in the back of Brandon's head. The boy had made too many mistakes, having nearly cost them their lives. First, he allowed someone to follow him back. Then he blew the attack at the tavern by shooting before they were ready. The final straw was leading them into an ambush at this house when he was sure that nobody would be here guarding it. The only reason he'd let Brandon live this long was that he might need the extra eyes until the rest of the men returned. Finding the other houses in the area would have to be done without Brandon's help.

From this house to the downtown area, DJ figured that it should only take about five minutes to get there by bicycle. DJ calculated that after dropping their bikes off, it was less than a three-minute walk to where Mouse and Okie were sitting. The occasional single shot signifying that nothing had changed came moments after the four rode away. Allowing enough time for Postal to update the others, he expected to see smoke within twenty minutes. The time he'd chosen to turn his rifle at Brandon would be when he saw the smoke.

DJ stood briefly, shedding his damp clothes and laying them out to soak up the sun's warmth. He glanced at the house and gardens; this was much better than the hospital where they'd stayed for the last year. There was no love lost the day that Mo was killed. That was the only good thing Brandon had accomplished. Mo was not an exemplary leader, not by any standard. He was lazy in that he didn't want to go out hunting for food. Instead, he waited for it to come to him. Because of this, they suffered through several periods of up to three or four days without anything to eat. Mo had also been unforgiving—if you crossed him, you would die. The men around him lived in fear. Had Brandon not shot him, somebody else would have. Now that he was in command, DJ had to be careful not to make those same mistakes. Keep these men happy and maybe they'd allow him to live.

Without a watch, DJ could only guess at how many minutes had passed since the others left. Only once had Brandon turned to ask a question. DJ responded by asking him to shut up. Irritated by Brandon's stupidity, he was intent on hearing any noises that might come from the downtown area, not wanting to miss anything. Time seemed to crawl as they watched and waited. Twice since they'd left, the periodical shots were fired. Several more minutes passed since the last one and there still wasn't any sign of smoke. Another shot rang out, only this time; it lacked the volume of the other shots. This caught DJ's attention. He stood as if it would allow him to hear more clearly. Then suddenly, there was a barrage of shooting going on. Both DJ and Brandon were on their feet glancing at one another. Several shots were exchanged before silence dominated again. DJ scanned the valley for any sign of smoke and found nothing. Again, a few more shots were fired followed by more silence. It was now apparent that it had not gone as planned.

DJ paced the deck as he tried to decipher the events that had just taken place. His hope was that his men would have easily handled those three, even if they came out running all at once. Had they missed the entrance with the Molotov? Whatever had gone down, there was no fire and there was no more shooting. He didn't dare abandon this place to go searching for answers. If either of them went into town, they could be walking into an ambush. No matter what scenario took place down there, their only choice was to stay here and wait to see who came up from the town.

This also meant that Brandon had earned a reprieve—for now.

CHAPTER 20

April 6ᵗʰ, 2031
12:30 pm

Knowing that both Lara and Lydia would be thirsty for any information, Ian sprinted for the house. Skyler had given him James' bow and .22 to carry. He didn't have the time to stop at the house. He needed to reach Thornton Road. Brandy would be wondering why he hadn't stopped, even if for only for a moment. Explanations would have to wait. For now, he was intent on reaching both the Lopatnikovs and Jensens.

Passing by the northern log barricade, Skyler was soon running up Thornton, jumping over downed power poles like they were hurdles. The Lopatnikov's farm, maybe a mile from the Church Road intersection, was just over the crest of the hill from the town. If they had heard any shots, surely they would have sent someone to investigate. Skyler now wished he'd gone to see them sooner. Their strength and numbers were his only hope. He felt a pang of guilt for wanting to stay until James returned.

Reaching the driveway, Skyler reminded himself to throw his bow over his back as a sign that he wasn't an aggressor. He remembered their pact about the red arm bands and wondered why no one, including himself, had followed through with this. Their security usually consisted of a lone sentry with a shotgun. Whoever had that duty took guarding this farm seriously. Even then, most all the men kept weapons handy no matter where they worked on the farm. As much as he wanted to continue to run, Skyler forced himself to walk up the gravel drive. It wasn't long before he heard the distinct sound of someone coming out of the bushes behind him to escort him in. He turned his head only once and recognized one of Dimitrey's uncles.

Someone else must have detected his arrival because Dimitrey and his father stood on the porch as he approached the house.

"I'm sorry to interrupt your day, but there has been trouble."

Dimitrey translated what Skyler had said to his father. As soon as the words came out of his mouth, all the men within earshot had dropped what they were doing to listen in. The older Russian wasted no time in dictating instructions to his son.

"My father wishes to know what has happened and why you have come here. Before he agrees to anything, he wants to know everything."

"Tell your father that a band of men, maybe seven or eight, came into Ferndale. James, Brent and John McBride rode down early this morning to corner them in a building and offer them the chance to walk away without their guns. Something went wrong, and they didn't come back." At this point, he paused to make sure that what he said was true and in order. "I think they are trapped somewhere downtown because someone has been shooting down there since this morning. Then, just an hour ago, six bandits with bicycles rode up to our house and forced me to leave out the back. I don't know if they stayed or returned to the town."

Dimitrey translated once again, and everyone listened intently. When he finished, all the men clustered together and spoke rapidly. One of them picked up his rifle and shook it as if trying to make a point. Finally, Dimitrey's father spoke to his son, but all the while he was looking at Skyler. This time it was briefer than before.

"My father wants to know what you want from us."

"I need help getting James and the others out of Ferndale if they are still alive. This needs to happen as soon as we can possibly get down there."

Again, following Dimitrey's translation, the men went into a huddle, conversing excitedly. This time it appeared more like they were arguing with one another. This went on for what seemed like minutes before, one by one, they were silenced either by satisfaction or seniority. The old man, all the time looking at Skyler, dispensed his final decree to his son.

"My father says that four of our family will help you. What do you need us to do?"

Skyler guessed that it was now early afternoon. The sun cut through the clouds revealing its position. It would be dark in five hours or less. It wouldn't be wise to launch an attack without preparation. "Tell them to be at the house on Church just before dark tonight. I'm going to scout out the downtown. When I return, we will be able to plan an attack. I must leave now and go see the Jensen's."

Before Dimitrey finished telling his father, Skyler was already running back down the driveway. Only at the last moment had he decided to reconnoiter the town to locate the bandits. Without knowing their whereabouts, he could be leading Dimitrey's family into an ambush. He also needed to know if there was any possibility that James and the others were still alive. For now, unless he had proof otherwise, he assumed that they were trapped and needed help escaping from their captors.

Approaching the Jensen farm still made him nervous. Then he saw Dag. The old man was outside tilling the soil with the others. They raised their heads when he entered driveway, but no displayed a weapon.

"Skyler, what brings you up here?" asked Dag Jensen.

Skyler had not seen the old man this healthy since the previous fall, yet his face showed the toll of his many years. He also noticed how quickly he leaned against his rake when he had the opportunity. "There has been some trouble. Bandits have moved into the downtown. Now I'm afraid that they are holding Brent, James, and John McBride prisoner somewhere."

"How many are there?" asked Dag. Like the Lopatnikovs, the others stopped working, taking an instant interest in the conversation.

"Seven or eight, we haven't been able to get an accurate count since they arrived."

"What do you know for sure?"

Dag's question sounded almost challenging to Skyler. He had to be careful with his answers, or he would lose the chance of enlisting their help. "Not much except that the Lopatnikovs have said that they'll help. As soon as I leave here, I need to make a quick trip to the edge of town to see if I can locate James and the others. I'll also need to see what we're up against. We'll attempt a rescue the rescue after dark."

"So, regardless of whether or not we'll help, you are still planning on trying to rescue them tonight?"

"Yeah, that's the plan," answered Skyler.

Carl looked at the old man and said, "I know what you're thinking Dag, but we can't afford to lose another person. I don't see how we can help and still guard this place."

"I haven't made any decision yet Carl. I know how vulnerable we are, but I also know how much more vulnerable we'll be if these men aren't stopped."

Skyler felt a wave of relief sweep over him. The old man hadn't confirmed that they'd help, but he did confirm that they should do something. He quickly jumped in with a suggestion. "What if one of you came over to guard the house on Church Road? That way, Petar would be freed up to help us. As it stands, without McBride there, he won't leave his house unguarded."

The old man smiled and said, "You can count on us for that. Expect one of us to arrive before dark."

Skyler thanked them for their time and understanding. His anxiety had been mounting as the sun drew closer to the horizon. Satisfied with what he gained in such a short time, he bid them good-bye and quickly took off back up the road. His next stop, intended to be as brief as possible, was to see Lara, Lydia and Brandy. They needed to be alerted to what had and what might happen. He was sure that both Lara and Lydia would be distraught after finding out that the men in their lives were missing. As

186

he ran, he thought about what he could do to reduce their fears. His only answer was to find James and Brent alive.

By the time, he turned onto Church and made his way past the barricade, the shadows on the road had lengthened. The sun, both his ally and enemy, would disappear within a couple of hours: twilight would last maybe an hour before it became fully dark. Knowing that the bandits probably occupied their house near Main, Skyler knew that on this reconnaissance mission, to avoid detection, he would have to stay off the roads. Maybe on the way back, the darkness would allow him to follow the roads.

Just before Skyler reached the street that led to Petar's house, Joe, Joel and Brandy stood up from nowhere and had their weapons drawn and aimed at him.

"Whoa, I'm a good guy!" he quickly shouted. He noticed that both boys carried the homemade crossbows.

Brandy lowered her arrow. "We knew that, I just wanted to show you that we had the drop on you. These two guys have learned a lot from you. I'm especially impressed with their crossbows."

"I don't have a lot of time, so I need to hurry. Can Joe and Joel stay here to watch the road while you follow me down to the house? I need to let everyone know what is going to happen tonight. Expect at least five men to pass through here. They are coming to help us get the others back tonight."

Brandy stepped out from behind the pile of dead limbs as the two boys sank back down and disappeared. She turned to Skyler and in a low voice asked, "How bad is it?"

"I don't know. Brent and McBride are experienced soldiers, and I'm hoping that this has helped them. I need to make a scouting trip down there before it's totally dark and see if I can figure out what's happening in town."

Nearing the yard, Skyler had her postpone the questions until they were inside. They were met inside the door by Lara; her eyes red and swollen, she'd obviously been waiting for him. Lydia came up behind her, placing a gentle hand on her shoulder.

"What happened?" she sobbed.

Skyler had expected her to be upset but wasn't prepared for this. She was truly fearful and worried. "I think James, Brent, and McBride are being pinned down by one or two men in town. I need to go down there to see if I can locate them. Six men took the house from Ian and me just this afternoon. This makes me think that there must be at least two men still in town. There were shots fired at something down there all morning. This is why I can assume that they are still alive."

Lydia stepped forward and said, "While we were waiting for you, there were several shots fired over a period of ten minutes. Since then, it's been quiet."

"All the more reason I need to get down there now. If James and the others get free and try to go home, they probably won't know that bandits have occupied our house. Four of the Lopatnikovs are coming to help later this evening. Dag Jensen said that one of his family members would come here and guard this place while Petar helps us."

Brandy reached for Skyler's hand and squeezed it before running back out the door. She was obviously going to pass the word to the two pairs that were guarding the road.

"That means that there'll only be six of you doing the rescue?" Lara's statement was more like a question.

"Yeah, but, hopefully the element of surprise will be on our side. Maybe James and the others can help us."

Before Lara could question him further, Skyler gathered a rucksack and packed it with some food and water. Only then did he realize that he hadn't eaten or drunken any water that day. He dropped his bag on the kitchen table and poured out half a bowl of carrots and a tall glass of water, downing it like a starved man. This would have to sustain him until he came back. The supplies in his rucksack might be needed for James and the others should the opportunity arise.

As he threw his pack over his shoulder, Lara reappeared in the doorway. They looked at each other for a long moment; no words were necessary. Skyler sensed both her fear and frustration of not knowing what the future might hold as equal only to his own. Finally, Lara stepped aside, allowing her friend to exit the house.

Pulling open the front door, he said, "I'll be back in two or three hours." Lara and Lydia stood side by side, watching him as he left. He was doing this not only for them, but for their whole community. They had to get their men back and as soon as possible. If James and the others were still alive, the longer they were in town, the odds of their survival diminished. If they didn't return, the three families that made up the Ferndale sector would probably not survive to see the next winter.

Instead of heading toward Church Road, Skyler went deeper into the development. He knew of a trail, seldom used, that would keep him hidden until he reached the edge of town. From there, he would alone and in the open.

CHAPTER 21

Their reaction to the only offer they received for freedom—that one of them could leave and return with thirty jars of food, caused a heated argument between the three men. James was the most upset that his co-captives wouldn't even deliberate the notion.

"Why can't we at least talk about it?" he pleaded with McBride and Brent.

"Because they're lying! What do they have to gain by allowing us to go free?" answered Brent. His frustration with James was not well hidden.

"Think about this," barked McBride. "They let you out of here, and one of them follows you home. You collect your thirty jars and when you come out, he shoots you in the back. These are bandits, not gentlemen. Once they know where you live and how much food you have, it will all be over with."

That last statement brought James back to reality. As much as trusting these men had gotten him into this situation, he needed to trust them to get him out.

An hour after taking refuge in the tavern, all three men were spread out with rifles pointed at the open door; aware that an all-out assault could be expected at any moment. Instead, once every ten to fifteen minutes, a bullet would pass over their heads only to lodge itself in the wall or ceiling beams. It was now apparent that their captor's intentions were to wait for them to come out.

"What do we have for food and water?" asked McBride, the irritation in his voice unmistakable.

Both James and Brent glanced at each other before Brent took the initiative to answer, "Nothing. We didn't pack a goddamn thing."

James lowered his head briefly. He was the lone holdout who didn't favor this raid until they enlisted more help. The blame for this was his; he allowed the other two to persuade him not to wait and to come along. Now, regardless of how he felt, pointing fingers was futile. He sincerely hoped that Brent's and McBride's attitudes weren't going to elevate into something they'd be sorry for later. That is, if they made it out of this mess.

McBride waited until the next round came through the door before he stood and walked to the back of the room. He showed no concern that several people had them cornered and wanted them dead. He looked at the metal and glass door that led to the fire escape. The stairway behind it sat between this building the adjacent one. The roof of the neighboring building had been ripped from its trusses and deposited on the fire escape. Since the door opened outward, there would be no way to open it. They could break out the glass window and start dismantling the large section of roofing, but they still wouldn't be able to get past the rest of it. Not to mention what would happen once they hit the street only yards away from where the bandits had rifles trained on them.

"The only way out of here is through the front," he exclaimed to no one in particular.

Both James and Brent kept their rifles aimed at the doorway while McBride inspected the rest of the aging interior. The only windows sat up high, difficult to get at. If they were able to point a rifle out one of these, the bandits could merely shoot through the wall to halt the attack. Once again, McBride's attention went to the front door. He dropped down onto his belly and began crawling head first across the tavern floor. Brent raised his head to say something, but was cut short when McBride raised his palm signaling silence. He continued his crawl until he was twenty feet from the open door. He stayed in that position even when the next round was sent to remind them that they were prisoners. Whoever had fired that shot had no idea that one of them lay prone on the floor watching their every move.

After fifteen minutes of spying on their captors, McBride crawled backwards until he was far enough into the dark room to stand.

"See anything?" James asked.

"They can't see in here. All they can see is a dark hole. I counted eight of them in that short time. A couple of them left, so for now, there are only six."

"Do you think we can take them?" asked Brent.

"No, four of them are positioned behind some power poles. If we were to rush out of here, we'd be sitting ducks."

"So what can we do?" James asked.

"Watch and wait. At some point, they'll leave themselves exposed. We wait for our opportunity to reduce their numbers."

James acted content with that answer, but he had suppressed the urge to ask 'what if'. He wasn't a former battle hardened soldier like these other two. This 'do or die' situation, then getting out alive, would require their knowledge and experience.

McBride dropped into a prone position and crawled back to the same place in which to view the proceedings outside. Using hand signals, he kept James and Brent informed when the two missing bandits returned and the other six left the scene. The two that returned had taken positions behind the logs.

James became instantly concerned; where were the other six going? Their house was maybe a mile up the road with only Skyler there to guard it. He thought about the boy. He was smart. He would have figured out by now that the mission had not gone awry. Skyler must have heard the many shots fired—too many for a successful attack. The continuous shots that came periodically through the door had to alert him that it was far from over. He trusted Skyler. If those men found their house, Skyler wouldn't be caught.

They waited for what seemed like hours before a flurry of activity caught McBride's attention. He rose up slightly, straining to hear what the bandits were saying. The bright sun highlighted the scene outside the tavern. Without turning his head, McBride raised four fingers signaling that four of the six had returned. Then he frantically motioned for Brent to crawl over next to him.

"It sounds like they are planning on burning us out," McBride whispered.

As both men watched, one of the bandits, standing, poured a clear liquid into a large green bottle. Another man, also standing, held the bottle steady. McBride dropped his face down and took aim with his rifle. Brent mirrored his position.

"I'll take out the thrower if you get the one standing with him," McBride whispered.

Not knowing what to do, James started inching toward the other two when Brent turned to him, shaking his head before returning to the scope. Retreating back a few steps, James attained his former position, rifle pointed at the lighted doorway. Seconds ticked by as he watched the two men on the floor lay still and focused.

McBride fired first with Brent's shot less than a second behind his. The loudness startled James despite his preparedness. Both men managed to squeeze off a few more rounds before scrambling from the floor and retreating to the back of the room. Screams from one of the bandits could be heard. Bullets came in through the open door, this time aimed lower than before. Someone outside fired repeatedly, forcing the three men to take cover alongside the stone fireplace. It was as if those few shots they fired had stirred up a hornet's nest. Bullets thudded into the wood all around them, but none found their mark. The bandits were angry over what had just taken place, and it showed.

"What the hell happened out there?" James asked in a hushed tone.

Brent smiled, "They made a Molotov cocktail. John waited until they lit it before he shot the bottle. It exploded in their faces. I shot the guy lighting it while McBride tagged the thrower as he tried to put out the flames. Two others had caught fire, but whatever fuel they used was pretty weak. I know we killed at least two."

McBride confirmed this with a nod and added, "We won't get the opportunity to move that close to the door again. Hopefully, someone has heard the shots and is mounting a rescue attempt. We'll have to be ready to charge out of here if those four are attacked from behind."

The rest of the afternoon and evening stayed calm except for the random bullet aimed at no one in particular. The tension between the three had dissipated after successfully reducing the number of their captors. Early on, adrenaline replaced the desire for food or water. Hunger and thirst gnawed at their hope. To their relief, the bandits abandoned any more attempts to create fire bombs. When darkness finally engulfed the street, McBride crawled near the opening and watched out the door briefly before retreating.

"They are all well hidden behind the logs," he reported to the others. "I think they're afraid to stand after that last attack."

"I've been thinking," whispered Brent. "Sometime in the middle of the night, we rush out of here and just run for it. By the time they figure it out, they'll have difficulty shooting at us in the dark."

"How about if you and James run," answered McBride. "I'll stay at the door and shoot at anyone who stands. Once you are in the clear, regroup and attack them on the other side of the logs. I think we'll have a better chance that way."

Both James and Brent agreed, staying in this place any longer lacked appeal. If McBride could force the bandits to stay down behind the logs, escape was possible. This new plan was viable, raising their optimism. Agreed, that decided to make their attempt sooner than later.

By dark, the random shots through the door had quit altogether. Were they running low on bullets? James had noticed that the sound of each shot had changed from the last. The bandits must have taken turns shooting through the open door. Now there was nothing. If six were out there earlier, what happened to the other two? They listened intently for those two to reappear, but nothing signaled this. If they did reappear, it might affect their plans for escape.

James had briefly traded positions with McBride when something came through the door and bounced off the back wall. All three men froze as they waited for more silent missiles to follow. James went as far as crawling forward, looking out the door and directly at the place where the bandits lay. Nothing had changed there. Brent groped his way to the back of the tavern, feeling the floor for what had just landed there. A hushed exclamation came when he found it. With the projectile in hand, he quietly moved near the front of the tavern to use the little bit of light that came through the door.

Holding the arrow up for James to see, he whispered, "Do you think this came from Skyler?"

In the faint moonlight, James took the arrow and rolled it in his fingers. The shiny aluminum arrow revealed a unique pattern painted on its shaft. The arrows head had been removed and replaced with a wad of cloth. McBride moved closer to listen in. James smiled. "Only Skyler could have shot this. It's my arrow."

"Then we wait," said Brent.

CHAPTER 22

April 6th, 2031
6:00 pm

With the waning daylight, Skyler traveled faster than he'd anticipated. His route traversed the south side of the small mountain in a downward diagonal line. For the first twenty minutes, he ran non-stop while leaping over tree trunks, following a trail once made by animals. Once when he was in an open section of field, he could see his house off Main. The daylight wasn't enough to reveal any details, but at this great of a distance, its occupants, if there were any, could not see him. Had he walked past it on the road, someone could have followed him, cutting off his retreat.

Staying on the high side of Main Street, the downed trees became fewer as the light diminished. A fence, followed by a ditch, separated him from a road that spurred off of Main. He wanted to abandon the trail, but it was still too light. Crossing the road, another field shielded by desolation, brought him to the intersection at Douglas Road without incident. A sliver of moonlight was all the light that could be called up once the night had truly settled in. He was now mere blocks from his destination. No shots had been fired since he'd left the top of the hill. He wondered to himself, "A good sign or bad?" No smoke drifted up from the town. "Was the battle over, the town now abandoned?" Regardless of the signs and his hesitation, he had to find James and the others. It was just as imperative to know where the bandits were. He ignored the thought that the worst had happened—finding them dead—but he also needed to know what had become of the bandits. If he couldn't save James and the others, then he needed to do this for the friends they left behind.

Skyler skirted the left edge of the asphalt until he reached Washington Street. He had not taken this road since the Change, only because he'd had no reason to. It was short, incredibly cluttered, and led directly over to Vista Drive. Nervous about approaching the downtown, Skyler saw the value of this road; it could allow him to enter the downtown from the back, an unexpected entry. It would take him longer, but that couldn't be helped. He was aware that if he took more than three hours to return, Lara's fears would amplify.

Trees and power poles lay across the road like the rungs of a ladder. The houses to his left, some of the oldest in town, were torn apart, each sending tail of debris stretching beyond the road. Taking Washington Street, three blocks in length, was adding only minutes to his time. With his bow ready to draw, aware of the dangers that could hide anywhere along his path, he moved on with a stealth that belied his age. Taking a risk, he stayed out of the shadows, steadily moving forward until the wreckage dissipated, and an open ribbon of asphalt welcomed him to the backdoor of Ferndale.

Vista Drive, a main avenue in this small town, ran parallel to the winds. This street brought back a painful memory from the previous year. When had that been? February or March? That period of late winter when the weather eased briefly, just long enough for James to bring him down here. Cautiously, he closed the gap, swallowing hard knowing that Third Avenue loomed ahead. This was where they'd found her, lying frozen in the street; her skin taut and gray from months of a tundra-like exposure. Any remembrance of that day made tears well up in his eyes. She was his mother, his whole world, his only world. Her death was the very reason he'd avoided this part of town. He loved the memory of her even though it came with much pain.

Now he was in enemy territory. Before him loomed the tall brick skeletons once harboring the businesses that made Ferndale a city. Silence and devastation were now the only occupants. Still, no trace of wood smoke could be detected. Had they left and gone elsewhere? Skyler felt the fear created by what he didn't know; a heartbeat away from breaking his courage. What lay in this darkness? What had happened to his friends? His right hand subconsciously dropped down to his quiver, unconsciously fingering its contents. He'd brought both his and James' arrows, ten in all. In a way, he wished that he'd get the chance to use each one; while on the other hand, he hoped that he would find no reason to draw back on the string.

Skyler made it a habit to turn and look behind himself frequently. Darkness became both his friend and enemy. This was not the time to make mistakes. The life of so many others now depended on him returning to the hill with an account of what he'd found. All of his senses were wide awake, yet still nothing appeared. No sounds or smells giving clue to what the darkness held. He needed to be one block over on Main Street. The old tavern was where this had started, so he had to look there first. He could follow Third Avenue to Main, but that would place him a block away from the tavern in possibly hostile territory. He had to assume they controlled the downtown and were watching that street. The alternative was to continue on Vista to Second Avenue. There would be less cover, but it might not matter. Its openness being the last place they would expect anyone. The fraction of moon that cast the scant light sat to the southwest. The buildings on the other side of Second would be shadowed. That darkness, growing on the north side of the store fronts, would provide his cover.

An empty parking lot provided him with a shorter route, allowing him to reach Second midway between Vista and Main. Skyler stood behind the corner of a brick building and peered out. From here, he could see most of the intersection and the front of the tavern. Still, he was too far away to detect any details. He needed to be closer. His plan had been to cross this street, creeping up to Main in the shadows. However, his intuition warned him not to do that. Something his senses picked up. What was it? What was out there? The tavern's entrance was as dark and lifeless as the eye sockets of a skull. Don't be in a hurry, he told himself. Then he saw it, the glow from a cigarette.

It was a little over half a block away, middle of the intersection in front of the tavern. Two large utility poles, one resting upon the other blocked the road. Skyler held his position behind the brick corner. Why is someone hiding on this side of the logs? They would be in clear view of anyone entering the town from the west, the way that he intended to bring the others later tonight. Another ember appeared, glowing as bright as any star. At least two were hidden in those shadows. Skyler didn't want to move closer, but needed to.

The sidewalk at his feet lay covered with junk left by the high winds. A narrow gap between the building's southern wall and the trash created a thin path most of the way to the sidewalk on Main. Skyler eased himself out of his sheltered cornice and dropped down on all fours. Each movement was carefully thought out, intentionally slow. Not a piece of debris could be disturbed. The tunnel along the wall provided plenty of cover from the street, but it also obstructed his view of what lay ahead. Inching closer, he now heard the tones of men talking. The thirty yards to the corner took him several minutes to cover, but he had done so without raising an alarm.

His new dilemma wasn't what he'd expected. The corner of the building lay fully exposed to the dim moonlight. In order to get a view of the street and its surroundings, he would need to rise above the detritus that hid him. If these men were as accustomed to this night's light as he was, they would surely notice his pale face appear. He'd come too far to turn back now. A steel awning above him had protected some of the sidewalk, enough so that the bulk of the debris was closer to the street. Skyler quietly laid his bow on the concrete and crawled to the edge of the clear sidewalk. He inserted his hand under a piece of sheet metal, being careful not touch it with his sleeve. He found the curb and felt the bottom of its vertical side—a half-inch of mud still wet from this morning's rains.

Three painstakingly slow insertions of his arm brought out enough to cover his face, neck and ears. The back of his hands, smeared with the mud, were nearly invisible in the low light. He crawled back to his bow and fit an arrow onto its string. He didn't want to use it, but held no qualms if needed. He didn't have the luxury of knowing what else lay nearby. If he was detected, it would afford him a shot that might allow him to escape. He had already wiped the muddy residue from his palms, only to find that they were sweating. Like a plant reaching for the sun, its movement undetected by the naked eye, he finally raised his head above the debris.

There they were, six of them, all prone or on their sides, some with rifles. Four were lying beneath the shelter of the logs, while two lay in the street. Were they sleeping? Skyler looked closely and could see no sign of weapons near those two bodies. Then he noticed that one of the bodies lay in a pool of blood. Those two had to be dead or as near to it that the others did not want to share their space with them. Two men whispered back and forth before one of them quickly lifted his head, aiming his eyes at the tavern's entrance, and ducked back down just as fast. Someone or something was inside that tavern holding them in their current position—enough so that they feared exposing themselves as much as he had.

James, Brent and McBride had to be the ones in the tavern. Skyler wished there was some way that he could let them know he was here, and that before the night was over, there would be an attempt to free them. But, short of alerting these four bandits of his presence, he could see no way to do this.

Skyler heard a click and a lighter flared up among the men before him. He froze as he took in the scene that had been previously shadowed in darkness. One had a rifle aimed through a gap in the logs with his attention focused on the tavern's opening. It was obvious to Skyler that this was a stand-off in which neither player could move forward or back. Someone inside must have a rifle aimed through the open door and had taken pleasure in killing the two that now lay in the street. Skyler was so tempted to draw and shoot arrow after arrow, taking the chance that he could end this stand-off for his friends. But again, he had to remind himself the importance of staying alive.

Having acquired what he'd come for, Skyler began backing out along the wall. He was again careful not to disturb his surroundings and was soon behind the building's corner. Looking back at the tavern, he wanted in some way to send them some hope without drawing attention. He pulled the arrow from his bow and unscrewed the razor-sharp tip; its blunt end still capable of harming someone at the speed with which his compound could shoot. Glancing around the corner, he noticed that the men behind the logs were shadowed from him beyond the other building's corner. If he shot from this vantage point, the twang of the string might not be heard. Even if it was, those men were not going to stand and take chase. With his pocket knife, he cut a patch from the bottom of his coat. Both Lara and James would not have approved of such an act. Pulling a piece of tape from the inside surface of the bow limb, Skyler used this to secure the wad of cloth to the end of the arrow's shaft. He wished that for this one time, he'd had one of those long bows he'd made. The ability to draw the string just far enough to get the arrow to its destination, would have been welcomed over using the compound. With this bow, to be at all effective, the string had to be pulled completely back, and the arrow would be released at its maximum speed.

He stooped low, aiming at the top of the gaping doorway. As soon as it left his fingers, the arrow disappeared into the darkness. Hopefully, it would make little or no sound as it passed the bandits on its way to the tavern's entrance. Even if it had, there would not be enough time to identify what had created such a faint sound. Skyler quickly drew a second arrow and headed back toward the intersection of Vista and Third Avenue. It was time to return to the hill, lay out the plans for the night, and end this nightmare. His hope now rested on the men promised to him earlier.

Skyler reached the intersection with Washington Street, retracing his path up that road. Upon arriving at Main Street, he made the decision that he would continue up Main until it intersected with Church. Cutting across the slope of the hill would be difficult and slow in this darkest of nights. Knowing he was near the two-hour mark, and that Lara would be counting the minutes, he chose the path of least resistance. Dark as it was, walking up Main Street should pose little danger. Along this route, he wanted to scope out James' house. He knew that there were at least seven bandits, maybe eight, yet only six could be accounted for. Could more have come into the area since this morning? Somewhere else, there was at least one and possibly more. He suspected that they lay in wait at James' house. They hadn't chased him and Ian out without a reason. They were looking for a place to relocate to. He was sure of it.

He came to a halt at the entrance of the cul-de-sac. From this distance, he couldn't tell if anyone was actually in the house or not. Smoke did not rise from the chimney and there were no burning candles to be seen. The house was a black silhouette against a dark sky. Then he thought to himself that if he was one of the bandits, what would he do? His answer came quickly—he'd lay in wait, somewhere high and outside, for anyone who could be a threat. He'd wait for whoever had shot at him when he attacked the house earlier. Someone was there. He just knew it. As if on cue, his question was answered as a match flared up. It was lit only long enough to light a cigarette before it was blown out; long enough for Skyler to see that someone sat on the deck, waiting in the dark.

On his way up the hill, his fear somewhat abated by the information he'd gained, Skyler managed a smile after what he'd witnessed.

CHAPTER 23

April 6th, 2031
8:35 pm

"It's me, Skyler, don't shoot!" The darkness dictated that Skyler approach the barricade cautiously with warning.

When given the okay, he scurried up the last short distance. Brandy and Joel were there to meet him. Hearing their voices surprised him at first; he'd forgotten that Petar would be a part of tonight's rescue. Skyler realized that because of the events, Brandy's value to her family was being tested. Something he helped her prepare for. In the twilight, he could see that Brandy carried a long bow with an arrow resting on the string. Joel held the larger homemade crossbow against his chest.

"What have you got all over your face?" Brandy asked.

Skyler reached up, touching his cheek. He'd forgotten that he'd plastered mud over all of his exposed skin. "Just some mud. It kept them from seeing me."

"You saw them?"

"Yeah, I saw four men, rifles aimed at the old tavern."

"Do you think James and….?" Her question trailed off, not wanting to broach the wrong possibility.

"I think they're okay. The only dead bodies I found belonged to the bad guys."

"You might want to wipe some of the mud off before going to the house."

Ignoring her suggestion, he asked, "Did the others arrive?"

"Sort of. Dimitrey came with four men. He's here to translate for his uncles. The only one from the Jensen farm is the old man."

This caught Skyler off guard, "Why him and not one of the others?"

"Petar asked him that very question. He says that since his time is short, he is the only expendable member of his family."

"I guess in a way that makes sense. Who's watching the other barricade?"

"Only Joe; Petar doesn't expect any trouble from that side." She ran her hand up his muddy cheek and said, "You better get going."

Skyler ran the rest of the way, rubbing some of the mud off his cheeks and forehead. A sliver of moon was just enough to light the road ahead of him. Probably perfect for what he'd planned tonight, allowing just enough visibility to lead them to the town and into position.

He made his way through the tangled path leading to the front door. When he pushed it open, he was met by several of the children, some overly excited about the strange events since that morning. Ian was the only adult in the living room, anxious to lead Skyler through the kitchen. Candlelight lit the way into the dining room where he found the rest of the adults, along with Petey and Dimitrey.

Lara was closest to him. She stood and gave him a long hug. Skyler felt her shudder before she finished her greeting. As she released him, Skyler looked around the room and spotted Dag Jensen. The older man sat in a corner with a pump-action shotgun across his lap, an overcoat stretched over the back of his chair. He didn't have that same tired look that plagued him earlier. Tonight's challenge must have invigorated the old man. The Lopatnikovs stood, backs against one wall, with Dimitrey in the center. The boy only nodded his head when Skyler looked in his direction. Everyone was apparently waiting for Skyler to speak.

"I made it all the way into the corner of Main and Second Avenue. There are four live men and two dead in the street hiding behind a couple of downed power poles. The dead are not our friends. The live bandits have their rifles trained on the front of the old tavern. That's where I think James, and the others are trapped." He waited for Dimitrey to translate before he continued. "If we come in on the east end of Second Avenue, we'll have a clear shot at the bandits."

Petar, a perplexed look on his face, asked, "Only four, I thought that there were possibly seven or eight?"

"Like I said, there were two bodies lying in the street. That accounts for six. There are also one or more bandits occupying our house. On the way up here, I witnessed someone on our deck light a cigarette. Once we free James and the others, we can focus on retaking what's ours." He spoke as if he had full confidence in the upcoming chain of events.

Dimitrey translated for his uncles. The four Russians began talking among themselves. Nods of approval followed, leaving no need for Dimitrey to translate back into English.

"I suggest that we split up into two groups and enter the town from two directions. That way, they can't entirely hunker down and hold us back. Who's coming with me tonight?" asked Skyler.

"Ian, Lydia, Ella and Dag are staying here," Petar announced. "Besides you, me and the Lopatnikovs, I want Lara and Petey to come along."

Skyler was a bit stunned at these new additions, but held his tongue, waiting for Petar to explain.

Petar must have sensed what Skyler was thinking and added, "We might need a medical person. We don't know the condition of our three friends. Ian was my first choice, but he pointed out that his value is as a surgeon and not as a medic. He suggested Lara because of her nursing skills. Besides, I don't think she'd let us go without her." He glanced up at her in time to catch a slight smile that had pierced through her immense pain.

"And Petey?"

"He's the oldest of the new arrivals, and he's a hell of a good shot," answered Petar. "We need more people trained in defense. I see this as an opportunity."

Skyler couldn't disagree; Petey was about two years older than him. By all standards, he was a grown man. "Will he be bringing that big cross-bow?"

"Not this time, I'm loaning him a rifle to use. While you were in town, I made sure he knew how to operate and aim it."

"From what I could see, this is how I think we should enter the down-town area." said Skyler. "Three of the Lopatnikov's will come in the east end of Second Avenue with me for the primary attack. Hopefully, James and the others will be able to join in once we start shooting. I want the fourth Lopatnikov to stay with Petar and Petey. The three of you will come in from Main Street. You will strictly be our back up, and should wait at Third Avenue."

"What about me?" asked Lara. "Where will I be?" She had a look of concern on her face.

"You'll be with me until we reach Second Avenue. There's a brick build-ing that will provide cover for you. If you are needed, I want you close by."

"How are we going to communicate? We won't have any way of know-ing if and when you need us for back-up," said Petar.

"Do you have any whistles?" Dag interjected. Everyone looked startled when the old man spoke.

"Yeah, we have at least two."

Dag stood and looked about, "Whistles can be better than yelling because your enemy won't know what you are communicating. One blast can mean to stay where you are. Two blasts means to come help and three blasts means to run like hell."

"Good idea. Thank you," said Petar.

"I wish that I had the energy to come with you. I think it's noble that you care so much for your friends. I'm honored that I am able to help out in some small way," said the older man.

Ian stepped up to the table and raised one hand to request a chance to speak, "What if this doesn't go as planned? What should we do up here on this hill?"

The room fell silent, each person waiting for someone else to speak first. Dimitrey quietly translated Ian's question to one of his uncles. This brought about a short discussion between his uncles before the oldest one responded back. Dimitrey raised his hand requesting permission to speak. "My uncle says that if anyone bad comes up here, you should all leave and go to our farm."

"As long as I have a destination, I'm content. I just don't like the idea of being homeless with a dozen children to care for," replied Ian.

Still on his feet, Petar looked among the crowd for anyone with something to add. Satisfied that he wasn't interrupting the conversation, he spoke to the group before him. "I want Joe and Joel to man the barricades while we are away. Dag and Ian will stay here in the house along with Lydia and Ella. Brandy's going to make rounds just to make sure the two sentries don't need anything. Should anyone approach this hill, you should have an adequate warning. If all else fails, there's a thousand places to hide within this development. Little Brent and Bekka know all the good hiding spots."

"Then that should be it. Let's get moving and end this tonight," said Skyler.

Coats and hats went on, men picked up their rifles. The cramped quarters forced them into a single line. Passing amid the children, they made their way to the door. They were followed by closely by Lara, the only member of the team not carrying a weapon. Her sole luggage being a backpack loaded with first aid supplies and water. Once outside, no one severed the silence as they moved up the street toward Church Road. Their nervous anticipation held at bay for now. Skyler had decided that they'd stick to using the main roads, wanting all of them to pass by James' house, not only so Dimitrey's uncles could see it, but also because if something went wrong, everyone should know the quickest way back.

Led by Petar, the rescuers arrived at the southern barricade where they were met by Joel and Brandy. Stepping around the logs, their travel slowed briefly as each one exited the security of the hilltop compound. Taking advantage of Skyler's proximity, Brandy reached out, touching his shoulder affectionately, knowing full well there were no guarantees tonight. Then, just like the others, Skyler disappeared into the darkness.

CHAPTER 24

April 6th, 2031
9:55 pm

Her small backpack, stuffed to the seams with as many medical supplies and water as it would hold, was all she carried. Lara, stricken by a terror so paralyzing just six months earlier, fought the agoraphobia that still gnawed at her every step she took down the steep hill. The near-total darkness did not help, but a stronger drive kept her moving forward; she could not imagine a life without James. He had rescued her from a lightless, cold basement where she lay in fear of being discovered by men who would think nothing of raping her, enslaving her for their continued perversion. Lara knew she was who had been trained to heal people, but it was James, whose quiet, steady presence and kindness had saved not just her, but the rest of their small community as well. She kept her feelings for James close to the bone; her participation in his rescue was driven by a deep love, not gratitude.

Although barely a whisper had been uttered by the group, when they reached the bottom of the hill, Skyler reiterated that from that point forward, absolute silence would be required, even their very physicality required them to tread seamlessly. No less than a hundred yards later, he stopped them all again. He scanned across the road and field toward their house. Lara watched as he gathered close to the Russians and whispered, "Moy Dom," my house, pointing at the tall structure barely visible against the night sky. Whispers and head nodding indicated the four large men understood.

They continued past the entrance to the short street. Lara couldn't take her eyes from the house. Skyler had told the group that only an hour earlier he had witnessed someone light a cigarette up on the deck. She loved that house; it was the home she and James had adopted together, had fought to scratch out some type of normal existence. It symbolized their survival and, besides James, had given her a reason to live. The very image of someone, vile and dangerous roaming within its walls, infuriated her.

They continued moving down Main Street for another half mile, Skyler leading the way, an arrow resting on his bowstring. He had made it clear that should they run into someone, his bow would be their initial defense. "The noise of gun shots could alert our presence," he had warned. Using rudimentary but well understood sign language to communicate with the Russians, he indicated the bow was number one, their rifles number two. They nodded in agreement, but Lara could not be sure that they fully understood. She was grateful that Dimitrey's father had sent them along. They showed no fear. They were peaceful farmers, hunting only to supply meat for their survival. Lara did not know their past stories, what their lives were like before the Change. Perhaps they had had to fight as soldiers once upon a time and simply did not wish to remember a past they would never live again.

When they reached the road that forked away from Main Street, Skyler brought the group to a halt. "This is where we split up," he whispered.

Lara experienced that strangest sense of déjà vu. She looked down the road. Washington Street. The road she used as a short cut between Vista and Main before the Change. She wondered how a landscape so vital to her lifestyle once had become a memory, one that may never well have lived on had the streets not still been there. Even in this near blackness, it looked impassable. Outlines of large poles and trees crossed the road resembling a childhood game of Pick-Up Sticks. Dark pockets of space between the downed timbers provided an endless array of spots for anyone wishing to hide. Seeing the maze before her as it was, Lara suddenly felt weak, her breathing shallow.

Skyler, understanding that Lara was well out of her comfort zone, touched her arm and whispered, "Don't worry. I've already walked this road twice tonight."

Just hearing him say her name and feeling his reassuring touch, brought Lara away from the abyss she was nearing. When Skyler was sure Lara was looking back at him from the present and not the past, he led the way into the darkness. She followed him like a child whose vivid imagination creates dragons in her sleep but who counts on her father to slay them.

Petar, Petey and the lone Russian had been quick to depart. Their next stop would be Third Avenue where they would wait for the signal. Skyler wasting no time, moved steadily ahead. Lara followed next, but found his pace uncomfortable. He was the only one who knew exactly where to go and what to avoid. The Russians silently followed Lara.

The short trek through to Vista Drive ended quickly and without incident. Once they made the turn onto Vista, the road ahead was illuminated by the thinnest filament of moonlight, as if the moon itself knew to remain tethered to the group. With just minutes remaining before they were downtown, they stopped infrequently to listen. By now, they were only a block away from Petar and the others who were lying in wait somewhere along Main. Skyler halted his group, pointing to a brick structure barely visible in the distance. Again using body and sign language, he showed them that the bandits were close by on the other side.

They crept down what remained of Vista, avoiding the cluttered sidewalk. Lara had fallen behind the Russians. She refrained from yelling out to James, reaching a kind of internal hysteria she found unbearable. She had to keep it together as she followed the men into what had once been a parking lot. Each step forward became more tedious as they trudged through the garbage of civilization. When they reached the building Skyler had pointed to earlier, he once again touched Lara's arm for reassurance. "Lara, wait here until we come back and get you." He knew by the way she looked him directly in the eyes, even with so little light, that she had understood clearly the full meaning of his statement. Superficial wounds, deadly wounds, friends, enemies, all possibilities she might be faced with. She held his gaze, showing that she was up to the task they had all set out to accomplish.

Like he had before, Skyler stooped down and pulled a handful of silt from a shallow puddle. He smeared the black sludge on the lighter parts above his collar line. The three Russians quietly followed suit. In an instant, they were all gone before she had a chance to accept their departure.

Lara, her backpack clutched to her chest, suctioned herself to the cold, brick wall behind her. With arms crossed, she dug her fingernails into her forearms as she fought for control. She was now in danger of losing both the men in her life. That sudden reality hit her like she had run full force into the very brick wall keeping her upright. Unable to handle the strain any longer, Lara drew herself to the building's edge. That guiding filament of moonlight provided her with just enough light to see all the way to the intersection. She had memorized Skyler's map in such detail before the group left that she instantly spotted the entrance to the tavern. Remembering the early post-Change days and nights when she and James had to live in total darkness for the majority of their nights and days. She tried to muster up hope as she looked at the dark tavern, praying that James was in there staying hidden.

For a quick moment, Lara made out the shadows of Skyler and the Russians who were almost to the intersection. Just as quickly as their silhouettes had appeared, they disappeared again. Lara was left with nothing but a howling silence. Several seconds passed before she saw a shadow rise at the other end of the building. She instantly recognized it as Skyler. He stood, his bow stretched out in front, fully drawn. A light twang reverberated in her direction before she realized that he'd released his arrow. At first, nothing happened. Then Skyler gracefully reached in his quiver for a second arrow. Lara was in awe at what was taking place right in front of her. The boy she'd comforted after his mother had died, now stood on a street corner willing to give up his life for the man and woman who took him in. His skill and precision were not as surprising to her as the confidence his body language proclaimed—that he would prevail. Before she was aware that he'd released his second arrow, she again heard the familiar twang. Skyler slipped from sight as, once more, she was left alone. Lara felt she was having an out-of-body experience, watching a grainy black and white film in which she was a bit player.

She was shaken from her reverie by a scream coming from around the corner. The street suddenly exploded with gunfire. The three Russians quickly stood, rifle butts against their cheeks. They shot with the same poise and purpose Skyler had demonstrated earlier, spraying a torrent of bullets at a target she still could not see. She continued watching the reels of her black-and-white film flicker in the moonlight, transfixed by the fearless performance of its heroes. They advanced until all three were out of her line of sight. The shooting continued and seemed to be moving further away at a rapid pace. Then she saw Skyler stand once more with another arrow drawn as he too disappeared in the direction of the arrow's head.

Like the call and response to a Sunday church service, Lara used to attend regularly before the Change when she still believed in God; she listened and waited, nerves taut as Skyler's bow. When she thought she would no longer be able to hold up in the surrealism, a familiar voice called out, waking her senses.

The location was unmistakable. It had come from the dark cavity across the intersection that she had been forbidden to approach. Three figures emerged with rifles ready, obviously tentative about their first steps outside in over sixteen hours. In the distance, Skyler's voice rang out an all clear. The trio lowered their rifle barrels to the ground and stepped into the street.

Lara, no longer like a blind person in unfamiliar territory, flew on feet that recklessly found their footing. She continued through the scene: to her right, four men lay in the street while to her left, her heroes emerged from the pitch black. From different parts of the intersection, the Russians and Skyler moved about, taking inventory of their victims. No longer in her surreal movie, she turned towards the left to see James, Brent, and John McBride walking in her direction. With a yelp, she ran into James' arms.

"I'm okay! I'm okay!" James whispered into her ear, golden hair soft against his lips, as he held her tight.

Lara knew then she would never let him go.

CHAPTER 25

April 6th, 2031
11:05 pm

Skyler's bow and arrow became an extension of his body; he learned to tread through any terrain or space with the lightness of a bird on a high wire. Intent on a mine field nature created; he forgot about the Russians behind him. They were as stealthy, silent and smooth as Skyler, if not more so, once again demonstrating a past experience they never discussed. When Main Street was two yards ahead of him, he motioned for the three men to stop their advance. A large corner sign made of plywood, faint letters of the family who owned the former grocery store—Flaherty's—torn down by high speed winds, still attached to the awning, a painting of a man holding a head of lettuce, stood in front of them. Small compared to a car, sufficient enough to provide some cover for the three Russians, but not Skyler and his bow. He moved closer than he dared, melting down behind a garbage can laying in the gutter. Rising up just enough, he counted six men sprawled out on the ground before him; nothing had changed. The two bodies he'd seen, like bodies carved out of stone, looked exactly as he'd seen them a few hours earlier. The other four, horizontal behind the power poles, were their targets. A snort followed by a cough alerted him that at least one of the men was sleeping. He couldn't make out which one, but he knew it would be a poor tactical move to shoot the easiest target. His first shot needed to take out the most dangerous, the one keeping watch.

Two, maybe three minutes, passed before Skyler saw one of the of the men change position. A pile of rubbish near the end of the power poles hid most of another from his view. He held a rifle that rested between the stacked logs; its barrel pointed at the tavern's door. Two of the men were using their forearms as pillows. Skyler figured they had been awake for more than seventeen hours. They had to be weak with hunger and needing sleep. Succumbing to sleep would be their undoing. The cold asphalt made for an uncomfortable bed, yet it would help fight off fatigue. The fourth man was tucked up against the logs. Skyler did not know his status: dead, wounded, asleep, or alert and guarding.

Skyler concluded that his first target had to be the one with his rifle aimed at the tavern. If a commotion erupted, any one of his friends might exit the safety of the building. This needed to be considered in his choice. The second target, should there be enough opportunity, would be the bandit tucked up against the logs solely because he too might be focused on the tavern.

Skyler had to rise up to his knees before he could draw his bow string. His view, partially blocked by rubbish, forced him into a full standing position, in full view of his targets. He drew his bow back, narrowing his gaze to that man. Amazingly, at a distance of maybe twenty-five to thirty feet, not one of the bandits had detected that he was in their presence. He preferred a head shot, but the shadow from the moon on the logs prevented this.

Skyler redirected his aim for the man's chest. The man lay half prone, half on his side. A spot about six inches below the man's armpit should be where his heart now beat. Without further hesitation, Skyler released the arrow, and in one fluid motion, reached into his quiver for a second. The first arrow met its target the same time the recoil of the bow string reached the victim. A sharp crack sounded as the arrow passed through the man's chest and met pavement, stopping it for good. The bandit released his rifle with his left arm to grasp at the protruding arrow. He did not scream out, neither did he attempt to wake another man sleeping only three feet to his right. Instead, he fought to get a grip on the arrow located in the one place most men were unable to reach. Not one of the other three bandits had so much as twitched.

Skyler had only a split second, with his second arrow drawn, to decide if he should finish off the first guy or aim for the next. The silence was suddenly pierced by a guttural cry coming from the wounded bandit, a sound of unmistakable agony. This stirred the man curled up against the logs. Rapidly, he raised his head, turning to face Skyler. Matching Skyler's fluid skill with the bow and arrow, he brought his rifle up, the barrel directed in Skyler's direction. Skyler wasted no further time. He took aim at the man's chest and released the arrow. Its razor-sharp head hit the rifle's stock, sending the arrow ricocheting into space. His location now revealed, the bandit raised the rifle's sight to his eye. Like a well-orchestrated dance, Skyler dropped down the same instant the three Russians stood and fired their rifles. The silent battle Skyler had engaged with the one bandit was replaced a rapid chorus of gunshots.

Skyler's first victim had ceased moving, his arm twisted back, frozen as it sought the arrow. The second one was knocked back by the barrage of bullets hitting him in mid-chest almost simultaneously. The remaining two sleeping bandits jumped to attention and were diving for whatever cover they could find. Their return shots, directed at the large sign where the Russians stood, were clumsy, forcing them to drop back again for cover.

Skyler stayed flat on the sidewalk, an unseen lethal weapon the bandits could not have located in their current situation. He was almost directly between the Russians and the two surviving bandits. Shots rang out from both sides. Staying hidden, the two foes quickly re-chambered more rounds. Skyler reached for his whistle to signal Petar's squad to come in behind the remaining bandits, but before it met his lips, both bandits stood, taking off up the street toward Third Avenue. The Russians, quick to respond, nearly trampled Skyler in their haste to go after the men. All the while, random shooting still took place as both sides sought out new cover.

Skyler stood as he drew a third arrow and walked in the direction of the shots. Darkness shrouded the battlefield. He could see the backs of two of the Russians as they hid behind an abandoned car on the far side of the street. The third appeared on his side, moving from car to car as he exchanged bullets with one of the bandits pinned down behind a car across from him. Where had the second bandit disappeared to? A sudden movement caught Skyler's attention. Someone rose up in front of the car where the lone Russian had taken cover. His rifle was pointed close range at the Russian's head. Before Skyler could yell a warning, another shot sounded from his side of the street. The bandit's head rocked once before, like a rag doll, he collapsed onto the hood of the car. The remaining bandit stood and ran toward a gap between two cars. A salvo of shots rang out as several bullets hit the man in the back, sending him face down onto the street.

All shooting suddenly ceased. Skyler took inventory of the men who had come with him. The three Russians were nearby and accounted for. Petar and the fourth Russian appeared from a concrete wall across the street, only twenty feet from where the last bandit had fallen. That one would have been surprised, had he had any hope of getting out of the fight alive, to run right into Petar and his Russian companion.

Skyler became concerned when he could not see Petey anywhere on the street before him. "Where's Petey?" he shouted to Petar. Petar raised his hand and pointed behind Skyler. Skyler turned to see Petey walking with his rifle raised and aimed at the man who had now slid from the hood of the car. Petey had been on this side of the street when the man was shot. The Russian, realizing the boy had saved his life, walked over to him, pushing aside his rifle as he lifted him in a giant hug. Skyler made out the mixed emotions on Petey's face. He would never forget killing this man, perhaps later in life he would be required to kill another, but this first time would stay with him forever. Accepting the big Russian's gratitude demonstrated so affectionately for such a dramatic and necessary final act seemed difficult for Petey. Skyler knew what he was going through. Killing someone, even to save another's life, impacted your thoughts for the rest of your life. Finally, a smile broke out on the boy's face when he realized he had been a significant part of the rescue, and could no longer ignore the large man lifting him.

As the rescue team re-grouped in the street, three men exited the tavern. To Skyler's relief, all three were walking without assistance. They carried their rifles ready; unsure of what took place outside their haven. Skyler raised his bow in the air, shouting an "all clear." Brent and James dropped their barrels to the ground while McBride kept his leveled. Waving with obvious enthusiasm, the three walked toward Skyler's side of the street. A sudden blur came out of nowhere, and before Skyler could raise his arrow, he saw Lara hit James so hard he stumbled back three feet as he sought to regain his balance. She clung to him, arms around his neck, legs wrapped around his waist, his head crowded from his neck by her own. Both McBride and Brent smiled, their first of the day, relishing in James' predicament. They gave them some space as James whispered in Lara's ear assurances that he was okay.

McBride broke the moment when he asked Skyler, "How many bodies are there?"

"Six."

"Christ, there are still two more alive somewhere. I counted eight of them this morning."

The smiles on both James' and Brent's faces disappeared. Lara released her grip and dropped her feet to the ground. The Russians knew without understanding a word of the English McBride had spoken, that tension had returned to the men they had just rescued, and that the group's work was not finished yet.

"They must still be at our house. Ian and I were chased out by six men. When I went past there a couple of hours ago, I saw someone on the deck light a cigarette," said Skyler. He then turned to the Russians and said, 'Moy Dom'. With no further explanation, the Russians understood. "They had to have heard the shooting and are probably expecting us. How can we get them out of there without shooting the place up?" asked James.

"We can fire a few bullets through the house," said Petar. "It would show them that the house itself might not be able to afford them any long-term protection. We'll need to leave them an escape route. Once they're out, we can resume the battle away from the house."

McBride nodded approval to Petar's plan and turned to James. "You went along with my plan and I damned near got you killed. Since this is your house, you should be calling the shots."

"Is there any reason we can't do this now?" James asked. He looked at his ten companions for confirmation.

"I don't know about you," Lara said, "but I'd like to sleep in my own bed again."

"I agree," added Brent. "We need to strike while the iron's hot. The sooner they're gone, the sooner we will all sleep again. Also, the Lopatnikovs won't be able to stay with us forever."

"Then it's settled," announced James. "Let's move up there now and surround the place. I want only three people on the north side with me, and since I know the house, I'll do the shooting. We'll have two watching the back, and when the bandits are clear of the house, they're anyone's game."

They quickly gathered up rifles and ammunition from the dead. Petar handed Petey a .22 caliber carbine. The boy had a look on his face like the gun was a gift beyond anything he'd ever received before, not just the rifle itself, but the trust he knew he had gained to receive it. Petar made some comment about it being the only rifle worth keeping. Six rifles in all were collected. Those with a limited amount of bullets would be disposed of later. For now, they didn't want them lying in the street. As a last thought, James had them drag all six bodies down the hill to the street below. The next flood would wash them away.

All eleven of them walked back up Main Street talking in hushed tones, aware that the road ahead could be a trap. Brent briefly relived their ordeal inside the tavern, and told how they had planned an escape until Skyler had sent an arrow through the open doorway. Their decision to escape was scrapped because it was a last resort.

It didn't take long before they neared the entrance of the cul-de-sac. The house could barely be detected against the darkened sky, the moons guiding filament of light, like a fine strand of hair, had almost disappeared. James had Lara fall back out of harm's way; he stuck two of the Russians with her to keep her company.

James, Petar, and Brent waited until Skyler and a Russian took a position on the west side, while Petey and another Russian hunkered down on the east side. Once he was sure that everyone was in position, James fired shots at both the deck and the house, being careful to place the bullets below the level of the windows. Brent and McBride kept their scopes directed at the structure as they waited for returning muzzle flashes. The only sounds were when James' bullets ripped through the house. No doors were slammed. No yells were heard.

Brent took advantage of the darkness and walked to the place where James had complained about a blind spot. From there, he walked straight in toward the front of the house. As he did so, James continued his occasional shots. When he felt no one was moving in or around the house, Brent waved his arm in the air to signal that he was going inside. He crept up the stairs, slowly at first, and then ran the last six steps in a sprint as he rushed the deck. Finding nothing there, he used his toe to push the already partially-opened front door, and waited for a response. Nothing happened.

As the others looked on, Brent disappeared inside the house. Moments later, he resurfaced through the front door to wave everyone in. James, glad that they didn't need to shoot up the house any further, was confused as to what they should do now. If the remaining two bandits weren't in the house, then where were they? Having two armed, hungry men loose in the neighborhood left him more than a little uneasy.

Petar and the Russians stayed outside as guards while everyone else, including Lara, went inside. A quick inspection found negligible damage from the bullets. The door to the furnace was open; their cache discovered by the bandits, but very little was missing. The beds weren't even messed up.

"If they're not here, then where could they be?" James asked McBride.

"Skyler said that they were out on the deck. I bet they heard the shooting and high-tailed it out of here."

"I wish we could count on that."

Brent was in a hurry to go back up the hill to let Lydia know that he was alright. The four Russians had done what was asked of them and were also looking anxious to return home. Petey offered to help Skyler with the watch for the remainder of the night, but Skyler declined his offer. Soon, Petey, Brent, McBride, and the Russians left for Church hill. Lara made James promise that he'd stay in their bed for the whole night, so that she could finally get a good night's sleep.

Skyler positioned himself out on the deck well aware that daylight wouldn't arrive for five hours. Soon, the frogs began croaking, filling the night air with their chorus. As long as they sang, he could be assured that no one walked among them. He was tired; he could not remember when last he slept. Slowly, the moon dipped below the horizon, making it as dark as night could get. The frogs were now his only forewarning of an intruder. In the morning, he would go up and see Brandy and the others. He hadn't spent much time with her lately and wouldn't blame her if she was a little angry. He wondered if it was appropriate that they should consider taking their relationship to the next level. Both were about to turn fifteen, and maybe it was time. He wondered if he should move up there on the hill, or if she would be happy down here. Either way, their future together would mean sharing a house with several others.

Sitting down onto the decking, his hand touched a small pile of cigarette butts. He thought it ironic that he chose the same place to sit as one of the bandits. Wherever the last two bandits had gone, they couldn't be more than an hour or two away. For the next few days, he didn't want the boys going out to the ponds. Everyone needed stay close to home or in groups with at least two people armed. Whoever they were, he hoped that they'd chosen to keep running.

He flicked a butt off the edge of the deck with this finger, and was moving toward a second when the unmistakable sound of a shotgun resonated in the distance from up on the hill. He had made it through the past several hours faced with losing his life or those of his friends without a nod toward fear, yet now a wave of terror engulfed him.

He knew exactly where the bandits were.

CHAPTER 26

April 6th, 2031
11:10 pm

DJ woke with a start when his chair rocked abruptly. He was instantly confused by the night's darkness. Brandon was nudging him. The kid has some nerve, he thought. His time is going to come sooner than later. The look on Brandon's moonlit face, however, displayed urgency, not insolence. It was then that DJ heard a barrage of gunfire. He leaped from his chair.

"When did it start?" he barked.

"A few seconds ago," Brandon answered, wishing he was anywhere but with DJ.

Neither spoke. They listened as the distant crescendo of several weapons trickled down to a final gunshot. They had expected a longer exchange, but it ended as quickly as it had started.

"Take your chair over there. My boys should be arriving here in about fifteen minutes." DJ's use of "my" was not lost on Brandon. He understood fully what DJ was doing, but it was going to backfire. Brandon had his own plans for DJ.

Brandon asked what neither wanted to think of. "What if they didn't win? What if someone helped those three guys?"

"What are you trying to say? We outnumbered them two to one." DJ wasn't in the mood to entertain the notion that one of his "boys" had been killed, yet it unnerved him.

Brandon continued, "I think we should wait somewhere else so we can see who comes up here. If it's our guys, we can walk in with them. If not, we run."

As much as he disliked Brandon, DJ had to agree with his solution. He fought the urge to finish him off and get on with business, because he still needed him. The kid had shown him this house, but had almost got him killed in the process. "Round up our packs and bring them out here. We'll wait by the road."

Like a dog minding its master, Brandon followed DJ's order and five minutes later both men stood in the moon's shadow between two crumpled houses, hidden from view by a collapsed section of a roof. From there, they could see down the road maybe a hundred yards at most. They had to strain to see anything in the darkness. Time slowed, each passing minute longer than the last as they waited and watched. At last, Brandon detected silhouettes on the road. It looked like half a dozen men. DJ almost made a fatal mistake. He momentarily assumed they were his boys. Just as he started to step out from hiding, the group widened; at least nine walked side by side.

"Not good," he whispered. "There're too many to be our men."

"What do you want to do?"

"Let's get the hell out of here before we get trapped."

DJ backed out of the tight place and started to bolt but stopped. "Where do you think we ought to go?"

It occurred to Brandon that the shift in power was favoring him. DJ was relying too heavily on him to escape alive.

"You know that road I pointed out this morning? The one that goes up that hill? The bottom of the road is just on the other side of that mess of dead trees."

"Are you nuts? What if they're headed that way now? We might back ourselves into a corner."

"No. In fact, I bet they're coming here to take this place back," he turned his head, jutting his jaw toward the house. "Remember how long it took us before we went up those stairs? They'll be busy for a long time. With this many men coming here, I'll bet there're only women and children waiting up on top of that hill."

"How are we going to get there? They'll be here in two minutes. We can't walk out to the road now."

"I think I know another way. Follow me."

Brandon took off in a jog with DJ following on his heels. They reached the house and cut across the parking pad to another yard with a gravel driveway. The only noises they heard were the sounds of their feet crunching gravel. One end of the unpaved ribbon led to the fresh framework they'd seen earlier. Brandon surmised that the other end had to come from the main road. They continued to follow it, running without knowing what exactly lay ahead. It was the better option, however. Emerging from two piles of dead trees, DJ felt the change from gravel to asphalt beneath his shoes. They'd reached Main, and Church lay just before them. Looking back toward the house they'd left, it was too dark to see anything. Although at least nine angry men were in their vicinity, the night was still absent from any sounds. The fact that no one was coming up Main meant that Brandon had been correct about where those men were headed. With no one in sight, they ran across the road and began walking up the long hill.

Somewhere along the seemingly endless hill, a gunshot reverberated from below them. Both men almost dropped to the ground. The first one was soon followed by more shots that sounded rather like someone doing target practice than engaging in gun battle. The sound resonated with both of them; it was not from a high-powered rifle.

The two men stopped briefly to listen.

Brandon was the first to break the silence. "I bet they're trying to scare us out of their house."

DJ began the climb up the hill again with only a grunt as acknowledgment. He realized they had left the house in such a hurry that they hadn't kept any of the food they found. They would need to find more by tomorrow at the latest. About five minutes later, the shooting from below ceased completely. The night sky only grew darker as the moon finished its trek across the sky. The only way they knew they were still on the road was because of the rough asphalt beneath their soles. Unexpectedly, Brandon was knocked backwards into DJ, nearly toppling them and sending both down the hill. They had walked blindly into a barricade of wall of logs. Quick on his feet, Brandon managed to catch himself. Pre-occupied with their near accident, they were shocked to hear a voice from their right ask, "Who's there?"

Both men froze. Brandon raised his rifle but then realized he recognized the voice. "Joel? Is that you?"

"Yeah it's me. Is that you Brandon?"

"Yes, and am I ever glad to hear your voice again. I've been looking for you."

DJ remained quiet. Whoever was there hadn't realized that Brandon was not alone; the absolute darkness shrouding his presence. He leaned in close to the logs and remained as still as a deer that senses impending danger.

"Brandon, what are you doing here? You were supposed to leave this area."

"I'm on my way back to Canada. I forgot to give you something before we got split up. It took me forever to find you."

Neither could see each other yet. Brandon judged that Joel was standing at the end of the log wall.

Joel, unaware of Brandon's involvement, ranted and warned him. "None of that matters. The people that live up here are trying to rescue their friends from a gang. I expect them back any minute, and if they find you here, they'll be angry."

By now, Brandon had honed his skills at thinking up lies in record time. "But I found a picture of a woman in my pack. I think it's your mother. I couldn't leave without giving it back to you."

Joel said nothing. He finally stepped out from the wall just enough for Brandon to detect his outline. That was when Brandon knew he'd conned him. He kept his rifle from view by hiding it behind his leg. When Joel drew close enough, Brandon pushed out his right hand to the silhouette. When Joel's hand touched his, Brandon grasped his wrist tightly, yanked him forward and spun him around. Startled by the sudden attack, Joel let the large crossbow fall from his free hand as it clattered onto the road. Before he could yell an alarm, Brandon's arm was around his throat like a vice. Someone else shoved a rifle barrel into his face.

"Make a noise and I'll blow your head off," growled DJ. "Now where's this house you're staying in? How many people are in it, and how many are armed?"

With DJ's rifle poised on Joel, Brandon loosened his grip on Joel's neck. He could only raise his right arm and point beyond the log wall.

"Just one," he answered hoarsely. "And he's an old man."

"That's good! Now, how about showing us this place?" The menacing tone of DJ's voice could not have been missed by even the most obtuse individual. Joel shook with fear.

With that, Brandon swung Joel around and pointed him toward the end of the barricade. His arm stayed locked about Joel's neck as DJ kept the rifle pointed at the side of his head. Joel walked slowly as the three of them moved like a lumbering three-legged insect. They maneuvered around the barricade and continued up the road in silence.

Joel steered the two men down the street that led to the house. DJ leaned in close and whispered, half chuckling. "No tricks and we'll be nice to everyone."

Soon, Joel led them into a maze of debris separated just enough to permit them to pass. The smell of wood smoke, thick and obvious, penetrated their nostrils. DJ kept the barrel's business end up against the boy's temple. They stepped up onto a porch where Joel, now free of Brandon's hold on him, reached out to pull open a large sheet of plywood that hid the front door. The hinged wooden sheet swung outward to reveal a solid wood door behind it. Before Joel could reach for the doorknob, DJ grabbed it, and slowly turned it until he felt the door come free, then violently swung it inward.

A chorus of startled children erupted at the sudden intrusion. Brandon pushed Joel forward as someone within struck a match to light a candle. DJ swung the barrel of his rifle at the old man as the room lit up. Brandon brought his rifle up and held it at Joel's head.

"What the hell?" yelled the older man. It was more of a statement than a question.

"Drop your shotgun right there, old man, or I'll start putting holes in these kids," hollered DJ. Around the large room, DJ judged that at least ten children were scattered about on a sea of beds and couches. Small voices could be heard uttering, "It's Brandon," as the light in the room increased. DJ's voice bellowed through the house. "I want everyone here in the living room now, or I'll start shooting!"

A second elderly man appeared from a kitchen with a look of bewilderment on his face. DJ motioned with his rifle for him to step into the room. Then two women appeared from the same doorway, one with two small children clinging to her legs.

With his rifle leveled at the first old man, DJ stepped over him and picked up man's shotgun, then backed himself into a corner. The woman with the children stood frozen in the doorway.

DJ announced to the entire group, "I want everyone in here and sitting on the floor." He swung the barrel of the shotgun in the direction of the women. They complied instantly. The other old man, DJ noticed, appeared to struggle to sit down, but something about the way he moved, and how he gave his attention to the children, suggested to DJ that he might worried about the children.

"Is there anyone else in this house that isn't here in this room?" His questioned was directed at the woman with the children. He kept his barrel pointed at her children to insure her honesty.

Her head barely moved as she nodded, no.

Brandon scanned the room at the crowd of kids. "Where are Joe and Petey?

The old man DJ was keeping an eye on said, "They aren't here; they're staying at another house."

"Alright, listen up everybody because this is how things are going to work from now on." DJ could see he was scaring them, but he relished in seeing their abject fear. "If anyone tries anything, we'll start shooting, beginning with the youngest." While he let that sink in, he fanned the room with the two guns. "We want half a dozen jars of food placed into each of our packs. Round up any ammunition and put that in our packs, too."

"I'll get it," said Lydia as she stood up, the two children getting up to follow her.

"They stay here!" DJ barked at her. The children became frightened and clung to her legs at once.

DJ pointed the shotgun at the old man next to her. "You get the food instead!"

"I, I don't know where they keep it. I don't live here."

"Oh for Christ's sakes, who does know where the food is kept?" he shouted, looking around the room. No one moved or tried to answer the question.

Finally, the woman said, "We keep some jars beneath the back bedroom floor. You have to move the bed that sits in the center of the room. It's crowded in there and the only way to move it is to lift it onto another bed."

Brandon said, "You take the old men back there. I'll keep an eye on the rest of this group."

DJ kept both the shotgun and rifle aimed at the two men as he motioned for them to stand. The trio walked quietly down the hall with DJ taking up the rear. The taller of the two older men held a candle out in front to light the way. When they reached the room, the two men, under DJ's careful guard, lifted the center bed and set it down on an adjoining bed. The trap door, hinged on one end, was swung wide. The candlelight showed open boxes of Mason jars sitting on a pallet about three feet below the floor. Ian, taking the initiative, and not wanting Dag to strain himself, hopped into the hole and began handing up jars.

"Hustle up, old man! We don't have all night."

Ian continued lifting until a dozen jars stood before him at chest level. He climbed out of the hole under his own power and was about to close the door when DJ stopped him.

"We don't have time for that." He laid his rifle on the bed behind him. With the shotgun pointed at the two men, he lowered his pack onto the bed. "Load this up with six jars and carry the rest into the other room."

Ian did the transfer to the pack as Dag collected four of the jars into his arms. Moments later, they re-entered the living room. Dag carried his load over to Brandon's pack. Brandon had a quizzical look on his face as DJ stepped into the room.

"Where's your rifle?"

DJ made a hard stop. He realized that he'd left it on the bed when they loaded the pack. He made an about face, returning to the back bedroom, picked up the rifle with his left hand, and was entering the living room just as the front door was thrown open, knocking Brandon and Joel onto one of the occupied beds.

Without any hesitation, DJ raised the shotgun and fired it with one hand. The gun, unaimed, jerked violently from the recoil, and flew from his hand. The blast of pellets hit the jamb atop the door's frame, splintering the wood, and showering the room with small bits of wood and pellets. The door slammed shut. Several of the children screamed as the room dissolved into chaos while DJ raised his rifle in an attempt to gain control. Brandon scrambled to maintain his hold on Joel as the smaller children continued to scream in terror. Whoever had pushed the front door open must have sensed that something was wrong and retreated just as the shotgun was discharged. Brandon gave up trying to hang onto Joel and jumped back off the bed with his rifle aimed at the boy. He used his backside to secure the front door, feeling for a deadbolt with his free hand.

DJ pointed the rifle around the room at no one in particular and yelled, "QUIET!"

Almost immediately, most of the children went silent with the exception of Little Brent and Bekka. The noise of the shotgun's discharge had frightened them so badly that Lydia could not calm them.

The two old men were the only quiet ones throughout the entire event. DJ allowed the barrel to sweep past them just as a reminder. He wasn't sure who had tried to come through the door, but whoever it was, they now knew that something inside this house was terribly wrong.

"Ah, Christ, now we're screwed," DJ thought to himself. If he'd only known then just how screwed they would become, he would have left in a hurry, making sure to kill Brandon before he did.

CHAPTER 27

April 6th, 2031
9:35 pm

Brandy, concerned about the situation, had watched silently as Skyler and the others vanished from sight through the curtain of night. She could not think about the next few hours. The future was alien to her; she had learned to compartmentalize her feelings. Sometimes when she and Skyler sat together under the warmth of a rare crisp spring day, she'd think that, after all they had lost before the Change—their family and friends, nature in full bloom, musings about boyfriends and girlfriends—and all that they had survived after it, that they deserved to mete out some kind of peaceful existence free from the constant fear of desperate and dangerous looters. She had a job to do. She was no longer the young girl the men of her family thought of her. A link now in the efforts of Skyler and Petar to rescue James, Brent and John McBride, her role was to keep in contact with Joe and Joel as they stood watch at the barricades. She took her duties seriously.

She stayed with Joel only a few moments before crossing the crest to check on Joe. Carrying the long bow gave her confidence; she was not afraid of what might happen if she should come face-to-face with a killer. She remembered the first week Skyler had started training her to use the bow and arrow; his patience with her neared tenderness. She struggled just to hold the bow, her arms not yet strong enough to pull the sting taught. Her hand shook slightly before releasing each arrow, their paths never the same, swaying as they tried to reach their target. Looking back, she knew it was her heart and not her mind that had been breaking her concentration, but with each passing day, her strength grew along with her skill. The most important rule he ingrained into her was to not hesitate—shoot first because you may not get a second chance. The men in her family did not take the long bows seriously. They thought of them as toys; a distraction to break the daily monotony the children faced when every chore, small or large, began to exhaust the optimism and childlike behavior they still conjured. Something as simple as a game of hide and seek did wonders to put smiles back on their faces. The adults had forgotten how to play, which is why, when Brent and Lydia moved out, Brandy was anxious to show her family that she, too, was no longer a child. She shot a crow at a distance of thirty paces, impressing both Petar and John McBride. No one had thought her capable of acquiring a skill that, up to that point, only Skyler had been capable of doing.

With an arrow resting on the string, she made her way following the asphalt ribbon over the hill to the north barricade. They did not expect any trouble from this side of the hill, but had kept Joe there anyway. Scott reinforced in them to 'expect the unexpected'. Near the barricade, she called out, "Joe?"

"Over here."

The reply was too brief for her to locate him. The wall of dark logs, now black as coal, kept Joe hidden. This is good, she thought to herself.

Joe, sensing her confusion, stood up and stepped into the murky dark.

"Pretty boring job, isn't it?" she asked.

"No, not really, I kind of like being alone. I've always been surrounded by the others. The peace and quiet is a nice change. Especially if I'm expected to keep my eyes and ears open."

"Do you need anything? I have some extra water in my pack."

"No thanks. Petar made sure Joel and I are equipped for the night. I could use a video-game console, a TV and a recliner if you have all of those things in your pack?" His way of joking, something he was becoming famous for doing, pierced the seriousness of their jobs.

"No, I dropped those things off with Joel. He'd conquered six universes and killed over a million aliens. I don't think there'll be anything left for you to destroy." Saying it without breaking into a smile, she enjoyed keeping the joke alive.

Joe turned sober, the joke having run its course for him. "Have you heard any shooting from down below yet?"

"Not yet. They just left the other side maybe twenty minutes ago. Petar said that it would be close to an hour before they were in position."

"I just hope it goes well, and they all get back alive, not just James, Brent and McBride. They're good people. What's it been now? Six days since we arrived? They took us in without question and have treated us fair ever since. They didn't have to do that. I'm grateful for all they've done. I'm just glad they didn't shoot us." Before the Change, Joe's comment would have been unfathomable: children grateful not to be shot. Their world had been turned upside down; their reality so unlike the previous generations. They were easy targets who wore their innocence like yellow stars sewn on jackets.

"What was it like before that? You know, when you guys traveled as a gang?"

"A guy named Brandon called all the shots. He was the only one with a gun, and he made sure we didn't take weapons when we stole stuff. As long as we came back with something, he was alright. But he didn't look out for us. Our group was larger a month ago. Brandon gave three younger children to a group of men, saying they weren't worth wasting his bullets over. The only reason Skyler found us was because Brandon had kicked Devon out of the club. Devon led Skyler to us."

Brandy had heard the story of their rescue, but had not known the details of their lives under Brandon's control. She'd been fortunate; Petar and Brent had taken her in, fed her, given her shelter and asked for nothing in return. She was proud that not one of her new family members had ever stooped to stealing food.

"I'm going to head back over and check on Joel again. Maybe by then there's some news from down there. I'm not sure if the sound of gun shots will reach this far, but keep your ears open anyway."

"I'm not using them for anything else. I'll see you when you come back. Be sure to bring good news, and see if you can wrestle that video game away from Joel."

"Will do!" she said as she turned to cross over the crown of the hill once again.

Trees silhouetted against the night sky outlined the road as she made her way back to the southern barricade. She let her thoughts drift to Skyler, all the while keeping alert to her surroundings. Skyler, close in age to these boys, was, like Brandy, on the other side of childhood. He was nearly a man in every way except by pre-Change standards. As such, he could mentor the boys, much as it seems James mentored him, giving them the chance to become men of character. Brandy shuttered to think of the moral sink hole they would have been fallen into if James and Brent had not saved them. She would take it upon herself to set a good example and mentor Gia, Bree and Marley. Brandy wondered, if they were to survive, have families of their own, if there might be future generations, would they all become part of a legend that people told each other around a campfire. Strange thoughts on a strange night, she considered, as she again channeled her energy into the task she had been set.

When she reached the southern barricade, she and Joel talked for about ten minutes, the kind of conversation where nothing is said and everything is inferred. They had just started to extol the virtues of standing idle for what seemed like hours when the sound of gunfire echoed from the river valley below. It shattered the quiet peace of the security. Furious shots rang out, until they were heard fewer and farther between, until they abruptly ended almost as quickly as they had started.

"What do you suppose happened?" Brandy asked Joel. Her question was rhetorical as hearing gunfire only meant that guns had been shot, but it was anyone's guess as the outcome.

"Don't know. I just hope that everyone comes back alive." Joel answered, pragmatic as usual.

238

They stared silently off into the still night waiting for more shots and wondering what was going on. When several minutes had passed, Brandy could only assume that it was over. She was anxious to tell Joe about what they heard and to see if the sounds of gunshots had traveled to that corner of the hilltop.

"You can probably expect them here in about an hour," she told him matter-of-factly. Then she added, "I'm going to make a trip over to Joe's side. I'll be back in about forty minutes. I want to be here when they arrive."

She placed an arrow on her bowstring and departed. She wanted to be back on this side before the arrival of the rescue team. Her pace quickened. She had to know the outcome. Her future, like everyone else's, might hang on the success of their mission. Her biggest concern was for Skyler; she needed to know that he was okay and that the danger had passed.

As she walked past the street leading down to the house, she realized that Lydia and the others would want an update. They were inside and probably didn't hear the gunshots. She made an about-face, running down to the house. She would quickly relay what she knew and then continue over to see Joe.

She opened the door and was immediately attacked by a flurry of questions from the older children. Dimitrey seemed terribly interested, asking if she had any knowledge about his uncles. She finally got everyone settled down to listen to what little she did know. Lydia had come in from the other bedroom, followed by little Brent and Bekka.

"All I can tell you is that we heard several gunshots. Shortly after it began, the intensity increased, and then it died off to nothing. Since that time, we've heard nothing else."

Ian, his prudence showing, stated, "So, I guess all we can do is to wait for them to return."

"If I hear anything else, I'll come back and let you know. I'm on my way over to tell Joe what I do know. After that, I'll go and sit with Joel until they arrive." As an afterthought, she went into the kitchen and filled a few water bottles. They'd been gone two hours, and she didn't know how much water they'd taken with them. A few minutes later, she waved good-bye to all the little children, and made her way to the door. Before leaving, she announced, "Don't be surprised if I come running back with more news!"

She reached Church and turned north. Moments later, she heard more gunshots, much fainter than before. This time it was different; they came from just over the hill to the south and only one rifle was being fired. The shots were also evenly spaced apart, almost as if it were a one-sided gun fight. The sound was not traveling from the downtown, but came from the area where Skyler's house sat. She stood and listened before continuing to the north barricade.

As she neared Joe's lookout site, she realized it was so dark she could very well walk right into a wall of logs. She stopped.

"Joe? Are you there?"

"What if I said no?" he replied.

She laughed nervously for a second and then remembered her haste. "Did you hear any of the shooting?"

"Barely and only about ten minutes ago. Someone was firing a gun about once every eight or ten seconds."

"I think that came from Skyler's house. I know they said they needed to chase one or two bandits from there before they'd be finished. I'm hoping that this means their trip into town was successful."

"Let's hope so. Are you saying that there were other shots fired earlier?"

"Oh, I forgot that you probably couldn't hear those. Yes, there was quite a bit of shooting from the downtown. It lasted maybe half a minute at the most. I'm anxious to cross back over to the other barricade and wait. I want to be there when they arrive." Even as she spoke with assurance, she felt anything but.

"Alright," he said. "Make sure someone comes over here and fills me in on the details."

"I'll make sure one of us comes to relieve you when this is over." With her task finished, she hurriedly said good-bye, and took off in a slow jog.

Crossing the crest of the hill again, she gauged the time to be sometime around midnight. Like all the major players of the night's drama, she

240

was running on an adrenaline rush. It would be hours before she would begin to feel fatigued. Regardless of tonight's outcome, she'd probably be on lookout until daybreak. She was more than happy to do it, especially if it meant that Skyler would stay with her.

As she neared the south barricade, she called out Joel's name. To her surprise, there was no answer. She called again, just a bit louder, and still there was no response. A shiver ran up her spine, and she feared the worst. Could something have happened to him? Then she realized that the rescue party may have returned earlier than what she had expected. They probably didn't need Joel or anyone else to act as a sentry, and he followed them back to the house. Sure of this, and not knowing what else to do, she immediately ran up the slope in the direction of the house. Skyler was most likely waiting for her there. She was almost sure of it.

As she reached the front porch for the second time within that hour, she noticed that the large sheet of plywood had been laid wide open, leaving the front door exposed. They had a strict rule about keeping this outer door closed to disguise the house. She bet that it was left this way by one of the Russians. They probably stopped in to retrieve Dimitrey on their way home.

She ran up on the porch to the door and, without hesitation, immediately pushed it open. She shoved it no more than eight inches inward when it collided with something on the other side. Through the gap in the dim candlelight, she could see Dag Jensen, seated in a chair, with a look of horror on his face. The children began screaming loudly at something, and she was unable to see what scared them. All she could see was that look on Dag's face as he tried to extricate himself from the chair. Her instincts instantly warned her that something was wrong. Before she finished pulling the door close, a shotgun exploded within the living room and the door jamb above her head erupted. Shards of wood splinters peppered her head as she dived off the porch.

As quickly as she could move, Brandy ran for the street and disappeared into the darkness. She was confused and scared, and didn't know where to go. This house had been the only safe haven she knew of. If she ran back over to the north barricade, Joe would be there—at least he should be. She couldn't be sure that she could meet up with Skyler or the others since their outcome was still unknown.

So she ran for the barricade that Joel had occupied and hoped that someone from down below would have heard that one blast of a shotgun.

CHAPTER 28

April 7th, 2031
12:30 am

Approaching the south barricade, Petar grew tense. It was still and quiet, more so than he expected. He would have thought that at least a few of the family members would be standing in front of the barricade upon their arrival. McBride, Brent, Petey, and the four Russians were accompanying him up the hill; the noise of their boots alone should have alerted the sentry. He called Joel's name aloud once. No answer. The sliver of a moon which had been their only visual aid, could no longer light their way. A whisper of an echo told them that the logs, unseen this night, were close before them. Petar knew that if the boy was within earshot, he would have replied. McBride stepped to the wall when his foot kicked something heavy. He picked it up.

"Petar! I've found his crossbow!"

"He wouldn't have left without it. Something's wrong. We'd better get up to the house!"

Just as they rounded the barricade, the stillness was interrupted by an explosion. The muffled report from a shotgun came from the area where the house was located. The men froze like statues, stunned and disbelieving.

McBride immediately assumed command and barked orders. "Brent, you and Petey stay here. The rest of us will head for the house and see what's going on. If a stranger gets comes through the barricade, shoot them."

The six men took off for the house. McBride stopped them when they reached the turn into the development. They had been traveling, hiding and fighting for so many hours with just outlines against the velvet back-drop of the night to guide them, but their keen hearing was now their eyes. They listened wordlessly, again as at the barricade, waiting for any kind of sound. Their investigation last only seconds as someone ran toward them, each footstep revealing a sense of urgency.

"Who's there?" McBride shouted and leveled his rifle automatically, his reactions working on autopilot.

"John? Is that you?" It was Brandy's distinctive voice, but laced with panic. She gulped for air, panting as she caught her breath.

He moved closer to her. "It's me, Brandy. What happened?" McBride's voice was uncharacteristically tender. Very little cracked his armor but, hearing her voice so stressed was gut wrenching. "Where did that shot come from?"

"From inside the house! I thought Joel had abandoned his post, so I ran to the house," she gasped for a breath again before continuing. "The outside door had been left wide open. I pushed the inner door open, and it hit someone. I could see Dag looking at me with fright, and then he looked off to his left. He reached out for something just as the door jamb above my head was shattered by the shot you just heard."

"Did you get a glimpse of who else is in there?"

"No, but I think I knocked someone over on the other side of the door. Dag was warning me about someone else to his left. All the kids were screaming which added to the confusion."

McBride filtered out what was fact and what was speculation. Back to the job he was faced with, he asked Brandy, "Who's watching the north barricade?"

"Joe, and I bet he's wondering what's going on."

"Go down there and stay with him. If anyone comes near that barricade without identifying themselves, don't let them pass. I've placed Brent and Petey on the south barricade for now. We'll send someone down to you as soon as we know what's going on."

"How are Skyler and the others?" Brandy had to know before she could move another step.

"Everyone is fine so far. Skyler stayed below to guard their house. James is catching up on some sleep. Now get going."

She slipped into the darkness. McBride wanted her away as quickly as possible. He needed to figure out how best to approach the house. Then he had to communicate that plan to the half of their men who spoke little or no English.

"How do you want to handle this?" asked Petar, deferring as before to McBride.

"We're going to walk down there and ask them who they are and what they want. I'm assuming that someone made Joel show them where the house is and now they're holding everyone hostage."

The Russians, during the past several hours, having struggled to overcome the challenges of communicating, seemed to understand McBride. They saw in him a man like themselves: one they could trust with their lives, a man who had learned to survive by eliminating any hurdles in his path. They followed the two men down the street, speaking in low tones in their native tongue.

McBride heard them say 'Dimitrey' several times during their conversation. When they were within a hundred feet of the house, McBride halted the group and in a whisper, he said, "I'm going to move in closer and try to make contact. I want all of you to stay back here. Understand?"

The Russians grunted their approval. Satisfied that they knew their role for now, McBride turned and approached the house. He stooped down until his hand found a rock, and gently threw it so that it met the front door with a thud. He waited a few seconds more before shouting in his booming voice.

"My name is John McBride. Who are you and what do you want?"

The house remained dark, quiet and ominous. There were no uncovered windows on this side of the house, not even on or around the door. Whoever was in there would need to come out the front or the back. Realizing this, McBride walked back to Petar and said, "Take one of the Russians, go around the block, and come in from behind. If someone tries to sneak out, drop them in their tracks."

McBride positioned the three remaining Russians in a semi-circle about twenty yards from the front door. He moved in closer and once again yelled to the house, "Who are you and what do you want?"

Finally, the front door opened and someone was pushed out onto the porch. Unable to see who it was, McBride asked, "Who are you?"

"It's me, Ian. There are two men in here with guns. All they want is to leave with some of the food. They haven't hurt anyone yet, and they say that they won't as long as you allow them a safe exit."

"What happens if we won't do that?" he asked the old man.

"They said that they will start shooting the children," he paused. "I believe that they'll do as they say."

"Are Lydia and her children in there?"

"Yes."

"Who else?"

"Besides Joel and Dimitrey, Ella, Dag, and all the small children are here."

Very quietly McBride asked him, "Do they know where the food is hidden?"

Ian whispered yes barely loud enough for McBride to hear.

McBride paused with his questioning. A plan was developing in his brain as he spoke with Ian. His next question was barely audible. "Is the trap door open?"

Once again, Ian whispered his answer.

That was what he wanted to hear. His hope being that no one else heard his questions. McBride didn't like being the only negotiator on the outside, but he had no choice. He was tired, stressed and impatient. Too much was happening for him to feel comfortable with. As soon as Brent found out that his family was in there, wild horses could not hold him back. His friend might not think rationally or logically. Petar's wife was also in there. McBride's dilemma was figuring out how to take out all the kidnappers without risking anyone's life. Yet, he wasn't about to let these men walk away free. They were the same ones who had led the attack against James, Brent and him earlier that day. They were also the ones who had attacked James' house and tried to kill Ian and Skyler. To allow them to walk away could mean that they'd enlist others and return for another fight. The next time, they'd know the location of their house. Yes, McBride thought to himself, they will need to be exterminated as swiftly as possible.

Looking up into the stars for a clue, he guessed that it was probably sometime after midnight. Dawn should arrive in only four or five hours. It had already been a long day; no end appeared to be sight. However, he needed to stall them as much as possible. Allowing them to escape under the guise of this dark night would be unacceptable.

"Ian, go back inside. Tell them that I am willing to accept their proposal as long as they let the children come out first. And tell them that they'll have to wait until daylight. No one is leaving here in the dark."

McBride heard the door open and close. He waited there a few more seconds before he was sure that Ian must have retreated back into the house to deliver his message. A moment later, Brent appeared out of the darkness. He'd run all the way from the barricade and was breathing heavily.

"Who's watching the road?" McBride demanded.

"Skyler is. He heard the shot and came running up the hill. James is staying down at his house to stand guard. That is, unless we need him. Are my wife and children in there?"

"Yeah, I'm sorry. They're inside, along with most everyone else. Ian assured me that no one has been hurt yet."

"What about Brandy?"

"She's the one that surprised them and caused them to fire that shot. She's a little shook up, but isn't injured. I just sent her down to the north barricade to stay with Joe."

"How are we going to get everyone out of there without anyone getting hurt?"

"Don't worry. I have a plan."

CHAPTER 29

April 7th, 2031
12:40 am

In the midst of chaos after the shotgun went off, DJ managed to regain control by demanding silence. The children were now more frightened than they were earlier. Seeing Brandon again had not dispelled those fears; if nothing else, it probably increased their anxiety. The children as a whole tried to stay apart from Brandon. Some of the children were fighting back tears, while others, like Joel and Dimitrey, were remarkably stoic, refusing to show any weakness to their captors.

Just as things had quieted down, they heard a rock hit the door. There was an eerie silence as everyone waited. What would DJ do next? They were taken by surprise when someone yelled from outside the house. It was a man demanding to know who they were and what they wanted. Brandon looked at DJ. The children watched and wondered whether he would respond to the man's questions.

"Before we let him know anything, we need to think about this." DJ whispered.

"It seems easy enough to me. We offer them everyone's freedom in exchange for our own." Brandon's plan was not thought through enough for DJ.

"Yeah, but what if they follow us out? What's to stop them from shooting us after we leave here? I'm not going out that door without any guarantees, and I'm not taking their word for it."

They continued to bicker back and forth until they heard the same man ask them, a second time, what they wanted. As Brandon reached for the door knob, DJ stopped him and turned to Ian.

"Hey, old man. Get up. You're going out there to inform them that we'll let everyone live if they let us walk out of here. Tell them that if they don't, we'll start shooting children, beginning with the youngest." DJ broke out with a smile as he motioned Ian to the front door with his rifle, confirming what Ian had suspected all along—they were dealing with a psychopath, not a hungry survivor.

Ian stood. "You wouldn't really do that, would you?"

"Damn right, I would. I'm getting out of here alive, one way or another. I don't give a shit about the rest of you."

Ian walked to the door, DJ keeping his rifle barrel pointed at him. "No funny stuff, old man. If you don't return, someone here is going to die in your place."

Ian tentatively opened the door and stepped out. Both DJ and Brandon listened to the exchange. DJ was satisfied with the way things were going until he heard the unidentified man demand that they wait until daylight. This part of the deal would have been unacceptable, until DJ realized the impact. If they were to try to walk away in the dark, they could unknowingly be followed, setting themselves up as targets. If they waited until daylight, each taking a hostage, they could refuse to release them until they were sure that they weren't being followed. This was shaping up better than he expected.

Ian stepped back inside the door. He had just started to relay the demands when DJ raised a hand to stop him. "Save it, old man. We heard everything. Sit back down."

Ian returned to where he had been sitting, yet he didn't sit down. He appeared to be waiting for something.

DJ was not impressed by Ian's defiance. Again with the barrel of the rifle pointed in Ian's direction, he sneered, "Do you have a problem?"

"Yes, I do. How are you going to leave here without someone stalking you?"

"Already thought about that, we'll each have a hostage."

"Then take me and him." He pointed at Dag, "We'll be willing to go with you."

DJ relished his control and power. "No, I don't think so. You move too slowly. I doubt those men out there will miss you if you die. They'll just have two fewer mouths to feed and less diapers to change. Now sit down and shut up!"

Ian did as he was told. Brandon had been scrutinizing one of the smaller boys. "I know who's going to be my hostage." He stood, pointing at Devon. "This little shit that caused all of my problems. I have a score to settle once I'm alone with him. Maybe we ought to take more than one hostage. Most of these kids were trained to steal for me. I'm sure they'd be happy to do it again."

"I'm setting my sights a little higher than you are." DJ stood and walked deliberately slow over to where Lydia and Ella were sitting. He reached out with his free hand, stroking Lydia's blonde hair. "I haven't been with a woman in over two years. My hostage is going to be nice and soft, willing to do anything I ask, especially if she doesn't want me to shoot her children."

Lydia, racked with fear, displayed nothing; she was not going to let a bully harm her children.

The room went deadly silent as the captives realized the bodily harm these two men would inflict upon them. Some of them would have to be released before those men could walk out of here, but two or more would have to stay and walk out with them. Whoever they chose may not be freed—at least not alive.

CHAPTER 30

Dag had been silently watching DJ's and Brandon's every move since their arrival. He had never been in a situation where his morals had been so tested. But he found it wasn't difficult when the opportunity presented itself—he would do whatever he could to get these children out alive, including putting his life on the line. By the way these men were ignoring him; they viewed him as nothing but a feeble old man. He needed to keep it that way as long he could. He'd almost blown his cover when Brandy's face appeared through the open door. Dag reflexively began to reach out for DJ's weapon, but stopped himself in time. DJ had fired the shotgun one-handed at the door. The gun had bucked and fired upward, tearing itself loose from his grip. Fortunately, neither DJ nor Brandon saw the old man reach out his hand. Had they, they would have killed him without a second thought.

DJ had made another critical error when he had Ian and Dag recover those twelve jars of food. He had laid his rifle down, forgetting it when he saw the food. Both men had seen it lying on the bed. Ian made brief eye contact with Dag while they were alone with DJ. Dag wanted to drop his jars and reach for the weapon, but the open trap door stood in his path.

Ian was quick to see it and made an attempt to close the door before DJ stopped him. When they'd left the room with the rifle still lying on the bed, Dag began forming a plan to go back there and retrieve it. The toilet was on the way to that room. Everyone knows that old men have to pee frequently. Dag's hopes were dashed when Brandon noticed that the weapon was missing.

The third error DJ and Brandon made was when they'd shared their plans with everyone in the room. They kept it no secret that they were going to take hostages. Ian seethed when he heard them discuss taking one of the children or women as if chattel, to be used or discarded at their whim. Ian and Dag had only met for the first time earlier that evening and discovered a mutual respect for the other as they shared stories from their past lives and learned how much alike they were. After hearing that Dag had been ill for months, Ian offered to listen to his heart and lungs with his stethoscope. Dag had declined, saying that would simply implant false hopes or reinforce his fears when he already knew he was on borrowed time. He was nearly eighty years old, having led a long and full life without regrets before the Change. He viewed himself as lucky. The children here could barely remember their past lives; who knew what the future would hold for them. The two old men knew that they were the only hope for saving the children. Ian made it clear to Dag that he was a pacifist and healer for most of his life. Would he resort to force if it was necessary?

Dag's first task was to open a line of communication with Ian, covertly in such a way that it would fly under the two thugs' radar. Trying to exchange or pass words in the living room was just plain suicidal. Dag had to get a note to Ian that he could read in private. The bathroom seemed the most logical choice. He'd been in there earlier and remembered seeing that a phone book was being used as their toilet paper dispenser. He patted his chest pocket and felt the outline of his pencil—something he frequently used for his woodworking. Now he had to think about what he could write in the least amount of words. Chances were that Brandon or DJ would get suspicious if either of them were in the bathroom any longer than needed.

Leaving no detail to chance, Dag noticed that DJ had leaned the shotgun up in a corner. Dag wondered if DJ was as stupid as his actions portrayed. Oh, he was smart—street smart and that had gotten him far, but he was slipping up, and Dag intended to catch him when the opportunity presented itself. And it would. Dag and Ian may have been nothing more than "old men" to DJ, but collectively, they had more life experience and education than the entire room of people. Dag was going to use that secret weapon to its maximum potential.

DJ appeared not to want to hold the shotgun after his failed attempt to fire it. The gun was old but dependable. There were four shells left in the magazine after the fifth had been fired. Dag thought it odd that he had not re-chambered a second shell. Was he not familiar with pump shotguns? The gun kicked badly when fired. DJ had been annoyed with its action. To his advantage, Dag had owned the gun since his youth, maintaining it as if it were an heirloom. He was accustomed to its violent kick. As he aged, it had become one of his favorite possessions, reminding him of the sacrifice his father had made to earn extra money to buy it for Dag's twelfth birthday. Remembering how his father had taught him to visualize hitting his target before he squeezed the trigger. Now, he closed his eyes and pictured himself reaching for the weapon. If DJ was holding his rifle, he would never have enough time to get to the shotgun before the younger man would notice.

Seeing that reaching for his old rifle would not work, Dag methodically started working on a new plan.

In the hour since Brandy escaped her failed attempt to enter the house, three of the younger children had already asked to use the bathroom. Before anyone could use it, DJ set down the stipulations; any offenders would be gravely punished. The door was to stay open. After each occupant exited, he would inspect the small room to ensure nothing suspicious took place. Dag measured out in his head the length of the hall which connected the living room to the kitchen. It was maybe five feet, six at the most. A door, the one for the bathroom, sat halfway along this hall. The toilet still flushed because someone in this household had rigged up a gravity-fed water system. It was something he had been meaning to ask Petar about, but he had no time for stray thoughts. He had to come up with a plan and, using shorthand, needed somehow to relay the message to Ian before dawn arrived; no small task indeed.

Dag used his keen observation skills to inspect every detail about DJ and Brandon. Both men were thinner than normal, but then, so was everyone. Every survivor paid for the lack of food by shedding weight. If it came down to it, Dag doubted that he had enough strength to take on either young man. However, Ian was different. He was thin, yet incredibly fit for his age. All Dag would need to do was buy Ian some time; as little as half of a minute might be enough. If he could keep DJ's rifle from being used against anyone, Ian could wrestle the rifle away from Brandon. Someone had to be outside, just waiting for a cry for help. His plan depended on Ian accepting the fate they had been handed, that their actions would most certainly be an endeavor in suicide.

Ian sat on the floor only about five or six feet from Brandon. Could he reach across and grab his rifle in a flash? He would have to act fast to overpower the younger man. Dag visualized him twisting the rifle so swiftly that Brandon would have to release his grip. Dag thought about Joel. Would he be brave enough to assist? Securing his help could not be expected because getting a note to him would be near impossible. Besides, he was young and had so much to live for. Like the other children, he held the survival of humanity in their hands. Dag could only hope for his help, but he thought he could make his plan work without the boy's intervention.

Dag reached for his chest pocket and pushed the pencil up through the opening, a weapon in its own right. Without glancing down, he could feel the top inch protruding. Once it was visible, he waited for both Brandon and DJ to look elsewhere. Ian had probably been waiting for the same moment because he looked at Dag with subtle anticipation. There was at least an eight-foot gap between them. Dag worried there might not be enough light for Ian to see the small object. Dag glanced downward toward the object sticking out of his pocket. He hoped Ian would see the pencil and catch on to Dag's intent. As DJ spun back around, both men were forced to look away from each other, but reconnected long enough for Ian to nod. He had seen the pencil.

The pencil. If one were to replay the events yet to be played out during the night, it would be the pencil seen as the hero. Dag would need to write just one sentence with as few words as possible containing concise instructions and asking for confirmation. If he were to enact this plan, he needed Ian's approval and acceptance. He played the same scene over and over in his mind until he was finally satisfied with how he would word it.

Ready to go forward, no looking back, no considering every possible outcome, the time had come to just act. Dag cleared his throat and asked, "May I use the bathroom to empty my bladder?" His question had been directed at DJ, but he hadn't spoken the young man's name. He didn't want him to know that while they'd sat there, he had learned everything possible about this man.

"As long as you leave the door open." Then DJ paused before adding, "If I don't hear you peeing, I'll come in and drag your ass out of there."

Dag stood and found that he had to walk in front of DJ to reach the bathroom. The younger man was not in a defensive position. Dag could have easily grabbed the rifle. It was a shame that the right set of circumstances had not presented themselves to Ian and him earlier. They could've made their move at that moment. Both DJ and Brandon were exposed and, with complete arrogance, not expecting any kind of retaliatory strike. Dag hoped another chance like this would present itself.

As Dag stepped into the hallway, he could see the window on the kitchen's east wall. Through it, he could see the faint outline on the horizon and the sky beginning to lighten along its edge. It must already be after three a.m., leaving him with maybe a little more than an hour or two in which to act. He briefly wondered what was happening outside. Had the rescue been successful? It must have been because the voice outside had identified himself as John McBride. They too could be formulating some sort of operation. However, this was not the time to dwell on the 'what ifs'. For now, he needed to get the note written and its message delivered to Ian.

Something he'd missed in his preparation was that the bathroom was black as coal. He wanted to request a candle but knew that it would only draw suspicion. At least in the dark, someone could not walk in and see him writing. He'd have to write the note without knowing where his words began or ended, the rheumy effects of old age working against his hand-writing, too. Then he'd have to make sure that Ian could find the note. Where would Ian find enough light to read it? It would have been much easier if the room had been lit up, even if only a little. He quickly dropped his pants and sat on the seat knowing that time was scarce. As his bladder relaxed and began to empty, he found the phone book, and quietly tore a section from a page. The noise of his urine splashing the water should be enough to drown out the sounds of paper tearing.

He jotted down the words he'd memorized, being careful to leave spaces between the invisible words. He finished in time and had to fold the paper as he stood. He quickly slipped the folded note under the seat onto the rim of the bowl. Just as he buckled his pants and turned around, DJ appeared with a candle in one hand and rifle in the other.

"Just making sure that you aren't up to something fishy," he said as he waited for Dag to exit. He then went into the bathroom and lifted the phone book as he tried to shake out anything hidden within its pages. Dag wanted to stand there and watch the rest of the inspection, but was aware that it might make DJ suspicious. He headed back to the living room, noticing that DJ came out close behind him. He'd obviously not found the note.

The note, carrying the weight of flesh and bone on it, was Dag's last effort to communicate his plan with Ian. While Ian was extremely sharp and might actually look under the seat, Dag needed to make certain he found the notice on his one and only trip in there. He thought about point-ing to his own seat, but knew that it too could draw attention from either DJ or Brandon. He finally figured out what would work and smiled briefly.

Some of the children had fallen asleep, cuddled up to one another for comfort. Both of Lydia's children lay on the floor with their heads rest-ing on her legs. She did not sleep, her eyes ragged around the edges as her resolve inched closer to cracking as the night sky began to lose some of its impact. Dag wanted to comfort her, to let her know that he'd do his best to stop these men from leaving with her or harming her children. He could do nothing now as he waited for Ian to ask to use the bathroom.

It was a half-hour before Ian made his short and quiet request. Once again, DJ spelled out the rules for using the bathroom as Ian stood to get circulation in his legs.

"Be careful in there, its dark and the seat is loose," Dag said in a low voice. DJ shot him an angry glance, but Dag had already finished what he wanted to say. Ian nodded signifying acknowledgment or thanks. Dag wasn't sure which.

After the toilet flushed, DJ entered the hallway to escort Ian back to the living room, but took the time to inspect the bathroom for any contraband before he did so. He appeared in a minute without seeming to have found anything out of the ordinary.

Several minutes passed before Dag was able to steal a glance at Ian. The moment had come when DJ had noticed that the kitchen was no longer a dark abyss; he called to Brandon to have a look. As both stared down the hall, Ian looked at Dag and gave a strong nod. Dag wondered when he'd had the opportunity to read the note and whether or not he was confirming he'd found it, or that he'd been able to read it. Time slowed and sped at all once. Dag would have to chance it that Ian was with him. His plan had to go forward now.

DJ moved over to the entrance to the hall and seemed content to stand there as he watched the kitchen grow brighter by the minute. His new location made it difficult, if not impossible, for Dag to grab his rifle. Any attempt from this position would be reckless. Dag tried to picture new scenarios in his mind. The part about Ian grabbing and twisting the rifle had not changed, but his own role had. Dag could see no way to get to DJ before he could bring the rifle around and knock him to the ground.

Suddenly, DJ stepped back inside the living room and threw his back against the wall. He was focused on something in the kitchen. Brandon also sensed that something was wrong and turned his attention to the lighted doorway. A voice outside the front door startled everyone as it boomed out loud. Those children who slept were quickly awakened by the others. The room came alive.

"Good morning! It's time to let everyone walk out, and we'll allow you to do the same."

The voice was the same one he'd heard earlier. It was John McBride. DJ seemed torn between answering the caller and glancing toward the kitchen. Something back there was not right, and both Brandon's and DJ's nerves had been jarred. Children were talking among themselves with fear in their voices.

Dag knew it was time to act. His last thought before moving was what a wonderful life he'd had.

CHAPTER 31

April 7th, 2031
1:45 am

"We get Dimitrey!"

His English was limited, but he had made his point. The large Russian needed no translation to show that he and his brothers were becoming impatient about waiting.

Brent didn't know how to convey that they were doing everything they could to free their nephew; that they had no other choice than to wait until they could get into the house.

"Please no. We must wait for morning!" He wished he had a clock or wristwatch so he could show them the time. The large man understood the word 'trouble', or at least he acknowledged it, but Brent could not explain the situation to them. All they knew was that Dimitrey was in the house being held captive by two men and there were four of them—two to one odds were good enough for them. They had handled the earlier events of the night following orders, performing battle knowledge and skill no one had expected, and now they were tired of waiting, wanting to retrieve their nephew and go home.

McBride returned just in time. He'd gone to check on Petar, informing him of the plan, leaving Brent alone with the three Russians, who he could see was having problems communicating with. McBride knew a few words in Russian, enough to point out that 'many children' were in danger. The largest of the men appeared to relax a bit and looked at his analog wristwatch. When Brent saw this, he reached for the man's wrist and pointed to the five. That was when they would enact their plan.

According to the large man's watch, it was almost three in the morning. Brent was on the edge since learning that his wife and children were inside, and now the Russians wanted to bust down the door. McBride hadn't fully shared the entire plan with him because he needed to confer with Petar first.

"Please explain to me how you think you can get Lydia and my children out alive?"

"You are going in to get them."

"What? Do you really think it's safe to rush in there?"

"I didn't say rush in. When the time comes, I am going to have them send everyone out. I don't expect them to comply. They'll want to keep at least two of the children hostage until they are sure that we aren't following them as they leave. I can't allow them to do that. While I am out here negotiating with them, you'll already be inside."

Brent said nothing, confusion written all over his face.

McBride continued, "Do you remember when we put that trap door into the floor? We also had to block off the shaft that led to the heat pump. I intentionally made it that way so we could easily remove that door. I thought that it could come in handy someday if we became trapped in the house. It left us a way to sneak out from under the house and out of sight of anyone watching the doors. That is how we'll get you in there."

Brent thought about it for several seconds before asking, "How far do I go in?"

"As far as you can without attracting their attention. I'm hoping you'll be inside the back bedroom by the time it's light enough to see. Ian was able to confirm that the trap door on the floor was open. Let's hope that they haven't closed it. Stay inside the opening unless you are sure that you can climb up through it silently. If things start falling apart,

262

you'll have the opportunity to take them out if they aren't cooperating."

"How will I know what's going on out front. We won't be able to communicate."

"I've already thought about that. Petar is going to watch you until you are under the house. When you are under the back bedroom, he'll signal me. When it's daylight, I will begin yelling instructions to those two bastards. I'm pretty sure you'll hear me."

Brent thought about the plan so far, and was game to give it a try. Still, he managed to come up with another question. "What if they do walk out with hostages before I get to them?"

"Don't worry; there'll be five of us out front. If they have hostages, we'll find a way to stall them before they can leave. I doubt that they intend to free the hostages when they're through with them."

Brent didn't want it to come down to this, but at least he was playing a major role in saving his wife and kids. Since finding out what had evolved, he'd had a difficult time keeping his anger in check.

He finally said to McBride, "I want to get moving as soon as possible. If things start falling apart in there before daylight, I think it's necessary to have someone who can respond within a few seconds."

"I was hoping that you'd want to go in now. Put some mud on your face and circle around the block. Petar can get you to the side of the house from the back. Every movement has to be done in baby steps. The slightest noise could throw the plan off in a heartbeat."

"Since it's going to be close quarters, can I borrow your pistol? I'll still have my rifle with me, but I prefer to have a weapon that can be maneuvered quickly."

McBride reached into his coat pocket and brought out his nine millimeter. He checked the magazine before handing it over. "It's fully loaded."

"Thanks." After pocketing the gun, Brent reached out with his free arm and gave his friend a hug. Not something he'd normally do, especially to another ex-soldier, but he suddenly felt a kinship with John McBride. This man was not only requesting that he take part, he was also being generous with one of his closest possessions. He turned and left to go find Petar.

The exterior trap door would be relatively easy to get to. During the previous year, they'd removed the neighboring fences to expand their garden. As dark as it was, finding the door was not difficult, but opening it without making any noise would be. The well in which the heat pump had rested within was now empty and covered with a thick sheet of plywood. Brent and Petar slowly lifted one edge before finally removing the lid altogether. As Brent dropped down into the hole, Petar held his rifle until Brent's feet were on the ground. Petar's new job was to stand by and keep an eye out. There were no open windows on this side of the house.

As if by Braille, Brent had to feel his way in the dark as he crawled along the three-foot shaft that would lead him through the foundation. The heat pump and large ducts had already been removed. McBride saw no need to leave them in place. True to the soldier he was, thinking ahead about escaping armed and dangerous enemies, decided it was the perfect escape tunnel should they require one. The door Brent had to pass through had been placed from the inside and was held in position by small wooden clasps. The clasps were made by taking rectangular pieces of wood and nailing them to the frame just around the door. The door itself sat flush within this frame, with the clasps swiveled to hold the door in place. The original design had been to make the door accessible from the inside and not the outside. Brent knew that if he could get something slim through the crack between the door and the frame, he could jimmy the clasps open.

Feeling around with his hands, he started on the right side of the door. His knife blade, small and thin, didn't fit on the first attempt. He tried the other side. The fit was tight, but he was able to squeeze the blade through. He remembered what McBride had said about baby steps. Pulling the blade down, he eventually felt the first of four clasps and pushed it aside. The plywood door instantly sprung inward a half inch. "Probably warped from moisture," he thought.

The next clasp was at the top edge of the door above the one he'd just freed. The knife slid easily until he felt resistance. He'd reached the clasp. His concern was that if he moved this one, the door would spring inward even further, possibly falling. He pushed the side out enough to slide his fingers between the door and the frame. Once the side was held in place, he pushed the knife blade up. The door moved only slightly.

The next step was to remove the door without dropping it. Even though it was still clasped on the right side, the left and top edges were free. He should be able to slide the door up and away from the two remaining clasps. Using one hand, Brent closed the folding knife and slipped it into a pocket. His movements were slow and deliberate. He would need both hands to prevent the heavy door from falling inward. While keeping pressure against the left side of the door, he slid his left hand up and onto the top of the door. Then he inserted his right hand under the lower edge. Shifting his feet to maximize his balance, Brent pushed the door away from him while holding it. He strained to control the weight while moving at a snail's pace. Eventually, he felt the weight swing inward as the door broke free. He gently lowered it to the ground and laid it flat. Sweat was trickling down from his temples.

Brent backed out enough to whisper, "I'm in," to Petar. At this point, Petar's instructions were to let McBride know that Brent was under the house. He then lifted his rifle and crawled back into the tunnel. After feeding the rifle through, he slowly squeezed himself through the small opening. It was so dark that he found it necessary to grope around so that he wouldn't bump into anything, including the joists above his head. The space varied from two to three feet in height, forcing him to stay on his hands and knees. The ground was cold and damp, easily penetrating his canvas pant legs. Brent also wasn't sure which way led to the trap door. According to McBride, it'd been left open, but the total darkness left him without any sense of direction. He finally had to back up and place his back against the concrete foundation. Closing his eyes, he imagined the layout of the house in conjunction to where he now sat. The tunnel came under the house on the opposite side of the house from the bedroom and a bit to the south. If he went straight in, he would end up under the kitchen. Knowing this, he aimed his body at an angle to his left and began a slow crawl. Each movement required that he feel just where his knee or hand would come to rest. The ground, still cold from the winter, threatened to numb his hands. His rifle had to be lifted and set back down ahead of him before he could move his right hand and knee forward. If any shooting started now, he wasn't sure how quickly he could find the trap door.

Brent had been crawling about ten minutes when his rifle barrel touched one of the cases of food. It surprised him that he hadn't sensed the obstacle. The noise it made was slight enough that it could only be heard within a few feet. Nevertheless, he chastised himself. Feeling the boxes, he discovered that they formed a wall. They had been stacked on a pallet made to keep them off the ground, but the cardboard felt soft and moist. He tried to remember if there was a place in this wall that he could pass through, but couldn't recall such a gap. He finally resigned that he would need to move two boxes and their contents in order to get past.

The first box he chose was only half full, so he started by reaching in and lifting out jars one at a time. At this pace, it could take a half-hour or more to clear the path. Luckily, McBride had not yet yelled his instructions to the men inside. He laid the jars on their side away from where he was working to prevent them from toppling over on the soft uneven ground. Once the box was empty, he gently lifted it off the next box. Suddenly, he froze. There were voices and footsteps above him. A dim light briefly appeared, allowing him to see that the trap door was open. Then he heard the noise of someone using the toilet.

The first box rested atop the second box, the one that needed to be maneuvered. At first, he tried sliding it on the pallet, but the moist cardboard began to tear. Once again, he would need to lift the jars out one at a time. It was a time-consuming job when all he wanted to do was rush, to let Lydia know that she and the children would come to no harm, that he was there. But he couldn't. Not yet. As he was close to emptying the box, another set of footsteps could be heard followed by the sound of someone using the toilet. He looked up and noticed a dim glow through the opening of the trap door. This was different than the candlelight he'd seen earlier. Much to his relief, he realized that the early morning light of dawn was beginning to make its appearance. A tiny sparkle of light reflected off his gold wedding band, reminding him of what was more important to him than anything left in this world.

Once the final box was out of the way, Brent sat on the pallet and waited with the pistol in his hand. So far, he'd done what he needed to do, and from his limited viewpoint, he knew he could be inside the house in just seconds. The house had remained quiet since the last person had used the bathroom. Could there be someone resting inside the bedroom? He waited. And waited. Waited for as long as he'd ever waited before as he saw the room above him grow brighter with the new day. Finally, he rose up and stood within the opening, listening to nothing but silence, scanning the beds for any occupants. It was as if the house were deserted. The air felt warm compared to the crawl space. The floor was level with his belt buckle. He felt certain that he could climb into the room silently. Enough light was coming in through the door to the kitchen to allow him to see everything clearly. To be effective in the plan, to free Lydia and his children, to be in place when the time came to act, he needed to be standing inside the bedroom when McBride made his move.

Lifting the rifle out first, he laid it gently onto the polished wood floor. The nine millimeter pistol went back into his pocket as he placed both hands on the floor's edge and lifted himself up into a sitting position. Still agile after the hours spent in the cramped crawl space, Brent slowly stood, retrieving the pistol with his right hand before picking up the rifle. The beds were tightly pushed together; he dared not try to climb over. He would need to go to the end and around the foot of the last one.

The glow from the kitchen made it possible for him to see his way around without bumping into anything. He finally reached the door and glanced through the kitchen. He could see the kitchen was empty, as was the hall leading into the living room. Since the bedroom door was not in alignment with the hall, he could only visualize a small gap between the two doorways. As he stood there, he could make out someone sitting on the floor just inside the living room. When that person raised their head, he recognized his wife. Brent did not want her to see him. Unsure of how she would react, he quickly stepped aside to hide his face from hers. As his weight settled behind the door frame, the floor creaked beneath his feet. The sudden noise was not the least bit faint. His heart sank.

Just then, McBride's booming voice sounded loudly outside, bringing the entire living room alive.

CHAPTER 32

April 7ᵗʰ, 2031
3:15 am

As soon as Ian was inside the dark bathroom, he lifted the seat and patted the porcelain rim with his left hand while fumbling with his pants with the other. He had only a few precious seconds to find the note that Dag had left for him. DJ stood just feet from the open door and would be listening to his every move. He knew this because he had watched Dag closely while he had been in here. The younger man nervous with good reason. Ian intentionally waited to request the use of the bathroom. His captors would have been suspicious if he did so right after Dag had been in there. His hand found the folded note. Without hesitation, he silently lowered the seat, and in one fluid motion, dropped his pants and sat.

He reached into his pocket and extracted a small cylinder. It was his LED penlight from his medical kit, and it still carried a charge. Always with him, and seldom needed, until now, he used it mainly to look into his patient's eyes and ears. Reaching down into the cavity of his open trousers, he unfolded the thin paper before turning the light on. The LED was not bright, the battery nearing the end of its life, but in this tiny room, its brilliance could be compared to a sixty watt bulb. Ian tried to keep the small light confined within the upper part of his open trousers. Should anyone look around the corner, he and Dag would surely be shot. As his bladder emptied, he read the message and pocketed the light before wadding the paper and dropping it into the bowl. As soon as he stood, he flushed the toilet before pulling his pants back up. Too dark to see if it went down with the flush, he stepped into the hall while fastening his pants.

DJ stood there holding the candle but said nothing. The message was clear; he was there to inspect the bathroom. Ian ushered past him without looking up into his face, and headed for his place on the floor. He dared not look at Dag just yet. The time would come, the light he'd seen come from the kitchen was still too dim to be labeled as dawn, but it was close. He'd already decided on his response. The note consisted of a single sentence. If given the chance, he wanted to commend the older man for his covertness. Its message was clear, "GRAB AND TWIST THE OTHER RIFLE WHEN I MAKE MY MOVE. YES?" The request was simple and concise, yet carried no guarantees. When Dag did whatever was outside of playing the captive, Ian's job was to grab and twist Brandon's rifle, wrenching it from his hands. He was sure that the old man wanted him to move on Brandon, since he sat only a few feet away from him. To simply grab the rifle would have put him into a tussle with someone of greater strength. But the twisting was ingenious. Twisting the rifle in a clockwise motion could force his opponent to lose his grip, and possibly buy him some time.

He had to wonder what Dag had planned for his role. DJ was younger, faster, and stronger. It would not be a fair fight. DJ also held the rifle that Dag would need to silence. If Ian was unable to stop Brandon from reacting, Dag would be vulnerable from behind. It was important that he make every attempt to move quickly, and to twist with every ounce of strength. He wasn't doing it for Dag or himself; he was doing it for the children. Whatever took place when dawn arrived would probably spell disaster for the children and Lydia. If McBride allowed them to walk away with hostages, they might not see those captives alive again. Why should they? The bandits would know the strength and numbers of this family, and would most likely return someday soon.

DJ had already made it clear that he wouldn't leave without using someone as a shield. For Ian, that was the defining moment when he'd made the choice to fight. All his life he'd walked the passive road, never willing to pick up a weapon against anyone. However, now it was as if it were his calling, being the only one that could assist the older man. His career had been focused on saving the lives of children, and tonight he would do that again, only by a different means.

The glow from the kitchen had caught DJ's attention; he called for Brandon. Some of the children slept through it, but others were disturbed by the break in silence. The two men moved to the hall, their backs toward Ian long enough for him to look at Dag. The old man was already waiting for his answer, wanting for the confirmation he'd requested. Ian shook his head enough so that there would be no doubt to what his answer was. Dag nodded back in return just before the two men re-entered the living room. Brandon returned to his station, but DJ remained in the doorway. If he stayed there, he would be two feet out of Dag's reach. Any attempt at that distance could be defended easily by the younger man. Regardless, Ian had set his mind and would follow through regardless of the outcome. Most likely, this action would have been suicidal anyway, but at least he'd be taking a bullet that may have been used on a child.

Ian sat there watching both Dag and DJ with the corner of his eye. He was ready to spring into action, having already shifted his legs so that he could rise up rapidly when necessary. As long as DJ stood in the doorway, he hoped that Dag would not react. The time would come when he'd enter the room again; he'd have to. It was just a matter of waiting. Regardless of what went down, Ian had already decided that as soon as his hands were on the rifle, he'd start yelling for help as loud as he could. Someone had to be just outside monitoring the house. Last night's rescue must have been a success, or at the very least, McBride had been freed. And surely the Russians would not have left without their nephew. Ian surmised that half a dozen men or more surrounded this house. To yell that single word over and over would bring someone through the door. As long as they held their captor's rifles from being aimed, the battle would end quickly. Ian no longer feared what lay ahead. He now looked forward to what was about to happen.

DJ eventually made his way back into the living room, but stood just inside the doorway. He was closest to Lydia and her children, yet still beyond Dag's grasp. Ian could not see a way in which the old man could rise up and reach DJ before he could bring his rifle around and block the attack.

A sudden noise caught Ian's attention. It had come from within the house, possibly as close as the kitchen. It was loud compared to the silence they'd been accustomed to. Everyone who was awake heard it. Heard it clearly. It was a distinctive creak of old floorboards. Someone was inside the back half of the house!

DJ responded instantly by swinging his body back into the hallway as he raised his rifle and pointed it toward the kitchen. Realizing that something had spooked him, Brandon jumped to his feet, the sound in unison with McBride's voice booming.

"Good morning! It's time to let everyone walk out and we'll allow you to do the same."

Ian looked over at Dag and saw that his hands rested in such a way that he was about to push himself up. He was held back by DJ's reaction to McBride's request—the younger man was swinging his rifle barrel back and forth as if he expected someone to enter from either direction.

Brandon made a similar move until he climbed over the small bed that separated him from Ian, obviously not wanting to have his back against the door. Ian, now sitting only two feet from Brandon and his rifle, was within reach without fully standing. He looked back at Dag just in time to see him throw himself onto the back of DJ, his forearm wrapping tightly around the younger man's throat. As if on cue, Ian reached for Brandon's weapon, and using his falling weight, twisted the rifle until the barrel pointed down. No longer able to watch what was happening between Dag and DJ, Ian began screaming, "Help! Help!"

Children cried out in horror as most of the adults in the tight space were entangled in combat. Ian focused on twisting the rifle like hands on a clock. Brandon was forced to release his grip with one hand. Ian nearly had the rifle wrestled from Brandon's left hand when a fist hammered the side of his head. The blow was so intense that Ian lost his grip and felt the weapon pull away from him. Looking up, fully expecting to see the barrel aimed at him, a blur passed through his field of vision and hit Brandon square in the torso. Joel was now on top of Brandon's supine body, pummeling his head with rapid punches, too fast for Brandon to block.

A gunshot erupted within the room bringing a sudden pause to all the chaos. Ian looked up in time to see Dag fall backwards with his hands clutched to his chest. Joel, startled by the noise, looked up see DJ swing the barrel in his direction. He dove off Brandon, seeking cover away from the screaming children. As DJ leveled his sights on the boy, another loud report sounded from within the house. At about the same instant, the front door flew open and McBride appeared with rifle raised, the barrel sweeping the room for a target. The second gunshot had come from the hall. Ian watched as DJ dropped his rifle and fell forward onto his face.

Brent appeared behind him ready to fire another round, but his rifle was not pointed at DJ. Ian turned to see what Brent was aiming at and saw Brandon. Somehow, during the melee, Brandon had retrieved his rifle and now lay on the floor with Devon clutched to his chest, the barrel resting beneath the boy's ear. Brandon's look was one of fear and determination.

Refusing to lower his weapon, Brent barked angrily at Brandon, "I remember you. I told you that if I ever saw you again, I wouldn't hesitate to kill you!"

"You better let me leave here alive, or I'll take this kid's life with me!" Beads of sweat had formed on Brandon's forehead.

Ignoring the scene before him, McBride crossed over to DJ's body and rolled him over with his foot. Even from where he sat, Ian could see that he'd taken a mortal wound to the back of the skull. Blood and bits of brain were splattered across the room. The children, some still crying out of fear, had quieted and were fixated on the standoff taking place. Gia cried out when she saw Devon, her only brother, being used as a shield by Brandon, the man they all loathed. She started to stand, but Bree held her back, keeping her from running to her brother's aid.

McBride stepped back and turned to look down at Dag. He squatted by the old man's side before looking around the room. As soon as he spotted Ian, he said gently, "You better get over here, Doc." The tone of McBride's voice was grim. Dag had risked his life on something worth meaning, and saving the lives of the children would be his legacy.

Ian crawled beneath the line of sight between Brent and Brandon to reach his friend. He grabbed Dag's wrist to check his pulse. Dag appeared to have lost consciousness, his face unmoving and eyes closed. Then his lips moved as if he were trying to form words.

Ian's attention was drawn away briefly as Brandon stood with Devon still clutched to his chest. Both Brent and McBride had their weapons raised but were stopped from further action by the threat to Devon's life. The boy did not whimper or cry as Ian expected. One of the Russians entered the room only long enough to grab Dimitrey and pull him from harm's way. Brandon walked sideways to the open door, keeping the barrel resting against the boy's head, squeezing him tightly against his body. No one made a move to stop him as he backed out the door. McBride followed as Brent took inventory of his wife and children. Finding them unharmed, he turned to Ian.

"Make sure everyone is alright. I have to help get Devon back." Then Brent disappeared through the front door.

Ian returned to Dag and unbuttoned his bloody shirt to find the wound. The single bullet had entered the old man's lower chest at the base of the sternum. It had severed a major artery. Like a lava flow, the blood, gushing at first, and then slowly coagulating, finally a last trickling as Dag was bleeding out. What children remained had now gathered around the physician as he inspected his patient. Dag let out an involuntary gasp. Thinking it was his last, Ian was about to cover his chest when he heard the old man whisper.

"Did we save the children?"

"You did," he lied, not yet knowing the outcome. "They are all safe thanks to you."

"Then I guess it was worth it." He winced, showing that it pained him to speak.

"I'm so sorry that I wasn't able to help you."

"You did what I needed."

With that, Dag gasped for air one more time but stopped in mid breath. Ian unconsciously held the old man's hand and felt it go limp as the life went out of him. Wee babes had died in Ian's arms before, but seeing Dag and realizing the breadth of his sacrifice, struck Ian in a way he could not have explained as his eyes uncharacteristically filled with tears.

CHAPTER 33

April 7th, 2031
12:50 am

It took Skyler less than fifteen minutes to reach the barricade after hearing that single shotgun blast. He was worried not only about Brandy, but all the children. A small army had preceded him up the hill, something that should have put his mind at ease. But he couldn't shake the feeling that something had gone terribly wrong. Brent met him at the barricade and had little to share; so far, McBride or Petar had not sent them any news. Skyler offered to replace him at the barricade, especially since his wife and children were in the house.

"I'm almost out of bullets." His statement was meant to inform the two boys, not request a solution.

Petey, lifted his rifle, the one given to him after the battle, and said, "Take this, it's loaded."

Without hesitation, Brent reached out and grabbed the carbine by the mid-section. Barely able to see in the moonless night, he turned to look at the two boys, as if he might not see them again. Wordless, he disappeared around the barricade.

An hour passed before McBride appeared in the dark. Looking tired and anxious, Skyler could only imagine what kind of day he'd been through and the fatigue he was experiencing. His previous military combat experience had been tested here for the last several hours. "What happened? Who fired the shot?"

"It appears that the last two bandits are up here, and somehow they took the house without much of a struggle. Nobody was hurt when the shotgun went off. They allowed Ian to come out and speak with me. Lydia and Ella are both in there with the children, along with Dag and Dimitrey. Petar is guarding the back of the house with one the Russians. Brent is covering the front while I'm up here."

"What do you suppose they want?"

"They want to walk away unscathed, and with their packs filled with food. Ian says that they've already found our food supply. They've said that if we won't allow them to leave, they'll start by shooting children."

"Are you going to let them walk away?"

"We can't. They know too much about where we live and how much food we have. As soon as they're hungry again, they'll be back."

Skyler asked tentatively, "Is Brandy in there?"

"No, right now she's with Joe at the north barricade. She knows that you are alright and what's happening up here. I told her to stay down there until morning."

Skyler was relieved to hear that she wasn't inside the house when those men arrived. He knew that she would remain there as instructed, but was also aware that she must be traumatized by what was taking place here tonight.

McBride excused himself and ran back to watch the house until morning. He'd said that everything was on hold until then. Skyler stayed at the north barricade through the night with Petey. They passed the time watching both sides of the barricade while waiting and listening for any signs of a change in the stalemate. Petey had found the large crossbow where Joel had dropped it. He picked up the weapon, and then searched the ground for possible projectiles.

Skyler was tired, having been awake for over forty hours. Some adrenaline still rushed through his veins, but it was quickly being replaced by fatigue. The fact that Brandy was in no immediate danger took a load off his back. Still, Ian, Dag and all the others were inside that house. Their lives were in danger. He felt especially worried about Dag and Dimitrey; they were there because he asked for their help. He had confidence in McBride and Brent, and the Russians, for that matter. For now, all he could do was to watch and listen while occasionally exchanging whispers with Petey.

About the time the sun was about to the breach the horizon, the boys heard two muffled shots, both from different guns. It signaled that something happened within the house. They waited, but no other shots were heard. Was it over or had something else gone wrong? Skyler, unable to stand the suspense, left Petey to watch the barricade by himself. He wanted to be nearby in case they needed his help. Dawn had arrived; one sentry on the barricade would be enough.

With bow in hand, Skyler took off in a run up the hill. By the time he reached the intersection, he was startled to see Brandy coming from the north; also running hard with her bow in hand. They met at the intersection, forgoing any physical greeting.

"What happened?" she asked him as she fought for her breath.

"I don't know. I've been at the other barricade. I just heard the shots and came running."

As he stood there, he noticed Brandy stare past his shoulder. Something down the street grasped her attention. Skyler turned to see a figure with the morning sun behind it, coming in their direction. The figure seemed to be moving oddly. At this distance, he couldn't make out what it was until he realized that this person was walking backwards. He stopped mid-breath; something *had* gone terribly awry. Then he saw Brent and McBride following from a distance along with two of the Russians. Petar and another Russian also entered the street from between two houses. Why weren't they shooting at him? How could they let this person walk away? Then the figure spun around revealing the burden he carried—a child, probably one of the boys, clutched tightly to his chest.

"What in the hell?" Brandy asked.

As he moved closer, Skyler now recognized the stranger. He was the same one that had tried to chase him down almost two weeks earlier; the very person that had forced the children to become his thieves.

"That's him. That's Brandon. The guy who made Petey and the others steal for him."

As Brandon moved closer, he spun around to show Skyler the rifle pressed up against the boy's head; his face wild with hate and desperation. Skyler recognized Devon, the boy whom Brandon had expelled from their club. Skyler could now see the sweat run from Brandon's temples as he fought to hold the boy's weight close to his body. Brandy placed a hand on Skyler's arm to restrain him.

"We'd better let him through," she said quietly.

Skyler could tell that if anyone made a move to stop Brandon, he would kill the boy before he could be mortally wounded. They had no choice but to let him pass.

The others caught up to him and Brandy. McBride looked more tired than the rest. They exchanged glances as Brandon continued walking backwards down Church toward the southern barricade; still holding Devon tightly against his torso. Skyler wished that there was some way of warning Petey of what was coming in his direction. He had to wonder how the boy would react to seeing Brandon holding Devon hostage.

"We need to stay back," said McBride, "or he'll never let Devon go."

They allowed Brandon to increase his distance between himself and them. Finally, when there was a significant gap between the two parties, Brandon lowered Devon, allowing the boy's feet to reach the ground and held him by the collar of his shirt; rifle still pointed at Devon's head. In the distance, the top of the barricade became visible as they reached the grade in the hill. Unable to do anything but watch, they followed until Brandon and Devon disappeared behind the wall of logs.

"I need to go back and get a bicycle. If Brandon frees Devon anywhere on the hill, I can get to him in seconds," said Skyler, not clarifying just who he would get. Skyler turned and ran without waiting for a reply. He heard footsteps closely behind and turned to see Brandy.

"I'll grab an extra bike so Brent can join you," she explained before he asked.

They ran together and found the two bikes that were kept at the intersection. Intended for emergencies, these were stationed centrally so they could quickly reach any side of the hill in a short time. Today was just such an emergency.

By the time they arrived at the barricade, Brent, McBride, and the others were standing on the uphill side of the logs looking over the top. As Skyler pulled up, he noticed that Petey was missing from the crowd of men.

"Where's Petey?"

"Don't know," answered Petar. "He wasn't here when we arrived."

Skyler was confused; the older boy had been so diligent about everything he'd been asked to do.

Unable to see past the row of men, Skyler dismounted and walked to the end of the logs to peer around. Since the grade of the hill increased as the elevation dropped, they could only see the top fifty yards of the road. Brandon was not in sight, and neither was Petey. Could Petey have decided to leave with Brandon or had Brandon taken him hostage also? He needed to get closer. He stepped back behind the barricade and picked up a bike.

Sensing what Skyler was up to, McBride said, "Be careful. The way this hill curves, you could be too close to him before you know it. If you're alone, he may not hesitate to shoot at you."

"I'll start out slow until I can see them."

With his bow slung over his back, Skyler wheeled the bike around the logs and threw his leg over the seat. Without pedaling, the bike quickly accelerated down the steep hill. The brakes squealed loudly every time he squeezed the lever to control his speed—something he hadn't planned on. As he reached the final rise and could see the intersection with Main Street, there was no sign of Brandon, Devon, or Petey. Skyler released the brake, increasing the bike's speed. It took only seconds to cover the final stretch of Church Road.

As Skyler applied the brakes, slowing only enough to make the turn onto Main, he realized that Brandon may not have turned and headed toward the town. Just as he locked down the wheels and was skidding to a stop, a blur out of the corner of his eye warned him of an impending collision. His right arm exploded with pain as a large rock knocked him off the bike, and sent him tumbling across the asphalt. He felt his bow crunch beneath his back. The contents of his quiver spread across the road as he rolled uncontrollably. When he finally came to a stop, a searing pain engulfed his right shoulder. He tried to stand but his injuries were quickly robbing him of his strength. His canvas pants, torn at the knees, were already soaked with blood. Both his hands had been outstretched as he fell; the asphalt chewed his palms like coarse sandpaper. He looked up to see Brandon stepping from the ditch with Devon pushed out in front of him. Brandon's rifle was no longer trained on the young boy as Skyler could look directly down the barrel.

"I was hoping that we'd get to meet again. In fact, isn't this just about the same place where I'd almost caught you two weeks ago?"

Skyler realized that his life, as well as Devon's, was in jeopardy. He made no attempt to stand, not wanting to appear aggressive. "No, it was at the top of that hill there. You didn't want your flock to get out of your sight."

"I just wanted to see if you would join my club, but you stayed out of my reach. Then you sent your friends after me, and they took what wasn't theirs!" Brandon's anger was increasing as he remembered the past. He seemed to be laying the blame on Skyler.

Knowing that arguing would only make Brandon more volatile, Skyler changed the subject. "There's no one else coming. Why don't you release Devon and take me the rest of the way?" The small boy was not crying, but Skyler could see that he was as frightened as anyone could be. He had to do what he could, even if it meant risking his own life.

"I'm not taking anyone anywhere. This little shit is the one that showed you where we were staying. Now you're both are going to die right here!"

"If you fire that gun, there are seven men up on that hill that will be down here in seconds. They will hunt you until they find you, and they won't be merciful. Just let the boy go, and you can walk away. I'll make sure no one follows you from here."

"No! I've waited for this moment, and I'm not just walking away. Brandon swung the rifle toward Devon, no longer interested in what Skyler had to offer. His rage overrode any chance Skyler had of negotiating with him.

Skyler reached for his bow, but found that its limbs were broken and hung loosely from the string. He tried to look for something to throw. Nothing of weight was within his reach. His right arm hung uselessly at his side. The pain in his head and arms was immeasurable. Making one more attempt to stand, he fought the sharp pain from his shoulder and was just able to get his feet under him when he saw Petey. The boy was no less than thirty yards up the grassy slope above the intersection, holding his oversized crossbow. He held it level with his face, looking down the sights at Brandon. Skyler had to draw Brandon's attention from Devon. He needed to give Petey another second. As he stood, he reached into his empty coat pocket with his left hand and yelled, "I still have my pistol!"

Alarmed, Brandon swung the barrel back in Skyler's direction and fired. Skyler jerked at the suddenness of his action. At that same instant, the heavy thunder-like twang of the crossbow was heard. Skyler felt the burn of the bullet as it grazed the back of his head. Then he saw Brandon's shoulders arch back in slow motion as the projectile impacted squarely against his upper spine between his shoulder blades. The jerking motion of his arms launched the rifle several feet out in front of him. His feet were lifted off the ground by the impact of the bone crunching projectile. As Brandon fell to the ground and rolled, Skyler could see the bloody cavity left by the projectile that Petey had loaded into the crossbow. It was obvious that Brandon would not be getting up again.

Skyler watched as Brandon's body stopped rolling only a few feet from him. He looked up to see Petey walking through the tall grass in his direction. The loaded crossbow held ready near his cheek. The tall blades swirled in unison with the wind, creating a surreal effect around the taller boy. The colors, once vibrant, were changing to gray tones as the scene progressed. Skyler realized that Petey must have seen Brandon approaching the barricade and shadowed him. He felt something wet running down his neck and into his coat. His hand came away covered with blood. Then he looked up the road. Someone was coming down to him on a bicycle. Devon ran to him. The small boy placed his arms about Skyler's waist and squeezed gently as he finally let out a sob. He must have faltered, because he felt Devon shift his hold. As Devon grabbed him around the waist, Skyler's knees buckled and the world around him went dark.

CHAPTER 34

Brandy arrived at the lower compound around mid-afternoon, just in time to catch Ian on his way out. As she was about to climb the stairs to the deck, Ian hastily ran down to greet her. This was her third trip down from the upper compound in as many days. The weather collaborated enough to allow the families to finish the planting at both compounds—a task surmounted following the decision to move the Jensens. The afternoon sun peeked through a thin layer of clouds. Today's warmth allowed her to leave her coat behind. This was the first trip she'd made alone; Joel and Petey taking turns as her escort. Since the events of four days ago, she had put in long hours completing her duties on the hill before making time for her personal treks. There was so much that had been done, yet still so much to do. Ian smiling at the sight of her greeted her with a bear hug.

"I think today would be alright if you wanted to take him out for a short walk," Ian said as he held her shoulders at arm's length. His words were fatherly, like he was giving her the use of his car for the first time.

"But you're leaving. I was counting on you being here when he got up," hesitated Brandy.

"I promised Carl and Robert that I'd help them move the last of their belongings. Besides, you won't need me; he's already been up twice this morning despite my restrictions. Just make sure that he doesn't attempt any stairs until I okay it. With that broken arm, we can't risk him falling."

"I'll make sure he sticks to walking the upper level. How's his pain?"

"He doesn't complain, but I know he has to be hurting. I think he's afraid that I might want to operate if he moans even slightly. I keep telling him that his arm will heal as long as it stays in the sling."

"By the way, thanks for helping Carl and Robert. It had to be difficult for them to move, especially considering their loss. We would've liked to have helped more, but the gardens became the priority. Skyler told me what their farm was like. Maybe someday it'll be safe for them to move back out there."

"I don't think they want to do that. I sensed that they feel safer living up on the hill. After Dag's funeral, Beth and Lindsey both said their privacy wasn't worth the security of living in your house. Besides, I think Beth has taken a shine to Mr. McBride. Have you noticed that they always seem to be talking while they work in the garden?"

"Everyone noticed. I'm happy for both." She paused and then added, "I'm glad to see something positive come out of all this."

"Well, I have to get going, and you have a patient waiting up those stairs for you. I'll probably see you later this evening."

She leaned up and gave him a peck on the cheek, a small gesture of her gratitude, before hastily taking two steps at a time. She liked Ian, as did everyone, especially the children. The events of the past week had changed the gentle doctor. He no longer spoke of traveling south, offering his services in trade for food. For now, this was his home and not just James' house. Ian seemed to spend equal time with each family, including the Lopatnikovs. He seemed a happier man. A man resuming his pre-Change life as the physician he once was. It was probably the children who gave him the most joy; their smiles eliciting the best in him. A hug from one of them, a toothless grin from a 6 year old, peals of laughter when he read a silly passage from a book. They were like manna for his soul. He taught

286

them about science, about nature, and most importantly; he taught them about healing and medicine. He knew that he would not be around forever and that grooming as many children as possible for life without a true physician could be beneficial for the entire community. They were a project with no end in sight. Fostering relationships built on love and attention made up for not ever having any children of his own.

When she reached the deck, Brandy silently opened the front door and found Lara in the kitchen. She quickly put a finger to her lips, silencing any greeting. Lara, mashing carrots, possibly for Skyler's dinner, smiled and nodded, knowing what was about to take place. Brandy made a habit of surprising Skyler with her visits. She had jokingly threatened him with solitary confinement if he wasn't following Ian's instructions to the T. She crept past Lara, placing a gentle hand on her forearm on her way to Skyler's room. His door partially ajar, gave way to a room black as night.

Pushing the door open a few inches, she slowly poked her head in, hoping to catch him awake, hoping he was waiting for her. Her eyes adjusted; he was asleep. Ian had warned her that until his body recovered further, he would probably be sleeping a lot more than usual. He had lost a lot of blood, another factor that might take weeks for him to recover from. She stepped into the room, leaving the door open enough to light her way. She stood beside his bed, watching him, listening to his every breath, thinking of how grateful she was that he was alive. Arriving at the scene of the final conflict shortly after Brent and McBride, she had feared Skyler was dead; another victim of that awful night. He was lying prone on the asphalt, face turned, his left cheek pressed against the pavement as if he was listening for the sound of horse hoofs, vibrations of the earth. Blood oozed from the wound near the back of his head, already forming a black pool on the asphalt. His upper-right arm clearly deformed and bent awkwardly, sent a wave of overwhelming fear through her. Devon, seated next to him, was crying as he shouted Skyler's name with no response. The scene before her had dashed all her hopes. Her worst fears, the ones she kept sequestered, had finally surfaced. Ian arrived moments later and swiftly went to work. Only after he'd examined him, explaining the extent of his injuries and what his recovery would entail, did Brandy feel she could breathe again. However, Ian made no promises as he set about bandaging the more serious wounds.

Looking down on him, so peaceful in the bed, Brandy felt a pang of longing, missing his companionship. She knew that their relationship had taken a turn in which they had come to the proverbial "Y" in the road, that they had bonded more intensely having relied on each other to stay alive. Skyler had asked for her each time he awoke, wanting to know when she would return to his side.

"Skyler!" She was certain she had yelled loud enough for Lara to hear her in the kitchen, but she didn't have the luxury of waiting any longer for him to wake on his own.

Before his eyes were fully open, he was smiling at the sound of her voice. He looked at her for several seconds, in that state between dreams and wakefulness, wanting her there. He finally asked, "How are you doing?" His voice raspy and weak from lack of use.

"Better now. We finished the gardens and can take a break. Ian assures me that you might live if you refrain from any more battles for the next few weeks."

He grinned, his physical pain lessened just by being in her presence.

"Seriously," Brandy asked, "how are you doing?"

He was slow to answer. "I'm good." He lifted his head and tried pushing himself up with his left arm. A barrier, probably created by the pain, halted his progress. He looked up at her and asked, "Can you help me sit up on the edge of the bed?"

"Are you sure?"

"Yeah, I want to walk around some more. I feel a lot stronger today than yesterday." He began to swing his legs over the side of the bed as he reached for her with his left hand. She instinctively grabbed it and pulled enough to allow him to do most of the work. Bandages covered both knees making them difficult to bend. He was wearing the same sweatshirt and gym shorts as he had on her last two visits.

Once up, he asked, "Fill me in on what's happening out there."

"Well, to begin with, Brent and James are out at the old aluminum refinery. They hauled some wagons out there to retrieve corrugated steel panels. The first loads will be for the roof of the second house on the hill. Carl and Robert have been busy finishing that project. They've decided to move to the upper compound. Ian's headed out to the Jensens to help them carry the last of their belongings back to the upper compound."

"What about Brent's house?"

"It's on hold for another week. James felt it was more important to get Carl and the others moved away from their remote farm."

"What else have I missed?"

"Not much. Now that the gardens are in, Joe, Joel, and Petey are rounding up whatever chain-link fencing they can find. Everyone agrees that we need to place fencing around the compounds. That's the next big project after the two houses are complete." Noticing the surprise on his face, she asked, "Hasn't anyone told you about this?"

"Only because they've been too busy. James occasionally sticks his head in the door, grunts once to acknowledge me and then says, 'Get better.' I think my injuries scared him enough that he's afraid to talk about it."

"Well, it scared the rest of us too."

"How's Devon? I haven't seen him since that day. You don't suppose he's afraid to come near me, do you?"

"He's doing all right. That first day was a bit traumatic, more than any kid should have to go through, but Lindsey has been working with him and forcing him to open up. She says the best therapy is being able to talk about your fears."

"Can I see him?"

"He would love that. I'll have one of the guys walk him down here in the morning. He's only staying on the hill because Lindsey is there." She paused briefly then asked, "Are you ready to go for a walk?"

Without asking for assistance, Skyler stood up using his own strength. He wobbled back and forth excessively at first, causing Brandy to reach out and encircle his waist with her arms. He then straightened up before smiling, letting out a small chuckle. "I did that on purpose."

She didn't know whether to be annoyed with him or happy, but kept her arm around his waist as he placed his good arm over her shoulder. Slowly, and carefully, they left the bedroom and made their way out to the deck.

The decking, warmed by the sun, felt delicious to his bare feet. As he looked out towards Main Street, he could see Joe and Joel rolling a bundle of chain-link fencing in their direction. Petey followed, carrying the .22 carbine that Petar gave him. Only then did he notice that they were working on their own without any adults nearby. He turned to Brandy and asked, "Why didn't anyone tell me about Dag?"

The question almost ambushed her. "We were waiting for you to get back on your feet. How'd you figure it out?"

"I overheard Ian talking about a funeral. I simply put two and two together."

"Ian says Dag sacrificed himself to save the children. He attacked one of the bandits and bought enough time for Brent and McBride to enter the house. Are you angry that we didn't tell you right away?"

"No, I only wish that I could have done something to prevent that whole chain of events. I really liked the old guy. Who would have thought that the people in the most danger would have been staying in the house?"

Lara stepped out on the deck holding a makeshift dinner tray. On it was a bowl of mashed vegetables and a spoon. She looked at the young couple hanging onto each other and asked, "Have you had enough exercise yet?"

Skyler smiled. "No, I'm just getting started."

EPILOGUE

The evening before they were to start canning their tomatoes and corn, James asked Lara, "Do you want to go for a walk?"

"Sure," she replied. She was in an especially good mood. The summer had been warm, and the garden had flourished with the temperate climate. The tomatoes had finally turned red following the longer growing season. "Where are we going?" she asked him.

"Down to visit the coyotes," he answered. This had become one of his favorite things to do when time allowed it. The wild dogs seemed to expect his visits, although they never approached him. Whenever there were table scraps, he would collect what he could into several small containers and place them in his pack.

Lara grabbed her coat, the evening chill ever present. They were able to walk freely down past the pond; the fence not yet in place behind the house. When they reached the development, James gave out a shrill whistle to signal his arrival. From various places, the coyotes appeared heads first, until they were sure it was James. Last year, he'd only counted the mother and her two pups. This year, there was a second bitch with pups and an alpha male, making for a total of seven in the family. They didn't share the same den, but they lived in proximity to one another. When James had come down here in the mornings, he often saw the four youngest hunting as a pack. Just as the humans had learned to do, the coyotes also formed families in order to survive.

He lowered his backpack to the ground and took out the seven plastic bowls; each half-filled with a small amount of fish, rice, and carrots. When he had first started feeding them, they were so skinny that he didn't think they'd survive. Now, heavy with a thick layer of fat and fur, they looked ready for another winter. He guessed that they mostly lived off frogs, mice, and anything else they could find. His joy was maintaining a relationship with them, offering them occasional meals, and making regular visits. He had learned early on that he had to provide each with their own bowl to prevent quarrels.

Afterwards, while walking back up to the house, the sun fell below the hill behind Church Road. The air chilled quickly, but neither James nor Lara seemed to be in a hurry to get back. Both were content to be in the other's company. As they crossed the field, James put an arm over Lara's shoulders after noticing her shiver. The orange glow in the western sky signaled both the day's end and the dawn of another winter. They passed Alder seedlings that would someday yield a forest. Before they reached the final climbing trail to the house, James stopped Lara and looked in her eyes.

"What's the matter?" she asked him.

"Nothing's wrong, but if I had to describe it, it's that I have everything, and yet I have nothing."

"What do you mean?"

"Do I need to spell it out for you?" James' wry smile gave clue that he was eager to share something particularly tender.

"Start by telling me what you consider everything," she asked softly.

"Okay. The last five months have been the best of my life. I don't mean since the Change, I mean forever. And it's not just because we've felt safe and have a family to be proud of, but because my life has more purpose now than it ever had before."

She thought about what he had just said and realized that those words could also have been hers.

They started walking again when she stopped him and said, "Now tell me about the nothing."

He smiled at her. "Without you here to share this with me, I would have nothing."

Lara reached around his waist and gave him a squeeze, one that she was in no hurry to let go. The world had collapsed and they had survived. Arctic winds, lack of food, and moments of truth. Death and regeneration. But through it all, she thought, they had survived the totality of their lives. Everything and nothing.

Made in the USA
Charleston, SC
14 November 2012